JENNY PATTRICK is a writer and former jeweller whose six published novels, including *The Denniston Rose*, its sequel *Heart of Coal*, the Whanganui novel *Landings*, and *Inheritance*, set in Samoa, have all been number one bestsellers in New Zealand. In 2009 she received the New Zealand Post Mansfield Fellowship. In 2011 she and husband, musician Laughton Pattrick, published the children's book and CD of s

JENNY PATTRICK

CATCHING THE CURRENT

BLACK
SWAN

A BLACK SWAN BOOK published by Random House New Zealand,
18 Poland Road, Glenfield, Auckland, New Zealand

For more information about our titles go to www.randomhouse.co.nz

A catalogue record for this book is available from the National Library
of New Zealand

Random House New Zealand is part of the Random House Group
New York   London   Sydney   Auckland   Delhi   Johannesburg

First edition published 2005
This edition first published 2012

© 2012 Jenny Pattrick

The moral rights of the author have been asserted

ISBN 978 1 86979 844 4
eBook ISBN 978 1 86979 857 4

Cover design: Kate Barraclough
Text design: Elin Termannsen

This publication is printed on paper pulp sourced from sustainably
grown and managed forests, using Elemental Chlorine Free (EFC)
bleaching, and printed with 100% vegetable based inks.

Printed in New Zealand by Printlink
Also available as an eBook

For my grandchildren, Ben, Alex, Arthur and Georgia

Reviewers' praise for *The Denniston Rose*

'A rollicking good yarn' — Gordon McLauchlan, *NZ Herald*

'An uplifting story of triumph and survival against seemingly insurmountable odds' — *Gisborne Herald*

'Violent, brash and colourful, *The Denniston Rose* . . . glows and flickers with energy' — David Eggleton, *NZ Listener*

'. . . an absorbing account of pioneer life and the incredible hardships faced by families attempting to carve a better future for themselves' — Whitcoulls' 'Guaranteed Great Reads'

'What a triumph this book is' — *Wairarapa Times-Age*

'You can really feel the wind coming up through the floorboards of the makeshift houses and hear the drunken shouts spilling out of the taverns' — *Dominion Post*

'Pattrick writes with the assuredness of a veteran . . . and has raised a simple story to a work of literary merit' — *The Press*

'With her winning smile, her waif-like ways and her ability to conceal the broad devious streak in her character, Rose becomes something of a mascot for Denniston and a peace token for a community which is deeply divided down sectarian lines' — *NZ Listener*

'It's hard to believe this is a first novel' — *Evening Standard*

'A sequel is on its way — I can't wait' — *Timaru Herald*

'This novel begs a sequel and I hope I don't have to wait too long for it' — *NZ Woman's Weekly*

'A sequel is promised — the prospect is one to savour' — John McCrystal, *North and South*

Reviewers' praise for *Heart of Coal*

'We have that sequel . . . and very good it is too' — *North and South*

'Spirited, memorable Rose is back . . . [*Heart of Coal*] is very different, but no less triumphant' — *Southland Times*

'*Heart of Coal* fairly rips along' — *Northern Advocate*

'Those of us who warmed to *The Denniston Rose* will be fired up by this gritty sequel' — *Next*

'. . . a superb yarn about love, loss and excruciating hardship' — *Daily News*

'. . . this sequel rises above its predecessor' — *Sunday Star-Times*

'Jenny Pattrick's unique and unsettling voice, and sharp turn of phrase, are just as strong here as in *The Denniston Rose*, and fans will be equally pleased . . . very New Zealand, very gritty, very recommended' —*Waikato Times*

'An unforgettable novel about loss and love, hope and despair, and most of all, the uncompromising spirit of a truly unique woman' — *NZ Woman's Weekly*

'*Heart of Coal* is a must. It is bound to be another bestseller' — Elizabeth Knife, *Timaru Herald*

'. . . an entertaining portrait of a society that rose and fell within one lifetime' — *Otago Daily Times*

'. . . a worthy sequel to the runaway success of *The Denniston Rose* . . . One can only hope Jenny Pattrick will oblige with a third book' — *Nelson Mail*

A GUIDE TO FAROESE PRONUNCIATION

æ	a as in hat
∂	y as in yes, or silent
ó	o as in oh
ø	ur as in fur
o	o as in long
í	ui as in ruin (but shorter)
j	y as in yes

ACKNOWLEDGEMENTS

Particular thanks to Karen Williams, great-great-granddaughter of Bishop D. G. Monrad, and her husband Bill, who gave me the Monrad story, together with the books that provided the detail. Also to Mrs Callesen of Valhalla, Karere; Anthony Lewis of the Palmerston North City Library; and the archive staff at Te Manawa, Museum of Palmerston North, and to Jim Lundy. In Wellington, Vicki and Tony Ellis for early Wellington material, and in Sydney, Tim Barlow for his tenacity in guiding me through second-hand bookshops.

For advice on Danish matters I owe a debt to Elin Bruhn Termannsen.

In the Faroe Islands John Eysturoy has been of invaluable assistance. Also thanks to Jøannes Patursson at Kirkjubøur, Regin Debess at Heima á Garði and the dancers and singers of the kvæði dance group Toekum Lætt in Tórshavn, who gave us a first-hand experience of chain-dancing.

To Harriet Allan and the staff at Random House New Zealand, thanks as always. And to my editor, Rachel Scott.

And a final tribute to my clear-headed reader, Laughton Pattrick, whose comments, as the work progressed, kept me on track.

It may look far, but one man can easily row across. It is a matter of catching the current. So here, if a person is late for a meeting or slow to understand, we say ha! — that one has not caught the current.

John Eysturoy, Streymoy, Faroe Islands

TRUTH AND FICTION

Bishop D. G. Monrad, prime minister of Denmark during the disastrous political events of 1864, was a real person who came to New Zealand with his family shortly after circumstances forced his resignation. The description in this novel of his life and that of his family is as accurate as I can manage. Other true historical figures mentioned are Monrad's friend the Rangitane chief Te Peeti Te Awe Awe; Titokowaru, the battle chief of the Pai Marire (sometimes called Hauhau) movement, Rev Duncan of Foxton and Rev Taylor of Wanganui. I hope that the words I have put into their mouths are reasonably true to what they might have said.

Major events, situations and battles, in New Zealand, Denmark, the Faroe Islands and Sydney, took place as I have described them.

All the main players in the novel, however, their journeys and their stories, are from my imagination.

Jenny Pattrick

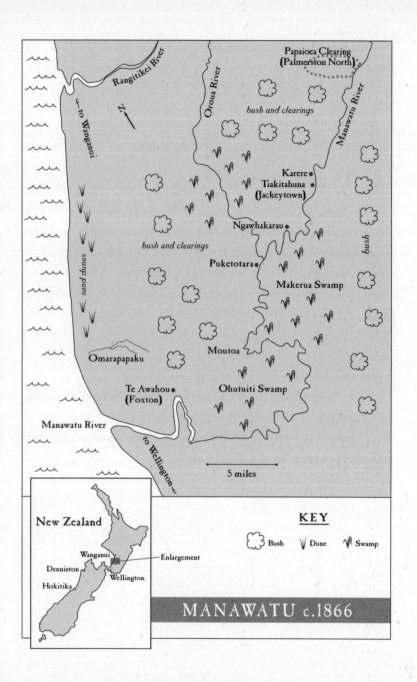

Rangitikei River

Oroua River

Papaioea Clearing
(Palmerston North)

Manawatu River

bush and clearings

N

to Wanganui

Karere •
Tiakitahuna •
(Jackeytown)

Ngawhakarau •

bush

bush and clearings

sand dunes

Puketotara •

Makerua Swamp

Omarapapaku

Moutoa

Ohutuiti Swamp

Te Awahou •
(Foxton)

Manawatu River

to Wellington

5 miles

New Zealand

Wanganui

Denniston

Enlargement

Hokitika

Wellington

KEY

Bush   Dune   Swamp

MANAWATU c.1866

1.
Visitor from the North

KARERE,
NORTH ISLAND, NEW ZEALAND
1867

1.

To: Bishop D. G. Monrad
At, or in the vicinity of, Wanganui
North Island of the colony of New Zealand

Conveyed to you by the hand of my son, Napoleon
Haraldsen.

March 1867

My dear old friend,

It is hard for me to think of you so far away! I can
understand your need to impose exile upon yourself, at
least until feelings in Denmark have subsided

somewhat, but would not the Faroes have served? Surely our islands are remote enough, and our people uninterested enough in politics to leave you and your family in peace? I cannot understand this punishing desire to bury yourself in a wild and uncivilised country somewhere deep in the southern ocean. Come back, my friend. Leave adventuring to others. Your skills will be needed again in Denmark, I am sure of it, and your voice of experience called for.

Already there is hope that the land lost to the Prussians may be returned to Denmark — or at least some of it. When that happens, you will be forgiven, and your decisions understood. I am sure of it. Time blurs the memory of even the worst disasters. Here on the Faroes we understand better than most that the simple matters of life — harvesting, farming, fishing, making clothes and shelter — will always take precedence, in the minds of the vast majority, over the actions of politicians and armies. (Forgive my presumption in saying this, but it is meant in good faith and as a consolation to you.) So begin your plans, my good friend, to return to your own people.

Now to another matter. I am sending my dear son Napoleon to you in the hope you may be able to help us. He is searching for a friend whom we believe has fled to New Zealand. He, too, is from the Faroes, so speaks good, though accented Danish, and our hope is that he has come into your orbit. The lad is a fine and good-hearted fellow from a respected family here. Somewhat high-spirited, alas, which has led to one or two unfortunate incidents both here and in the Danish navy, where he served for some time. Our belief is that he fears retribution, and has 'disappeared' to New Zealand. We know him as Enok of Sumba, though I understand he is prone to changing his name. In the navy he called himself Køne. Hardly a clever disguise. Or he may use the patronym Rasmussen. At any rate, he is quite unmistakable, so any change of name will scarcely deter his discovery. Look for a giant of a young man, as blond as any true Viking and wearing his hair long like a hero. He has a laugh to carry across wide fjords and a wonderful voice for a song or a saga. A big lad in every sense of the word, who is sorely missed here by family and friends.

There is a fresh feeling here in the Faroes, initiated by the young students returning from Copenhagen. A new national spirit. Enok should be part of this resurgence. He has been considered from an early age to be a potential leader. In particular his facility with our kvæði — our ancient sung sagas — is an asset we can ill-afford to lose. Napoleon is sent to entice him back. (I am hoping that this voyage will satisfy my son's adventurous nature enough to reconcile him to a farming life here. More and more I rely on him. Give him some work to do to earn his keep. If you can, let him see that work is no more exciting in the southern ocean than in the northern!)

If you know of Enok, please help Napoleon to meet him. I have written to the authorities in the navy and am reasonably confident that they will overlook his 'indiscretion'. The boy is a magnet to women of all ages: I will say no more. My daughter Clara —

I believe you met her when she was a student in Copenhagen? — is most anxious that he return. Despite his past I would have no hesitation in blessing that union. Clara and he are admirably suited.

You write that many Danes visit your holding in search of work or news from home in a familiar language. I feel certain Enok will have contacted you, for he is a sociable lad. Encourage him to tell you something of his story. It is an interesting one, and he is a born storyteller. You will have an entertaining evening, I promise you!

In return for this favour I offer you a book to add to your excellent library. I trust Napoleon has carried it safely. We are rather proud of it — the first book published in Faroese. You will be interested — the great **Sjúrðar kvæði**. The ballads are similar to the Danish sagas about Sigurd, but the differences give the tale a distinct Faroese flavour. Our language has now been given a written form — the young ones are quite fervent on the matter and argue the long nights over spelling systems: whether to favour the Danish or Icelandic texts. I fear they are foolish to believe that our small islands can keep their language intact. Denmark and the Danish language are the way of the future. At any rate, see what you can make of the book. An educated Dane like yourself will understand a good part of it, and Napoleon will help you. For myself, I prefer the old sung forms; Enok of Sumba, though young, is already a kvæði master.

I have been most interested in your letters. What a strange, wild place New Zealand is. I can scarcely imagine a land completely covered in trees! It has made me wonder whether the Faroes themselves were once tree-clad. I doubt it. Grass has enough trouble growing. Anything raising a higher head would surely be mown flat by the wind in a week!

Best wishes to your wife and family. You are a brave man to take them all so far. I commend my son to your care and trust you to make sure he returns as planned, with or without young Enok. Napoleon is a good sailor and will work his return passage. He will have no trouble finding a ship, I imagine. Nor, please God, Enok.

God be with you.
Your friend,
Harald Haraldsen,
Streymoy,
Faroe Islands, Kingdom of Denmark

2.

ANAHUIA WALKS DOWN from the bishop's house through his
wife's vegetable garden and into the patch of great trees. She stands
for a moment, enjoying the shade, and listens. She will hear his
singing before she sees him, but birdsong is all she hears yet. This
little island of bush is the last to remain between here and the fringe
of trees by the river. Only three years ago she could walk the whole
distance without lacking shade. Out in the open now, she strides,
head down in the heat, around the end of the lagoon. This shining
half-circle of water was once a curve of the Manawatu River, so Te
Peeti says, until one winter of many floods, back in his grandfather's
time, the river cut through, and raged on out towards the sea,
leaving the still water of the lagoon isolated — a paradise for water-
hen and eel. And of course mosquito. They will be bad tonight. On
the edge of the water, red-beaked pukeko wade through the reeds,

the blue of their stubby, flightless wings flashing in the sunlight. Anahuia would like to stop, pull off her wretched clothes and wade in among the birds, but the bishop's family do not allow nakedness.

Again she pauses, standing among the stumps, the felled wreck of branches, to search along the dark line of the standing bush. The tall trunks, straight as spears, stand close together — an army waiting for the sign to advance. Except this is no advance; more a slow and sad retreat. Every day the land lies more open, the great stretch of forest she loves, diminished.

Now she hears him. He is ahead, in the bush somewhere, roaring out a strange, wild song as he works. She picks her way with care through the tangle of browning foliage not yet burnt; the precious material of the dress must not be torn. She longs to run into the cool dark ahead but walks sedately, aware that the bishop's wife or daughters — or one of the other workers — might be watching. All the time her eyes look this way and that, searching for the flicker of movement that will show where he is.

At the edge of the bush, standing at last between the dark trees, she hears him clearly. He sings in a deep voice, more chant than song, in a language both familiar and strange to her. Not quite Danish but close. The song stops for a moment and now she hears the thunder of his axe. Not far away, surely. Her fingers, resting against a trunk, feel the shock of his axe blows coming up through the ground. The wood of the giant kahikatea under her hand echoes each stroke: Thock. Thock. *Thock.* A small seedling beside her shivers — a tiny movement that unsettles the young needles over and over again.

When the axe blows cease and the heavy rasp of the saw begins, she suddenly sees him on the other side of a small clearing, stripped to the waist, his white skin and ash-blond hair shocking against the dark bush. Back and forth he draws the cross-cut, feet planted wide, both hands on the wooden handle, s*craw scraw*, *scraw scraw,* eating through the soft white wood. None of the other workers is strong enough to draw the saw single-handed.

Anahuia sighs. She loves to watch him. Everything he does is different, somehow: more noticeable, larger. Yesterday she watched from the bank as he joined a party of men from the river villages in an eel drive. He jumped into the muddy water with a bloodcurdling cry that had even the strongest warriors laughing with admiration. He thrashed around, the one white body in the boil of brown ones, making so much noise, the great boy, that no one noticed how he kept to the shallows. Only she understood his fear of swimming. And later, when the hundreds of eels were safely netted and brought to the bank for the women to split and smoke, when it was time for the men to play and eat and sing, there he was, understanding scarcely one word in twenty, but fooling around with the other young lads, making them laugh, teaching them new sea-songs, as if they had all grown up blood-brothers.

She smiles still, remembering. Slowly now, lest she attract his attention too soon, she removes bonnet and bodice, lays them on a mossy stump. Rolling her damp shoulders in the cool air, she stretches up to unpin the long hair — darker than Conrad's, but still light enough to attract ribald jokes downriver — to let it fall free down her back. At ease now, naked to the waist like him, she steps out into his line of sight.

Conrad sees her immediately. His instincts and reactions are always quick. Perhaps he has been watching all along. He stops his sawing for a moment and raises one great arm, all his teeth showing in a grin wide as a dog's. With the raised hand he now indicates the line along which the tree will fall, and motions her to move a little to one side. She waits. The crack, loud as a musket volley, comes a few moments later. Conrad steps back quickly as the bushy canopy high above sways forward, slowly at first, then with frightening speed. Whump! Down it comes, filling the little clearing with thrashing branches, exactly along the line Conrad has indicated.

'Aha! Ha!' his triumphant shout echoes off the standing trees. He scrambles onto the great trunk and for a moment poses there, fists high, like a prize-fighter. Then he flips into a handstand and proceeds along the fallen tree, hand over hand, sure as a cat, towards her. With another flip he is back on the ground, right side up, red-faced and laughing. 'See that, Ana? Look, I have let the sun in!' He lifts his head as if to drink the bright shaft of light. Already fantails are cartwheeling through the sunlight, feasting on the clouds of insects disturbed by the fall.

'Yes, you big show-off, and by nightfall you will have destroyed all this cool shade. There is more than enough sunlight out beyond.' But she can never be truly angry with this fascinating young man, who has so changed her life.

'You don't like sun?' he shouts across to her, grinning because they have often argued the matter. 'Sun, warmth: they are the gift of God. That blue sky, eh? Deep as oceans!'

He picks his way through the fallen trash of branches to take her arm and lead her to a mound of moss. For a while they are quiet together. He strokes the warm brown skin of her back, and the curve of her belly where the baby grows. But when he tries to pull her into his arms she holds back, smiling.

'Conrad, this is not a pleasure visit. I am at work.'

'And I. But a lad must rest between felling trees.'

'Then rest.'

'And how is a servant of the bishop's working when she takes off her clothes and visits a man alone in the bush?'

Anahuia frowns. 'I am not a servant, Conrad. I choose to work there.'

'Oho! You choose?' But he will not push this dangerous matter further.

They speak mostly in Danish, hers heavily accented and laced with Maori words, his coloured by a curious lilt, different from the bishop's but clearly understood by her.

Conrad, not one to rest for long, now stands and stretches his full height. Damp blond hair curls from his shoulders to his navel; his muscles are firm under pale skin that never browns. He opens his arms to her and grins his invitation. His arousal is quite evident. The successful felling of the tree, the sight of her naked skin and heavy breasts have excited him, but he knows better than to force her; despite her status, Anahuia is always a woman to be reckoned with.

She stands now too. Not as tall as him but remarkable for a young woman. She is not beautiful. Her people at the kainga find her ugly — the smoky eyes unnerving in her pale brown face, the body too scrawny, the fact that she is a good head taller than the chief, insulting. Conrad — this young wanderer who can sing a hundred sea-songs and tell wonderful stories, who can carve wood or bone into any likeness that takes his fancy — this popular giant of a fellow is the only man to have shown any interest in her as a woman, and she loves him for it. But now she places a hand against his bushy chest.

'Later, perhaps. With luck. I am sent by te tihopa, the bishop. He wants you to come up to the house when you have finished work.'

'Why?'

'A visitor has come from Wanganui.'

Conrad frowns. 'That is no reason.' In the twelve-month he has worked breaking in this land he has visited the house rarely — for the feast of Christmas and the like.

'I think he said the visitor knew you.'

Conrad breathes in sharply. Anahuia notices with interest that he has completely forgotten about any lovemaking.

'Did you see the visitor?' he asks.

'No.'

'How did the bishop seem?'

'The usual.'

'Not angry? Disturbed?'

'No. More . . . what is the word? Like he is with a new book. Sharp, and pleased.'

For a moment the big man is silent. Then he groans. 'Ah, sweetheart, I have a bad feeling about this. Should we run off now? Would you come?'

'You know that's not possible.'

Conrad is silent again, thinking. Anahuia, fearful that he might indeed run off as abruptly as he appeared over a year ago, is sharp with him. 'Conrad, you are a big strong man and this is a country where people make their own lives . . .'

'You do not.'

'Don't bring me into this. That is different. Go up to the house. Meet the visitor. It may turn out to be a great pleasure. Or, if it is a fear, better to face it here.'

'Ana. No one — *no one* — could have followed me. Not one soul knows I am in New Zealand.'

'Who said it was a visitor from the old world? It could be some drinking friend from Wanganui.'

Conrad looks up at the patch of blue sky unveiled by the fallen tree. 'Ah, no. There is a different feel here.'

Anahuia snorts. 'You are worse than my kuia down at the kainga, reading signs and portents into every simple event. A visitor, the bishop said. Visitors are rare and to be welcomed. You would think some executioner had arrived.'

'Oh God, Ana, don't say it!'

She has never seen him anything but confident and carefree: a blond giant who would argue and sing all night and then do the work of three next day. This mood of his frightens her. Whenever he has spoken of his past, the story has been laced with fabulous beasts and magical adventures to make you laugh and gasp and end up with no idea where the truth, if any at all, lay.

If there is something dark in his past, she wants him to face it here. 'The bishop,' she says carefully, 'is an important man and a fair one. You are a valued worker. If there is something — or someone — to fear, what better ally to have than the bishop? Or what better judge if there are . . . matters . . . to be answered?'

Conrad laughs suddenly and she laughs with him, relieved to see his mood change. 'Jesu, sweetheart, *you* should be the bishop. You would persuade a block of stone to move uphill. Well, we shall see who on earth thinks he knows Conrad Rasmussen, eh?'

'There is a clean shirt drying on the roof of your hut. And wash off the sweat before you come. The bishop is a man for dressing in the evening.'

'And will you be there?'

She laughs. 'Ae! I will think of some work to keep me late at the house tonight. I'll be watching somewhere, count on it. And Conrad . . . be polite. The bishop likes good manners.'

She is teasing him and he knows it. Conrad Rasmussen roars through life with no regard for status or the conventions of society. Mostly his charm and high spirits earn him forgiveness. The occasional reprimand rolls off his back like rain off a leaf.

Which make his odd disquiet now all the more puzzling.

3.

UP AT THE big house everyone is shouting and running. Louise is dashing towards the pataka where the tobacco is stored; Olga, the daughter-in-law, charges out of the house, holding her little son with one hand and flapping wildly with the other. The child is screaming. Bishop Monrad himself stands in the yard directing operations, while his wife and younger daughter bring him burning candles. In the fading light of evening the scene resembles a wild dervish dance: pale figures, dressed for a quiet evening, capering through the flower-beds and vegetable gardens, arms whirling, never still for a moment.

Conrad, striding up past the lagoon in his clean shirt, hair neatly tied back, can guess what has happened. Someone will have left a shutter open and mosquitoes have invaded the house. The maddening little pests are very bad this evening; near the water they hang in thick curtains, and only his constant movement keeps him ahead of them. He grins to see the pandemonium, glad to arrive when the centre of attention is elsewhere.

'Louise! The leaves here!' instructs Monrad. The smoke from burning tobacco leaves is his own discovery as a potent destroyer of mosquitoes. Now he damps the leaves with water from the rain barrel and gives them to Anahuia. She takes them and a candle and calmly goes into the now empty house to light the leaves in a pot on the hearth.

Soon clouds of smoke are streaming out of the door. No one will be able to go back inside until the choking fumes have dissipated, but at least the mosquitoes will be dead. Monrad places another bundle of leaves ready at the door against further invasions, and leads his family in a brisk walk away from the lagoon and towards the newly cleared field, where sheep are grazing among the stumps.

'Karen, let me hear your English lesson,' says the bishop as he walks. His younger daughter answers clearly, in the language Conrad still finds awkward. He stands in the shadow of a tree and searches the faces in the half-light. None is new. All are family. The bishop and his wife Emilie, the two daughters, Olga the daughter-in-law and the grandson Ditlev. The two sons, Viggo and Johannes, are away up north. Where, then, is this mysterious visitor? Conrad decides to hold back from joining the party just yet, and slips around behind the house in search of Anahuia.

This is the largest house in the district: four rooms downstairs, two above. Bishop Monrad was an important man back in Denmark — prime minister as well as bishop. He has bought property and built a house worthy of his past status. Already the homestead at Karere is a magnet to other Danes driven out of their homeland by the war or simply looking for a new life in New Zealand. Some, like Conrad, have been employed by the bishop; others have visited and moved on. Conrad had heard about this determined, strong-willed politician, admired in the early days for his hand in establishing the first Danish Parliament but later vilified for his part in the war. Here, in his new country, the bishop has become an inspiration to others struggling to make their way. The Monrads don't sit down and weep over the past. Every member of this family works like the devil.

Conrad, who took part in the Danish war unwillingly and whose interests lie in directions other than politics, admires the stern man for his work habits and his fairness as an employer, but has never become a friend, choosing rather to mix with the Danish workers who come and go and sometimes with the Maori from Anahuia's kainga and those downriver at Jackeytown.

He finds Anahuia outside the back door, tossing a shovelful of dead mosquitoes into the evening air. She smiles to see him neatly dressed, and draws him quickly into the house, kicking the door closed behind her, before further swarms invade. Inside the door an oven dish heaped high with the pests is ready for the same disposal.

'Quick now,' says Anahuia. 'Open and close the door for me!'

'But where is he . . . ?'

'She smiles at his impatience. 'Wait till this is done. Now!' And out she whirls, tosses the insects and is back in again as fast as he can heave the door this way and that.

Inside, the smoke is less thick, though the tobacco stench is powerful. Anahuia wrinkles her nose. 'It's all very well for the bishop. He loves his pipe. How will they enjoy this piece of mutton when it is laced through with tobacco smoke?'

'Ana! The visitor?'

She indicates the stairwell. 'Shh. He's upstairs sleeping, behind a door, under a mosquito net. No idea about all this fuss! He'll be down in his own good time. Te tihopa says not to disturb him —

he's had a long trip.'

'Did you see him?'

'For a moment. Not to notice much. Small man. Dark hair.'

'Naval? I mean, in uniform?'

'Conrad, what is all this about?'

'Just tell, woman.'

'A seaman maybe, by his walk. But then they all walk that way after months on the water. I wouldn't know naval or no.'

'Ah, sweetheart, what'll I do?'

Anahuia's grey eyes narrow. They can be iron-hard sometimes, in her brown face, beneath the fine dark eyebrows. 'Conrad, you will stay and find out. Te tihopa Monrad is pleased about the visit. There is maybe a *happy* secret about it. Not some bad thing. That is how I feel it.'

Conrad grunts, thinking. He drums his fingers on the rough wool of his trousers, then nods. 'Let us see, then. Ana . . .' His blue eyes, in a face a world different from hers, are anxious. 'Ana, there are things in my life . . . my stories are sometimes not quite . . . well, maybe you need to hear other things.'

She faces him squarely. 'Your life *here* is what is important, not what you came from.'

'Easy for you to say that.'

'No!' The word is fierce. 'Not easy. I could fill the air with laments. A sad saga with weeping and howling like a dog. But what use is that? Today is more important. And tomorrow.'

He smiles at her. 'Well, maybe true, sweetheart. But sometimes my yesterday knocks, wanting to come in. I try to forget it, that life in another ocean. But there it is.'

She pushes him through the big living room towards the front door. 'Tell or not as you wish, you big ox. And I will listen. But now is not the moment. Light these leaves at the door to help them all get back in safely. Here comes Louise, singing to keep their spirits up.'

He sighs, then kisses her with unusual tenderness and lets her go back to the kitchen.

NAPOLEON Haraldsen has been in a deep sleep, upstairs in the bishop's house under his mosquito net, for twelve hours. He heard neither the rumpus over the insects, nor the voice of his old friend below. For four days he had ridden south over the most unsettling terrain he has ever encountered. Even that terrifying battlefield at Dybbøl had been open land — you knew where your enemy was. Here, everything was strange and unknown. Hidden. God knew what or who might be lurking behind the densely looming trees. Also, his progress was atop a horse. Napoleon could manage any kind of water transport, from full-rigged sailing ship to tiny rowing boat, but the jolting, creaking gait of a horse was an utterly new experience to him and it seemed that every bone and muscle in his young body complained of the treatment. Sometimes he dismounted and walked beside his horse, but then the scale of the trees towering above him, his own insignificance among all this lonely grandeur, began to intimidate him, and he would remount, just to feel bonded again to a creature of flesh and blood.

Wanganui itself was not so difficult. The small town on the river seemed familiar enough, with its streets and houses and noisy businesses. The captain of his ship allowed him to live on board in return for occasional work, and the gentle rise and fall of the ship, its knock, knock against the solid wood of Taupo Quay, comforted him each night. For a week he wandered the streets enjoying the new sights, asking — in a colourful English learned from a Cornish sailor during the journey out — after Enok. Always he drew a blank. Bishop Monrad, though, was well known. The local

31

preacher, Reverend Taylor, a kind man and a good friend of the bishop's, helped him to buy a horse and provisions and described the fifty-mile journey down to Karere.

'There are rivers to cross,' he said, 'which require some care. The bishop has lost a good friend, drowned in a river crossing. Do you swim?'

Napoleon nodded, too ashamed to admit that he couldn't. Swimming in the cold waters of the Faroe Islands was considered a foolish activity, and none of his friends had learned the skill.

'If the river is shallow,' said Taylor, with a shrewd look that made the lad blush, 'stay on the horse, leave the reins slack and let him walk you through at his own pace. If the river is deep, it is better to dismount and hold tightly to the saddle. Your horse will swim sturdily and you may float safely alongside him.'

Napoleon wanted to ask how many deep rivers lay in his path, but only frowned in what he hoped was a manly fashion, and nodded.

'And if the river is in flush from a storm — if large logs are tumbling downriver — do not under any circumstances attempt a crossing till the waters subside. The rivers in this country are surprising and dangerous. They rise and fall quickly. We are not used to such moods, as many settlers have learned to their cost. They call it the National Death here — drowning.'

'Ay then, thanks to you,' said Napoleon, hoping the warnings were over. And that he had understood the crisp English words fully. His sailor friend had spoken slowly, with much thought and chewing of his tobacco between one sentence and the next.

Taylor smiled and clapped him on the shoulder. 'You look a lively lad, you'll do fine. All your countrymen seem to thrive on the settler's life, even Monrad, who must surely have been used to more refined conditions. Take your time. The natives are mostly friendly down towards Foxton and will help when you need it. If they invite you to sleep or eat with them, accept gracefully.' After a pause he remembered another piece of advice. 'And don't call the town Foxton. It's not a popular name down there. The old name is Te Awahou.'

'Te Awahou,' said Napoleon, wondering what 'mostly friendly' meant. But Reverend Taylor had other business to attend to. He indicated the track leading south along the coast, shook the boy's hand and strode back towards his house, leaving Napoleon to struggle with the problem of mounting his horse.

He made slow progress, sometimes walking sometimes riding, unable to impress his will on the fortunately placid horse, which would stop to lower its head and graze at every opportunity.

On his second day the towering trees gave way to more open country, covered in tall flax and low bush. For some time Napoleon walked his horse along the beach, loving the smell of salt air and the sight of an ocean horizon. His spirits rose again at the first large river he encountered. Two natives were there to ferry him and his horse across on a crude barge. They were indeed friendly, and offered him fresh vegetables and an egg, which he cooked in his skillet over a driftwood fire in the sand dunes, singing aloud with pleasure. He half expected Enok to stroll casually out of the dunes. Enok would be near the sea, surely. Napoleon hoped to find his friend quickly, without having to stay too long in the dark interior of this huge island. Back home, he could walk right across his island of Streymoy in an hour or two; could stand on its highest point and see almost all of it, laid open to the wind and the sky. To Napoleon, this great land, empty of people and crowded with trees, had some kind of menace at its heart, like a muffled drumbeat, scarcely heard.

On the third day he crossed a small river by ferry. He looked enviously at the river craft drawn up on the bank. Now *there* was a proper method of transport! He watched the natives pole their narrow dugout canoes upriver through the shallows, admired the way they controlled their craft through the rapids. I could learn that, he thought, but had not the words to ask. Already he was forgetting his English, much less learning any Maori words. Smiling, nodding his thanks for the ferry trip, he headed inland again. Here the bush became more and more dense, the track a thin line between towering trunks. Often the horse plodded up to its hocks in mud. To Napoleon it was as if the world were pressing down on his head. All day he saw no one.

At one time a large river lay in his path and for half an hour he stood at its edge, unable to decide whether to ride his horse through it or stay dismounted and hold onto the saddle as the Reverend had advised. Finally he mounted and set across. His hands shook with a fear he couldn't understand. Climbing aloft a ship's rigging in a storm with the mast heaving this way and that and the roaring sea far below held no fears to him. Yet a muddy river flowing with far less drama terrified him. When the horse stretched its neck and started swimming, Napoleon almost slid from the saddle. He lay across the horse's back, his legs trailing in the warm water. Moaning like a baby, he clung to the mane until his horse found its feet again with a rearing jolt that toppled Napoleon into the shallows. For some time he sat on the bank, too shaken to remount. Later, tired and saddle-sore, he slept badly on damp moss, both he and the horse twitching and slapping at the whine and sting of mosquitoes.

At last, on the fourth day, a more familiar landscape emerged. Every few miles through the bush he would hear the ringing sound of axe blows and would emerge into sunlight — a clearing — with sheep grazing among the stumps. Sheep! Strangely white like so many maggots on a great carcass. Nothing like the shaggy, long-legged Faroese sheep, which wore blobs of brown and black and white — every one an individual. But still, these were sheep — as white and out of place as himself, yet seemingly unconcerned by this wild, dark landscape. Napoleon could have hugged the dear placid beasts. One sturdy farmer gave him a wedge of bread and mutton to eat as he travelled, another a letter to take to the bishop. Now the path was easy — straight as a die through the bush, in and out of these clearings, until the larger holding of Bishop Monrad's came into view, the house on a rise, imposing after the simple log-and-mud cabins he had passed earlier.

Napoleon presented his letters and gifts, apologised for his muddy clothes. Ladies chattering in familiar Danish crowded around, welcoming him, praising his journey, full of questions about the homeland. His head swam with it all — his voice too loud, his grin too wide — but they didn't seem to mind. Once he had to turn away to hide foolish tears. Later, washed and well fed, in a clean nightshirt belonging to one of the sons, he fell asleep and dreamed of the wide, windswept hills of Streymoy.

'WELL now, young Rasmussen,' says the bishop, eyeing Conrad sternly, 'shall we have a word in my study, mmh?' This is not really a question; the bishop has already entered the small room, leaving Conrad to follow.

Everywhere the rank smell of burnt tobacco leaves hangs in the air, but perhaps the Monrads are used to it. Conrad can hear them banging pots in the kitchen and the rattle of cutlery, someone tapping out a tune on the piano. He would like Anahuia to slip into the room behind him, but of course she is not invited.

This tiny study is full of books. On a small table a folio of etchings lies open. Other paintings and drawings hang on the walls. Shelves, some beautifully crafted, others simple rough-sawn planks, hold more books and papers than Conrad has seen in his whole life.

The bishop sits heavily on the only chair and plants his hands on his knees. He leans back and gazes at Conrad. The expression is not unkind — quizzical rather, and penetrating. Conrad can imagine the great man sitting in Parliament in Copenhagen dealing with grave matters of state.

'I seem to recall,' says Monrad at last, 'that when you first came here seeking employment, you mentioned the Knud Rasmussens of northern Jutland? Relatives, you said, of the late King Frederik's wife, who, as we all know, was a Rasmussen?'

Conrad looks out the window and says nothing.

'The ring you wear: did you not suggest it connected you with an ancient line of noble Rasmussens from that area?'

Conrad covers the ring with his other hand and remains silent.

'Perhaps I remember incorrectly? Did you not mention that your accent was on account of your mother, who is Icelandic and descended from Vikings?'

Conrad shrugs his wide shoulders. He is too big for this room. 'Herr Biskop, is it a crime to invent colourful stories? Surely I am not the only one who arrives in this country with a past he would rather forget?'

A cheeky answer that does not help matters. The bishop frowns. A silence develops. Then he sighs and nods.

'Forgive me. I should not tease you. But you have misled me, have you not?'

Conrad tries to smile, but there is too much anxiety behind it. His face twists.

'In God's name, sir, I have worked well for you. You would not turn me over to the officials? A man's past —'

'Rasmussen, take heart, I will do no such thing. Nor will your visitor. You are in fact from the Faroe Islands?'

Conrad takes a slow breath. 'I am,' he says. 'I am a Faroeman.' He grins and this time the pleasure is clear. 'By God, it is good to say that again.'

'I have received a letter from Haraldsen of Streymoy. The name means something to you?'

Conrad is amazed. '*Haraldsen* is your visitor?'

'He is not.' The bishop stands. He is a big man, though shorter than Conrad. His hairline has receded — or perhaps it has always left his great forehead bare. He is wiry and sunburned from his months breaking in his land, but still there is a gravity about him — the mark of a scholar. He looks tired — or is it discouraged? The voice is pleasant but reserved, a little remote. 'I think our man is awake,' he says now. 'That will be his step on the stair. Shall we . . .'

In the hallway, Conrad looks up. Someone is descending but his face is in shadow. The visitor has no such problem, as an oil-lamp glows in the hall. 'Enok!' he shouts. 'Enok!' And clatters down the stairs to trip at the bottom and fall headlong into his friend's arms. 'Gud signi teg! Enok!'

For a moment Conrad cannot recognise him. Something sad and tired in the eyes. A bitterness, perhaps. Then Conrad lets out a roar of astonishment. 'Napoleon? How is this possible?' He holds the boy at arm's length to make sure, then folds him in a bear hug that knocks all the wind out of the smaller man. 'Napoleon Haraldsen, what in the name of Thor are you doing here? Jesus and Mary, man, you could knock me down with a blade of grass!'

The bishop shepherds the two men into the front room, where the women are gathered. Anahuia stands in the doorway, smiling. The two young men, though, have eyes only for each other. They shout questions and answers in their native Faroese, then break into laughter. Conrad drapes an arm over Napoleon's shoulder and the two dance a few steps together, smiling at some shared memory.

'No, no,' laughs Napoleon, 'I am not on the run. I came to find *you*! Clara sends her love, by the way.' He winks.

Conrad casts an eye sideways to see if Anahuia has heard. He cannot tell.

The visitor's eyes are shining with excitement. He has travelled to the other side of the world and found this friend whom he has idolised since he first set eyes on him. 'Enok, I have come to take you home, you dolt!' he cries. For a moment he tries to look solemn. It seems as if he will salute. 'You are needed.'

Conrad frowns. 'Home? No, it's not possible. There are things you don't know. The navy —'

Napoleon laughs. 'Yes, we heard. Whatever possessed you, you idiot? But my father has had a word with the authorities. The officer . . . well, the officer now realises it would be more . . . suitable . . . if the matter were buried. Ha! At any rate, Enok, things are different now. A new government . . .' He glances quickly at Monrad, who is listening with interest, trying to catch the half-familiar words.

'It seems,' says the bishop, 'that we have some interesting stories hidden away here. Perhaps after the meal we may hear them?'

Conrad blushes and switches quickly to Danish. 'That story is not one for the ladies. Nor anyone, sir. I'm not too proud of it.' He turns back to Napoleon. 'But how can I come home? How am I needed?'

'Magnus is dead.'

Conrad releases a long sigh. 'Ahh . . . but Otto?'

'What about Otto?'

'I damaged him. Badly.'

Napoleon shakes his head impatiently. 'Otto is fine. Too fine. Didn't you read your mother's letters?'

'What letters?'

'No, no, no!' Monrad interrupts. 'This is too much! The ladies have no idea what is going on and nor have I. We need not forget manners just because we are in this wild place. Louise, bring Karen from wherever she is and we will have our Bible reading. There are fresh eels and a pukeko in the pot, and our own potatoes. After a good meal (and some general news from Denmark, please, young man), perhaps we will forgo our Shakespeare and hear young . . . Enok's . . . story. If not the navy incident, your earlier life. Haraldsen suggested it was of interest.'

'Get him to sing!' cries Napoleon. 'He is famous!'

The bishop's wife, Emilie, who has sat, tired and pale, through all the excitement, looks up with interest as Napoleon mentions music, but the Bible is now in Monrad's hands. He takes them all in with a stern look. Here is someone who expects to be listened to.

'I will read from Genesis, Chapter 22. God's testing of Abraham . . .'

As they sit quietly listening to the familiar words read in the bishop's beautiful, strong voice, Enok and Napoleon exchange frequent looks. There is so much to say! But while Napoleon's face beams with pride and excitement, Enok's smile is troubled. He never imagined returning home would be possible. There is Anahuia to be considered. No, a return is not possible. He looks for her but she has gone from the doorway.

The bishop's voice rises and falls. '". . . and Abraham built an altar there, and laid the wood in order, and bound Isaac his son and laid him on the altar . . ."'

Images from Enok's youth crowd into his head. His island. His family. The time spent studying at Tórshavn. Memories that he has not dared to dwell on now creep back, warm and insidious. The rolling lines of the great sagas he has learned swell in his ears until he is lost in their ocean.

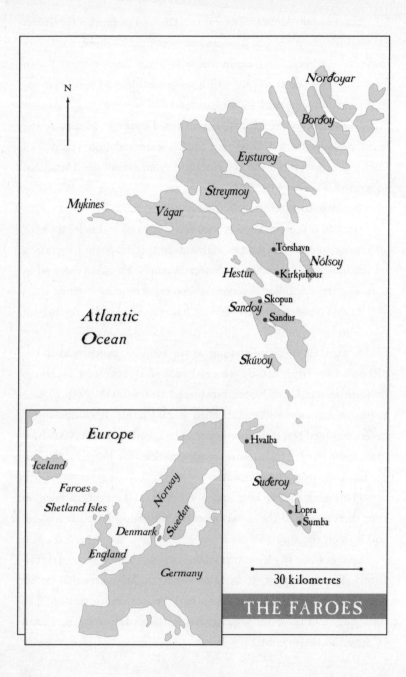

N

Norðoyar

Borðoy

Eysturoy

Streymoy

Mykines

Vágar

Atlantic
Ocean

•Tórshavn

Nólsoy

Hestur   •Kirkjubøur

•Skopun

Sandoy

•Sandur

Skúvoy

Europe

Iceland

Faroes

Shetland Isles

Norway

Sweden

Denmark

England

Germany

•Hvalba

Suðeroy

•Lopra
•Sumba

30 kilometres

THE FAROES

2.

Feuds and Ballads

THE FAROE ISLANDS
1862–64

1.

OLD NICLAS PATURSSON scratches his head and says the sight of that boy being rowed in brings ancient heroes to mind, and the teacher Johannes Müller has to agree. What a sight! The lad comes into the harbour this long summer day, standing up in the bow as if he were spearman at a whale kill. Pale hair shining, grin splitting his face. Is he singing — or shouting, perhaps? Something with excitement and pleasure about it, certainly.

'He's going to upset the boat,' says the teacher, 'flinging his arms around like that. Silly boy.'

Old Niclas laughs. 'Not he. That's young Enok of Sumba. From Suðeroy.' As if that explains everything.

For three hours Niclas Patursson has been sitting here on the stone bench at Tinganes, partly sheltered by the bulk of Parliament House, most famous building in all the Faroe Islands. Sooner or later the boat would come in and he wanted to be the first to greet the boy. As it turned out, the wind had blown up from the north. A small boat beating up the sound would always find the north wind heavy going, so the arrival was delayed. Niclas lit his pipe, pulled his woollen cap down over his ears and waited. They would come around the headland from the south. He watched the expanse of white-capped sea between the island Nólsoy and this small town where he had lived all the seventy-two years of his life. Not so small a town now, in fact. When he was born, Tórshavn housed forty families; now there were nearly two hundred. The place was bursting at the seams! Old Niclas shook his head, thinking of the speed of it. The land wouldn't cope — any fool could work that out. Faroese soil was poor, the warmth of the sun in short supply. You couldn't just say to the barley or the potatoes, 'Grow faster and richer this year — there are more mouths to feed.' The young ones and the foreigners believed fish would be the shining future for the Faroes, but how many people would the fish support? And for how long? Old Niclas knew in his bones that the old rules were sensible. A man shouldn't be allowed to marry and set up house and have children just when he felt like it. The population had to be kept in balance with the land.

Johannes Müller, walking down to the stone landing dock at the end of the school day, saw the old man there, shaking his head and muttering. For a while the teacher breathed in the fresh salty air, enjoying the rare sunlight, the sea-birds wheeling and crying in the wind. Then he approached the old man, as was expected, and greeted him with respect.

'Good evening, Niclas Patursson. I have watched you sitting here and shaking your head. Does something trouble you?'

The old man looked up sharply, but then grinned and wagged a finger. 'Now then, teacher, would you make fun of an old man who has gained much wisdom over many years? Years during which this teacher was neither on these islands nor even born?'

Müller laughed and the old man joined in. Foreign teachers were acceptable, in the old man's strict view of matters. Niclas Patursson was a famous and argumentative conservative, for many years a powerful speaker in the Løgting, though no longer a representative on that council. He had led the resistance to every change of policy, had deplored the influx of Danish fishermen, had given a memorable and entertaining speech ridiculing the proposal, by some Danish farming expert, to introduce — 'yet again!' — the use of the plough on Faroese soil. But a Danish teacher, like a Danish priest, was traditional, so Niclas had no quarrel with Herr Müller. This serious young man, with his brown hair and brown eyes, his quiet voice and polite manners, would stay for another year, perhaps two, until the Danish government sent another teacher just like him. That was the way it had always been, and Niclas felt comfortable with it.

But now he narrows his old eyes and stands for a better view. Here comes the boat around the headland, tossing and yawing in the choppy sea.

'They should take down the sail,' says Niclas, and at that moment down comes the sail, leaving the work to the ten sets of oars. 'A Suðeroy boat,' he explains to the teacher. 'They build them bigger for crossing open sea. You don't see them so often these days, now the Monopoly is disbanded and any sort of person may set up a shop. Even a landless man!' He shakes his head to rid it of such gloomy thoughts. 'Yes, this will be our boy. Your pupil and mine.'

Müller has not caught up with this news. How information travels around the eighteen islands is a mystery to him. The fishermen seem to be fiercely self-contained and secretive when rowing in and out, and yet how else could the Faroese learn all the minute details of everyone's life almost before it happens? An extra pupil will be welcome, though, in his new — the first — high school. Families from the outer islands have been slow to accept that a high-school education might benefit a son who is destined for farming or fishing.

'Is that him?' asks Müller. 'The boy in the bow?'

That's when old Niclas makes his remark about ancient heroes, and the teacher, watching that upright spirited lad, feels an excitement coming from both the old man and the boy. An excitement that he would like to contain.

'Silly boy,' he says.

But now old Niclas is walking slowly down to the dock. Müller follows. The eight rowers heave the beautiful white boat through the water. Its prow juts clean and square above the curving sweep of the overlapping planks. Even the oars are painted a brilliant white. The man at the tiller shouts an order and one bank of oars flicks upright as the other bank brings the boat around to touch, with scarcely a bump, against the dock. The boy — he is a man, surely, given his height and the breadth of his shoulders — leaps ashore, shouting something the teacher cannot understand, to tie ropes fore and aft. As he helps to unload barrels of train-oil and salted klipfish and canvas-wrapped parcels — knitted goods and feathers, no doubt — he is talking all the time, joking with the oarsmen, shouting instructions, though he is surely the youngest aboard.

Niclas Patursson turns to the teacher. 'Look at him!' There's pride in his voice as if the boy were his son. 'A leader already. They say Enok of Sumba will be important for our islands one day. Already they say he is the best ballad singer in all Suðeroy. I can see greatness in him even now.' Then he frowns as the tall lad shouts an order to the oldest of the oarsmen. 'But it may be that both you and I will need to teach him a few manners. Enok!'

The boy turns, quick on his feet for all his size. The fair skin of his face is wind-burned from the long trip and his smile open, ready for whoever calls. He squints up against the pale summer sun, which will set today for only two hours. For a moment he looks at the two men standing on the steps above him, then he comes up to them with his hand outstretched as if he were man greeting friend, not boy meeting, for the first time, his teachers.

'Herr Patursson, is it?' he says, and when the old man nods, the boy grasps his hand in both of his own and shakes vigorously. 'Gud signi teg! It is a great honour to meet you. My stepfather sends warmest greetings and my mother has sent something more substantial. Wait!'

He turns to run back for the parcel his mother has sent but old Niclas speaks sternly.

'Enok, the gifts can wait; is there some reason we are so pressed for time that you ignore the man who stands at my side?'

The boy stops in mid-flight, turns back with a groan and slaps a hand at his forehead. The dismay is so genuine and so comical that even stern old Niclas cannot keep a straight face.

'The problem is,' says the boy, grinning now to see he has won them over, 'that it is all so exciting. So new! So many houses! All these boats! How will I ever get to know them all? I'm sorry. My apologies.'

Again he holds out a large hand as if greeting a friend. 'Gud signi teg! I am Enok Rasmussen of Sumba, Suðeroy.'

This exchange has all been in Faroese and Müller has had difficulty following, but he understands the introduction.

'And I am Herr Müller, of Sønderborg, Als, Denmark,' he replies in Danish. 'Teacher at the realskole here in Tórshavn.'

'Ah. I am pleased to meet you.' Enok switches to good Danish. His smile, though, becomes uncertain. 'My mother wishes me to

attend the realskole, but perhaps this other study will not allow time
. . . Also,' and his face brightens as he looks around at the houses,
the green fields sloping up this way and that from the shore, the
jutting cliffs of Nólsoy across the sound, 'there will be much to
explore and learn in this new place.'

'You will attend to my teaching and to realskole, both,' says old
Niclas firmly, 'and no doubt find time for exploration as well. The
days are long at this time of year. Now, finish your work and then
come up for a meal.' He indicates his house, on a rise a little isolated
from the rest, built in the old style: low to the ground, its wide
sloping roof covered in grass. 'There is much to discuss.'

As the boy runs backs to the boat, waving and shouting again
to his friends, Müller turns to the old man. 'Did I miss something
in your conversation? You are to teach him?'

The old man nods; sighs. 'Yes. It is ambitious. A Faroese matter.
I am to teach him the middle section of a special kvæði — one of
our ballads. I have always been known for this one. It is very, very
long. His father was famous for the first section.'

The teacher waits for more, but Niclas is ready to move now, up
towards the houses.

'The boy's own story,' says Niclas, 'is also a long one, like the
kvæði he is to learn. I will tell you another day. You will need to
know it. You will also need to be careful where Otto is concerned.
Otto may cause some trouble.' After uttering this peculiar warning
Niclas smiles. 'But then they are young and perhaps I am fearful
only of old ghosts.'

2.

ONE WEEK AFTER Enok Rasmussen's arrival, Johannes Müller realises that his promised talk with Niclas is already overdue. He watches from the window of the schoolroom as his pupils run through the misty village during their midday break. Enok has led them out, shouting and laughing and goading them on. The fifteen boys and one girl have followed him readily, but had never thought of going so far themselves. Müller watches as Enok kicks the ball high, then runs after it, dodging the tiny jumbled plots and gardens of the infield, nimble as a cat at avoiding men and women at work. The others follow, with less success, earning a few shouts and threats. One farmer turns to glare back at the schoolhouse. He shakes a fist when he spots Müller at the window.

Over the stone wall and free to run on the sloping grass of the outfield, the young men kick the ball back and forth, setting the sheep running this way and that. There will be more complaints, no doubt. But Müller is pleased to see his pupils active. He has been trained by the modern techniques recently set in place by the new Danish education minister, D. G. Monrad; he believes the mind works more quickly if the bloodstream is well oxygenated from time to time. If there is no flat land for a school field, then the stony, lumpy outfield, farmed jointly by all the landowners, will have to serve.

This strange land still surprises Müller, who is used to the flat farms of his native Denmark. Here the smooth grassy fields tilt this way and that, like giant choppy waves. Dark cliffs rise from the sea to meet, abruptly, the sweeps and crags of the fields; not a tree to break the line: sea, cliffs, fields, crags repeated and repeated. Then the slash of a fjord and another island, with choppy fields and towering cliffs and a small village or two set wherever the land swoops low enough to provide access to the sea. Villagers must augment the poor results of farming with the riches that sea and cliffs provide, so it is important to live near the sea, and to own a boat.

This small footprint in the Atlantic Ocean, nearer in distance to the Shetland Islands, and in language to Iceland, but traditionally part of Denmark, is interesting to Müller, but only up to a point. He finds the people too resistant to new ideas, too conservative in all their ways. He will be ready enough to leave when he has served his two years. Meantime, he will encourage some of these pupils to break away, to continue their studies back in Denmark and perhaps bring back some fresh ways of thinking. In his view the minds of the Faroese are as clammed up as the foggy weather.

The girl, Clara, could well be one to escape, he thinks, though her father is unlikely to consider a girl's education as a priority. Clara has not joined in the antics of the boys. She sits on the stone

50

wall, looking back to the village and the sea. In Müller's opinion she is the best scholar in the school — much brighter than her brother, Napoleon, and more open to new ideas than Otto, who is also clever. But Enok? The teacher sighs. The boy's mind is like quicksilver — always on the move, and rarely on the subject at hand. In discussions he will contribute — dominate, even — presenting views that are challenging and occasionally pertinent. He loves to talk and the others enjoy listening to this engaging newcomer. Old Niclas is right — the boy is a natural leader. But pinning him down to his bookwork is another matter. After two minutes of copying or writing his essay Enok will be fidgeting. His fair head will rise, his blue eyes searching the room for a soulmate. If all the other heads are down he will throw a smile at the frowning Herr Müller, shrug and try again. But a minute later his head is up again to address the quiet classroom with some provocative idea or other.

'Why do they write it like this in Danish? It doesn't look like it sounds.' Or 'Frederik, Christian, Christian Frederik — what about a new name for a king? How can we remember all this? What about Olaf? Or Sjúrður? They should choose heroes.'

He can usually provoke a discussion, the wretch, and Müller himself is often drawn in against his better judgement. But the boy will not pass his exams — and the work of the others may suffer — if the situation is allowed to continue.

Müller steps outside to ring the ship's bell, salvaged by a fisherman, gifted to the school and set in a painted frame outside the door. Enok leads the charge back down the hill, grinning and whooping, and the teacher finds himself smiling in response. When the boy trips leaping the steps up to the classroom, and comes crashing down in a heap, Müller is among the crowd of concerned pupils who pick him up and dust him off and gently probe the scraped skin for deeper bruises.

Otto is the only one who stands back. He watches the scene quietly, and the teacher, moving away now that no disaster is apparent, notices the boy's agitation. With forefinger and thumb Otto plucks at his knitted jersey just above his heart. Pick pick pick, the fingers pinch the wool as if a burr is caught there. Otto is slightly built and tall — not as tall as Enok, but still taller than his teacher. He leans against the wall of the schoolhouse, one knee bent. The stance is casual but the look in his green eyes is intent. Pick pick, go the fingers as Otto watches. Enok, the centre of attention, laughs ruefully and rubs the spot where the skin is now beginning to ooze blood.

Müller admires Otto; he is a striking lad, athletic and confident, reserved and polite to his teacher, but open enough with the other pupils. He is fair, like most Faroese, though his hair is more honey-gold than ash-blond, and his skin a little more deeply coloured. There is an odd alertness in those green eyes now, as Otto watches Enok. It's as if the boy is waiting for something, Müller thinks. He is on edge, expecting — what? — and is puzzled, perhaps, that nothing happens. Müller remembers again old Niclas's warning and resolves to invite the old farmer to the schoolhouse for a drink.

'Well then, my pupils,' says Müller. 'It seems no one is going to die around here, so perhaps we can resume our studies?'

Serious Napoleon offers Enok an arm and Clara quickly steps to his other side. The wounded scholar leans more dramatically than is necessary, especially on Clara's arm. His smile of thanks would melt solid granite, which Clara most certainly is not. The teacher is not the only person to notice that Otto draws in his breath softly as if he is the one in pain.

THE lesson this afternoon is modern Danish history — the vexed Slesvig/Holsten problem. Should the Danish kingdom allow the more German duchy of Holsten to separate and become part of Germany? Some Danes think so, says Müller, but none believe that the Germans should claim any of Slesvig, even though the majority there now, it seems, are German-speaking. Müller, who was born on the island of Als, which is generally considered part of North Slesvig, becomes more and more animated as the afternoon progresses. He is adamantly of the belief that not one inch of either duchy should be ceded to Germany.

'Where is the precedent? What do the past statutes say? The duchies have always been Danish, ruled by Danish kings since ancient times. And so it should stay!'

Even Enok is captured by the teacher's rhetoric. Müller can feel that the class is with him, which is not always the case. He marches over to the map of Denmark that hangs on the wall, beside the framed portrait of King Frederik VII. He stabs with his ruler at the more northern of the two duchies, Slesvig, whose boundary adjoins Danish Jutland.

'Here I myself grew up, a Danish boy, speaking my native tongue, honouring our Danish customs and heroes. Those Holsteners from the south wanted to make us all speak German as first language in all the schools of Slesvig! True, there are many German-speakers in Slesvig, but since time immemorial that land has been governed by Denmark. It is hallowed Danish soil. Imagine our anger at such a proposal! I saw, with a boy's frightened eyes, my father march out to join with the Danish army. I waited with my mother, anxious for news. Those Holsteners have powerful allies. Who?'

'Prussia,' says Otto.

'And our brave Danes marched to repulse them. Date?'

'1848 Holsten invaded Slesvig,' says Otto, before anyone else has time to take breath.

'*Tried* to invade, Otto. We repulsed them. And again, gloriously and against the odds, two years later. Name of battle? Not you, Otto.'

Another lad finally comes up with Isted Heath. But now Enok is on his feet, hands sketching new theories in the air.

'But sir, you are surely inconsistent!'

Müller frowns. He does not expect to be challenged on this, of all subjects. As usual Enok's thoughts have taken him on a tangent.

'The language, sir. You are saying that everyone in Slesvig should learn Danish in schools, even if Danes are fewer in number than the German-speakers?'

'It is their *right*, Enok. Think, think, boy! If you lose your language, you lose your culture, your identity with your past.'

Enok smiles broadly. His enthusiasm for his argument carries him to the front of the classroom, where he towers over the teacher. 'Ah, then. What about me?' He indicates his fellow students. 'All of us? We are Faroemen, every one. We have grown up speaking Faroese. Our language is at the heart of our culture, yet all we learn is Danish history and everything we learn is in the Danish language. Where have *our* rights disappeared to, then? There is your inconsistency.'

He looks in triumph to the rest of the class. Most of them, however, have their eyes lowered, embarrassed by such a bold outburst against a respected teacher. Enok, puzzled and hurt by their lack of support, rails at them in Faroese.

'You know I'm right! We have our own stories and songs in our own language.'

Otto, however, meets his eye and, as usual, is ready with an answer, before Müller can gather his own defence.

'You are not right, Enok Rasmussen,' Otto says quietly, in Danish, from his seat. 'Perhaps you should wait at least a few weeks before you bring down the education system.' This earns him a laugh from everyone. 'Over the centuries Denmark has supplied us food and bought our goods. Without her support the Faroes would surely wither and perish.'

'Yes, but —'

Enok is ready to argue. To him the exchange is an entertainment. But Otto is deadly serious and overrides him easily.

'If we do not speak the language of the Danes, trade with her, learn her culture and history, we will be shutting ourselves in a box labelled Extinct. We have no written history, no tradition of writing down our songs and stories, no books. How can we learn in Faroese if there are no books to learn from? You should sit down, Enok, and show some respect to your teacher.'

The words are innocuous enough, but the heavy tone carries more than a hint of a threat.

Enok is suddenly angry. He takes a step towards Otto, fists clenched, breathing hard through his nose. Otto stands quietly to face him but makes no sound, shows no sign of anger or fear. For a moment the two boys eye each other. Then Clara reaches up from her seat at the front of the room and plucks at the sleeve of Enok's beautiful knitted jersey. Enok looks down at her, then around at the other pupils, and the mood is broken. He clears his throat, looks at Müller, then back at Otto. He shrugs.

'Well, there is something in that, certainly. I am only putting forward a view.' He grins. 'Something in both sides of the argument, eh? Sorry to interrupt, teacher. I am not used to being always on the listening side!'

Enok walks to his seat at the back of the room and makes a rather exaggerated performance of sitting and listening attentively.

The lesson continues. The rights of the Danes living in Slesvig are revisited and this time Enok is silent. But a new atmosphere has entered the room. It is as if Otto and Enok have grown in size and the others have shrunk. The pupils listen quietly but Müller feels that only half their attention is on him. They are also listening to silent vibrations bouncing back and forth between Otto and Enok.

3.

The story of Róland of Suðeroy
and the whale kill

OLD NICLAS WEARS his knitted cap and his thick jersey inside the schoolhouse. The air is chilly, even though it is near midsummer, but Niclas does not expect a warm room. The fire smouldering quietly in the firebox is tiny — a large fire at this time of year would be considered wasteful. Dried peat is a hard-won and therefore valued commodity. The old man's cheeks, though, are on fire from the teacher's imported brandy and he is ready now to tell his story. He has declined the offer of a meal, saying he knows his own stomach and will prepare his own food. In fact he chose to eat in his own home because of Enok. Niclas likes to coach the boy while the two eat their meal. He has found that Enok's memory works best on a full stomach, and is reluctant to lose a precious minute of the task in hand.

Now old Niclas is seated on the bench nearest to the fireplace in a room which, like most on these islands, is practical — severe, you might say: stone and timber walls, the bare necessities of furniture fashioned from the timber of shipwrecks and driftwood, the one softening effect a woven wool rug dyed in the muted colours of the landscape. The teacher sits against the wall on the other side of the firebox. Niclas considers this a modern room — there is a table and a chair in the corner, and an iron stand above the firebox for cooking. Müller occupies the upper storey of this house; below live the primary school teacher, his wife and three children. The windows are small and lack curtains. The pale night sun casts an eerie light into the room, almost as silver as moonlight. Outside a single guillemot rides the wind for a moment, then slants abruptly west, heading for the cliffs.

The old man rolls the wine glass in his hands and brandy tips this way and that, catching the low sunlight and shooting golden flecks across the room. He looks across at Müller.

'Enok of Sumba,' he says, 'is the son of a famous ballad singer. In our hearts, you must understand, the ballad singers — those who can perform the best and oldest of our kvæði — are held in the highest esteem in these islands. Those who hold *power* are Danish, usually, and of course we honour them . . .' Old Niclas is not being diplomatic; he believes in this order of things, '. . . but among our own people the ballad singers carry our stories in their heads. We have no way to write them down, as you know.'

Johannes Müller nods and smiles to himself. Where has he heard this recently?

Old Niclas takes a small sip of his brandy, shakes his head as if arguing with himself over something, then places the glass carefully on the floor beside him. He is ready, at last, to tell the story. He closes his eyes and begins.

'RÓLAND of Sumba was a Rasmussen — a Faroeman from Suðeroy. Suðeroy, you understand, is the most southern of our islands and the most isolated. The other islands are separated one from the next by narrow channels. With some you can hold a conversation across the fjord without raising your voice, but Suðeroy is different. A stretch of wild and open sea separates it from the rest of us. So in that southern island the people are more independent — and more conservative, if you can imagine that! — than up here. Old ways die last in Suðeroy, and last of all in Sumba.

'Róland was the younger son of a landowner who had only one mark of land to pass on. That mark went to Róland's elder brother, as is the custom and the law here. But Róland was not one to be defeated by such a misfortune. Imagine Enok twenty years older, perhaps a little wiser, but certainly no less hot-headed, and you have his father. Energy to burn. Tall, fair like Enok and very strong. He wore his hair long like the heroes in the ballads he sang. Sumba folk are large people and mostly fair. Some say a Viking hero spent time there long ago and fathered a special breed. Who knows? Look at me. I was once dark-haired and have always been small. I believe that here in the northern islands our blood is mixed with that of Celts from the Shetland Islands. Well, that is by the by. Certainly Sumba people sing their kvæði with such fervour, stamp the dance so energetically that no other Faroese village can match them.

'So then, Róland, Enok's father. He made his living as a fisherman until the law was passed to abolish the Monopoly. You understand about the Monopoly?'

Müller nods. The system by which the Danish government supplied the islands with their needs and bought their goods at fixed prices in return had been in operation for centuries. Often grumbled over by both the government (poor investment) and the Faroemen (too restrictive), it had no doubt saved the Faroes in years of failed crops or poor fishing. Müller is of the opinion that it was unwise to abolish the Monopoly; that the fragile economy of the tiny Faroes is now dangerously exposed.

Obviously old Niclas thinks the same. 'A foolish move,' he mutters. 'The Monopoly, with its trading post here at Tórshavn, united us. All Faroemen, even from Suðeroy, had to come here to buy and sell. We exchanged stories and passed on news. No good will come of this fragmentation. No good.'

He picks up his brandy glass, looks into it, then smiles up at Müller. The dour old face lightens and the teacher is suddenly warmed by a charm he has not seen before.

'Oho,' says Niclas, 'I had better not take any more of this excellent liquor or I will be off on every side-road and lost in some bog before I get to Enok himself. That is no way to tell a story, as I should well know. Now. Sumba.'

As the story unfolds, the old man's voice grows stronger. The face is impassive but the words rise in pitch, then fall away with the rhythm and emotion of the tale. Almost, he is singing. Müller is drawn into the tragedy. This man is a true storyteller. The teacher can picture the events, though he has never been to Suðeroy and will perhaps never sail that far south.

'Róland Rasmussen,' says old Niclas, 'may have been landless, but his good looks and his skill with the ballads and his fine, open ways made him a favourite with everyone, especially the girls. He could have chosen any of many for a wife, but the stubborn lad had to set his eye on a Dahl. Else Dahl. She was willing enough, too — a sweet thing, lively and open-hearted, nothing like the rest of the family. The Dahls are a powerful family, as you may know, owning five marks of land in Suðeroy and, through careful marriages, several marks of crown-lease land here on Streymoy. Old Magnus Dahl, Else's father — he's still alive — is a formidable man to this day, admired and hated in more or less equal measure by most Faroemen.

'It is never wise to cross a powerful man like Magnus Dahl, but wisdom was not a virtue held in high esteem by young Róland. He courted Else Dahl and won her heart, despite the black looks of the father and her two brothers. Else, the only daughter, had been set down for a sound marriage — to a wealthy farmer, owner of several marks of land, on another island. Magnus liked to have a finger in many pies. To make matters worse, the headstrong Róland arranged for his friend Hans Høgnesen, son of a wealthy and powerful priest, and newly ordained as a priest himself, to marry the couple without the knowledge or consent of Magnus. A very, *very* foolish matter, but then young people in love are blind to reason and imagine that all the world will forgive them; that their love is both a shield against ill-will and a magnet to kindness and warmth.

'To a certain extent that was indeed true. Róland and Else Rasmussen were popular and loved on the island, which only served to rub salt into the anger of the Dahl family. Magnus acted as if his only daughter no longer existed. In every way within their power, he and his two sons made life difficult and uncomfortable for the young pair. Not one fleece from the Dahl share of the annual sheep-shearing was presented to Else for carding and knitting. No small plot among the many belonging to Dahls in the infield was made available to the couple for growing crops or vegetables. The Dahl brothers, a surly pair, took every opportunity to ridicule the status of their sister.

'And yet the young Rasmussens thrived. Imagine the wrath of the powerful Dahls! Róland was a fine fisherman. His family's one possession was a good Suðeroy boat, which he and friends regularly rowed out. Róland knew every hidden reef, every rocky outcrop in the seas around the island — places where cod and haddock and coalfish were waiting, it seemed, to throw themselves upon his long-line. He favoured the Scottish practice of long-line fishing, which was suited to the open sea. More cautious fishermen kept to the old practice of two or three hooks on a short line — fine for the narrow fjords where a long-line would tangle, and safer in stormy weather, which was three days out of five — but young Róland was not one for safety, as we shall soon see.

'Well, so here was all this fine klipfish, split and salted by the Rasmussen family. Also pickled puffin chicks. Else's pickle was famous: a recipe her mother had handed to her as the only daughter. The loss of this recipe was another deep thorn in the Dahl side, Magnus's wife having died some years back. What provisions Else and Róland could not eat or sell on the island they brought up here to Tórshavn to sell to those who had business connections with Denmark.

'But Róland was not satisfied with this state of affairs. Not he! He set his heart on opening the first trading store on Suðeroy. If he had to make the long journey up to Tórshavn with his fish, why not return with a load of barley and salt, honey and liquor to sell back home? He and Else saved every skind. Róland combed every lonely cave and rocky inlet for driftwood. Our custom is that the first man or woman to lay hands on a piece of driftwood owns it, no matter where the log comes ashore. With these logs, and with stone gathered from the beach — for he possessed no land, remember — Róland began adding a large room to his mother's house, letting it be known that he was providing extra rooms for his growing family. In fact this was to be the trading post, but he kept his plans secret for fear the Dahls would move to set up a rival post before he had enough money for the initial stock.

'This was the state of affairs at the time of the fateful whale drive. The trading post half built, not quite enough money saved, two fine daughters born to them and Else again pregnant. You have not yet experienced a whale drive, I imagine?'

Müller looks up in surprise. He has been staring at the floor, lost in the story, and is now startled that the old man has broken the narrative to address him.

'No,' he says, 'not yet.'

'You will not forget the sight. A marvel of skill and excitement. Every Faroese boy lives for the day. It is like St Olaf's Day and Christmas and your birthday rolled into one. You must realise that though we Faroemen may be considered peaceful — phlegmatic, even — our blood runs high at a whale drive. The whales are like a precious gift that we all share. For years sometimes no pod comes near, and those are hard times for us. Even landowners with title to several marks of land can scarcely make ends meet without the bounty of train oil and whale bone to sell, or the flesh and blubber to eat. On the rare occasions when violence or worse breaks out on these islands, you may be sure that the incident is in some way connected to a whale drive. Well.'

Old Niclas takes a sip of brandy — 'oil the voice!' — winks at the teacher and resumes his tale.

'It was near midsummer — a time like this — and St Olaf's Day approaching. Róland Rasmussen was in a state of high excitement. (At no time could *Róland* be considered phlegmatic. He was a Sumba man to start with, and had high blood by nature.) Róland had finally accepted the challenge to sing the first two sections of the great Sjúrður ballad at the St Olaf's celebrations. Both in one night. No one had attempted such a feat of memory. His father knew the first section; I and another man from Nólsoy were known for singing the finest and longest second. The third was usually sung in the north, on Viðoy and Borðoy.

'Young Róland had lived with me at his father's request for the year before he married, in order to learn the middle section. A pleasure to teach he was — such a quick memory! It is important to teach the great kvæði early, while the mind is supple enough to absorb not only the accuracy of the words but the *spirit* — the weight and importance of the ballad. Cadence, intonation and tempo are of course left up to the brilliance — or sometimes the lack of it — of the individual. Róland's *Sjúrður Fafnirsbane* should not sound exactly like mine, but the *spirit* must be captured exactly.

'Now Róland felt ready to perform both kvæði. Villagers from all over the island would soon gather to listen to and dance the story. Even old men who had not attended a dance for years would come this time. There was much conjecture as to whether Magnus and his sons would attend. They were not singers, but of course they danced the kvæði. Who could stay away from a celebration like this? I myself was on the island to hear, and, naturally, to judge his performance. The priest Hans Høgnesen had offered his house for the dance. He had built a fine klingran — a sprung floor — especially for the purpose. If you dance all night, a good klingran is a blessing, especially for the old. And of course every housewife in Sumba was busy preparing food.

'The day before St Olaf's Day, Róland and his brother rowed out, hoping to bring in a good catch for the feast. Imagine their surprise and delight when, not far offshore, they found themselves in the centre of a large pod of caaing whale. A grind, we call it. Five or six hundred was the estimate. It was the first time for eighteen months a grind had ventured into their waters. And at St Olaf's! It seemed a sign to the excited young men. The sea was reasonably calm and if the sky glowered, well, what was unusual in that?

'No time to lose. The boys shipped their oars for fear of startling the beasts, and Róland hoisted his shirt up the mast, as is the custom, to signal their discovery. Flap flap in the breeze, the dancing garment was soon spotted by some bright lad watching sheep in the outfield. He ran first to the beacon set ready on the highest point above him, with tinder and wadding ready under a dry rock. This lit, he leapt down the field, feet flying among rocks, to bring the news to his village.

'"Grindabo∂! Grindabo∂!" he shouted, and soon the call was taken up by all. "Grindabo∂!" Oh, the excitement! Away sped fresh lads — all the fastest runners — to villages that might see neither the first beacon nor other fires lit by sharp watchers on more distant high fields.

'Soon boats were launched into the sea from every bay and jetty, men rowing with one hand while they fastened their sea-jackets and pulled their woollen caps low over their ears. Six or eight men rowing, depending on the size of the boat, and one in the bow with a spear. Those who had no place in a boat — mainly young boys and older men like myself — reached for spears and hooks and ran along the beach looking for where the whales would beach. The women and girls stayed inside, of course — to show themselves to the whales would bring boundless bad luck. Róland's wife Else, being pregnant, dared not even look out the window for fear she might jeopardise the drive. But be sure that the girls peeped as they prepared boiling water in abundance for the kidneys that would enrich their feast day. "Grindabo∂!" they sang, and praised God, who had sent such a gift to honour St Olaf. The priest, Hans Høgnesen, ran to the church, ready to fling wide the west door, facing the sea, that the good Lord Himself might welcome the whales to Sumba.

'Róland, standing tall in the bow of his boat, sang softly to the whales, of sea journeys and quiet summer days. "Lie basking there, dear brothers," he sang. "Enjoy a well-earned rest in this quiet bay." It would be a disaster if the grind changed direction and headed out to open sea before the foreman arrived to direct the little flotilla of boats. But here he came, wise old Sørin, nodding with approval at

65

the way Róland had quietly kept with the grind. Using hand signals, old Sørin directed the boats as they rowed in, sending them wide this way and that, until the grind was contained. Róland was in a fever to start the drive but the foreman waited patiently until all the slower boats rowed into place.

'At last the moment arrived. Sørin raised his hand, in it a stone tied by string to the boat. Carefully he threw it to splash behind a whale he judged to be a leader. Róland, tense with excitement, threw his own stone. Soon the sea was alive with the gentle splash of stones or the quiet smack of an oar. Yes! The grind turned lazily and began to swim towards the shore. Every rower bent to his oars, while every spearsman quietly encouraged the whales as Sørin directed.

'Slowly the grind turned and headed around the little island at the entrance of the bay. Róland turned to smile at the foreman. If they could be herded in here, where the beach shelved gently, they would run ashore without panic. A perfect spot, and close to the village. Yes! Yes! Shoreward the whales swam, the sea behind them churned white by the driving oarsmen. The men and boys on the shore, seeing where the grind was headed, silently moved away, left or right, leaving the beach open and quiet. On the hill above, the priest flung open the church door and sang a hymn of welcome.

'Just before the entrance to the bay was reached, a wily bull turned sharply, heading towards a rocky outcrop. Immediately his sonar told him danger lay ahead and he headed away, taking perhaps a hundred whales with him. If more followed, the operation might end in disaster. But an observant spearsman shouted the warning and nearby rowers bent their backs to plug the gap. The remaining whales were once more contained; they swam steadily in. At the perfect moment, old Sørin gave a mighty shout, striking the hindmost whale with his spear. Onto the sand the whales ran and stuck, flailing their tails and rolling in panic, but to no avail.

'The slaughter was quick and deadly. From the headland above I saw the sea turn red. The spearsmen leapt from their boats and, waist deep in the rosy water, thrust again and again, one quick cut behind the blow-hole, until not one whale was left alive. Shouting, I ran with the boys down to the shore to help drag the precious animals in. Bare hands grabbed at dorsal fin, gaff-hooks took hold in the tough hide, and whale after whale was dragged up onto land. It was a wonderful whale drive, yielding close to five hundred beasts, classic in every part of its execution.'

Old Niclas's voice has risen during this description. His feet twitch as if he wished to dance his story, which has become almost a sung ballad. But now he pauses and sighs.

'Alas, the next stage could not be described as classic in any way. As had happened so often in the past, tragic events followed the excitement of the whale kill. Foolish Róland. If only his good sense had matched his skill . . . but then . . .'

Niclas lowers his voice in telling the next events. Müller marvels at the old man's ability to make the tale come alive. He also wonders whether some embroidery of the truth may be creeping in. Nevertheless, he leans forward, eager to catch every word.

'No time could now be lost in preparing this great catch. Men and boys set to with a will, cutting the many whales, dividing blubber from flesh, and flesh from bone. Róland worked with a will, knowing that, as the one who gave the first call, he would receive an extra whole whale above his share. Perhaps now his dream of a trading post would be possible.

'But suddenly a rumble of discontent spread among the workers. Róland looked up from his bloody work and saw a large group of men — Magnus Dahl's farm labourers — dragging whale after whale off to one side, and preventing, with threatening gestures, other fishermen from approaching. Magnus stood above, on a grassy slope of his own land, while his two sons, Daniel and Poul, directed operations. Their intentions were clear — as landowners of the bay where the whales beached, they wished to claim half the catch.

'Róland let out a roar of fury. He leapt over half-flayed carcasses and bloody sheets of blubber to confront his two brothers-in-law.

'"This is illegal, what you do! We share equally! That is the new law and you know it!"

'Daniel stopped his work and stood, feet apart, hands on hips. He was a big man and something of a bully. He laughed. Not a comfortable sound.

'"What new law?" he said, with a wink and a grin to his brother. "We go by the old ways here. Everyone knows that Suðeroy changes its habits slowly."

'From his position on the hill, Magnus shouted at his workers to make haste. Poul gestured to some of his men to continue taking the whales, while another group came to guard their actions, standing firm behind the elder Dahl son.

'By now Róland was in a great rage. If half the catch went to the Dahls, the portion to share with the rest of the villagers would naturally be greatly reduced. The old system, which gave half the kill to the landowner of the beach where the whales came ashore, had been changed — to general approval — years ago. How dare the Dahls take the law into their own hands like this?

'Of course Róland should have waited for the king's bailiff, who should surely be hurrying to the scene. But for one thing the king's bailiff was a close friend of Magnus's, and might well have been encouraged to dally, and for another, alas, Róland was lost to a rage that no doubt flared all the wilder from the past years of taunts and sneers from his wife's family.

'"These beasts are the property of all!" he shouted, brandishing his whaling spear at Daniel. "We will not allow this arrogance!" He turned to gather support from the crowd, who roared approval and moved towards the Dahl men.

'Daniel was not a man to be cowed. He stood firm, with his own spear at the ready. Again he laughed, directly into the face of the furious Róland.

'"This landless herring who brings dishonour to our sister thinks he can control the Dahls? Dream away, singer."

'The cutting words released all restraint from Róland. With a wild cry he lashed out, meaning, he later insisted, to thwack Daniel across the shoulders with the shaft of his spear. But at the same moment Daniel swung around to shout something to his brother, moving directly into the path of the razor-sharp blade. His throat was split ear to ear, cutting windpipe and jugular both. For a moment he stood clutching his neck, red blood seeping between his fingers. His mouth opened wide but no sound could escape, nor any breath be drawn in. Oh, it was a sight to still the heart of every man and boy there as the big man slowly, slowly buckled at the knees, never once taking his eyes off the horrified Róland. His last gesture was to take one hand from his neck and point a terrible red finger at his sister's husband, as his blood gushed to mingle with that of the whales.'

For a long moment there is silence in the bare room. The night sun still slants through the window. Below a child is singing. Old Niclas stares into the empty fireplace.

'And Otto?' says the teacher at last. 'My pupil?'

'Daniel's son,' says the old man. 'A child not more than a year old at the time. He has been brought up to consider vengeance is his duty. I would like to hope that he can resist that call of duty, but who knows? Certainly he is not like his grandfather. Nor his Uncle

Poul, who has done his best to instill in the boy a fierce hatred of the sister's family.'

'The father, Róland? Where is he now?'

'Dead, long dead,' says Niclas flatly. 'He didn't live to see the birth of his son, Enok. What happened was a sad, quiet end. The king's bailiff arrived to a scene of mayhem. Shouts and threats from all sides, half-butchered whales lying on the shore, a dead man and a broken killer standing among the bloody wreckage. Fortunately I was present and at that time commanded a certain respect. The bailiff turned to me in all this uproar, as a voice of impartiality. I recounted the scene as I had observed it, and was able to say, with truth, that I believed Róland's blow had been hot-headed but not struck with intent to kill. Several others agreed. Róland was a popular man and Magnus less so — especially after his attempt to steal whales that were not his right.

'The bailiff believed my version and acted quickly. A wise man — dead whales wait for no one. He decreed that Magnus had acted illegally and the whales should be shared equally. But also that Róland would forfeit any share at all, as punishment for his act. And that he would work for Magnus one day in every week for a year, and that the coming kvæði, in which Róland was the star attraction, would no longer take place.

'It was a good judgement and seen as fair by all except the Dahls, who loudly demanded Róland's imprisonment or deportation to Denmark. Else took her stunned husband by the hand and was leading him away when Magnus spoke out.

'"Let this be the first day of the wretch's work for me. Take up your knife, singer, and prepare my share of the catch, and render my train oil."

'It broke Róland. There is no other way to describe it. The sudden descent from the brightest day of his life to the most humiliating was too steep. While the rest of the villagers gathered to sing and dance the life back into their icy limbs, while the women boiled up a steaming stew of whale kidneys for their heroes, Róland, cold and alone, was set to cutting strips of whale meat to hang and dry under the eaves of Dahl houses. Whale meat that should have been his and his family's.

'Poor Róland. His spirit was not strong enough to withstand the further humiliations the Dahls heaped upon him in the following weeks. They say he became quieter and quieter, avoiding even his wife and daughters. One stormy morning he quietly put into his wife's palm his ring. It was a beautiful thing, old and heavy with gold, an enamelled design on its upper surface, which he had found, he said, among salvage goods washed up against a rocky outcrop half a day's row to the south. He used to joke about its past and make up stories about its powers, and he would never be without it.

'"If you have a son," he said, "give him this ring. And if he has my voice, see that he learns the Sjúrður kvæði. And," he said, smiling sadly, "if he has your tenacity, see if he can learn all three parts to the ballad. That will show your family that even landless fools like me have gifts they may pass on."

'Before Else could take breath he was gone, down to the shore and around the headland, running as if the dragon Fáfnir were after him. Else, deadly afraid, called to him and ran too, but, heavy with child, she made only slow progress. By the time she rounded the headland he was gone. No sign at all. When, two days later, his cap and a boot were washed ashore, she took them both to her father's big house on the hill, laid them at his door and left silently. She never spoke again to father or brother.'

Again there is silence in the room. Niclas nods slowly at some unspoken thought. He picks up his brandy and sips again. Müller reaches out to add a little more and the old man smiles his thanks.

'Yes,' says the teacher, 'I can see why you warn me about Otto. Some strong blood between the boys. But Otto lives here, surely?'

'He does. He was brought up by his uncle, Poul, who now looks after the Dahl land here in Tórshavn. Magnus stayed in Suðeroy and has remained set hard against his only daughter all these years. If it hadn't been for the priest Hans Høgnesen, goodness knows what would have happened.'

'I have heard Enok speak of him. With affection.'

'Oh, indeed. And well he might. The priest married his mother a year after Enok was born. Høgnesen is the most senior priest on the island and second only to Magnus in wealth. He shielded Else and her children from the wrath of the Dahls. What is more, he encouraged Else to continue with the plans for the trading post. She and her daughters now run it, quite successfully, and soon Enok and his two half-brothers will take it over.'

Niclas smiles. 'That post is an ever-standing affront to Magnus's pride. It stands at the shore of his village like a lightning rod to his wrath. The store is a gathering place for gossip and laughter, a happy centre to the village. And it is run by the family who killed his eldest son. In his mind the death of Daniel Dahl has never been paid for. That is the way he thinks. "My son's blood will never rest easy in the soil of Suðeroy until retribution is made." To Magnus, Róland's death was a cowardly escape from punishment — a punishment that now should be suffered by someone in that family. If not his own daughter, then the son. And yet they prosper!'

The teacher nods. 'An understandable attitude. Naturally, I would not condone it.' Müller is proud of his modern views. 'But in the matter of a violent death some punishment is to be expected. The king's bailiff was perhaps too lenient in his original judgement.

So Otto is expected to carry on this animosity? Surely this is a heavy burden to lay on a boy?'

'Not in the mind of the Dahls — Magnus or the uncle, Poul. Enok has led a golden life — talented, admired, open and friendly — as you have surely noticed. They will try to discredit him in some way, count on it. If not worse. Otto, poor boy, will be torn. On the one hand he will be attracted to his cousin and schoolmate. On the other he will be urged to bring him down in any way he is able, no matter how false.'

'Well then,' says the teacher, 'Otto is the one I fear for. Enok draws all into his orbit. In my view he is too flamboyant, too confident, but they all admire him. Otto will find himself the outcast in my small class.'

Old Niclas rises. He steadies himself against the bench until his legs return to his body and he is confident they will bear him outside.

'You may be right,' he says. 'I am not so sure. Otto is clever and studious, but there is a devious side to him. Enok, for all his flamboyance, as you call it, is ingenuous. He feels no ill-will and does not expect to find it in others. We will see whether that becomes a strength or a weakness in his dealings with Otto.'

The old man thanks Müller and walks, staggering a little, to the door. He stands in the doorway, one hand on the post, tut-tutting at his own weakness. 'Your brandy and my old legs are unsettling partners! Will you take care with Enok? Don't be too hard on the boy. He carries a precious burden in his head: all those words. I would like to see him succeed in his task. He is even more brilliant as a singer than his father. You will be amazed when you hear him.'

Müller nods and smiles. Privately he considers the old Faroese kvæði over-long and rather dull compared to the tuneful Danish ballads he has learned; however, he knows better than to say such a thing to this man.

'I will watch them both,' he says. 'Don't worry, old man.'

But Niclas Patursson, walking out into the cold sunlit night, fears that his warning has not been taken seriously, and that harm is bound to come to his precious pupil.

4.

CLARA HARALDSEN ORGANISED the fowling day, though she made sure her hand in the event was unnoticed. Boys and men went fowling, not girls, but somehow Clara is in the party and somehow Enok is the one who walks beside her, admiring the way her hair flies back from her face and her woollen skirt swings this way and that with every dancing step. Enok is in high spirits — this is the first time old Niclas has allowed him to leave Tórshavn. Up over the outfield they climb, west out of Tórshavn, then the long tramp across the stony headland until they look steeply down to the grassy roofs of the Haraldsen farmhouse and its many outhouses. Harald Haraldsen, Clara and Napoleon's father, holds three marks of land here on Streymoy and one across the sound on the small island of Hestur, whose cliffs will provide the day's fowling. Harald Haraldsen is a powerful man, a landowners' representative on the

Løgting. He was sent as a boy to Denmark for education and so knows the ways of the world. When Harald Haraldsen sent a note with his son to the teacher, Müller, asking for a two-day break so that the pupils might return home and help their families with the fowling, Müller knew he would be foolish to demur, even though the school would also close for St Olaf's Day celebrations in a few weeks. The teacher, wrote Haraldsen, was welcome to accompany any of the class who wished to come with his two children. Surely, he wrote, it would be a good opportunity for those who had not experienced the excellent sport that the cliffs on Hestur offered.

As Clara hoped, most of the class have disappeared back to their own villages for the excellent fowling their own cliffs provide. So it is only Enok, Clara, Napoleon and Otto who walk with the teacher over the hills. Otto's uncle, Poul, has good hatcheries near his marks of land, but Otto has decided with an easy smile to 'have a look at how your cliffs compare with ours'. Often, in the year since Enok arrived, he has joined this group. The tension he feels in the presence of the Suðeroy boy is clear to everyone, and yet he cannot stay away, it seems. The four have often been seen together around Tórshavn, arguing, laughing, helping unload a catch at the wharf, the boys sometimes rowing out in a Haraldsen or Dahl boat, testing their prowess against that of other youngsters. A strong man on the oars is next best to a good ballad singer, so naturally every Faroese boy practises when he can. A casual spectator would say that the four were good friends; the elders, who know the history, wait for what they consider to be the inevitable disaster. They shake their grey heads and mutter that Else Rasmussen has been most unwise to send her good boy up here, where no Rasmussen or Høgnesen can protect him. But for a year, apart from certain tensions and niggles, Enok has remained unscathed. He has learned his kvæði and will soon perform it. Meantime he continues — somewhat reluctantly — his schooling.

Now, down on the shore, four other men from the village are waiting near the boats, sorting poles and oars. Haraldsen himself is striding down from the church with the ropes, which he stores in the sacred air of the church belfry, gathering blessings in between expeditions. Enok bounds onto an outcropping rock to wave his own tall pole and halloo to the men below, as if he were a castaway and they rescuers to his sea-bound rock. Haraldsen's laugh booms back over the whistling wind as he joins in the play.

Otto, standing beside Clara, murmurs into her ear, 'What a show-off. He should show more respect to your father.'

Clara looks away. She prefers to ignore the rivalry — and worse — between the two boys. Sometimes in class Otto will set the class sniggering at Enok's Suðeroy-accented Danish or his fanciful answers to scholarly questions. Once, up in the outfield, Enok lost his temper and flattened his cousin with a single back-swipe of his arm. Otto, with blood dripping from his nose, only smiled, as if he were the victor. Both boys fancy Clara; she knows this, but will not become involved in their spats.

She runs after Enok as he leaps down the last stretch of grassy slope, and arrives, puffing, to introduce the boy to her father.

'Oho,' laughs Harald Haraldsen, clasping the boy's offered hand. 'And I thought *I* was a big man! They breed giants down in Suðeroy, I see. Welcome, then, Enok Rasmussen! I danced your father's kvæði once and have never forgotten it.' He lowers his voice as the rest of the party arrives. 'But we will talk of your family later. Now is not the moment. Welcome, Herr Müller, and to you, young Otto! Come to see whether Haraldsen puffins taste as sweet as Dahl ones, eh?'

The big man gives both his children a quick slap on the

shoulder, hands Clara a basket of food and beer to stow, then, anxious that they will miss the current, directs men and boys into the two boats. Soon there is no further talk as they row hard across the choppy water to Hestur.

The sky has clouded by the time they have climbed across the island to reach the top of the cliffs, and the wind coming off the sea has a sharper edge. Below them puffins are circling and calling. The cliffs, white with nesting birds, fall sheer to the grey Atlantic Sea. Harald Haraldsen tests the air with a finger and nods his approval.

'This is excellent. The wind will bring the birds circling towards this side. We should make a good catch. Does the teacher wish to try his hand?'

Müller shakes his head, wary of the sheer cliffs below him. No tree or even shrub breaks the sharp line between grassy tops and the sudden drop. Far below, cold waves break and swirl around jagged rocks.

'This teacher will be happy to watch and learn,' he says, backing off a few steps and sitting abruptly on a pile of sacks. The dizzy edge has his head reeling.

'Well then, Napoleon, you shall go first, and show how a Haraldsen snares a bird, eh?'

Napoleon is alive with excitement. He can hardly stand still while the rope is tied firmly around his middle. Clara is sent to sit with the teacher, but as soon as her father's attention is on the rope she is back at the edge, urging her brother to snare a fat one. Haraldsen winds the other end of the rope halfway around his big body. He and the other ropeman, Thorval, pay it out slowly, taking the weight of his son, who walks backwards over the edge and down the cliff as if on a Sunday stroll. Halfway down the cliff Napoleon reaches a rocky spur with a few clumps of grass clinging to it. Here he turns outwards to face the open sky, then lowers himself carefully to sit astride the rock, the rope hanging slack beside him. In one hand he holds his eight-foot pole — Napoleon is not tall like Enok and Otto so his pole is not full-length. Clara shouts encouragement as Napoleon shakes free the V-shaped net attached to the end of the pole and holds the long snare ready, sloping outward but not yet fully upright.

'Clara, would you scare off our catch with your screeching?' says Haraldsen with a frown. 'I knew it was a bad idea bringing you along.'

Behind her father's back Clara turns to Enok with a smile and a shrug, but she falls silent all the same, and settles close to the edge, leaning over to watch the progress. Quick as a fish, Otto slips between Enok and the girl to sit beside her.

Clara sees his triumphant glance at Enok and thinks the whole manoeuvring silly. She watches her father as he braces himself against a rock, close to the edge. The two ropemen plant their feet firmly in front of them, preparing to hold Napoleon steady at the lunge. Clara loves her large bear of a father and knows better than to earn his disapproval. His education in Denmark has made him less strict when it comes to this daughter and the old ways. His approval of her schooling is unusual to say the least; for this alone Clara owes him her deepest gratitude. She loves to study and knows she is good at it. To be allowed on this expedition is also a rare favour. Her mother and sister will be at home preparing food for the returning men and have never been invited to join a fowling expedition.

Clara has a feeling that it is not only her own wiles that induce this leniency in her father, but some plan of his: that he sees some future for her beyond the life of a good Faroese wife and mother. The thought is both exciting and unsettling to her, and Clara is sharp enough to recognise her own divided nature. Yes, she is excited by her student status and the new ideas she is gaining, but she does not hanker for the wider life her father perhaps sees for her. Her father is avid for news of the outside world and will no doubt discuss politics with the teacher this evening, but when the adventure on the cliffs is over, Clara will be happy enough to help in the kitchen, serve a good meal — and look her best for Enok Rasmussen.

At this moment Enok's attention is not on Clara but below, where her brother is slowly raising the pole upright. Now with a quick stab he shoots the net upwards into the flight path of a good-sized bird. A perfect catch! The puffin's wings are caught in the folds of the net and held there as Napoleon lowers the now-heavy pole, takes the bird out by the head, breaks its neck with a smart flick, and hooks it to the rope around his waist. Haraldsen raises his hand in approval and the boy below signals that he will take several more before coming up. Haraldsen nods.

Still the birds wheel in the steady wind. The hatchery is below Napoleon, on an almost inaccessibly sheer rock-face, but as the birds leave their perches to forage, they ride the air currents up and past the boy and that is when he must lunge with the netted pole. A precarious action. Napoleon waits for the perfect moment.

Above, Enok is intrigued. On Suðeroy they do it a little differently. He explains the system to Haraldsen, who laughs and shakes his head.

'You southerners would make a rats' nest out of any simple operation!'

'No, but you see,' says Enok, eager to explain, 'we hold the pole this way, so the net hangs at an angle to the wind.' He demonstrates expansively, lunging with his right hand and turning his body, then whoops in alarm as he trips and nearly goes over the edge.

His laughter as he regains his equilibrium is covered by a wilder scream. Haraldsen, who has momentarily turned his attention away from his task, is nearly jerked over the edge as Napoleon's rope goes taut. The boy on the cliffs has lunged at almost the same time as Enok's demonstration. Perhaps the shout from above diverted his attention; perhaps he heard nothing but simply lost his balance. Whatever the cause, Haraldsen and Thorval are now taking all the boy's weight.

'What is it, quick?' Haraldsen pants, straining back from the edge, his boots making deep rucks in the turf. Enok throws himself onto Haraldsen and grips the big man's shoulders, adding his weight to the burden. Clara and Otto peer over and are horrified to see Napoleon dangling face down at the end of the rope. His pole has smashed far below on the rocks. They can't see his face. His fingers grab for the cliff-face but they touch only air as he circles slowly above the sea.

Haraldsen, Thorval and Enok lean back against the rope but it won't budge. Otto adds his weight but still there is no movement.

'No, wait! Stop, stop!' Clara, looking down, is suddenly aware of the danger. 'The rope is caught! You will cut it!'

'Clara, don't panic,' grunts Haraldsen. 'We have been through this kind of thing many times before. He will come up safe and he knows it. We must be patient. Otto, run and fetch the others.' He indicates with a nod of his head a place on the headland where the other men from the farm are already set up.

Otto sprints away. The teacher stands transfixed. He is no use at all, unable to approach the cliff's edge, not knowing whether his added weight would help anyway. Across the headland Otto shouts his request. The startled men look up and immediately understand the danger. Otto helps them bring the lower man up from the cliff. All are experienced at fowling and show no fear. Now they race back to the others, coiling their ropes as they run, preparing for the new task.

Haraldsen grinds out the orders. 'Petur, help me with the

weight; you are heavier than this boy. Símun and Jacob, lower Enok down to release the rope.'

'I could do it,' says the panting Otto. 'I will be quicker than him.'

'You are out of breath. Thank you, Otto, but we may need Enok's broader shoulders if the rope is hard to budge.'

'But I know our ways better —'

Haraldsen cuts him off sharply. 'Otto Dahl, this is not the time for arguments. You do *not* know our ways if you waste breath at a time like this. Watch at the edge and call when the rope is free.'

The boy colours at the rebuke; glances over to see if Clara has heard, which she has. His brows lower but he goes, quiet now, to the edge.

Already Enok is roped. Down he goes, sure as a goat, hardly needing the support. Símun pays out steadily, then slackens as the boy reaches the ledge. Enok lies flat on his stomach across the rocky protuberance, his long legs dangling into space. An arm's length away a puffin sweeps past, orange bill and neat clown's face clear between the spread wings, but Enok pays no attention and neither does the bird.

'Hey, Napoleon!' Enok speaks quietly, not to startle his friend below. 'Your rope is caught. Try not to swing while I try to free it.'

Napoleon nods. His face, when he twists it upwards for a moment, is bright red. The rope is clearly cutting into his sides but he is calm enough, and hangs as still as he can as Enok reaches down, feeling for the snag. There it is — a small crevice into which the rope has wedged. Enok tries to loosen it, but the tension makes the task impossible. He feels for his knife, then picks delicately at the rock to see if he can enlarge the crevice. The stone will not yield.

Enok turns his face to Otto and Clara above and signals that he should be lowered further. Otto nods and speaks to the ropemen, who lower again. This is tricky. The cliff is undercut here, so Enok must free the rope while hanging in mid-air himself. But nothing seems to worry this big agile boy. He is humming to himself as he works. Clara does not hear the song but can see the wide grin on his face. She would not be able to say whether the beating of her heart is fear for her brother or admiration for his rescuer.

Reaching for Napoleon's harness, Enok hooks his fingers around the rope and heaves upward with one hand, while the other releases the now-slackened rope from the crevice. It is an impressive feat of strength for a boy not yet grown into a man's heavy frame. Now both boys swing free. Enok, whose harness allows him to hang upright, takes Napoleon's arm and holds him so that he, too, may face the cliff instead of the sea below. Napoleon closes his eyes and sighs with pleasure as the blood drains from his head.

'Oh, that is good. My eyes were going to burst out of their sockets if I stayed that way one more second. Thank you.'

Enok grins but does not speak. The strain of holding them both upright is beginning to tell. Napoleon gives the signal and both ropes move upwards. As soon as they are hauled past the ledge, both boys can assist the men above by walking against the cliff, using their fingers in the tiny cracks and seams in the rock.

'Hey,' whispers Napoleon as they climb, 'you should watch out for Otto. He's set to destroy you.'

Enok laughs. 'Jesu, man, you are climbing up from an almost death and you warn *me*?'

'But it's true! I heard his uncle —'

Enok will hear none of it. 'You heard old people retelling old stories. I have listened to them all before. All my life. But Otto and I are not our fathers. Now, save your breath for reaching the top.'

And up they go, guided and hauled by ropes, to emerge, two heads together, one dark, one blond, both grinning, to receive hugs from Clara and a gruff slap on the back from Haraldsen, who is not inclined to over-dramatise the rescue.

'Now,' says that man, 'perhaps we can get on with some real fowling before the day is over. Napoleon, you will need to regain your confidence with a good catch, but meantime, Otto, let's see what you can do.'

As Otto is roped and prepares to be lowered down the cliff with his netted pole, Clara is watching the other two boys. Napoleon looks up at tall Enok with something like awe. 'You saved my life.'

Enok rolls his eyes at Clara, shrugging off the adulation. 'Hey, friend, any one of us would have done the same. And could.' He laughs and Clara has to join in. His moods are infectious.

The last thing Otto sees as he backs down the cliff is that scene: Clara and Enok laughing together, and little Napoleon looking up at a hero.

5.

IN THE BIG Haraldsen house the meal of roast puffin, potatoes, barley-bread and greens is over. The men have drunk good Tórshavn-brewed beer with their meal, but now Haraldsen brings out Danish brandy to help the flow of conversation. Upstairs, in this solid box of a building, the younger children are asleep. Across the yard in the smokehouse the surplus birds — puffins and guillemots — are curing under a smouldering peat fire. Clara sits with her sister, mother and grandmother knitting jerseys. The beautiful Faroese designs grow under fingers that have no need to count stitches or concentrate on the intricacies. The mother smiles as she knits, pleased to have visitors under her roof, pleased at the contentment she has engendered among the men with her good food and warm hospitality. In a corner of the room the grandfather, who is now too deaf to join in the talk, cards wool in preparation for spinning. Clara's attention is more on Enok than the general conversation; her face is bent to the wool but her eyes slide sideways.

Enok fidgets. His stool is too small and his long legs feel cramped. He wants to go outside into the wind-blown evening light. He wants to talk to Clara about his coming kvæði; is it possible she and Napoleon might come to Suðeroy? He tries to concentrate on the conversation, which has turned to Danish politics, but always other thoughts break in: snatches of song, memories of the past months on this island. He takes from his pocket the piece of bone he has been working. The rhythm of carving will perhaps spread up through his hands and settle his ears to the talk.

'War is inevitable in any case,' Müller is saying. 'The only way to secure the boundary is to fight for it. The Prime Minister is right. Let Holsten go; fight for Slesvig.'

Haraldsen disagrees. He has friends in Copenhagen who write to him regularly. 'Bishop Monrad is a friend to our family but I must admit he is not a popular choice as new prime minister. He will not easily form a strong Cabinet. New king, new prime minister: bad combination at such a time.'

'But look at our allies! King Christian's daughter Alexandra will be queen of England. His other daughter married to the Czar of Russia. His son now king of the Hellenes. Our new king is related to all the crowns of Europe.'

Haraldsen laughs. 'But not to Prussia. Not to Austria. That is where an alliance would be useful. The Germans want Holsten *and* Slesvig. Do the other crowns of Europe care enough to come to our assistance? I doubt it.'

Otto is interested. History and politics are fascinating to him. He wants to show off his knowledge. 'Queen Victoria of England would surely favour the Prussian argument. Look at her own

German connections. She won't let her son's beautiful Danish wife sway her in our favour, surely?'

His teacher considers the argument but rejects it. 'No, Otto, these days it is politicians who decide matters, not kings and queens. England will not let Denmark fight alone. Right is on our side and the British believe in justice. And anyway, look at our army! Didn't we fight alone last time? And didn't we win against the Holsteners? We have the best navy in Europe and the bravest soldiers. It is time Slesvig enjoyed full citizenship with Denmark. If we have to fight to hold Slesvig, so be it. Bishop Monrad is a clear thinker and a great patriot. He says we must not compromise and he is right.'

'But war?' says Haraldsen. 'I hope not. I would not like to think I was sending young Napoleon here into battle. I have just enlisted him in the navy. See a bit of the world, yes; learn the seamanship and discipline, certainly. Not killed, though, for another country's argument. That would make no sense at all.'

'But Father,' says the lad, flushed and proud of his new status, 'we are part of Denmark. I would fight for her.'

'No, no, son, you will be needed here on the farm in a few years,' rumbles Haraldsen. 'But we will see, we will see. A war may not come. More to the point, will the potato blight arrive? Now, there's a danger!'

'Potatoes?' Müller frowns at this sudden change of topic. He is just getting into his swing.

Haraldsen, though more cosmopolitan than most Faroese, still puts Faroe matters first. He considers the agricultural change from barley to the far more productive potato a dangerous move. 'Look at Ireland — their famines, their blight. We must be vigilant. If the blight arrives on these islands we may suffer the same fate. Now, *I* still plant a decent crop of barley in my best section of infield . . .'

And so the conversation goes on. Otto joins in and, now that the talk has moved to farming, so does Napoleon. Enok at last manages to catch Clara's eye and jerks his head to the door. She nods — the smallest movement, but enough for Enok. He rises to stretch and saunters to the door, making as if he is headed for the outhouse.

Outside he walks a little way towards the shore, breathes with pleasure the salty air. The sky has cleared and a pale full moon, just risen in the east above the hills, mirrors the low western sun. Enok reaches upward and out, then flexes his cramped knees. He wants to run. Or row out. Fly, even. Until he has sung his double kvæði he will feel like this — full to bursting with an excitement that is also deep apprehension. All his life he has been brought up with this dream ahead of him — his dead father's wish. And the third part? Will he ever manage to hold all three in his head? Even for one performance? He hums a line or two, then stops. The words want to roar out of him, and that would never do. Impatient, he looks back at the big Haraldsen house, solid and substantial, set aside a little from the other houses of the village. Why doesn't she come? The house juts squarely up from the hillside, a forbidding, uncompromising building, quite different in style from the low, grass-covered house of old Niclas Patursson, which has been his home this last year.

But here she comes, Clara, running down to meet him, her pale hair turned silver in the evening light. She could be out of a ballad herself: the pale beauty whom Sigurd roused with a kiss. When she dances up to him, Enok holds her shoulders still and kisses her cheek with such gentleness that she can find no words of rebuke, but kisses him back.

'Clara,' he says, loving the sound, 'Clara.' And kisses her again. 'Can we walk up a little? I want to talk with you and there is never a time. And soon it will be St Olaf's Day and I will be back on Suðeroy —'

Clara lays a gentle hand over his mouth to stop the tumbling words. 'You know I cannot walk up with you. We would surely be missed. My father may relax some of the rules but never that one.'

Enok's feet dance on the gravel of the shore. Tonight he feels like a lightning strike that has no place to ground. 'Just for a few minutes? Clara?'

She reaches for his hand, holds it between both of hers. He grips her — too hard — and she almost cries out as the heat from him runs up her arm and through her body.

'Come early in the morning, then,' she gasps, 'up to the peat-house. I will be watching the barley.'

Without another word or backward glance she runs back to the house, where the lamps have just been lit. The flickering lights in the windows soften the severe building but do nothing to ease Enok's mood. He bounds across the beach, kicking up shingle, until he comes to the rocky headland. Out of sight and ankle deep in the moonstruck water, he tears at his clothes then leans, half naked, hard up against the black stone of the land. There, hands spread wide and clutching at crevices, forehead laid against the cool surface, he thrusts again and again at the unyielding rock until, with a moan, he releases.

Much later, calmer but ashamed, he creeps into the quiet house and finds a place to sleep.

IN the morning he finds her in the smokehouse. The cured birds have already been taken away to the dry store and now it is the barley's turn to enjoy a little heat. In this cold climate the barley rarely ripens in the field but has to be brought to full readiness over a smouldering peat fire. Clara, bare-armed and barefoot, is raking the trays of grain, the warmth in the little shed making her skin rosy and slick with sweat. Enok creeps up behind her and plants a kiss on the first part he can reach, which is a bony elbow. She jumps backwards, nearly knocking out one of his teeth. Enok clutches his mouth, hopping in pain and rolling his eyes, while she laughs until the tears run.

'Enok Rasmussen, you will bring the whole family running! Get out of here, in the name of God, before you scatter the barley!' She pushes him to the door and out they both tumble, into a morning that for once is clear and sharp. Behind the shed they are in the lee of the westerly. The wind scuds over the brow of the hill behind them, but they lie on the grass, sheltered and warm.

Clara allows a kiss, then another. Her breathing is now as urgent as Enok's but her will is stronger. She moves away a little and sits up, head to one side like an inquisitive bird. 'Is this the talk, then, that can't find a time?'

Enok grins. The fingers of one big hand walk gently up and down the bones of her spine. She shivers with pleasure but won't lie down again.

'Enok?'

'Mmm?'

'Wake up, man, you are half asleep in this sun!'

Enok lies back, eyes shut, and speaks so quietly that she has to lean in to hear.

'This moment, this morning is so perfect — you here, the sun — don't you feel it? It seems best just to drink it in. Forget about plans and futures. Kiss me again.'

'What plans and futures?'

'There you are! Planning already!'

'Enok!'

Enok opens his eyes and smiles at her. 'Marry me, then. Shall we ask your father?'

Clara makes a sound that is half laughter, half despair. 'Oh, you are truly impossible. Are you serious?'

'Of course I am.'

'We are still at school. We are children still.'

'Seventeen is a man.' Enok jumps to his feet and stretches his full height. 'Look at me! Won't I do?'

Clara pulls at one of those long legs. 'Well, you won't do quite yet. Sit down or they will see that great length of you.'

Enok crashes to the ground. His calm of a moment ago is shattered; now he is ready to argue. 'But we have nearly finished our schooling. What now? Wouldn't I make a good husband? I lack land, yes, but there's the family business. I am a top fisherman and share a boat with my half-brothers. Suðeroy is a beautiful island. I have a reputation as a ballad singer . . . Clara?'

Clara sighs. 'You may feel ready to settle but I don't. I feel a girl still. Don't you want to go to Denmark? Set eyes on something more than these islands?'

'But the Faroes — I still haven't visited half of them! What more could you want?'

'How can we know till we get away and look back?'

'You want to leave? I can't believe it. I thought you loved the islands.'

'Enok . . .' Clara speaks slowly now, frowning as she thinks. 'I love the Faroes, yes, but I want to know other things too. Other kinds of people — how they think and do things. Don't you? We are so small. My father wants to send me to Copenhagen next year to stay with a friend of his. Maybe go to a realskole there. One year, maybe two. But of course I will come back.'

'Two years?' Enok touches her arm gently. His tender smile

would melt an iceberg. 'What would I do without you, Clara? Two years?'

'You could come too.'

He shakes his head. 'How could I? I must learn the third ballad. Also I will get no scholarship to Denmark like you and Otto. And I am the oldest son. My stepbrothers are young. I will be needed.'

Enok sees to his dismay that Clara is impatient with him.

'Enok,' she says, 'use your own will; think for yourself. You do not *have* to learn the third part. It will be a triumph if you manage two! Your mother has no right to expect —'

'It was my father's dying wish.'

'And then he killed himself and left the burden to you.'

'That's not fair!'

'Isn't it exactly the truth?' Clara is engrossed in her own argument now, and doesn't notice the effect her words are having on Enok. 'Isn't it? He couldn't face his own failure, so left the righting of it to his unborn son. Walk away from it all, Enok. You say you are a man now.'

Enok jumps to his feet, raging for all the village to hear. 'You are wrong, Clara! I *want* to sing! Want it for myself!'

'How can you know that? It has been drummed into you all your life. I feel so sorry for you, Enok.'

'*Sorry?*' The word comes out as a roar.

'Everyone knows your story. How could you escape from it?'

'Clara, I don't want to escape! I *want* to live that story. I'm proud of it. I want you to live it with me. Ohh!' Enok kicks against a rock and then hops with pain until he tumbles down beside her. 'Oh, this is all wrong. Shall we start again?'

'The words need saying.'

'No. Not like this. They have the wrong flavour. Can't you hear that? You are saying them in a cruel way.'

Clara looks down at her hands and says nothing. Enok fidgets beside her for a moment, then stands up again.

'Clara, would you at least come down to Suðeroy to hear me this St Olaf's?'

Clara raises her head then. There are tears in her eyes. 'How can I? We will be celebrating here and I must be here to help. You know it is impossible.'

'So I must break away from my obligations but you must not?'

Clara beats the grass with her fist. 'Oh, you stupid ox of a man! Can't you see how different the two are?'

'No, I can't. I can't!'

Enok turns and runs away from her up the hill. He leaps rocks and blunders past the placid sheep, muttering furious arguments to himself as he climbs. He doesn't notice Otto, who has been watching the scene and who has now climbed lower, to stand directly above Clara.

'You were right to say that to him,' murmurs Otto. 'He should go away from it all.'

'Oh, what do you know about it?' screams Clara. 'Get out of my hair, both of you!'

And down she storms, back to the smouldering peat and the ripening barley.

6.

AS ST OLAF'S Day approaches, the village of Sumba on Suðeroy is brimming with people and excitement. Every day for the week before the festival another boat rows in bringing visitors for the celebrations. In the handful of houses at the head of the bay, children are bedding down on sacks of feathers out in storerooms, to make room for visiting adults. Anyone with a remote family connection to someone in Sumba has decided, it seems, to leave their own island and 'come home' this year. Isn't that handsome young Rasmussen boy going to attempt what his father never achieved? Who could miss the chance to dance two of the longest Sjúrður ballads sung by this talented fellow?

And what will the Dahls think of the event? Enok is, after all, Magnus's grandson. Surely it is time for old grudges to be buried? Though, come to think of it, has that powerful bastard ever shown generosity of spirit? The old skinflint was born grasping with both hands and has never stopped reaching out for something more. For one thing, he wants his daughter's trading post, but that is secure now in the Høgnesen line; for another he desires more sons and grandsons to inherit his many marks of land, but there is only Poul in Tórshavn, who is more interested in trading than farming. Now it is rumoured that his precious only grandson, Otto (for Enok will never be acknowledged), is turning his back on farming too, and talking about going to Denmark to study! Oh yes, there haven't been such rich topics for gossip on Suðeroy since — well, probably since the whale kill, when Enok's father killed Otto's. Now wouldn't *that* add salt to the feast, if the whales paid a visit this time too?

To increase the excitement, the Danish army and navy recruiters are on the island. At this time of year, if a naval boat is free, it will bring last year's recruits back to their homes for the celebrations. These young lads arrive in their smart uniforms, accompanied by a few older officers to keep them in line. Their commanders wisely believe that young men returning home at festival time with stories of foreign sights and new experiences will excite admiration and envy and be the best possible advertisement for the armed forces. The boys are expected to persuade their friends to enlist, and receive a bonus for every recruit they bring in.

The officers are quartered with Magnus in the big Dahl house. For two days they have enjoyed his food and hospitality and left the returning recruits to roar around the island, drunk every night and telling wild tales of their adventures in the navy. Recruiting is going badly, though. There is talk of war — Slesvig/Holsten yet again — and what father wants to lose a much-needed son fighting over land that means little to a Faroeman?

The night before St Olaf's, Magnus entertains the officers lavishly and nods sagely as they outline their concerns.

'I tell you what,' booms Magnus, 'your lads need to show a bit more initiative. Falling about drunk doesn't help the cause.' He offers more brandy. 'I've heard them out the back singing those new Danish songs. Much more catchy than our own old dirges. Get them to go around the villages in a group. Sing and dance the latest tunes from Denmark. That'll bring the young ones in.'

'But isn't there a special — what do you call it? — your kind of ballad dance here tomorrow?'

Magnus laughs dismissively. 'Oh, that's not important, really. Relic of the old days. Our village needs livening up. They all do. Tell you what, Otto will come with your lads. He won't be enlisting, mind, but he'll be interested in the new songs. Otto! Come in here, boy. I have a proposition for you.'

Later Otto tries to argue with his grandfather. He points out that the villagers love and revere the kvæði; that they will not take kindly to an interruption; that the Dahls will be unpopular if they are linked to such a break with tradition. But Magnus only laughs and claps his lanky grandson on the shoulder.

'The tide is beginning to flow in a different direction, lad, and I intend to catch the current. Look at *you* — off to Denmark! You'll bring back new ideas, no doubt, new ways to further the Dahl holdings. New customs. Now, I want you to take those young sailors down to Høgnesen's when the kvæði is on.'

'They are from this island. They will want to be at the kvæði too.'

'Tell them I will pay them two skind each if their songs prove more popular than Enok's. Turn it into sport! A contest. They will love the idea.'

'It's not wise, Grandfather.'

'Rubbish. You do what I say! Get them to sing outside the Høgnesen place. We'll see who is more popular. The young will leave their dreary dance and come out to jig.'

'They won't.' Otto keeps his voice low. He shows no emotion but his words leave no room for doubt. 'Enok is popular. *He* will be the hero tomorrow, not the sailors. Not the Dahls. Everyone loves Enok.'

Magnus is suddenly angry. 'A boy should not speak back like that, Otto. Your grandfather knows these islanders better than you do. You have been away too long.'

That is the end of the argument. Otto gives that quick, hunted smile of his, nods without looking into his grandfather's face, and walks away.

THE first hours of St Olaf's Day are cool and windy but more or less clear. Thin wisps of high cloud stream across the wide sky; birds circle in flocks over the sea, plunging again and again to feed. Fishermen grumble that such a perfect fishing day should present itself on St Olaf's but the complaint is only routine — rain today would not be welcome.

In the Høgnesen house activity has reached fever pitch. The trading post is besieged, everyone wanting a last-minute measure of sugar or barley flour and another kande of beer. Else and her daughters, all three beaming with pride, are trying to meet these needs while preparing food and drink for the kvæði, which will take place late in the afternoon and go on well into the long summer day/night. The boys have stretched two canvas sails over the courtyard of the priest's house to provide shelter for those who cannot fit inside.

Else runs from store to house with a trencher of her pickled puffins. She is a big woman, strong still and with a rosy sweetness that comes from a happy marriage and busy life. Her silvery hair, which started the day firmly plaited around her head, is already breaking from its moorings. A rope of it now swings free as she runs, giving her the look of a much younger woman.

'Say a special prayer for clear weather,' she says as she sees her husband setting off for the church. 'Look, here comes another boatload! They will never all fit in.'

Hans Høgnesen laughs. 'The good Lord will no doubt shed a tear or two sometime in the day, overcome by the quality of the singing. The sails will provide some cover. And what Faroeman has not danced in wet weather?'

'But this singing will be so long! The old men will find it hard.'

'The old men will be inside. We'll try to keep Enok dancing near the doorway so that he can sing to those in and out.' The priest touches her sleeve gently, then takes the heavy dish of food from her. 'Don't worry, Else, he will be fine; the day will be a great triumph. I have heard him practising. He is a performer. You know that.'

'He is so tense. Have you noticed how jumpy he is? What if he forgets? Have we driven him too hard?'

Hans laughs again. 'My dear, anyone would think it was you performing! It would be a sin if the boy were *not* tense on the morning of such a performance. If he forgets some line he will cover, like any good singer. And who is there to recognise a mistake?'

'You. Old Niclas.'

'You think we would breathe a word of criticism? Else, let us prepare this house and the food and trust the boy to do his bit.'

'And there is Magnus . . .' Else has long given up calling him father.

The priest sighs. 'There is Magnus, yes. He will be at church this morning. He won't miss *that*. I'll have a word with him.'

'It would be so good if he could come: praise Enok, break the silence . . .' Else's voice tails away. Her hope is too unlikely.

Hans is a forthright man and an optimist, like any good priest.

'One day he will come to it; perhaps this is the day. Magnus's anger damages only himself — it rolls off Enok like water off a sea-bird's back. He hardly notices.'

'Which angers Magnus the more.'

Hans laughs suddenly. 'Listen to the two of us. This is a great day for the family. *Our* family. Let us enjoy it. What can Magnus do?'

Else smiles, straightens her back. 'You are right, my good husband. I'm foolish to let worry cloud this day. If Magnus wants to sulk, he will surely be the loser. Here, give me that dish. You will be late for the service.'

'So will you, my dear!'

Else smiles at him. 'The Lord will forgive me if I tiptoe in a few minutes late. You would be a different matter. Now, off with you.'

She turns away, already calling for the boys to beg a few stools from the nearby houses on their way back from church. The older dancers are bound to need a rest now and then.

Upstairs Enok sings a phrase, grins and tries it another way, but softly. He wants the strength of his voice to make a dramatic impact from the first word he sings. He can feel the blood humming through his body. His breathing is slow and deep as he has been taught. The bustle and banging below are a world away. He is lost in the great tale he is about to sing.

BY late afternoon the wind has turned to the north and blows chill. A bank of mist is rolling into the bay. When the sun breaks through, village, sea and mist are illuminated in purple and gold as if they were a fabulous setting for a grand opera. A minute later the sun disappears and colour drains from the landscape, leaving it cold and stark. Again bright, again the fade, over and over as clouds and sun play hide and seek, though Magnus is perhaps the only person in Sumba who watches these dramatic changes. Everyone else is crammed into the Høgnesen house and courtyard, intent on a drama of their own making.

Enok stands in the doorway. His head touches the lintel, the long blond hair tied back and secured with a bone ornament carved long ago by his father. The scarlet waistcoat — his father's also — is embroidered in intricate patterns. The rows of silver buttons glow against the rich cloth. His blue eyes look from inside to out and back again, gathering everyone into his orbit. The buzz of conversation dies; beer mugs are grounded. Else holds her husband's hand tight as everyone watches Enok. Out go his arms, stretched wide as if conducting an orchestra, which in a way he is. This is the signal for the dancers to join him in a long chain, elbow to elbow, hand in hand, one foot planted, the other resting lightly on the toe, ready to move.

Enok smiles left and right at his dancers — here is a different sun (and son) illuminating the scene! Once, twice, his shoe rings on the fine wooden floor, setting the rhythm. Stamp, stamp, sixty feet take the beat, then pause, waiting for the right place in the ballad to start moving. Enok draws out the moment, then takes the first deep breath of his kvæði. He is away.

Faroemen, welcome from your fjords and valleys, he sings, his voice strong and compelling.

> *Encircle this hearth, hear me sing*
> *Of the hero Sjúrður, his mighty deeds*
> *The dragon's treasure and the dread ring . . .*

Feet rooted to the ground, Enok dances with torso only, moving his broad shoulders to one side and then the other — strong, graceful sweeps, building a rhythm to his words. Then, as the welcome comes to an end — thump! Down goes his foot, and sixty others take their first step with him.

> Brave Sigmund lay sore-wounded and weary,
> Sundered in three parts his sword.
> Dark Queen of the Dead, Hel, called to him
> Crimson his life's blood poured . . .

Enok's chorus is a little different from the one the crowd knows. His is the ancient version, rarely sung. Forward, forward and back they step, listening to Enok sing it, memorising the words:

> Sjúrður braved the lair of the dragon
> Claimed the golden treasure hoard
> Smote the beast with his father's sword
> Sjúrður braved the lair of the dragon . . .

By the last line they have it and roar it out with Enok. The kvæði is under way.

> Un-born, in his mother's belly,
> Lay son of Sigmund, Sjúrður, doomed
> Before even he breathed first breath in the land . . .

The crowded dancers shout and stamp. Forward, forward and back; forward, forward and back, the rhythm already beginning to cast a spell. It is going to be a great night!

Enok sings with his eyes open, unlike some older ballad singers. He watches the dancers, face alive with the tale he is unfolding. The tempo builds and falls away, builds and falls again. The hypnotic rise and fall of the tune, the rich rolling lines of the great Viking saga, the slowly snaking line of dancers — all are utterly compelling. Sumba kvæði are renowned in all the islands for their drama but tonight Enok has drawn the dancers into a deeper, richer state, close to intoxication. He can feel his audience with him and plays them wonderfully; they are fish hooked to his ancient mystic line. After each verse they sing the chorus as one — quietly if tragedy is in the air, more often with a great roar and a stamp and a shaking of fists as Sjúrður prepares to fight the dread dragon Fáfnir.

At the end of the first fifty verses Old Niclas leaves the circle and sits to listen. Tears roll down his wrinkled cheeks but his eyes never leave Enok's face. Slowly he rocks back and forth on his stool, dancing in his mind. The saga rolls on. Whenever a dancer drops out of the chain another slips in to take his place. Slowly they step and circle, living the story through the movement of their bodies. Occasionally the dancers shout in unison — a wordless exclamation underlining a dramatic moment.

> *Brave Sjúrður lunged to broach dread Fáfnir's belly.*
> *Freshly flowed the dragon's blood*
> *Good fortune that the war-gear held*
> *Against that dire and fiery flood . . .*

From time to time, when the story takes a fresh turn, the dancing feet also change direction to circle back the way they have come. On and on Enok sings, his voice never faltering, driving the story into the hearts, into the very souls of his listeners. Else and Hans, who have heard him sing this before — have taught him this section, are, even so, spellbound. Together, shoulder to shoulder, they dance, lost in the chanted drama.

As the kvæði finally draws to its triumphant end, as the birds warn Sjúrður of Regin's treachery and Sjúrður draws his mighty sword, once broken in three parts by Sjúrður's dead father but now welded by the same Regin — at the very moment the sword descends, the low evening sun breaks through cloud. Its long rays reach beneath the canvas roof of the courtyard to illuminate the young singer. A theatre director could not have managed a more dramatic finale. Enok's blond hair and pale skin turn deep gold; the feet of the dancers slow and still; the last words of the saga roar to a close.

And then, on cue, the sun also is obliterated. For a long moment there is nothing, then the silence is shattered with whoops and clapping and stamping. Enok is surrounded by admirers who want to touch him, to pound their congratulations into his tall body. Enok himself shouts and laughs with the excitement of it all.

Else and her daughters, their eyes still streaming, run to bring out the trenchers of food and drink. There is barley bread and potato bread, fatty sheep sausage and delicious strips of dried sheepmeat, chunks of Else's famous pickled puffins alongside boiled and stuffed puffins and guillemots. Neighbours have brought trays of fresh fish and salted klipfish, boiled potatoes and precious slices of dried whale meat and blubber. There is butter cake and half a tun of imported mead. Hans and the boys hang whale-oil lamps to light the big room and the courtyard. The evening is young yet: the second kvæði is still to come. Oh, this is a night to be remembered long into the future.

Indeed.

Later, when night has finally turned dark, Enok has settled to his singing again. His deep and resonant voice chants the story of Sjúrður's magic horse, Grani, and the great leap through the ring of fire to claim beautiful Brynhild. As the dancers are quickening their steps to match the pace of the saga, as evil magic is woven and the hero seems doomed, at that high moment a different sound niggles at the attention of the courtyard dancers. A sweet merry tune played on a pipe, distant at first, but coming closer.

Those on the outer edge of the listening crowd shake their heads, as if an annoying fly is buzzing, and press in closer to the ballad singer. But the piped tune comes closer and now male voices take up the jaunty melody, giving it words.

> *A drummer boy by a lake saw a beautiful swan*
> *Fly down to swim in the water there . . .*

The sailors sing in Danish, their rough voices blurred with drink but tuneful enough.

Enok sings on, raising his voice to meet the challenge and never missing a beat.

> *Trapped within the circle Brynhild waited*
> *Around her leapt the magic fire*
> *Up and upward surged the horse*
> *Sjúrður urged great Grani higher.*

Those inside the house cannot hear the interruption; they dance on, entranced. But outside it is a different matter. A few younger lads and a girl or two, tiring perhaps of the long evening of chanting, have broken from the chain and turned to listen to the jig. Someone claps in time with the sailors, which encourages them to sing louder. An angry farmer tries to chase the little band away.

'Hey there! Move away! Hendrick, I know you — show some respect for a decent kvæði. Off with you!'

His outburst only draws attention to the rival singing. A few more turn to listen. Someone laughs at the ribald chorus . . .

If you beat on your drum,
Young drummer, she will come . . .

Enok, dancing near the doorway, can hear the lilting tune clearly. For the first time in the whole evening his voice falters; a dancer or two from the inside ring stumble as the rhythm is broken. Else is not dancing but listening in wonder to this kvæ∂i, which her first husband learned but never performed. She sees her son's face redden but thinks the emotion is coming from the scene he describes. Her hands clench tight as she wills him to continue, to carry the audience with him at this important climax. For another stanza — and another — Enok carries on, but the magic is no longer there. By now even those inside can sense some kind of commotion out on the street.

The angry farmer has spotted Otto among the singers, 'Otto Dahl! You should be ashamed of yourself. Be off!'

The singers are already moving away, still piping their tune, when Enok hears Otto's name called out. His concentration — and his control — breaks.

LATER, sitting alone on a high rock, far from the village, Enok looks down at the crawling sea and beats his damaged fist against the stone until it bleeds all over again. Stupid, stupid, *stupid*! If he had held on a minute or two longer the crisis would have been averted. Already the crowd outside was turning back to him. He could easily have drawn them in again and carried the day. But for once he had let his cousin get under his skin. *Stupid*!

Enok has downed a good measure of mead and his head swims, but nothing can obliterate the memory of Otto's odd, pleased smirk as Enok charged through the crowd, roaring like a bull seal. Or the way Otto stood, unflinching, to receive the crunching blow — not even raising a hand to defend himself, and the sickening backward snap of his head as he was flung to the ground by the force of Enok's rage.

Enok groans and sucks blood from his bleeding hand. He tries to stand but the liquor and his misery have overcome him. For a while he lies on his back, watching the sky lighten. A curious skua approaches, step by step, head cocked sideways. Enok lunges with one hand but the movement is clumsy. The bird flies away. He tries to imagine what happened after he struck the blow and then ran off, snatching a jug of mead as he went. Consternation over Otto, no doubt. Was he dead? Disfigured? Had the blow lost him his mind? Else and Hans would be distraught — not to mention all those who had come for a great celebration. He could imagine what they would be saying: *Enok didn't even stay to survey the damage. It's his father's story all over again.*

Enok finally staggers to his feet. Lurching, sometimes falling, sometimes crawling, he makes his way back towards the village. At the edge of the infield he is met by three naval officers. Two hold the staggering boy upright, one on either side of him. The third speaks kindly.

'Come on, lad; celebrations are over; ship's waiting.'

Enok shakes his head, not understanding. He tries to pull away but is too drunk to control his actions.

The officer frowns and consults his list. 'Enok Rasmussen, isn't it?'

Enok nods.

'You've enlisted. Paperwork's all here.'

'No . . . No . . .'

One of the others speaks. 'Lad's too drunk to remember, sir. Can't even keep his feet.'

The first officer chuckles. 'Well, St Olaf's Day is like that. You can't blame them. Tough year ahead. Come on, lad, let's get you aboard.'

'No,' says Enok, finally getting his tongue around a word or two. 'I don't want . . . Didn't . . . didn't sign.' But there's no spirit in the words.

The officer holds a sheet in front of Enok's unfocused eyes. 'Here. Your signature. Your grandfather as witness. You'll remember it all when you've slept this off. Come on, now.'

Tall Enok, head hanging, feet dragging, lets himself be taken.

Storms and Disasters

KARERE,
NORTH ISLAND, NEW ZEALAND
1868

1.

CONRAD'S HOME FOR the past year has been a small hut that he built himself on Monrad land down near the river. It is a cunning construction — everything Conrad makes with his hands is beautiful. The framework is of ponga logs, lashed together with stripped flax. Between these dark red and fibrous uprights Conrad has placed walls of river stones, so neatly interlocked that there is no need for a plastering of mud. The roof consists of many layers of ponga fronds laid over a sheet of stretched canvas.

'I'll not be staying long,' he said when he arrived many months ago, 'or I'd build something more substantial.' But here he has stayed, missing the sea, dreaming sometimes of his other life on the Faroes, but content enough with the hard work — and with Anahuia's company. Often Anahuia sleeps here with him. She comes and goes according to other calls on her time, calls that Conrad has learned not to question.

On this evening she is with him, and so is Napoleon. The three friends sit around a fire that Anahuia has lit on a hearth of stones at the entrance to the hut. They all sit close to the smoky warmth — the night is cool, and the mosquitoes are kept at bay by the swirling wisps of smoke, which Anahuia fans this way and that, making sure all three are protected.

Napoleon is laughing as he tells them of his day spent searching for the bishop's sheep. 'Even the sheep here are wild! Here I am stumbling over stumps and branches,' — he jumps up to imitate his clumsy advance — 'calling them by all the sweetest words I know, and they simply run further away! Back home, Ana, our sheep are more like members of the family. They love us. They come to our call. How can you manage sheep that run off all the time?'

Ana smiles at the lively fellow. 'You use a dog to fetch them.'

'A dog!' Napoleon is horrified. 'Surely that would drive them further away? At any rate, the bishop is surely losing his flock. I can count only sixty where there should be two hundred — or so he says. Two hundred is scarcely believable. I have never heard of two hundred sheep all belonging to one man.'

Conrad grins at his friend. 'This place is full of surprises. Have you looked closely at the wool? Curly and fine all the way through. These sheep don't grow outer wool at all. Nothing coarse and straight for coats or sails. And watch the way these people take the wool. Cut it right off the sheep's back with huge shears. The whole fleece! For weeks the poor ugly things run around half naked, pink skin showing through. You wait, you'll see.' He reaches out a lazy arm to pull Ana closer. She leans against him, her blanket falling open to reveal one brown breast. Napoleon turns away at first, but then his eyes are drawn back. His look is anxious, though.

'Enok, I don't want to wait much longer,' he says. 'Even to see naked sheep. Friend, when will we leave?'

'Use Danish, Napoleon. She should hear what you say.'

Napoleon frowns. He shifts a little, as if to shrug away some thought, but repeats formally in Danish: 'Enok? Is my friend ready to leave? This wanderer cannot go without him. The mother at home says it is important.' He looks away again into the night. A single bird calls, long and mournful, once, twice, a third time. 'Others say it is important. You are needed.'

Anahuia gathers her blanket and stands. Even with the heavy weight of the baby she stands straight, her bare feet planted firmly. Her strange grey eyes are dark in the firelight, their expression stern, perhaps. Or calm? Difficult to read. She touches Conrad on the shoulder.

'Talk to your friend in your own language. Make a true decision.'

Conrad rises and follows her. 'Ah, stay, sweetheart. I thought you could stay tonight?'

'I am able to, yes, but your friend is anxious when I am here. You are a hero to him in some way. Be careful with him.'

Conrad groans. 'Ana, I am no good at big decisions. Stay and help me.'

She wraps her arms around his chest and holds him tightly for a moment, the bulge of the baby pressing into his groin. Conrad feels a small kick and then another more impatient one, and despite himself he stiffens in response.

'Jesus,' he murmurs, 'my own child is enticing me. This is not proper, surely!'

She laughs and releases him. 'Conrad Rasmussen — or whatever your name is — you are a good man and a true one.' She grins. 'And sometimes a foolish one. Let the true man make the decision, not the foolish one.'

'I couldn't leave you.'

'That is what I hope. Then tell him. But gently.'

'He should know your story.'

'I will tell it. But later. Ka kite.'

Anahuia turns and walks steadily into the dark — downriver, back towards her kainga.

Conrad returns to the fire. He sits for a while, looking into the flames, then picks up a piece he is carving and begins to work.

Napoleon smiles in recognition. How many times has he seen his friend carving at bone or wood when he is trying to untangle a thought.

'What is it?' he asks.

'This? A wood they call manuka. Hard and sweet-smelling.' He hands the piece across to Napoleon.

'No, I mean what will it be?'

'A boat, I think. A little whaling boat.'

'There — you see? You are missing your own island!'

Conrad laughs. Takes the piece from Napoleon and works again in silence. 'That woman,' he says at last, 'she has become . . . important. Can't you see that, Napoleon? How strong she is?'

'She is very strange sometimes. Scary. The baby is yours?'

'Yes.'

'Are you sure?'

'Yes, of course.'

'I thought maybe they weren't so . . . strict . . . as us about that sort of thing.'

'Napoleon!'

'But how can you *know*? I mean she is often down with her own people. Perhaps there is another . . .'

Conrad stabs his knife into the ground. 'I know because she tells me so! The baby is mine. I am *happy* for it to be mine.'

Napoleon will not give the matter away. 'She wants to keep you here, can't you see that? She has cast some kind of spell over you. It's uncanny. How can you prefer a . . . a half-caste like that, before your own mother? Before Clara? Before all of us?'

Conrad leaps to his feet, too blind with anger to notice the tears in his friend's eyes. For a moment it seems as if he will strike Napoleon, who cries out and rolls away in fear.

'Don't you dare call her a half-caste! It's bad enough they say those things down at Jackeytown. Leave it. Leave it alone, Napoleon!'

He snatches his knife from the ground and crawls through the low entrance to his hut. There he lies on the mattress of fern fronds, frowning up at the dark roof.

Outside, Napoleon cries silently. Again the low hoot of the morepork sounds; again it is echoed from further away, two-toned and lonely. The boy wraps his blanket tighter against all the pressures of this strange, frightening island — so large, so gloomy — which seems to have captured his friend. He thinks of the wide, grassy fields of the farm on Streymoy, the windswept sky, his mother knitting by the fire and his bright bossy sister, now assisting the teacher at Tórshavn. The excitement of the voyage has disappeared. His pride in accomplishing a difficult mission — finding Enok — has vanished among these dark trees. A harsh, rasping cry sounds somewhere nearby and he starts in fear. But before he can move back towards the security of the bishop's house, a jaunty whistle comes from inside the hut — a seaman's jig the boy recognises. Quickly he wipes his fist over his wet cheeks. His lips, though, are still out of control; they will not form the return phrase.

'Ah, Jesus.' Conrad's voice comes out of the dark. 'What are we doing, Faroeman, arguing? Come inside this minute. I have not heard even half of your story. My woman has walked into the dark so you will have to do for warmth, eh? Come on in and bring your blanket, Napoleon Haraldsen.'

Inside, the two young men snug down together. Conrad hugs the smaller boy to him, punches his shoulder. 'God bless you, my friend. You have travelled half the world to find me and I repay you with curses. They should string me to the yard and flog my wretched temper out of me! You know what I am like, Napoleon. Forgive this mad fool. Eh?'

Napoleon is too happy to speak. The tears are flowing again, for a different reason. He returns the punch and hopes that his grunt of assent will pass for words.

Conrad whistles the tune again. 'Did you learn that one?'

This time Napoleon manages a wavering return.

Conrad laughs. 'We all learned that one! Join the navy and learn a new ditty every day.' He sings the snatch of another tune and Napoleon responds immediately with the chorus. Soon the two are singing and laughing like young boys, vying to remember the rude sailor versions of the old folksongs.

Conrad stops mid-song to ask, 'But, friend, I never once saw you! Every ship I came near I asked for you. You went into the navy?'

'I did. For a while only.'

'What ship?'

'*Frederik.*'

'Jesus, man, we were alongside at least twice! No boy aboard called Napoleon, they said. Did you change your name too?'

'They drafted me out, the rats. It turned out I was a good shot with the rifle, and they were desperate for more land troops.'

Conrad snorts. 'Why waste a Faroeman on land? What use would we be in the army?'

'What use were any of us except to die?'

Conrad suddenly turns on his elbow and peers at Napoleon. 'They didn't send you to Slesvig? You were at Dannevirke?'

'I was.'

'Jesus. At Dybbøl and Als?'

'The whole bloody mess. The bishop up there in his big house has a lot to answer for. Different orders every day, different leaders. Advance. Retreat. Hold fast. All we could do was die by the hundred.'

'Napoleon Haraldsen, tell me the story at once. You are a bloody hero just to come out alive. Did you see the bishop's son? Viggo? He was a captain there.'

Napoleon stretches, smiling in the dark, warm and secure now in his friend's admiration. 'They said he was there. I never saw him. Müller was there too — you remember our teacher?'

'How could I forget?'

'He caught the first ship back to Denmark to fight for his land. He came from Als, didn't he?'

'Yes, or somewhere in Slesvig.'

'Well, he died there. On that retreat from the Dannevirke. Enok, I have never been so cold in my life as on that damned retreat. The officers had fired us all up to hold and fight for king and Denmark. They boasted that we had beaten the Germans before and had the best army in the world, that our brave navy had blockaded German ports so the enemy would soon be crippled. They said we had important allies who would come rushing to our defence — Sweden, England, France . . .'

Conrad laughs. 'We got all those speeches too. Along with a measure of rum!'

'And then,' says Napoleon, still bitter at the memory, 'this order comes to retreat. Not a shot fired! I was ready enough to get out, I suppose — not my war — but some of the Danish soldiers were furious. They wanted to stay anyway and questioned the order. Later, an officer told me that General de Meza had two sets of orders — one to hold the Dannevirke line but another to keep his army whole, to be ready to fight in the spring. The story was that the crumbling old Dannevirke fortifications were impossible to hold, so de Meza chose to save his army. Well, no one explained all that to us.'

'Was he a good general to you?'

Napoleon laughs. 'Good enough, I suppose. The older soldiers liked him, thought it a shame he was removed. But a dandy! Fuss fuss about his uniform. I saw him once tear strips off a man who splashed mud on his white gloves. But for all that, a brave man. Every morning without fail he'd ride out to inspect the lines. Right in front of the enemy sometimes. You'd think he was daring them to shoot. But after the retreat they recalled him. Had to have a scapegoat, I suppose.'

Conrad growls. 'Isn't it the same always? Who would want to be an officer?'

'Surely,' says Napoleon stoutly, 'you would be officer material? You are born to lead people, Enok.'

'I am not born for anything but to blunder around like a bat in the daylight. Knocking all hell out of my friends. Look at tonight! But the story, Nap, the retreat.'

'God in heaven, that terrible retreat. You can't imagine the blizzard. We never had anything like it in the Faroes, Enok. The ground hard as iron, no purchase for your boots. We had to drag the great field-guns uphill and down again in the dark, wind and hail cutting into our faces. Once I tore the skin off the palm of my hand when it froze onto some metal part I was pushing.

'Two days and two nights we marched. I saw grown men just lie down and die, Enok. That's how Müller went, they say. Never had a chance to fight for his beloved land. Just too cold to go on. But you couldn't stop to help or you'd be the same. That was the worst time. Dybbøl and Als were awful too, but that retreat . . . no one understood. That broke our spirit, I reckon — not understanding. Feeling that our officers didn't understand either. I still don't really know why we were fighting at all.'

'Ask the bishop. He'll have his reasons.'

'That's what father says. There were important reasons, he says, and not to blame the bishop. He says Monrad believed it was the only way. That the ancient fortifications at Dannevirke were broken down, not able to be held. Father says the English are to blame — that those traitors let the Danes down, promising an alliance and then going back on it.'

'Don't talk to me about the English,' says Conrad.

'Why?'

'That's another story, friend, and a good one — happier than yours, at any rate. Let's hear about Dybbøl, then. We heard you fought well but it was hopeless.'

Napoleon is silent for a moment. 'Hope? I suppose you had to feel hope of some sort — that help would come, or that the enemy might be called off, or at worst you yourself might survive while others died. Mostly we didn't think about hope. Just kept going day after day, doing what we were told, going where the officers said, eating when we could, loading and firing our rifles. It's only looking back you can see it was hopeless.'

2.

Napoleon Haraldsen's story of
the Battle at Dybbøl

NAPOLEON HARALDSEN, FAROEMAN, lying next to his friend in a hut on the bank of the Manawatu River in New Zealand, tells of his part in the battle of Dybbøl. Not far away, Bishop Monrad, once prime minister of Denmark, the man who could not agree to a compromise position and who, with King Christian IX, gave the orders and made the decisions during that terrible time, only four years ago, writes in his study while his daughter plays the piano in the quiet house.

STRUGGLING back through snow and icy mud, Napoleon had never felt so miserably alone. Men tramped next to him but the easy talk and banter of the training days had been eclipsed by the bitter taste of defeat. Older soldiers were resentful, the young recruits frightened and discouraged. No one felt like sharing a joke or even smiling a greeting. Every man retreated into a silent monotony of hauling, slogging, snatching odd moments of sleep, and always, always giving ground — the sacred Danish territory of Slesvig — to the enemy.

At Sankelmark the Austrian cavalry caught up with them and the Danish rearguard turned to engage with them. Napoleon, near the tail of the long, straggling line of the retreating army, heard the sounds of the guns. For an hour they were cheered at the news that their soldiers had turned the Austrians back, but the order was still to retreat, endlessly, through that bleak winter landscape. The Prussians and Austrians followed them at a distance, occupying Slesvig as they came, mile after precious mile.

Once, when the blizzard cleared enough to see a few yards on either side, Napoleon realised they were walking close to a newly laid railroad. The lines ran in the direction they were tramping. But where was a train to carry them and these damned field-guns to safety? The boy cursed all stupid officers and politicians and vowed at that moment that if he survived he would never again volunteer to serve in any war.

Finally at Dybbøl they halted, their backs to the sea, the strategic island of Als behind them across a narrow neck of water. Here was the only high land for miles, overlooking the flat fields to west and north. Here were fortifications. To the south, the wide bay of Vemmingbund gave them some protection. A fitting place, the leaders decided, to make a stand against the superior force of the advancing Prussians. There they waited, behind the fortifications at Dybbøl, all of Holsten, much of Slesvig gone, the Prussians now free to move into Jutland.

The order came to cease fire: a conference was to be held in London. Surely now the big powers would see sense. That wily Prussian Bismark with his massive army should not be allowed to run loose on sovereign Danish land. That's what the officers said, and it brought a little hope, but the sickening shame of retreat — the proud Danish army! — cast a pall over the following weeks.

The weather warmed. Napoleon's heavy greatcoat, saturated most of the time, began to smell; everything about him smelled. They all had fleas. Everyone was sick of it. Some soldiers slipped away, crossing the bridge to Sønderborg, ostensibly to attend church, and then made their way through the trees to find a boat or a friend — some way back to normal life again. A few took the risky route overland to farms and families in Jutland. The cavalry were sent deep into the swamps and wilds of Jutland and told to keep out of the way of Prussian soldiers. Most of the soldiers stayed, though. Prime Minister Monrad sent stirring messages to the troops about fighting to the last drop of Danish blood. But Napoleon, who felt his blood to be Faroese, longed desperately to go home. He dreamed of rocking gently in a fishing boat on a clear, windswept morning, and woke to an officer's boot kicking him awake where he lay on the hard earth of their entrenchment.

At Dybbøl, Napoleon became friendly with Nils Amundsen, a Norwegian volunteer. Nils had been a fervent advocate of the Scandinavian Movement in his own country — had published a student broadsheet arguing the advantages of a strong union of Scandinavian countries. When Norwegian politicians refused to join Denmark in the battle for Slesvig, Nils had been outraged. He and a group of young friends came south to join the battle. Nils was a fiery young man, red-headed and freckled, and given to argument, a habit that earned him disfavour with some of the more stolid soldiers. But Napoleon liked him; their mutual foreignness was a bond, perhaps. Napoleon found himself digging trenches and adding to the meagre fortifications alongside the talkative Norwegian. Nils was interested in the Faroes, its government and its affiliation with Denmark. He was interested in *everything*, in fact. How better to keep their gunpowder dry, the best height for the new fortifications, what Napoleon's sister looked like (and did she have a sweetheart?). Nothing seemed to get Nils down. He whistled as he built the walls, and earned a cuff from their officer, who thought the enemy might hear.

'No, but,' argued Nils, unwisely, 'the wind is from the south — can't you see? We may hear them but not the reverse. Besides, a high sound carries less far.'

Napoleon kept his head down so the officer wouldn't see his grin.

'Keep your breath for the work, loudmouth!' shouted the officer, aiming another cuff.

Nils looked up earnestly. 'Now, *that* sound might well carry, Sergeant. The lower register, you see. I would be careful if I were you.' Then he staggered off with a shovel full of dirt before he attracted worse than blows.

Napoleon loved to stay near the cheerful fellow (*He reminded me a little of you, Enok*) and would take care to sit near him when they ate their rations or settled for the night.

'We'll win out here, young Nap,' he would say. 'The man who fights for his own land will always win over the invader, who cannot help but lack passion.'

'But it's not our land exactly, is it? Not yours and mine?'

Nils made a pretence of outrage. 'None of that talk, Faroeman! We are all Scandinavians, are we not? We are all bred of Vikings and Norsemen? This soil,' and here he would stamp his boots one-two-one in a patriotic dance and give an exaggerated salute, 'belongs to the north, not to those guttural lowlanders!'

BUT then the news came that the conference in London had failed; that Prime Minister Monrad had refused to agree to the terms of a treaty. Immediately, as if they had known all along that war was the only answer, the Prussian army attacked.

When the bombardment began, Nils realised at once the failings of the Danish artillery. His ruddy, freckled face paled. 'Here's trouble,' he muttered. 'Big trouble. Come over here, Nap, and keep your head down.'

From across Vemmingbund Bay, from a direction in which the whole Danish army had felt secure, protected by the stretch of water, Prussian guns began to fire on Dybbøl. Incredibly, the cannonballs travelled clear over the water to thud into the fortifications. Round after round smashed at the walls, shattering the army's newly built protection. Then the heavy shot began to fall behind the entrenchment.

Even then, Nils was intrigued. 'That would be half again as far as our guns can reach! How is it possible? I've seen their field-guns — no bigger than ours, I'd guess.'

Napoleon had no such interest — only dread. They were stuck here behind crumbling walls with no ability to retaliate. Surely they would all die.

And so they did — many of them. After that first appalling bombardment the Prussian soldiers attacked fiercely on foot from their trenches below the hill, and the Danes retaliated. Nils and Napoleon were not in the advance guard; their orders were to hold the redoubts to the north. He and Nils loaded and fired, loaded and fired, ramming powder and shot down the barrel of their field-gun time after time, heads ringing from the percussion, muscles aching with the heavy work. They aimed over the heads of their own men, with no idea whether their shot reached the enemy. Beside them, two young gunners lay moaning, a leg and an arm smashed, bleeding to death and no one to care for them. Napoleon shat himself without even realising it. Afterwards, when the Prussians retreated and they could rest, Nils took him gently down to the sea and washed him off, the air all around ringing with silence. The boy was shaking so hard Nils had to pull up his wet trousers for him.

'I'm not much better myself,' said Nils ruefully, holding up his own shaking hands. 'This will not be a pretty time, my friend. They have the better of us. A stronger desire is the only weapon in our favour. We will do what we must, but also try to survive. Agreed?'

Napoleon tried to smile and nod, but his legs suddenly gave way and he slumped to the ground.

Nils managed a wavering laugh. 'Ah, now, soldier, up with you. Surely we have earned a hot meal and a measure of beer! Let us march in search of sustenance.'

Later that night, Nils came back to the refuge they had found for themselves in a hollow, well behind the fortifications. He had been sent out to bring in Danish wounded, and found as well a Prussian rifle. The two young men examined it. Napoleon was puzzled — couldn't make head or tail of the bolts and slides — but Nils groaned.

'No wonder. This is how they do it. Look.' He slid back the bolt, pushed one of his own shot into the open slot, closed the bolt again. 'You can do it fast as lightning. You and I, Nap, would be still ramming our second shot down the muzzle while these fellows are firing off eight or ten more. Bet you my lucky stone against yours their big guns are loaded the same. God almighty, this is too clever for us.'

It was the first time either had seen a breech-loader, but not the last. Days turned to weeks and the pounding continued as the Prussian army dug in. In hand-to-hand fighting their superior weapons gave them no advantage, so they concentrated on the barrage, with occasional sorties. Gradually their trenches crept towards the Dybbøl fortifications. Soon almost all the Danish soldiers were doing the same as Nils and Napoleon: at night they sneaked out of the trenches and back down into the fields, out of range of those big guns. There they could hope to sleep in some kind of peace. In the morning the fields were full of the dark coats of Danish soldiers, doubled over, running back to the noisy chaos of their lines.

That's how they were caught, the last terrible day. Nils started by laughing at the sight, but soon wore a different expression. He and Nap were woken by the shouts and curses of their officers, more urgent than usual. The Prussians were advancing from their positions very early in the morning. The blue-capped heads of Danish soldiers popped up from hollows and dug-outs, like rabbits scenting danger. Suddenly everyone was running back to the lines, pulling on coats, dragging rifles and powder-horns. The Prussians were running too. It was more a race than a war, those first few minutes. Who would reach the Danish lines first?

For a while the Danish army held its position. Then it was a rout.

Napoleon lost Nils. He had no idea where he should be or what he should be doing. He had lost his powder so his rifle was useless. Shot whistled this way and that over his head. In his fear he stood still, screaming for Nils as if for his mother. Suddenly the big Norwegian was beside him, arm around his shoulder, driving him forward.

'We are to retreat! Down you go, Nap, down to the bridge.' He pointed to the two bridges over Als Sound, connecting the mainland to the town of Sønderborg. Napoleon could see the tide of soldiers pounding down the hill; already the bridges were dark with moving bodies and guns. He started down the hill but then realised Nils was not following and ran back to drag at his friend's sleeve.

'I'll follow soon,' shouted Nils. 'I am ordered to counter-attack for a short while. Some of our men are cut off and need time.'

Napoleon cried out at this. 'You'll be killed, Nils. What's the point?'

But Nils was gone, running back into the fierce fire.

Slowly Napoleon joined the retreat. He let others pass him, hoping Nils would join the column. Tears ran down his cheeks but he felt no shame: half the soldiers were in the same state. On a rise, General du Plat himself was standing, watching the retreat, taking no cover. Napoleon saw an officer run up to him, clearly urging him to join the column, but the general shook his head. The next time Napoleon looked back the general was on his knees, his tunic gashed, blood staining the fabric.

Napoleon kept his head down as he staggered across the heaving pontoon bridge and into Sønderborg. On either side of the street townspeople watched in silence. None of the soldiers could meet their gaze. The church doors were open but no bell rang to welcome them. The army had failed to protect this ancient town. Napoleon thought of his teacher, Herr Müller, how he had died on that cold march, the stories he had told of his beloved Sønderborg. And now the proud Danish army — what was left of it — could only delay the inevitable invasion by blowing up the bridges.

Exhausted and hungry, he wandered among the dispirited soldiers asking for news of Nils. Finally he found his friend, laid out with the rows and rows of crying, dying soldiers in the grim Sønderborg castle. They said a king of Denmark had once been imprisoned here and certainly it felt more like a prison than a castle. Its tiny slits of windows looked out across the sound to Dybbøl hill, where the Prussians now camped in triumph. Nils had been carried down with a bullet in his chest, one of the last to cross the bridge. Napoleon sat among the wounded and dead, a cold stone wall at his back. For hours he held Nils's icy hand, watching his friend's face turn blue-grey and the freckles stand out almost black as he fought for each breath.

'Take my lucky stone, Nap,' he wheezed. 'Then you will have two pieces of free Scandinavia to help you out of this mess.'

Later he whispered, 'Damn all politicians.' And died.

NAPOLEON couldn't eat, spoke to no one. He realised now that if Nils had been ordered to counter-attack, then surely the order was for him too. Nils had protected him and probably saved his life. Dazed and exhausted, he lived through the final, mercifully brief defeat and retreat from Als. Monrad was forced to resign, and a new Danish Cabinet was formed which accepted disastrous peace terms, losing all of Slesvig and Holsten to the Germans. Denmark had lost thousands of soldiers and over a third of its kingdom; Napoleon cared about none of it. All he thought of was getting out of the army and home to the Faroes.

A year later his mother cried out to see the silent scarecrow walk down the fields from Tórshavn, his sister Clara bringing him home to the farm. That night he sat by a peat fire listening to the long drumroll of waves breaking against the stony shore. He ate barley porridge and dried mutton and, in time, began to smile again.

3.

A MONTH AFTER Napoleon's arrival at Karere he has still not managed to persuade Conrad to leave with him. Underlying their friendship, and the easy way they work together on the bishop's land, is the constant pressure of that question. Napoleon tries not to mention it too often, but he is also aware that the thought of leaving this flat inland farm appeals more and more to his friend. He sees the distant look in Conrad's eyes when he turns west and lifts his head as if to smell the salt. Napoleon shares the longing. Oceans are in their blood; when they remain too long away from the sea it feels as if a limb were missing.

First Conrad refused any notion of leaving. He had a duty to Anahuia, and a love for her. Then he suggested they wait. Perhaps something could be worked out. Perhaps Ana could be freed from her . . . obligations . . . in some way. Napoleon, who knew his sister

Clara's heart, and who jealously wanted his friend as brother-in-law, could not take Anahuia seriously. Also, she disturbed him: her fierce, free ways, her height and her straightforward talk. Conrad hinted that she was bound in some way but she never gave that impression.

'Her people will look after the baby, surely,' Napoleon would say. 'You can't expect to be tied forever to people so different from us. We are wasting our lives here.'

Conrad would frown, uncharacteristically silent.

But increasingly Napoleon feels that his friend *will* leave this dark inland place. Soon the pull will be too great.

ONE afternoon the two friends, working in the bishop's tobacco patch, look up to see the bishop himself standing among the rows of leafy plants. He leans heavily on a stout stick, still recovering from an injury that has been slow to heal. He was thrown while riding and then the horse stepped on his leg. Monrad nods at them in his serious way.

'Would the two of you come up to the house when you have finished the row?'

Conrad straightens, wiping sweat away with his forearm. 'We'd be glad to, Bishop. This work breaks the back of a tall fellow like me.'

Napoleon draws breath at his friend's cheeky response but Monrad simply nods again. 'I would help,' he says, 'but as you see, I am in no shape. I find it distressing to be so idle when so much needs doing.'

Conrad protests. 'Ah, Bishop, I wasn't asking for your help. Everyone knows you work harder than most when you can. We two young Faroemen can cope with these few weeds.'

Monrad smiles, a sight not often seen around the farm. 'You are both good workers,' he says, 'and I am glad to have you, but there are matters that need discussing.' As he turns to leave he adds, 'Come up as you are, lads. No need to change your clothes.'

Napoleon hopes that the question of setting out for home might be raised, and he is not disappointed. But first Monrad raises another issue. As soon as the two men are standing in the quiet study, the bishop looks up from the book he is studying and comes to the point.

'Conrad — or should I call you Enok?'

'Conrad will serve well enough.'

'Conrad, you are a ballad singer of note in the Faroes?'

The tall young man shifts from foot to foot. Again he feels uncomfortable in this quiet, ordered room. 'I was just a learner, Bishop.'

Napoleon can't let this pass. 'A learner? You were famous in all the islands! Who else could attempt two long kvæ∂i . . .'

'Attempt, yes. Finish, no.'

'You were famous, though. You can't say no to that.'

Monrad silences Napoleon with a raised hand. The bishop is used to conducting his interviews without assistance. 'Let us accept that you have exceptional talent. Now. The ballad you specialised in concerned the legend of Sigurd?'

'The slayer of the dragon Fáfnir, yes.'

'Interesting. We call the dragon Fafner — but the story is no doubt similar. Would you sing me some of it?'

Conrad looks startled. 'What — here? Now?'

'Yes. If you please.'

Napoleon and Conrad exchange a grin. The bishop, for all his wisdom, doesn't understand. But then Conrad, never one to turn down a challenge, thrusts an arm through his friend's, grasps his hand, then strikes a pose and takes a breath. Napoleon wants to giggle — this is ridiculous — but tries to join in. He raises one foot ready for the first step.

> *Faroemen welcome from your fjords and valleys,*
> *Encircle this hearth, hear me sing*
> *Of the hero Sjúrður, his mighty deeds*
> *The dragon's treasure and the dread ring . . .*

His voice roars into the small room. The bishop leans back in his chair as if a wind has struck him. When Conrad reaches the moment for the first step of the dance, the two young men stamp on the wooden floor with gusto and move two paces forward, one pace back.

In the second verse Conrad lowers the volume, then pauses for effect. Napoleon can't take it seriously — he is shaking with silent laughter. Then without a change in expression Conrad neatly turns the phrase and he is singing a popular sea shanty:

> *And we're rolling rolling, over the sea*
> *And we're bound, oh, we're bound for the shore . . .*

He turns to his friend, grinning through the words. Napoleon changes his step to the hornpipe and then the two men fall about, laughing and slapping their thighs.

'Sorry, sorry, Bishop,' gasps Conrad, 'but it can't be done. Not here. Not like this. Kvæði are for special occasions. They are for the Faroes. The spirit of that place. I need a crowd of Faroemen to dance me through. Ah, Jesus!' He roars with laughter again and slaps his friend on the back until he hiccups.

Monrad sits calmly through all this. If he is annoyed he doesn't show it.

'Well, well,' he says at last. 'You have made your point. But here,' and he holds up a book finely bound in leather, 'is your kvæði, all the sections of it, inside these covers and on my desk here in the colony of New Zealand.'

Conrad frowns. 'A Danish version of the Sjúrðar kvæði?'

'No, no, no. In Faroese. *Your* version. The words you sing.'

'Not possible, Bishop. My version is that of my father Róland of Suðeroy and of old Niclas Patursson. Neither could write Faroese. Who could? The words in your book will be different.'

Monrad smiles. 'Indeed, they may. See for yourself. You will be interested.' He offers the book.

Conrad stays where he is, frowning, but Napoleon takes the heavy volume and turns the pages. For a while he is silent, reading — or seeming to. Then he hands it to Conrad, his expression blank. The tall Faroeman holds it in his hands without looking down at the page. He stares out of the window at the broken fields and the flowering garden.

'Read, read,' says the bishop. 'I would value your opinion.'

Conrad sighs and begins to study the page. All the liveliness and fun of the last few moments have gone from him. Napoleon watches anxiously.

'I understand,' says Monrad, 'that you have learned two of the three sections. Perhaps you could learn the third from this book. When you return to the Faroes you might surprise them?'

Napoleon is delighted at the idea. 'Yes! Enok, what a plan! You could learn it on the long trip back!' His voice falters as he sees the stubborn look on Conrad's face. 'I could help,' he says quietly, touching his friend on the sleeve.

Conrad closes the book. Hands it back to the bishop. 'The words mean nothing,' he says. 'Nothing.'

'A different version?' suggests Monrad.

'How would I know?' shouts Conrad. 'Those symbols on the paper are nothing I learned. We learned to write Danish.'

Again the bishop raises a calming hand. 'Ah. I see. But you will pick it up quickly, I am sure. You *speak* the language, after all.'

'Yes, I speak it and think in it and sing it. Some Dane, I suppose, has tied it down and put it into a book?'

Monrad is becoming testy. His worker is overstepping the rules of politeness. He had imagined a very different reaction to his kind proposal.

'Now, now, that is uncalled for, young man. This book is a fine work of scholarship. You should be delighted to see your language take its first step into the modern world . . .'

Conrad snorts and would have left the room if Napoleon, embarrassed by his friend's rage, had not barred his way.

'Enok, Enok, you are too angry. There is no need. The bishop makes an offer, that is all. Calm yourself.'

Again Conrad stares out of the window in silence. But he breathes more quietly. The other two wait. He has a presence, thinks the bishop, that is hard to explain. A quality of leadership, is it? A strength, at least. Monrad would dearly love to hear this young man sing the Sigurd ballad seriously.

Finally Conrad turns back to face the bishop. 'I apologise for my outburst, sir. But can you understand how I feel? I have been taught to value greatly the tradition of passing down the kvæði from master to pupil. From one voice to one pair of ears. How can you possibly capture the feeling, the music, the *spirit* of a great ballad on a piece of paper? Don't you see? Now anyone can read those words . . . well, some people will, I suppose . . . but what will they find? My great, living kvæði is robbed of its life: dry, withered as the paper it is written on. They will have no way of understanding. This book,' and Conrad points dramatically to the volume, which now lies on the bishop's desk, 'will kill what it seeks to preserve.'

Monrad is impressed with the oratory if not the content. 'Come now, lad, there is no need to be so black and white. I am sure this book will do no such thing. It will help many to value your traditions. We should value scholarship when we find it. I imagine that in finding a way to write your language, the writer has helped to preserve Faroese.'

The bishop sees that Conrad is inclined to carry on the argument so he moves quickly to his next point.

'Well, so be it. You may borrow the book — either of you — if you change your mind. Now. Another matter. Your father, Napoleon, asked me to see that you returned safely to him. I have heard today that a sailing ship will leave Port Nicholson Harbour in three weeks' time. There would be positions for you and Conrad in the crew. Would you like me to arrange this for you?'

'Yes! Yes, please!' says Napoleon, almost dancing with excitement. He turns to Conrad. 'Say yes, Enok. You know you want to.'

Conrad moves his head slowly from side to side as if looking for a way out. The smell of freshly oiled wood is sharp in his nostrils. He twists the cap in his hands into a tight ball. When he speaks, it is to Napoleon, not the bishop.

'Jesu Maria, I am no good at this kind of thing. You are right, I do want to go. It's the sea I miss. And other things. And I would miss you, too, my good friend, if I stayed.'

'Then come! Say yes! Here is the chance.'

Conrad turns to the bishop. 'It is Anahuia. I am . . . attached . . . to her.'

Monrad frowns. 'Her baby is yours? I had thought . . .'

Conrad smiles. 'Mine.'

'Are you sure?'

The smile disappears. '*Yes*! In fact down at her kainga they rather suspect *you* are the father, Bishop.'

Monrad snorts. 'What rubbish!'

'Well, yes, we all know that. But her people don't fancy her — not as a woman — and since Te Peeti offered her to you, as a help and translator, they assumed . . . other things.'

Napoleon's face is red with embarrassment. He prepares to be bundled out of the study, along with his friend.

Monrad, however, is clearly interested. 'Anahuia. She is bound to Te Peeti's family in some way?'

'To a relative of Te Peeti's, yes.'

Monrad frowns. 'Some kind of slavery?'

'No, sir, not slavery. Anahuia is very firm on that.'

'A native custom, then? A matter of utu?'

'Yes, Bishop. A muru party took her some years back.'

'Ah. I have read of such occurrences. We must hear her story. I would like to add it to my papers. Now then, young man, do you wish to marry her?'

It is Conrad's turn to be embarrassed. 'Marriage? I had not thought . . . They would not allow . . . She is not Christian . . .'

The bishop is stern. 'But surely you are, Conrad. Surely?'

Conrad manages a small nod. He glances sideways at Napoleon for help. In fact neither young man has been to church in six months.

A silence develops in the room. The bishop rises with difficulty and walks to a desk where a book of etchings lies open. He turns a page and regards the image, taps the paper. Napoleon, looking out the window, breathes in sharply. Anahuia is there, her bare feet in the soil of the garden, standing stock-still, looking in at them. Conrad has seen too, but makes no sign. Does she know what they are discussing?

Monrad, still regarding his etching, speaks to them. 'If I spoke to Te Peeti he might release the girl?'

Conrad nods slowly. 'I have already asked the man who has . . . taken her. He refused. Te Peeti said it was not his decision to make or break. He might feel differently if you asked.'

The bishop frowns. 'I am not about to sully my reputation to save yours. If she were freed would you take her back to the Faroes *as your wife?*'

Conrad spreads his hands, palm up. 'Sir, I have no money for a passage for her. And I am by no means sure she would come. We could live near the coast, maybe. *This* country's coast. Where she would be comfortable and I could find work that involved the sea.'

'Returning to your homeland is not in your plan?'

'Ahhh.' Conrad moves impatiently. 'Plans. Mine mostly go grievously astray. I . . . to be honest with you, I am not a planner.' He grins. 'One day, perhaps. I was forced to leave in such a rush. My mother . . . Yes, one day I will go.'

Napoleon grabs at his sleeve. 'Now! Come now. It is the right time.'

Monrad frowns a little. 'Your friend is right. The homeland is always important. A man has a duty to serve his country if he is called. It would seem you are needed.'

Conrad bridles at this. 'Bishop, you have left your country at a time of need.'

The bishop clears his throat, taps a finger impatiently against the black and white drawing on the page. 'Denmark has need, yes,' he says, 'desperate need. But she does not want or call me.'

'And you are settling your sons in a country far from their homeland. Am I so different?'

Monrad sighs. 'Yes, you are different. My sons are good and upright men. They will make fine farmers here; safe from the slurs that may be cast upon them because of the . . . recent disasters. You, on the other hand, will be welcomed home. Your knowledge of kvæði and your ability as a singer will help build and preserve a language that is in danger.' Monrad turns at last from the page he has been studying to look directly at Conrad. If he feels bitterness or anger over his lot there is no evidence of it in his calm and straight gaze. 'If I were called for such a reason, I would go. Gladly. So should you, my friend.'

The stern words make no impression on Conrad. He walks to the window; raises a hand to the woman who still stands there, at a distance but looking in. 'Thanks anyway, Bishop,' he says, 'If you can persuade Te Peeti to intervene in her release we would both appreciate it.'

He walks out of the room, leaving his friend marooned. After a silence in which the remaining two, man and boy, regard each other in some disarray, Napoleon reaches for the precious book.

'May I take it, sir? He will come around to it, surely.'

'You may take it.'

'He is concerned for that woman at the moment. But the kvæði . . . our old customs . . . he was born to them, schooled from a small boy in them. In the end that will be the most important to him.'

Monrad nods with serious approval. 'Good. I hope so. But do not underestimate the power of a new young country and fresh experiences. My own boys . . .' He smiles briefly; the change in his face is a revelation. Then he waves a hand in dismissal. 'Well, off you go. The work remains to be done.'

As Napoleon turns to leave the room the bishop asks, 'Will you go back without him?'

Napoleon cannot answer.

4.

Anahuia tells her story

THEY ARE ALL there, in the bishop's parlour, even the older son, Viggo, on leave from the fighting in Taranaki. He has travelled south to visit his wife and children. The room is filled with the delicious smell of æbleskiver, which Olga is cooking to mark the occasion. She has heated the heavy iron pande over the fire in the parlour, so they can all enjoy the sizzle as the batter drops into each buttery depression. Tonight Anahuia does not help with the cooking but stands in the doorway watching. Olga turns the golden treats with her knitting needle, waits for the second side to brown, then hands them to be dipped in sugar and eaten still crisp and hot.

The bishop clears his throat. It is time for the Bible reading. Tonight he reads a passage from Jonah, his fine voice bringing the old story to life. When the passage is finished they all sigh and settle, ready for lighter entertainment. The bishop motions with his pipe for Anahuia to come forward and be seated, but she shakes her head.

'I will tell it standing.'

Anahuia is not dressed in her usual European-style dress but has draped a plaid blanket over one shoulder and pinned it in place with a bone ornament. Her hair falls straight down her back, the dark and shadowy brown of it glowing in the lamplight. She looks with her strange smoky eyes towards Conrad, who nods and smiles from his seat in the corner. Napoleon sits on the floor beside him, resting his back against his friend's knees. The wind is quiet this night and the air blessedly free of the whine of mosquitoes. This is a peaceful scene. All the women, even young Karen, have a piece of cloth in their hands and are stitching quietly at mending or at new garments. On a table beside the bishop, paper, quill and ink are laid ready for any notes that may be made.

'It is fitting,' says Anahuia in her soft accented Danish, 'that you have read tonight, tihopa Monrad, from Jonah. I am the daughter of a whaler. The child I carry has whaling twice in his ancestry. Conrad,' she speaks with pride, 'also belongs to a whaling family, and is the father of this unborn child.'

Anahuia tells her story simply and without emotion. She holds her head high as she speaks, and looks over the heads of her audience. Once or twice she turns towards Conrad and pauses, as if searching for the correct expression. Sometimes she uses an English word, occasionally Maori. The meaning is always clear. The listeners seem spellbound. They lean forward to catch every quiet but powerful word.

'My father was Danish,' says Anahuia. 'His name was Johan Gerhard Jensen. Jutland was his home — a land, he said, of rain and mist and bogs. He could not name any mountain as his, but used strange names of seas and lakes to describe his place. There were seven boys in the Jensen family. The land of their farm was sour and damp: seven men could not make a living there. So my father left Denmark with his two brothers for a life at sea. These three youngest were only boys when they left, my father just twelve years old and his brothers a little older. Work was available for all three on a sailing ship bound for Australia — a convict ship, but one that also brought free settlers to Botany Bay. They were strong and adventurous fellows in those days, I think, not yet ruined by too much strong liquor.

'At Botany Bay they left their ship to work on a coastal trader. My father never said why they ran away from their ship but I think it was something bad they did — or had done to them. For two years they worked trading up and down that coast — Botany Bay to Hobart and other places in between. My father was happy talking about that time, and would have stayed, I think. But his brothers became restless and wished to try whaling. My father, with no other family but those two brothers, followed their wish. They signed all three with a whaler bound for New Zealand. My father's oldest brother said he was experienced, which was not quite true, but the owner of the trading ship was desperate for men and he accepted my uncle's word.

'They were set down at Wharemauku, a shore whaling station on the coast about three days' walk south from here. Just opposite the island called Kapiti. Their task was to search for the whales at the time of year when they came close to shore, to harpoon them and drag them to land, where the rich fat of the whales was boiled down and barrelled up for oil.'

Anahuia has used a Maori word for whale — tohora. Conrad sits forward.

'Tohora — is that a kind of whale?'

Anahuia smiles. 'I have forgotten the Danish word. In English *a whale.* Not the big one — paraoa, who dives deep and is caught further south. Paraoa did not come close to our station. Sometimes the other big ugly ones came. More often the black whale — not so big but with good oil and bone.'

'Grindaboð!' shouts Conrad, 'Grindaboð! *Our* whales were the smaller sort, too — and black!' He jumps to his feet and, humping his back, shapes with his hands a narrow dorsal fin. 'Do your fish also have this fin?'

She nods, and Conrad leaps around the room in excitement, imitating the curving passage of the pilot whale. 'It is the same! What if our whales swam the whole ocean to visit this place? What if I have seen the same whale off the shore of my Suðeroy as you have seen off your Kapiti?'

Monrad clears his throat. He is trying not to smile. 'That is not a likely idea, young man. Why would a whale swim from one cold sea to another, and not stop when it finds the warm ocean of the tropics? Eh? Also, one whale would no doubt die before it completed such a heroic journey.'

Conrad stops to think. He is about to put forward a theory when the bishop's raised hand halts him.

'Are we to hear this young woman's story, then? Enough of the mythical journeys of whales.'

Anahuia has been laughing at Conrad's antics. Now she sighs, arching her back against the weight of the baby. Even so, she will not sit down. Conrad's interruption has relaxed her, though, and now as she talks she does so to her audience, and moves a little this way and that as she explains her early home.

'My father came to our place about three years before I was born. The brothers had changed their names to English-sounding ones. My father was known as Johnny Jacks. I never knew the names of the others. I called them uncle when I was little, and then they went away.

'The whaling station already had two boats and the new whalers, my father and his brothers among them, were dropped ashore with two more. They were left there for the season, which was about four months. The boats that chased the whales were not big — three people could manage one boat. My oldest uncle was headsman, which meant he gave the orders; the next uncle was steerer, which meant he threw the harpoon; and my father, in those early days, was commonman, which meant he rowed all the time. By the time I was born he was headsman of his own boat, and then for a short time chief headsman.

'The whales have gone now and the stations with them, but when I was growing up the whales still came.

'My mother is Paora of the Pukeroa hapu. Our tribe is Te Ati Awa. We call our mountain Taranaki, though we no longer live under it. We came south when there was fighting among the tribes. My mother's family is influential and it was felt fitting that a Pakeha–Maori be added to the hapu. So she was offered to my father as wife to him.'

Anahuia smiles at the shocked look from the bishop's wife. 'This was the custom. And in some places still is. An alliance with a white man is an advantage for trade and other connections.'

Napoleon digs Conrad in the ribs and slides his eyes towards the bishop, who is examining his pipe with great concentration. Perhaps he is remembering their conversation in the study yesterday.

'Two other families,' continues Anahuia, 'gave wives to the older brothers. My Danish uncles both had Ngati Toa wives, related to Te Rauparaha's hapu. The other tribe from the area — Ngati Raukawa — were angry that they had missed out but Te Rauparaha still had a little mana in those days and they kept their peace.

'The young brother, my father Johnny Jacks, was pleased with his wife, and excited to have a woman of his own at such an early age. My mother told me she was proud of him in the early years. At seventeen he was very tall and strong, his hair the colour of scraped and bleached flax, his head full of stories and songs that she did not understand but still enjoyed. He worked hard at his rowing and spent much time with Paora and her family. At the end of the season, when the trading boat came for the barrels of oil and the whale bone, Johnny Jacks decided to stay on shore and wait for the next season. His brothers were eager to return to Botany Bay, so away they went, leaving Johnny with his share of the profits — his lay — as commonman, one one-hundredth part. The uncles received more.

'After he had been with us for three years, I was born and named Ana for my Danish grandmother and huia for the bird whose white-tipped feather is prized by Te Ati Awa. My mother and father and all our hapu planted many potatoes each spring to sell to the trader when he returned, and my father suggested to the elders that they might build a small trading boat for themselves so they could take their potatoes and flax down to Port Nicholson, where new settlers were arriving every day and there was a strong need for food. Oh, my father was full of great plans and good ones in my first three years.

'The family respected his views. The boat was built, and Johnny Jacks sailed it with some others down the coast. My mother said there was a great welcoming feast when he returned with blankets and nails and liquor and tobacco. He did not bring guns. Te Ati Awa had turned Christian a year or two before, and anyway the way of guns was not popular at that time. I was two years old. Te Rauparaha, our great leader and neighbour — and a cousin by marriage to my grandfather — had just been returned to his people at Otaki. That great chief was humiliated and lacking in mana after his ten months in jail. The rule of guns was no longer a path that most Ngati Toa or our own Te Ati Awa felt to be profitable.

144

'So my father was well loved. His brothers returned for three more seasons but then disappeared. Johnny Jacks became headsman of his own boat. My first memory is of the whaling station. The smell! The sight! It is like a nightmare in my memory. Our kainga — our village — was a little distance from the whaling station. There we had our own dwelling, built by my father. Most days my mother would walk over the small hills with food for my father. Sometimes my little brother and I came too and we would all sit with my father to eat it. We would sit at the top of the . . .' Anahuia turns to Conrad. 'What do you call a hill all of sand with stiff grasses and flowers growing on it? Is there a word?'

Conrad shrugs. 'A hill of sand? There is no Faroese word for such a sight.'

'A dune,' says young Karen, who is eager to show off her English. 'A sand dune.'

'Well, we would sit on that tahuna and look down at the black smoke from the trying pots, the black bodies of whales spilt open to show the pale and shining fat that foreigners would pay so much money for; the red blood, worth nothing, soaking into the sand. Men with knives on long poles slashed at the dead whales and many, many seagulls screamed above them. The skulls of the great fish and the ribs and backbones lay everywhere, jutting out of the sand like the timbers of a village that has been destroyed by flood. The smell and the smoke and the flies made my little brother scream in fright and I was not much better. My mother told me that once my father had wanted to take me down to the shore to show me to the other whalers, but I beat him with my small hands and struggled from his arms to run back over the dunes to our kainga.

'The earlier years were good for Te Ati Awa and Ngati Toa. They shared in the good money for whale oil and bone, and made their Pakeha whalers welcome. But then the whales became fewer and fewer. The year I was six no whales came at all. Not even if my father rowed all day and searched the sea far beyond the protection of the island.

'After that year our station closed and the trader ship took the whale boats away. My father had no work except the potato planting, which, so my mother said, was not in his nature. Fearing that he might leave, she spoke with her Ngati Toa relatives and they gave him whaling work at Waiorua, the one remaining station on Kapiti Island. But it was not the same. No longer was he chief headsman. Even out on the island few whales came. My mother said they had learned good sense; what whale, she said, would willingly come towards the shore, year after year, to be slaughtered? Another old man — a Pakeha–Maori of the Ngati Raukawa — told me later that the way the whales were taken was sheer madness. And that greed had blinded the common sense of Pakeha and Maori whalers both.'

'How was it done, then?' asks Conrad, who is interested as always to compare techniques and new ways of performing old customs.

'In the time when the sun sets directly out from our shore, not north or south,' says Anahuia, 'the female whales came close to the shore to give birth. That was always their custom. Perhaps they needed to give the newborn a warmer sea for their first days. The whaling boats would row out looking for the spouting whales and then wait until they saw a newborn. This they would kill and haul towards the shore. The mother would not swim away with her own family group but would stay close to where her young had been born. She is a constant mother. The whalers would then harpoon the mother also, and drag her to shore, where the heavy ropes attached to the shears at the water's edge would drag her body to land.

'As the old man, who had himself once been a whaler, said,' (Anahuia uses a grating, angry voice for the old man) '"Killing the

146

mothers and babies year after year was the work of idiots! The heart of the group destroyed. Breeders, future breeders. We were greedy bastards, myself included, and deserved what we got. Or didn't get. The whales themselves did not deserve such a savage cull." Those were his words.'

Conrad shakes his head, striking one fist into the other palm to emphasise his words. 'Mothers and babies only! Bad. Very bad.' He looks down at Napoleon. 'But are we any better? We take all! Fathers, mothers, babies young, old. If we can get the whole group, then good! But the whales still come.' He hesitates. 'Sometimes.'

Again the bishop's hand is raised for silence. Anahuia continues, but now she sits on the stool that has been placed beside her. She settles her bare feet wide apart to give space to the baby, rests her hands firmly on her knees, the plaid blanket, cream and brown, reaching down almost to the floor.

'For us that was the end of the good times. My mother and her family were disappointed that their Johnny Jacks was now only a commonman who brought little mana and less money to the kainga. There were many days when no whales came, even in the season. My mother said that all the good whalers had gone — to search for gold or to begin farms of their own — and that only the wasters had stayed, to drink and make nothing but trouble all day. She would point to other whalers who had accepted land from their hapu and developed good farms for their wives and families; who were now prosperous men, respected by Pakeha and Maori alike. When my father turned his face away from work on the land, my mother shouted at him to turn then to the sea. What about his grand trading plans, she asked. Why did his trading boat lie idle week after week?

'Drink — strong liquor — was my father's problem. He had grown to love it. Sometimes he would become soft and gentle with the drink and tell my brother and me stories in his own tongue. He encouraged us to speak back to him in Danish and we did, though my mother was angry and said we should go and work in the garden and not encourage him. Other times he would rage and swear and pick fights with Paora's brothers and uncles, until she screamed at him and beat his back, and then he would hit her too.

'I think he was too young a man to be left with no kin of his own except us — my brother and me — who were too small. I have thought about him leaving home so early and growing up on a harsh ship with no person to be father or mother to him. He said that in his country it was the custom for boys to go to sea very young. Who, then, could teach them right ways of living? My thought is that he was a good man who took one wrong turning and then another.

'So, the end came on a trading trip inland.' Anahuia smiles sadly. 'Near here, not far from Tiakitahuna, which you call Jackeytown. My mother had begged my father to go with her brothers and uncles on a trip to sell potatoes for flax and other things that we needed. He went, grumbling and already drunk, and that was the last I ever saw of him. At the kainga where the party stopped my father was offered more drink by some foolish Rangitane man. During that night my father, it is said, stole into the hut of another man's family, dragged out his daughter and made . . . takahi wahine . . . to her.'

'Rape,' whispers Conrad to Napoleon, who nods. There is no need for translation; the way Anahuia growls the words makes the meaning clear.

'The girl screamed and the father and mother came running. My father was a big, strong man. The others of the village let the father of the child fight on his own because his own honour demanded this. My uncles should have dragged Johnny Jacks away but did not. I don't know why. At the end of a long and bloody fight, the father of the girl lay dead and my father on his hands and knees, still drunk, still cursing, a wound in his arm bleeding onto the ground. Out ran the mother of the dishonoured girl, out from her hut where she had been sheltering. At the sight of her dead husband she screamed curses and abuse at my father. She flew at him, clawing at his skin, reaching for his eyes to gouge them out. My father, they say, went to defend himself, and even hit out at the distraught woman, but then, *then* my uncles held him and let the woman have her way. The woman took a knife from one of their warriors and, while Johnny Jacks' kin held him, she stabbed many times in her rage and grief until he was dead.'

Monrad clears his throat and looks to his wife to see if this gory tale should be curtailed. She in turn looks to Karen, whose eyes are glued to Anahuia.

'Go on,' whispers Karen.

Anahuia speaks calmly, but there is a tension in her voice. 'That was the end of the killing. The death of the husband had been avenged by the wife, as was proper in our custom. But the matter of the . . . other thing . . . with the young girl — that wrong was not settled. The Rangitane people let my uncles go home but both sides knew a muru party would soon be sent to finish the feud. My mother cried all night when they returned, and tore at her breasts with her fingernails. My brother and I watched in silence. We had never seen our mother so wild. I think now that she was more upset at what she knew would happen than at the death of our father, Johan Gerhard Jensen, known as Johnny Jacks.' After a pause she adds, 'But I cried for him. I loved his loud laugh and his beard that was like dry tussock-grass, and the stories of his childhood in Jutland. He was not a good man, I suppose, but I cried for him.'

'The muru party?' The bishop brings Anahuia back to her story. He has his pen ready poised over the paper. This is the part that interests him. 'Muru means the same as utu? Revenge?'

Anahuia considers this. 'Not the same. But it can have the same result. A feud or a debt is ended after a successful muru party.

'At this time I was nine years old. Ten years ago. We Te Ati Awa had become Christian so we no longer killed and ate our enemies. Rangitane were not yet Christian. You have made some changes in their thought since you came, tihopa Monrad.'

The bishop smiles. 'I do what I can. Your chief and I have many talks.'

'But Christian or not,' continues Anahuia, 'some customs remained. Still remain. A wrong deed must be paid for, even after many years. My mother knew that the bad thing my father did to the dead man's daughter must be paid for. She thought it was better to settle sooner rather than later, when the deed may be exaggerated or provoke a lasting feud for generations to come. So when she heard that the muru party had set out she was relieved, I think. All our hapu met together to plan. I remember the day, but did not guess the way it would end. I hope that my mother also did not guess. Some of the uncles and great-uncles were angry with my mother for her stupid Pakeha husband. I remember that my grandmother kept looking at me with sad eyes. Only later did I realise why.

'The family agreed what gifts they would prepare for the party. My mother, hoping the party would spare her house, carried all our best possessions outside. Our cooking pot, my father's gun and his axe. His woollen trousers, washed and folded, his pipe and all his supply of tobacco. But what liquor there was she poured in anger into the stream. My grandfather brought two sacks of potatoes and my uncles sent a sack of smoked eels and one of dried fish. My grandmother worked all night to finish a beautiful cloak that she had been making for me. It had dark and light patterns and feathers in the old style. It was beautiful. I had helped her make it and cried to see it laid out for that other girl to wear. Two young pigs were also tethered by their legs just outside the door to our house. My grandmother looked at the big heap of goods laid out there and nodded and said yes, this was a good price, but her eyes still looked sadly towards me.

'Then our hut was left empty of all its homely things, even the blankets and mats we slept on. Even the table my father had made was carried outside. My mother, my brother and I went to our grandmother's hut to wait for the muru party. They came silently as night fell and I was very frightened. There were many men standing just beyond our kainga. Some were dressed in the old way and some carried guns. Also they had brought horses and baskets. My grandfather stood in his doorway and nodded in satisfaction to see so many. He saw it as a compliment to his family's importance that a big party was sent. My grandmother called a welcome to them, and many of our women joined in. But the voices sounded strained and anxious to me, not the usual strong and ringing karanga that shows the pride of a family.

'The men came forward suddenly. They came with shouts and many threatening thrusts of guns into the air and kicking up the sand with their feet, but they did not shoot or fight. At our hut they stopped and walked around the pile of goods. The pigs squealed in fear, tugging on their ropes. The tether of one pig pulled out of the sand and my brother laughed out loud to see one Rangitane warrior chasing the little fellow in and out of the piled goods. My grandfather slapped my brother hard and told him to turituri. Usually he would not do such a thing, but even he must have felt fear.

'The leader of the muru party was the brother of the dead man. A harsh and a cruel man. He is a relative by marriage of the chief Te Peeti, who is your friend, tihopa,' Anahuia looks with hard eyes at the bishop, 'and not such an honourable man, although he now has been baptised into the Christian church. He walked all around the pile of all our possessions and the gifts of food from the family. Then he shouted an order and at once two of his men came to my grandfather's own cooking fire. They thrust bundles of dry tussock-grass into the embers and when these torches were flaming they tossed the fire into our house. My grandfather and grandmother and all our uncles and aunties watched without a word as our hut burned to the ground. Even my mother stayed silent.

'At last the leader — I do not like to use his name — came forward and stood before my grandfather. He asked where were Johnny Jacks' children. At this my mother cried out but someone held her back. My grandfather pushed my brother and me in the back, but we were frightened and would not move. "Go! Stand high!" said my grandfather sternly. We had been brought up to obey him always, so I took my brother by the hand and we both stepped one pace forward, while all the Rangitane looked at us. My legs were trembling but my brother, who was seven, held his head up and frowned like a man. When the leader reached out to take us, my grandfather spoke. "Not the boy," he said. His voice was powerful and ringing. "Not the boy," he repeated.

'My brother, you see, is brown-skinned and dark-eyed, like the rest of the family, and strong-spirited. My grandfather, who is dead now, was very fond of him. He did not value me so highly.

'For a long moment the two men, one grey-headed, the other black, looked into each other's eyes. Then the Rangitane nodded once. He took me roughly by the shoulder and made a sign to the others in the muru party that they should gather the goods. I was very frightened and tried to pull away but they held me tightly. My mother cried out but she did not come for me. Only my grandmother came forward and spoke softly. "We will remember you, little Anahuia, but you must go with them. This Rangitane is a hard man to take you. But you must stay with him and be like a Rangitane now, even though you are Te Ati Awa. Just think that you are going by your own brave act to save others in your family. Never let them call you a slave. Think that you have chosen to go. This is a true thought." '

Anahuia sighs. 'I have tried to keep that thought in my head. It has been explained to me that if I leave this Rangitane man's kainga they will take my brother or my mother in my place.'

The bishop frowns. 'Surely not. This colony is now under English rule. Slavery is not permitted.'

Anahuia rises slowly to her feet. 'I am no slave. I stay by choice. These days my life is fortunate. Te Peeti has asked my . . . the man . . . to lend my services to you because I speak your tongue. So that I can translate your ideas for Te Peeti and can carry his wishes to you.' She speaks without looking at Monrad. 'There was some thought when you first arrived that you might wish to add a Maori wife to your present one, and that an alliance would bring benefits to both important families.'

Anahuia turns at Emilie's abrupt movement and speaks to the wife. 'I have explained that one wife only is your custom. But forgive me, please . . . I have not spoken to Te Peeti or the other man about who the father of my child is. It is to my advantage, perhaps, if they think he will be a Monrad.'

Monrad rises and speaks firmly. 'Thank you, Anahuia. You may leave now.'

She remains unmoving.

'Thank you,' he says again, 'for your sad story. But this talk is not proper in front of children.'

Still she stands in front of them all, her fierce eyes fixed on his face. The bishop looks towards his wife. Even he is uncomfortable under her stare. Conrad is about to make some remark — anything to break the silence — when Anahuia, without any change in expression or movement, other than to take a long slow breath, starts to sing. There is little tune to it — a slight rise, an abrupt fall and then a continuation, the words, in Maori, rolling on, inexorable as the sea. As the chant grows stronger Anahuia's hands at her sides flutter a little and then vibrate steadily, faltering only when she pauses for breath.

Monrad leans forward, listening intently. He has studied the language and can catch some of the meaning.

Conrad also listens closely, but with a different intent. Gently, not wanting to break her concentration, he draws a tiny pipe from his pocket. It is made from a hollow cow-bone, holes drilled in a line down the length of it and etched all over, as sailors do, with scrimshaw patterns. He puts the little whistle to his mouth and begins to accompany her, blowing softly. The notes come out high and sweet above the lovely depth and warmth of her voice. Anahuia's eyes widen at the sound, and though she does not pause there is a new lightness to her singing — almost a smile. Sometimes she sings alone, sometimes she waits for the piping decoration to finish before she continues. Then, mid-phrase, she stops. Conrad waits. She looks to the ceiling, down at the floor, then shrugs.

'Aue,' she says. 'It's gone. That is my mother's and my grand-mother's song. A Te Ati Awa chant. But I never learnt it all.'

In the silence Conrad pipes a cheeky little snatch, more like chattering birds than song, and they all laugh. Anahuia, laughing too, goes to stand by him and from this safe position turns to face the bishop.

'Will you speak to Te Peeti on my behalf?' she says. 'I would like to leave.'

'We will see. Thank you for your story. Goodnight, goodnight. God go with you.'

Anahuia leaves then, acknowledging each of the company in turn with a slight nod before she goes. Conrad smiles to see her dignity. He is proud of this woman. He and Napoleon take their leave too, and follow her.

'I don't think the bishop will speak for her, do you?' whispers Napoleon.

Conrad frowns but says nothing. Outside he takes his leave of Napoleon, who will sleep tonight in the hut beside the bishop's house, and follows Anahuia into the moonless dark.

She takes his arm and they walk in silence. Conrad feels her shake from time to time and wonders if she is crying.

'No,' she says, 'you cheeky man. I am laughing.'

'Cheeky?'

'Interrupting my solemn song with your squeaks.'

Conrad pretends outrage. 'Squeaks? I have seen you dance lively enough to my pipe before. What was so solemn then in your song?'

'It was my mother's ancestors — who they were and where they come from.'

'Well then, I added comments from your father's Danish blood. Eh? Was that not proper?' Conrad grins in the dark. 'Ancestors are not always so solemn, are they? We should laugh sometimes.'

Anahuia hugs him closely as they walk. 'My dear one, you are better at laughing than me. Yes, we should laugh sometimes. When we do not cry.'

Later, in Conrad's little hut by the river, Conrad dons his scarlet military coat and tells Anahuia a story. The coat is a secret he shares only with Anahuia. Every time he wears it a different story about its history is told. Sometimes he is the son of a Danish prince; sometimes the heroic captain of a warship; tonight he is a famous explorer sent by his king to discover new lands. His ship sinks, cracked by ice and all his men lost. Conrad floats on an iceberg, then clings to the back of a polar bear until he reaches Greenland. Finally, after more adventures he reaches home and is rewarded with the highest honour in the land — a magnificent silver star set with diamonds and sapphires, which the king himself pins to the red coat.

Anahuia sighs. 'Your stories have happier endings than mine.'

'Ah, well, sweetheart,' says Conrad, stroking her fine breasts, 'only because I make them so. No harm in dreams, eh?'

After they have made love, gently for fear of the baby, Anahuia cries. She sobs loudly and heavily while Conrad holds her close on their bed of sweet manuka branches. He has never seen her break before; she is the self-possessed and proud one while he has often floundered in this new land. He can't think what to say. Conrad is better at arguments or theories — or with music. He sings to her now, from the beginning of the first Sigurd ballad, but sings it softly, as if it were a lullaby, not a saga of great feats and doom.

Anahuia sobs harder. 'You will go,' she cries, 'back to your home.'

'I will stay.'

'You will not stay and I cannot go.'

Conrad holds her until the sobs die away, then he says, 'I have a plan.'

She listens.

'If you were to die, would the Rangitane send another muru party to take your brother or mother?'

Anahuia thinks about this. 'I am not sure. If I took my own life, Rangitane might demand another in my place. If it were an accident or illness, perhaps even my own hapu might demand some token for my loss. Perhaps not. I do not understand all the ways, and also these days Pakeha make other rules that might or might not be obeyed.' She sighs. 'Since I have lived with Rangitane I have not had my own mother to teach me the ways. I am neither Rangitane nor Te Ati

Awa now.'

'What about Rasmussen?'

'What about this famous plan?'

'If the bishop does not speak, or if he speaks and your people will not release you, this is my plan. We wait until the next big rains and when the river is high we will report that you have accidentally drowned. I will carry the story of the tragedy to the Monrad family and to Te Peeti. We could let some pieces of your clothing be found in the river. I will pretend to be very upset and after searching in vain for your body for many days, I will go away in despair.'

'And where will I be all this time?'

'Sweetheart, the plan is not finished yet. This idea has just now arrived in my head. Trust me, we can work this out. You swim like a fish.'

'And you do not.'

'Exactly! I will not be able to save you and will blame myself bitterly for your sad death.'

Anahuia is silent for a while. Conrad is drifting into sleep when she murmurs, 'Let us hope the rain comes before the baby.'

Conrad grunts. That could be a complication, certainly. But he is happy enough with this kernel of a plan. Where they would go after the faked death, and how Napoleon might fit in, are matters for thought another day.

5.

TOWARDS THE END of May a heavy storm drives up from the south, bringing hail and high winds. The bare fields at Karere become waterlogged and sour. Pools lie between the black stumps of felled trees. At the boundary between cleared land and bush, tall trees — kahikatea and rimu and totara — unaccustomed to bearing the brunt of the wind alone, keel over one by one. Their great root systems, wrenched from the mud, thrust upward unnaturally — giant half-moons of matted root, soil and seedlings, twice as tall as a man. The Manawatu River rises rapidly and where it rushes past the boundary of the cleared block at Karere it begins to eat into its own exposed banks. Muddy water tears into the unstable tangle of roots and saplings and newly cleared land. At each bend the roaring river enlarges its banks, claiming freshly sown fields to the east and west.

Standing trees are undercut. Anahuia, watching the devastation from a patch of higher ground, sees an ancient totara that has often given her shelter topple slowly, slowly, with helpless dignity, into the torrent, to roll and thrash its way seawards as if it were no more than a branch. She thinks then about Conrad's plan and knows it to be hopeless. These last few days he has been so happy, so excited with his scheming — storing food, putting together a roll of blankets and a few cooking implements for her — that she has found it impossible to voice her doubts. But she knows the baby's birth is too close. The weight drags at her terribly. She would find it difficult to travel or to hide. And who would deliver the baby? There are rumours that Maori not far from here have become followers of Pai Marire; if she and Con travel alone outside their tribal boundaries he might be attacked. She herself might be taken for a Pakeha and killed. Anahuia, accustomed to being self-sufficient, does not like to admit to this feeling of helplessness. The coming baby, she feels, is undermining her courage and her independence. She has weakly smiled at Conrad's chattering, as if he were the child, and put off any serious thought of action.

But now the river is swollen. If the pretence of drowning is to take place, this is the moment. Anahuia suspects that Conrad himself is more on edge than he admits. Napoleon is the difficulty; he doesn't fit neatly into Conrad's plan. When Anahuia raised the question Conrad avoided her eyes and changed the subject. She knows he cannot give up the unlikely hope of somehow persuading his friend to stay in New Zealand. Certainly he has not spoken to Napoleon about the drowning scheme. Anahuia recognises the anxiety but does not share it; she wishes Napoleon would go, quickly, back to his own land and leave her Conrad in peace.

Three days ago, head against the flank of the Monrad house cow, bucket between her legs and the wall of the shed to hide her,

Anahuia heard the two friends arguing. The strong words easily drowned the steady swash of the milk against the scoured metal. Monrad, perhaps unwisely, given that winter would soon be here and fodder scant, wanted two men to ride to Foxton to pick up a small herd of cattle that Viggo had bought there on his father's behalf. Napoleon, now reasonably adept on a horse, had volunteered and wanted Conrad to go with him.

'Just the two of us!' he said, his voice full of excitement. 'It'll be an adventure, Enok. A night at Foxton with a bit of singing and dancing and a drink or two. Like old times.'

Conrad had mumbled something low and uneasy.

'But I asked the bishop if you could come. He said yes. He will release you from that old chore.'

Napoleon's words were clear and high. Anahuia let her hands rest for a moment as she listened for Conrad's reply.

'It doesn't suit me, Nap. Sorry.'

Anahuia knew then that Conrad was ready to put his plan into action. She thought of the rain that had fallen all last night. Otherwise he would surely enjoy such an expedition.

Napoleon wouldn't leave the matter. 'But why? Is Ana not well?'

'She's fine.'

'Have I annoyed you, friend? Hey, sorry for whatever, but let's go anyway!'

'The answer is no, Haraldsen. This man is not coming.'

Napoleon gasped at the formality of the words. The anger underlying them. 'What is eating you, Enok? You're worse than a wounded seal. Come on, spit it out. You're in a mood over something, I know you.'

'Leave me be!' shouted Conrad. Anahuia felt the smack of his fist on the side of the shed. The startled cow kicked her tethered leg violently and over went the stool — and Anahuia with it. When she had heaved herself upright again Conrad was still shouting.

'. . . expect me to follow you everywhere like a dog! Always whining and pleading! Go back home in the name of God and leave me in peace!'

Another blow to the side of the shed — this time a kick, by the sound of it — and then no sound except for the crunch of boots on gravel. When Anahuia dared to look outside, Napoleon was still standing there, watching his friend go, his expression puzzled, shoulders drooping, a lifeless look to him as if he were some toy abandoned on the path. Anahuia went quietly back to her milking. She smiled into the flank of the cow. Later she would remember with pain the sharp pleasure she had felt.

BUT now she stands near the river waiting for Conrad. He comes from the direction of his hut, whistling. Across the river to the east the sky is dark and rain hangs like a curtain above the bush, but over the Monrad block the sun has broken through for a while. The damp earth steams and in the eerie brightness a rainbow forms over the river.

'A sign!' shouts Conrad, beaming just as brightly. 'God is blessing our plan!' His arms are full of parcels: a neat bedroll, a kete of food and a bundle of woman's clothing. Anahuia recognises her own best dress, given to her by Louise Monrad.

'Conrad,' she begins, but he interrupts, eager to show his clever idea.

'Look here . . . your dress . . . see how I have tied this bundle of straw? For a while the dress will float, held up by the straw. I have torn it a little, too, as if you had struggled to release yourself. Someone will find it downriver — perhaps even at Jackeytown — and your death will be accepted. It's a neat job, eh?'

'Conrad . . .'

'The straw will become sodden in the end and break free. Don't worry, I have made it carefully. No one will suspect. Now, this canvas strip will keep your bedding dry; you must stretch it over a branch and tie it with these ropes. See how I have made it so one person can do it easily. You will be snug and warm, sweetheart.'

'Conrad, this will not work.'

'Of course it will. You are a strong woman. Clever.'

'I am a woman close to giving birth. The baby is heavier than I imagined. A big boy, like his father.' She tries to smile but the strain of her words is too great.

'I will be with you in a week. We will manage together. Think of being free, Ana!'

'Listen, my dear one. I should have spoken earlier and am ashamed that I did not. This plan is like a story from one of your sagas. It will not work here, in our real world.'

'But why not? I have thought it all through carefully.'

Conrad looks so crestfallen that for a moment Anahuia falters. Perhaps he is right; perhaps this man's energy and invention will carry it through. But she is too tired. 'Conrad, look at me. I cannot hide in this condition, or run quickly. I will be seen, and then all the pretence and your story will come down hard on us. On my family, too.'

'Your family have not shown much concern this past ten years. As far as they are concerned you could be dead already.'

'Don't say that!' Anahuia speaks sharply. 'They would know. They would care.'

Conrad leaves the subject of Anahuia's family; he has learned to his cost that Anahuia will always defend them fiercely, despite evidence that they have indeed turned their backs on her. Carefully he places his bundles under the protection of a bush and prepares to argue seriously. He is not about to back away from this adventure.

'There is no need to travel or run. Haven't we planned a good place? Where you will not be seen? Take heart, Ana. You will not be alone for long. You like it in the bush. Listen, sweetheart, I have never seen you afraid, even when others are shaking from some sound or sight. Why now, when we can so soon be making a free life?'

He speaks persuasively, gently; takes her hand and strokes it as if soothing a nervous animal. Puts an arm around her shoulders to draw her into his warmth. To Anahuia it is like a drug she feels she must resist.

'There is much movement among our people these days,' she says, shaking free. 'Some are moving secretly through the bush to join Titokowaru and his Pai Marire. Others are meeting to discuss whether to fight with him or to support the Queen's Maori. It is not safe, Conrad. I will be found.' She does not speak of her deeper fear — that the baby will come while she is alone, and with no woman to assist her.

Conrad moves impatiently. He steps away from her and picks up the bundled dress. 'You are starting at ghosts and shadows. This is the time. Look how swollen the river is — it has come almost up to my hut. The plan will be believed, I know it!'

He walks toward the river and goes to throw the dress. Anahuia lurches after him and takes his arm.

'Kao! It is not the right way!'

'Ana! I am trying to help!'

'Wait till after the baby comes. We will try again to persuade the man. He may change, then. The bishop may help. Wait, please.'

'You are afraid!' Conrad shouts the words.

Anahuia accepts the taunt. 'Yes. I am afraid. Also, it is a false thing. I will not do it, Conrad.'

'Ah!' With a sharp cry, which is as much despair as anger, Conrad swings back his arm and hurls the dress and its bundle of straw into the swirling river. 'So I am to be trapped here, along with you? I need to leave, Ana. Can't you see that?'

For a moment Conrad and Anahuia stand watching the blue and white of the fabric as it bobs and weaves its way downstream. The green branches of a tumbling log reach for it and for a while the two — dress and tree — travel together; then they separate and continue on around the bend and out of sight. Abruptly, without a word, Ana walks away, downstream too, towards her kainga. Conrad watches her go. He slams a foot into the bedroll, then picks it up and, groaning, presses his face into the rough canvas.

LATER that day news reaches the big house that Napoleon Haraldsen has been swept away in the river and cannot be found. Evensen, the Dane who accompanied Napoleon on the trip to Foxton, arrives at the house dripping wet and distraught, leading Haraldsen's horse.

They had picked up the herd, he reported, and made the crossing safely before the river rose. Progress was slow, because of the mud and the rain, the cattle preferring to take shelter and wait out the storm, but they struggled on. At Jackeytown, Evensen suggested they stop, yard the cattle and enjoy a dry evening at a friend's house, but Napoleon, who had been 'down in the dumps all day; not his usual self', was keen to get on home. Not far from the Monrad block one of the beasts broke from the herd and stumbled towards the river. Napoleon followed on horseback. Evensen shouted a warning about the danger and Haraldsen raised his hand to acknowledge.

The strange thing was that he succeeded in diverting the steer and seemed about to turn back himself when something else took his attention. With a shout he pointed towards the swirling water, ran his horse at the river and plunged in. Halfway across the horse plunged and reared, throwing its rider. The river was not deep, said Evensen, but running very swiftly. For a moment it seemed that Haraldsen would hold on to the saddle, but he must have lost his footing or been struck by a log. The last Evensen saw of him was a distant thrashing of arms and legs as he was tumbled downriver. By the time he reached the bank Haraldsen's panicked horse was lunging back to shore. There was no sign of the rider.

For an hour Evensen rode downriver searching the banks but saw nothing. Finally he gathered the herd and drove them as hard as he dared, home to Karere to get help. Evensen feared the worst, he said, but there was the possibility that Haraldsen had been thrown into the shallows and survived.

Conrad is among the search party that sets out. The light is fading fast and before they reach the place where Napoleon went in the southerly strikes again, bringing driving rain and a cold wind. The searchers can scarcely see beyond their own noses. When the others finally give up, Conrad will not go home with them. He shrugs off their advice and stumbles on, calling to Napoleon in his native Faroese, the words carrying no distance at all in the roaring dark.

The river rises further during night, flooding the low-lying fields, breaking its banks where Conrad had built his hut, and sweeping the whole construction, including his few possessions away. In the morning Conrad and Anahuia find sodden blankets, the bedroll and Conrad's fabulous red coat scattered along the riverbank, but no sign of Napoleon. In silence they spread the wet bedding and clothes over manuka bushes to dry. Both know the thought of the other: the fear — the dread — that Napoleon saw Anahuia's dress floating, mistook it for the woman, and plunged to his death in an effort to save her. Why else would Napoleon, notoriously fearful of even small rivers, let alone raging torrents, be so foolhardy?

The appalling possibility is too dire to voice. They work in silence.

Towards noon the sun breaks through. Thick mud lies over the bishop's river-fields, and some sheep are missing. An acre or two of land has been claimed by the river. The situation would be retrievable, but for the loss of Napoleon. Again a search party scours the banks. They soon meet a silent party on horseback coming up from Jackeytown. Draped across the back of a big white mare is the dead body of Napoleon Haraldsen, Faroeman, beloved only son of Harald and Thora Haraldsen of Streymoy.

6.

ON THE NIGHT before Conrad leaves, Anahuia asks for a story.

'Put on your scarlet coat,' she says. 'Tell me a story to remember you by.'

'Until I return,' he says.

'Until you return.' Her voice is uncertain.

'Ah, sweetheart, look where my stories and plans have landed me. I am not in the heart for high tales.'

'Tell me a true one, then. Tell me truly how you came to be here in this country.'

Conrad looks at her quietly. They lie together under a makeshift shelter of canvas and ponga fronds. Anahuia lies on her back, her belly mountainous under the blanket. Outside, a sharp wind tosses the trees and sends leaves clattering against the canvas.

Slowly Conrad reaches for the coat. The epaulets are edged in cords of gold, golden tassels hang from one pocket. The stiff, high collar, marked with silver scrolls, cannot enclose Conrad's wide neck, nor can the gold buttons reach their intricately decorated toggles. On the breast a many-pointed silver star is pinned, at its heart a darkly gleaming jewel. Conrad shrugs into the coat. His smile is the first Anahuia has seen since the death of his friend five days ago.

Napoleon's body has been buried in the little graveyard at Tiakitahuna. The bishop said the prayers and spoke of Napoleon's father and his homeland. Conrad could not utter a word, nor sing, though he tried.

After the funeral the bishop called Conrad into his study. 'You will be going back,' he said.

'Yes.' There was no question now. News of the death had to be delivered and Conrad was the man to do it. No one else had spoken of the floating dress; no one had suggested that a silly game might have caused Napoleon's death. This was a private agony that Conrad must suffer.

Monrad pointed to a neat bundle tied with rope that rested on the floor just inside the door. 'His possessions. Not much, but Haraldsen will be pleased to have them.'

'Yes.'

'Among the articles is the book of sagas. Keep up your studies, Enok Rasmussen of Suðeroy. Learn to read your language as you travel. Learn the third section of the Sigurd saga. Your friend was eager for you to memorise further. Think of it as a tribute to him.'

For a moment Conrad considered arguing, but the breath he took petered out as a sigh. 'Perhaps,' he murmured. 'Yes, perhaps.'

Finally the bishop held out a fat packet of letters, secured tightly with red tape. On top of the packet was a single envelope. 'This one,' he said, 'is for my friend Haraldsen. The others are for colleagues in Denmark. Will you send them on their way when you reach Copenhagen?'

'I will.'

'It seems there is some interest in my return. A year, two maybe — we'll see.' The bishop nodded, kind and sympathetic. 'Perhaps — who knows? — I will visit the Faroes one day and will hear you sing. I hope so. God speed you and keep you safe, young man.'

Conrad tried to clear his head of the deadening guilt. 'Will you take care of Anahuia? Of the baby?'

Monrad frowned a little. 'Her place is with her people. They will undoubtedly care for her. Of course if she wishes still to work here she will be welcome. She may, of course, find that difficult once the baby arrives.'

'I plan to return to her.'

The bishop smiled gently. 'The Faroes are a long way distant from here, Enok. Many things may keep you in your own country once you are there. Do not make promises or raise hopes that you cannot fulfil.'

'Ah, Jesus!' Conrad reached for the packet of letters, hoisted Napoleon's bundle onto his shoulder and stumbled out of the room without a word of farewell.

The bishop, standing at his window, watched the tall young man, blond hair flying, stride down past the lagoon and felt, perhaps, a little relieved. Monrad was accustomed to seeing young Danish men come and go, was always ready to give them work until they moved on to make an independent life in this country. He felt it a duty, and it gave him pleasure. This volatile Faroeman, though, had proved a bit of a handful. A good worker, certainly, and richly talented with hands and voice. But unpredictable. The business with the native woman had been unwise. Monrad had always considered those from the Faroe Islands to be solid, God-fearing people; phlegmatic, even. This Enok — or Conrad — didn't seem to fit the pattern at all.

NOW, lying on fern fronds, clad in his scarlet jacket, Conrad leans over his Anahuia and pushes into her hands a tiny purse of coins.

'Keep this safe,' he says, 'and use it when you have need. It is all I have left from my wages here. I wish it were more, but I am not wise with money . . . or with other things.'

Anahuia holds tightly to the purse. Touches his face with her free hand. 'I will treasure it. If possible I will keep it safe till you return.'

Ah, sweetheart,' groans Conrad, 'I am frightened. I cannot see the future clearly. Can you?'

Anahuia strokes his face. Moonlight glows against their canvas roof, turning Conrad's pale skin and hair ghostly. 'No,' she says. 'I am very frightened too. But I think you will return. I think so.'

'Truly?'

Anahuia does not answer. After a while she whispers, 'I will wait here if I can, with the Monrads. Or if I am freed — which will surely happen if we are patient — I will wait at my mother's kainga further south.'

'I will find you.'

Anahuia feels with her fingers the tears that slide silently down the cheeks of her poor lost man.

'The story,' she says. 'Give me something cheerful to remember, not tears.'

Conrad sighs. 'Ah . . . my dear one.' He wipes his tears and lies back beside her. The silver star on his chest gleams in the pale light. He draws a long breath.

'This is the story,' he says, 'of Køne the Tall and the Battle of Heligoland.'

'A true story?'

'So far it is true. Tall Køne was my name in the navy.'

'Keep it true then, you terrible man.' Conrad grins.

'I will do my best. But a good story, you know . . .'

'A good story can also be true.'

'Enough! Listen.'

Norway

DENMARK

Skagerrak

Sweden

North Sea

Jutland
(Jylland)

Zealand (Sjælland)

Copenhagen
(København)

Funen
(Fyn)

N Slesvig

Als
●Sønderborg
Dybbøl●

S Slesvig
Isted●

Lolland

Heligoland
Dannevirke

Holsten

Prussia
(Germany)

.... Ancient Danish boundary
|||||||| Boundary after 1864 war
- - - - Present boundary (restored 1920)
===== South boundary of Holsten (now Germany)

4.

Conrad's Tale of the Battle of Heligoland

THE NORTH SEA AND COPENHAGEN
1864

1.

KØNE HAD BEEN in the Danish navy only two days when he resolved that military life was not for him. He was sick at heart — that would have to be part of the trouble — but also the rules, the discipline, the bloody-minded officers all rubbed him the wrong way.

Køne was in trouble from the moment he stepped onto Danish soil. That first step was at the naval dockyard at Nyholm in Copenhagen. The dockyard rang with the sounds of industry: iron hammer on iron rivet, the rasp of saw on timber, rumbling carts carrying mountains of cannonballs. Close to Køne, a plank thicker than a handspan was being bent to fit the curve of a half-built hulk. The dripping plank rested on trestles above a smouldering fire. One man with a huge wet mop plied the wood with water, while two others used great tongs to bend the ends. Despite his misery, Køne paused to see the great mass of wood miraculously curve, centimetre by centimetre, down towards the ground. To the west, the long thin bulk of the rope-making building blocked the view, while closer the anchor-smiths shouted warnings as a cauldron of molten iron poured its blinding contents into the waiting sand-mould. The air hung heavy with the stench of sulphur: one of the buildings must have been manufacturing powder for the cannons.

A sense of urgency drove all the sights and sounds: shouted orders, running feet, horses straining against harness. War was in the air. Several great ships lay dockside, their masts and rigging intricate against the morning light, the gap-toothed squares of their open gun-ports black and sinister. Men swarmed over these fighting frigates, repairing rigging and timber. Ordinarily Køne would have been agog at the new sights and sounds but the tall Faroeman stepped ashore from the recruiting gunship, head down, dragging his feet, conspicuously silent among the chattering recruits.

When it came his turn to face the officer, he failed to salute. The lieutenant, accustomed to homesick boys, gave him a little leeway.

'You are . . . ?'

Silence from Køne.

The recruit next in line said, 'He says his name is Køne, sir, but actually he's Enok Rasmussen from Suðeroy, sir.'

That earned him a black look from Køne.

The officer checked his list. 'I've got an Enok Rasmussen.'

'Køne,' said Køne.

'Konig? King who? Related to royalty, are we?'

'Køne.'

'Kone, is it? Some kind of woman in disguise? You trying to be clever with me?'

Silence again.

'He doesn't talk much,' said the obliging recruit.

'And you make up for it,' said the officer. 'On your way, lad; I'll deal with this.'

He turned back to the surly Køne. 'Now, lad, any name will do in a storm, and if you're set on Køne it's all the same to me. Make a new start if you will, but I won't have insubordination. I want a salute and a "sir" from you.'

Køne saluted in slow motion. 'Yes, sir.'

'Better. Now. Do we have another name?'

'No . . . sir. Just Køne.'

'Trouble at home? Left a sweetheart behind? Recruited against your will?'

Silence.

'Dear God,' said the lieutenant, 'there's no time for sulking in the navy. You'll have to grow up quick, Køne. Now get out of my hair.'

That was the most sympathetic voice he heard for the next week. Køne was in the dumps and he let everyone know it. He was slow to respond to commands, repulsed friendly advances from other boys; once he was put in irons for answering back and told it would be the lash next time. It made no difference. Køne lost his temper over some minor argument, hit a rating and earned twelve strokes. It was clear he had no intention of settling. His commanding officer, at his wits' end but reluctant to lose such a big strong fellow, suggested the difficult Faroeman be put to sea immediately.

'Perhaps the ocean will bring him to his senses,' he said. 'Give him a month and then we'll see.'

Tall Køne and two boys no more than eleven or twelve years old were assigned to the frigate *Jylland*, which was about to leave dock at that time, having had her upper-deck guns refitted.

'He's handy with tools and can row like the devil,' said the lieutenant as he handed Køne's papers over. 'Never make a naval officer, if you ask me, but could be a useful sailor.'

'We'll see,' said the first lieutenant, grinning and winking at the two boys. He had his own methods. 'Stand back now, lads,' he said, hauling the boys aside by the scruff of their necks. 'Make way for the ladies. Gutter manners won't do in the navy.'

Down the gangway came a good dozen women, the last very fashionably dressed in burgundy skirt and jacket with hat-feathers to match. The first lieutenant, standing aside at the foot of the plank, let go his two charges to touch his cap as she passed. The woman nodded, her eyes sharp and friendly.

'God speed, Lieutenant. Bring my husband back safely,' she said.

The lieutenant kept his eyes on the dock. 'We will all do our best, madam.'

The woman took a step and then paused. By this time the other ladies were well away down the dock. 'And who is this, then? A new man?' She raised a slim arm to her hat and held it there against a ruffling breeze while she looked Køne up and down. Køne returned the stare.

'Mmmm,' said the lady. It sounded like approval. Almost as if she were inspecting a good specimen of horseflesh. Or tasting a favourite sweetmeat. 'Mmmm.'

The lieutenant, still keeping his eyes lowered, hustled his charges on board, leaving the lady behind. Køne, looking back, saw her standing there, one hand still raised to her hat. For a moment he thought she was waving to him.

'Was she beautiful?' asks Anahuia.

'Very beautiful,' says Conrad, 'but in a cold and dangerous way, not like you at all, sweetheart.'

'So you say, you bad man. Go on, then.'

THE lieutenant spat over the rail. 'Watch your step with that bitch,' he said to Køne. 'She may be a well-bred lady with friends in high places, but she is pure trouble, and poisonous to boot. As I know to my cost.'

If Køne was listening he didn't show it. He followed the lieutenant below deck, stooping low to see where he should sling his hammock and where to eat. All the time the lieutenant talked to the silent cadet, telling him which watch he would join, and who headed it, which gunner would lead him and where that gun was stowed. Suddenly he turned to face Køne and grabbed at both the big fellow's hands, turning them palm up for inspection. He nodded, grunting approval.

'That's what I like to see. A decent callused set of paws. Some lads come aboard with hands soft as silk purses. You'll do, Tall Køne, even if you've lost your tongue. Now, stow your gear while I see to these boys. Then report to the ship's carpenter. I hear you can use a chisel.'

TALL Køne, as you would know, was not one to sulk for long. Hour by hour the new sights, the crowded shipboard life, the skills he was learning wore away at his misery. He began to forget the humiliating failure on St Olaf's Day, and the killing (as he thought) of Otto Dahl.

Three things in particular rekindled his interest in life. The first was the ship's boy, Mikkel Waag, who had arrived on board with him. Mikkel was thin as a bundle of sticks and small for his eleven years. You might judge him to be eight or nine. Dark eyes and black hair. More than a dash of the African in his dark skin, though he spoke good Danish. To start with, Mikkel was as silent and withdrawn as Køne. He carried aboard a battered violin case and, as far as Køne could see, little else — no bundle of food or any little comforting memento from home. That bound the two, for Køne had arrived just as destitute.

Mikkel was to sleep with the other boys — in a coil of rope or tucked against the warm brick of the galley-fire for warmth: any place where they would be quickly on hand when called. This was hardship enough in the warmer months but particularly so this cold winter, given that Mikkel lacked a decent coat or covering. Also he was picked on by the other boys for his dark skin and skinny legs. On his first day aboard Køne saw a bigger boy whipping Mikkel around the ankles with a bit of rope to make him dance. Køne put down his chisel and mallet (he was repairing the beautiful carved fruits and sheaves that adorned the stern boards of the *Jylland*), walked over and picked up the bully by the scruff of his dirty shirt. The boy hung there, eyeball to eyeball with Tall Køne, for a full minute. When the boy squirmed and whined, Køne snapped him roughly as if he were a scrap of canvas that needed shaking out, then lowered him to the deck again. No word was spoken, but the message was clear — and little Mikkel's undying devotion kindled.

That night as Køne lay in his hammock, swinging gently and squeezed head to toe with the other sailors on the lower orlop deck, he felt a little scratch under his buttocks. It felt like a rat was trying to gnaw its way through the canvas. Køne reached down to slap the thing away, but encountered a small cold hand, which clung to his. In the dark he gave the hand a reassuring pat, guessing it to be young Mikkel. Immediately the little fellow grabbed the canvas edge and by some trick of feet and hands flipped himself upside. Without a word he cuddled into the older boy's side, bony and cold, the dark head tucked into the crook of Køne's arm. They slept that way all night — each giving heartsease to the other, dreaming of homes and mothers and hearth-fires — until the bell rang for the morning watch. Then Mikkel reached up to kiss his friend on the cheek — an offering sweet and light as air — and disappeared over the edge of the hammock, scuttling beneath the pendulous sleeping men before anyone could notice or disapprove.

It became a habit that both enjoyed. Once, when Køne found the hundreds of sleeping bodies on the orlop deck oppressive, he unhooked his hammock, tiptoed up the companionway and slung his bed between timbers on the empty gun-deck. Sure as a shadow, Mikkel joined him there, giggling at their secret.

The second event that contributed to Køne's recovery was also enjoyed by the two. The day before they set sail for open water and the blockading of the North Sea against Prussian ships, the *Jylland* left dock in calm weather to sail a little distance from shore.

'Now, lads,' said the first lieutenant, 'you are going to learn a thing or two about this floating marvel.'

The order was given for the funnel to be retracted and full rig to be set. Up aloft scurried the men, Køne and skinny Mikkel among them, to set sail after sail, from top-gallant down to headsail on all three masts, then the triangular gaff and studding sails between masts. When all eighteen sails were set, and the ship making very slow headway in the light winds, the first lieutenant gathered all the new men — sailors and boys, a young officer and three marines.

'Captain wants a boat drill,' he said. 'Hop to it, lads!'

The 'lads', hardly knowing what to do, made a mess of lowering the long-boat, but finally got themselves into the rocking craft, which remained tethered by a long rope to the ship.

'Row out now!' ordered the lieutenant, and then a minute later he had to tap Tall Køne on the shoulder to cut his stroke. The Faroeman rowed so strongly that the boat ran in circles! The new officer, rowing his best, gave Køne a hard look. Clear to see that he did not enjoy having his strength bettered by a raw rating.

Finally they were out at full stretch of the rope. The lieutenant gave the order to ship oars and turn all eyes back to the *Jylland*.

'Now, lads, look back and marvel,' he boomed. This was a well-practised speech but the old sailor believed every word. 'You'll never see a more beautiful sight from cradle to grave than that what you see now. A full-rigged ship — *your ship* — full set in all its glory. Forget about your iron ships and your paddle steamers; our *Jylland*, which will be your home, your safety and your pride, is a bloody miracle, built by the skill of Danish craftsmen. Just sit and look, lads; feast your young eyes and don't never forget.'

Køne looked. That old officer knew a thing or two. The heart swelled to see her. To a Faroeman, accustomed to small traders and single-sailed rowing boats, the *Jylland* was indeed a creation of great beauty. Hauling and straining at those great sheets of canvas and the heavy ropes that moved them, you had no idea of the symmetry and style of the whole. Naturally a woman who grew up on a far south-sea island would also have no idea.

'Get on with you,' says Anahuia. 'Speak for yourself. I've seen whalers in full sail when I was young.'

'Ah, no, sweetheart, your whaler is a dirty poor sort of a ship, more often a schooner than a square-rig. You can't compare. Jylland *was a true lady of the sea.'*

'Now you're in love with a ship. God help me.'

'Laugh if you like; it was a love, yes — a pure kind of love, which I still hold for any square-rigger. Not for the war that I fought aboard her, no, but for the sailing: the heel before a following wind, the creaking moaning song of the rigging. You are something close to a god, sweetheart, when high aloft, singing your own song maybe, alone with the wind and the rain or shoulder to shoulder with good men, and your ship swinging far below. I learned to love all that. Still do.'

'Enough of ship-love. Is this a story or not?'

WELL now. The lieutenant finished his speech with an inventory of the ship: sixteen hundred great oak trees were felled to build her, each tree close to two hundred years old. A native of New Zealand would have to think of a giant totara, but harder wood: a spreading tree whose leaves blazed with colour and then dropped before winter like the elm tree the bishop's wife planted in her home in Karere. (Naturally, the lieutenant did not mention the bishop's tree!) The *Jylland* carried forty-four guns, he said, though of course Køne had already counted the gun-ports: fifteen each side of the gun-deck and fourteen on the upper deck. The third and fourth guns from the stern on the lower deck were to be Køne's concern, and Mikkel's also. They fired thirty-pound balls.

Full complement of sails numbered eighteen, which Køne's own sore hands could attest to. *Jylland*, said the lieutenant sourly, was the first ship he ever heard of to use wire for her standing rigging. Hands callused for rope were now having trouble with wire shrouds. Shrouds, he added, are not sails as some of you land-lubbers might expect, but the fan of ropes from mast to the side of the ship, holding mast firm and also strung across with ropes like ladders, (mercifully of hemp, or your feet also would be cut to ribbons). The lieutenant never said one word about the steam engine, its funnel now telescoped below deck. Engines were for war or emergencies and rated lower than bilge-water in his eyes.

So the newly awed lads rowed back to their ship and prepared for war. *Jylland* sailed out of the Skagerrak into the open water of the North Sea to join the blockading squadron under Admiral Suenson, charged with keeping Prussian ships out of their own ports, capturing any German merchant ships and assisting — when they were able — in battles on land.

There was a third part of ship life that lifted Køne's heart like a fresh breeze after a calm. The music. In every part of the day the sailors sang. The shanties came from all over the world. Head man of the watch led a hauling shanty when they set sail; there were several pumping shanties with grunting responses and a long, long English shanty — 'Black Ball Line' — for bringing up the anchors. A hundred and twenty men were needed for this, leaning all their weight against the long arms of the capstan. First they had to haul the ship until it lay above the anchors, then hoist the two-and-a-half-ton monsters alongside. Round and round they tramped, the verses of the song groaning down the length of the gun-deck. Sailors made up extra verses in Danish and soon Køne was known for his wild and roaring additions.

One night, when the men were singing and dancing to an old sailor's accordion, Mikkel shyly brought out his violin. He sat on Køne's knee and followed the tune by ear, grinning and rocking from side to side, his fiddle like a live thing under his chin. Another sailor pulled out a tin whistle and soon they had a band going, one sailor after another taking the centre of the circle in an effort to dance faster or more intricate steps than the one before.

'By Thor and all the ancients,' shouted Køne, more than a little drunk on rum and excitement, 'I must get my hands around one of these little beauties!' In the Faroes he had grown up with unaccompanied singing and dancing. Instruments were never used. 'Lend me that fiddle, Mikkel!'

But Mikkel dodged away, still playing, his black curls bouncing in the lamplight. 'You have a chisel and a pair of hands,' he said, flushed and cheeky at his sudden success. 'Make yourself a pipe; my fiddle will be too hard for you!' And danced heel and toe to his own music.

A young officer came down to the orlop deck to see what the commotion was.

'Join in, take the floor!' roared Køne. 'Show us how nimble an officer's feet can go!'

But the officer spoke brusquely to the men, ordered quiet and lanterns doused. A day of hard preparation on the guns lay ahead. He frowned especially sharply at Køne.

'You are in one of my gun crews,' he said. 'You had better be up to it tomorrow.'

Køne, foolish as always, spread his hands. 'A bit of fun, Lieutenant, never did a man harm. Music is good for the soul, they say. We will be right for the morning.'

'Sir,' prompted Mikkel in a soft whisper.

'*Sir*,' said Køne. The heavy emphasis was not well received.

The men hid their grins behind hands, or looked the other way. Lieutenant Dahl had a reputation for strict discipline and heavy-handed punishment. For a moment the lieutenant looked as if he would order Køne into irons for the night, his look was so black. Then he turned on his heel and climbed up top, leaving the men grumbling.

'That Dahl would turn milk sour,' said one.

'Pity anyone who earns his bad books.'

'He has his eye on you for some reason,' said Winther, the old accordion player. 'Hold your head a little lower, lad. Never does to draw the fire of an officer.'

'Dahl?' said Køne. 'By God, don't tell me. Is that officer a Faroeman?'

'Speaks like a Dane,' said Winther, 'acts like someone important from Copenhagen. Why?'

'There are Dahls in the Faroes with long and bitter memories.'

'We don't want to know, lad,' said Winther sharply. 'Grudges, personal little wars are pure poison on board a ship. Forget your bloody grudges.'

'You tell that to the officer. D A H L, is he?'

'I don't read, lad. Any rate there's plenty of Dahls in Denmark, whatever way they write it. There's a war on. Think about that.'

2.

PREPARING FOR WAR was a different matter altogether. Tall Køne, who could nip up the shrouds faster than any sailor, who enjoyed dangerous tasks like reefing the royals in a storm, that strong and confident Faroeman lost all his new-found pleasure in life when practising on the guns. To start with, his height was against him below decks. Køne had to perform every movement bent almost double. When the officer shouted at the men to work faster, tapping the hourglass angrily, Køne would forget his height, surge forward with cannon-ball in hand, crack his head on the timbers above and end up, often as not, flat on his back, the heavy ball rolling away down the gun-deck to trip the other gun crews.

Even little Mikkel, nimble and at ease in this confined space, grumbled at his friend's clumsy movements. Firing the big thirty-pounders was a competitive matter, and every crew wanted to be the fastest and the first to earn the extra ration of rum. Again and again the thirteen-man teams went through their paces, ramming powder, wadding the cannon-balls down the barrel, using wedges and rocking bolts to aim their unwieldy weapon at an imaginary enemy, while Winther called the aim and waited ready to spark the charge. As the lethally powerful recoil drove the heavy gun back inside, Køne had the dangerous task of steadying it with ropes while others cleaned the barrel and prepared for the next round. Heads ringing, shoulders aching, the men ran the heavy guns back to the gun-ports for another round.

'Once more, to my count!' roared Lieutenant Dahl. 'Crew three is still too slow. I want a round every minute. If Admiral Nelson's crew could do it, so can you!'

'He'll use up his shot before we see enemy at this rate,' muttered Køne, rubbing his bruised forehead. 'I thought we were meant to be sailors, not bloody cannon-feeders.'

That earned him a crack on the back from the officer's stick.

'Keep that mouth shut and your eye on the job,' shouted Dahl, his dark eyes sharp as nails, daring the big man to strike back.

If it hadn't been for Mikkel, hopping up and down, shouting and pointing at some imaginary sight and thus creating a diversion, Køne would no doubt have lost his wretched temper and flattened the officer, but the moment passed. Indeed, the imaginary event turned into a real one, for the rest of the squadron was sighted and all hands piped on deck to set sails and make a good showing of the approach.

That night it was all singing and dancing above and below deck. Admiral Suenson came aboard from the frigate *Niels Juel* to discuss tactics with Commander Sommer and his officers. Mikkel, who with the other boys had been serving at the captain's table, reported that half the officers were drunk and the other half too nervous to eat their food. A sea battle was almost certainly in the offing, he said.

'There's a squadron of Austrian ships on the way,' said Mikkel, enjoying his role as informer to the men below deck. 'They are come all the way from the Mediterranean. Admiral Suenson says they are fools to think they can surprise us when they have taken five weeks to get here and half a dozen countries have reported on their progress to our prime minister. They have joined with three Prussian frigates and hove to a day's sailing south of us.'

This was grim news to the sailors, who shared Køne's fear of being trapped on the gun-deck and smashed by enemy cannon-balls.

'How do they seem up there on the poop? Does he seem a good fellow, the admiral?' asked one of the men.

'He does,' said Mikkel, and the other boys nodded, solemn and round-eyed. 'He is cursing the English up the mast and down again for being two-faced traitors. They are supposed to be neutral, he said, but they have let the enemy squadron sail clear up the channel, and even now have a man-o'-war off the island of Heligoland as if ready to referee a sporting match.'

'Are there ships-of-the-line?' This question asked with apprehension. The big seventy-gun ships with three gun-decks would be too strong for the Danish forty-four-gun frigates.

Mikkel shrugged. 'I dunno. But he said our squadron would be about an even match, save that their guns might have the edge on ours for distance.'

'No ships-of-the-line, then,' said the sailor with satisfaction. 'It'll be frigates like us. What else then, lad? Come on, master sharp-ears, we need to know all this.'

Mikkel put on a serious frown to mimic the admiral. 'He moved his knife and fork and his glass of port around on the table to show how our ships would lie. He said we would meet them in open sea, which should give us an advantage as they are not familiar with the North Sea's moods. Maybe tomorrow, he said, maybe next day. He said they would be tired from their long voyage and we are fresh. He said we know the shoals and shallows and can run them aground with good planning. He said Prime Minister Monrad is counting on us to rescue the good name of the Danish military might.' Mikkel grinned. 'Or some fancy words like that. The admiral's face was all solemn and the officers suddenly sobered up and frowned too.'

'And so had we better sober up,' said old Winther, hooking up his accordion. 'A sea battle is no party, especially for us on the gun-deck.'

TWO days later, as they moved south under sail, Køne, up the mizzen mast securing a loose yard, heard a shout from the watch up the main. Following the midshipman's pointing finger he caught a distant glimpse of the enemy squadron, sailing north in line ahead. The call was given and immediately all hands were running. Up the rat-lines ran the men, furling sail after sail until the *Jylland* was proceeding by steam alone, her funnel belching black smoke as the engineer cranked up the fires below.

'Clear the gun-decks!' came the order, and down below ran the men. Already their hammocks were stowed. Now tables were collapsed and everything else moveable cleared away or lashed down and the great guns rolled out to their ports. The sea rolled beneath them — not rough enough to threaten the opened gun-ports but a trial when it came to securing the guns in place. Lanterns were lit and hung from the rafters so the men could still see when gunsmoke thickened the air. Mikkel and the other boys ran back and forth over the deck scattering sand.

'There'll be blood,' said the lieutenant sombrely, 'and we must keep our firm footing. Injured men, recoiling guns, gunsmoke thick as hell — you don't want to be slipping over when all that lot hits us.'

Køne with his thirteen-man crew primed their guns. After the first salvo the team would split — half cleaning and preparing gun three, while the other half aimed and fired gun four. Now all thirteen stood silently, peering out the gun-port. They were all afraid: you could feel it almost solid in the stuffy air. Even Mikkel's dark skin had a greyish tinge to it. They could now see the Austrian and Prussian ships, trimmed for battle, pluming smoke, darkly sinister in the distance. They waited as the line turned in a wide curve, still in line ahead, to come up broadside against the Danes. They would fight port to port, as the admiral had planned. Køne couldn't see the rest of his squadron, to know whether the *Jylland* might be first, last or whatever order in line. All he could see was the heaving foam-flecked water of the North Sea and the black shapes of the enemy ships, framed in the dark square of the gun-port, growing clearer and larger minute by minute.

Even Lieutenant Dahl stood silent. This was his first sea battle too. He waited just below the companionway, so as to hear better the order to fire and relay it to the men.

The Germans were first to fire. Still distant — well over three thousand metres, by the look of it — the frigates plumed gunsmoke. Moments later came the boom, and then a hiss and splash as the balls hit the sea, alarmingly just short of the *Jylland*.

'Come on, come on,' muttered Dahl. 'We have the advantage now, while they reload.' He strained upwards to hear the order, but none came.

'God help us, we are way too short yet,' grumbled Winther into Køne's ear. 'That lieutenant has no idea.' Old Winther, the only experienced man in their crew, though no longer strong, could aim a gun with a dead eye. 'They will get in another round before we are in range.'

True as he said. The two lines were closing fast.

'That is their flagship, the frigate *Schwarzenberg*,' said Winther. 'I heard another sailor tell of her. She is bigger than us, and her guns fire further. She will be a hard nut to crack.'

He spoke on, calm and quiet. Perhaps to steady the men against the obvious jitters of their commanding officer, perhaps to calm himself. 'We will aim for the water-line first,' he said, 'and their gun-ports. Our guns up on top deck will deal with the rigging. *Schwarzenberg*'s the one to take. Keep your eye on her and count the hits.'

At that moment the Germans fired their second salvo. Again the roar came a good count of five after the puff. This time the shot found its mark. Køne jumped to hear the sickening thud of metal against wood almost directly below him, and another crash up ahead. Dahl was dancing in his anxiety to give the order.

Winther smiled grimly. 'Steady down, lad. Still too early, see? That ball was almost spent. All noise and no splinter. And now we are in range, while they must reload. Now, *now* the admiral will give the order. He knows what he is up to. Look to your gun.'

'Fire!' yelled Dahl at last. The *Jylland*'s fifteen port guns roared and the gun-deck filled with smoke. The lighter guns on the deck above added their higher boom. Køne hit his head on the rafters and almost went under the recoiling gun.

'Reload, reload!' shouted Dahl in a frenzy, as the men choked and staggered. Reloading seemed much more difficult when the war was real and the answering salvo seconds away. Winther peered through the port, directing the aim, while Køne and the others cleaned barrels and rammed home powder and ball.

As they readied to fire, the German salvo hit them squarely.

Further up the deck a well-aimed ball came through a gun-port. Men and gun went sprawling amid screams and shouts.

'Fire at will!' shouted Dahl, and the guns belched again, this time out of unison. Fresh screams came from someone hit by the recoil.

'Mikkel!' shouted Køne into the black smoke, fearful that the lad had been caught. But there he was, eyes popping with fear, zigzagging up the deck with a new measure of powder.

'There's an arm over there all on its own and spouting red,' he wailed, 'and a dead man too!'

'It'll be over soon. Take heart,' said Køne, the boy's fear steadying his own.

He was wrong, though. For two hours the battle continued. Køne reloaded and fired over and over again, never knowing whether they found their mark, or indeed which ship they aimed at. For a while the *Jylland* changed tack and the men rushed to prime and fire the starboard guns, then it was back to port at a much closer range.

'Ha!' shouted Winther once. 'We have holed her below the water-line!' And later, 'Her rigging's shot to pieces. We have the better!'

But to Køne the whole two hours were nothing but pure nightmare. Again and again he hit his head; his back ached from the bending; two of his team had been felled by splintering timber and were dragged away — alive or dead Køne couldn't tell — to the ship's surgeon. Køne must now fetch cannon-balls, load and ram them by himself. He heard several others further up the deck screaming in the dark. Everyone was coughing and retching. Another salvo crashed against solid oaken timbers. Another man screamed to see his own hand shot away. No one sang at this work.

Suddenly there was an almighty explosion. Everyone stopped in fear. If the ship went up they would be trapped below. But the sound was too distant for that. Winther stuck his head out of a gaping hole where a gun-port had been and peered up the line. His blackened face came back grinning.

'It's *Schwarzenberg*! She has taken a shell amidships and is broken. She is backing off. Now we will have the run on them!'

The men were too weary even to cheer.

'Reload! Fire!' shouted Lieutenant Dahl, in a dancing frenzy to see his men relaxing. He rushed to the gaping hole to see for himself the lie of the battle and at that very moment a thirty-pound ball smacked into the timber above his head. The shock sent him out of the hole, one scrabbling boot catching in the crook of the split timber. There he hung, face to the water, exposed to enemy fire and screaming his head off. His flailing arms found no purchase against the ship's side, the weight of his body slowly pulling his leg out of its boot.

Mikkel saw it and dragged Køne over. The tall Faroeman steadied himself with one hand against the broken timber. He leaned far over the foaming sea and clamped strong fingers around the dangling man's knee above the trapped boot-top. With a grunt he drew the leg out of its boot and heaved the ashen fellow back on board.

'Fire! Reload!' shouted the lieutenant, out of his mind, his smart trouser fronts wet from his own fear.

'Conrad Rasmussen,' says Anahuia.

'What, woman? You are interrupting a great flow here.'

'Is this some story of your northern heroes and gods or a true battle in which you fought?'

'A true battle, I swear it.'

'Every word true?'

'Ah well, sweetheart, as true as may be. A pinch of salt now and then to add flavour, you know. But true in its backbone.'

'You bloodthirsty northern men with your big guns. You are worse than the Ngapuhi. Go on, then.'

KØNE grinned, laid the shaking lieutenant flat and went back to his gun. As did the rest. The kindness, the grin, Dahl's own irrelevance: all this was an insult too heavy to be borne by the young officer. Up and down the deck he ran in his one black boot and one white stocking, shouting and laying about with his quirt. Completely mad he was, worse than an idiot. The men ignored him and went on with their loading. What else could they do?

Later Køne would realise — perhaps begin to understand — that his act of kindness had made an enemy, if indeed a Dahl grudge had not been festering there before. Weak men cannot bear to be shown up for what they are, especially by such casual heroism. Poor Dahl was in command over men much older and more experienced than he. Under pressure the officer showed himself to be what he was — a silly strutting boy, gone mad with fear.

But the sea battle was coming to an end. Køne took the initiative to climb to the top deck and listen for orders. It seemed that a ceasefire had already been called and another officer was on his way to see why the gun-deck was still active. Køne stood in the sweet, clear air, his head still ringing. Across the water the *Schwarzenberg*, blazing fire, her main mast at a crazy angle and the foremast rigging cut to ribbons, peppered with holes above and below water, had hove to, with the rest of the squadron gathered to protect her. The screams could be heard in the sudden silence. Køne watched in horror as German sailors and officers, their clothes and hair ablaze, hurled themselves overboard. Long-boats from the other ships were already in the water, but could only wait at a distance from the blaze and hope some could swim to their rescuers. Slowly, still protecting their crippled flagship, the whole German squadron began to withdraw.

Admiral Suenson on the *Niels Juel* gave order to give chase. If they could cut off the Germans or drive them onto the shallows, a whole squadron could be claimed for Denmark as spoils of war.

But it was not to be. Køne, now aloft to break open the main foresail, heard old Winther alongside him growl in fury.

'Almighty bloody God, will you look at that Englishman!'

Køne, new to naval rules and to politics, had no understanding of the treacherous action, but all the Danish officers and half the men knew and understood.

The *Aurora*, an English man o' war, had entered the fray. Full set, she sailed between the Danish squadron and the crippled Germans. Denmark was not at war with England: quite the reverse. The traditional expectation was that in any action England would — both diplomatically and militarily — support its northern neighbour. Admiral Suenson could not fire on the *Aurora*, but had to stand aboard his flagship gnawing his lip in rage, while the English ship shepherded the stricken *Schwarzenberg* and the other damaged ships of Austria and Prussia into the safe haven of English waters around Heligoland.

'Damn the bloody bastards to hell and high water!' swore old Winther, high aloft, tearing at ropes and unfurling sails with a rage that surprised Køne. 'We have lost every battle on land and now those traitorous English are denying us a decent victory at sea. I could spit and roast the lot of them!'

Winther was a loyal Dane who had been outraged and then deeply dismayed by the retreats and defeats in Slesvig and Jutland. His own beloved ship, the *Jylland*, bore the name of his own province, whose sacred Danish soil was now overrun by Prussian armies. Unthinkable! And now the bloody English were protecting those same Prussians at sea.

Køne, less patriotic, thought of the dead and the dying, the bleeding and burned men on both sides, and was simply glad that the stink and the black nightmare of those hours on the gun-deck were over.

That Battle of Heligoland was in fact the end of fighting. Next day news came that a ceasefire was in place. Admiral Suenson sent words of congratulation to his men. The Danish victory at sea had forced the Prussians to stop fighting and agree to a conference. There would be an important meeting in London, he said, with the Danish prime minister, Bishop Monrad, negotiating on behalf of Denmark.

'A conference in London!' muttered Winther. 'I wouldn't trust those English to skin a fish, let alone sort out an agreement fairly. They are clearly on the Prussian side. And that Monrad! He gave the order to retreat at Dannevirke, didn't he? What can we hope for from him? Denmark is done for, if you ask me.'

Which no one did, naturally.

The ceasefire meant that the Danish blockade was lifted. The battered ships of Suenson's squadron were free to head back to the dockyard for much-needed repairs.

And what a sight to see so many ladies waiting on the dock, waving and smiling, dressed in their Sunday best, ready to come aboard and bring comfort to the heroic victors! Right at the front of the chattering crowd, resplendent as a peacock in feathers and ruffles, was the woman Køne had met earlier on the gangway. Boline Fomisen.

3.

BOLINE FOMISEN HAD, so she said, a husband on board — a high-ranking officer, she hinted — but none of the ratings was quite sure which one. She dined at the captain's table, that was certain, and her screams of laughter were often heard coming from the officers' quarters, but she seemed free enough to wander the ship and to join with the ratings 'tween decks when singing and dancing were in the air.

At first Køne thought her wonderful. She knew all the songs in the world and would pick up her skirts to dance a jig or hornpipe when the men brought out their instruments. Little Mikkel's fiddled tunes were a particular favourite with her; she would dance around him, touching him here and there as if he were a pretty toy. Mikkel would grin and duck away. He had been warned about her and wisely took heed.

But Køne, the great fool, fell for her flattery hook, line and sinker. It was clear to all the men that Køne was her favourite. When he was up on deck, set to mending rope or repairing damaged timbers, she would seek him out, standing close by and remarking on his skill, his strength, sometimes asking for a special song. Køne would squint at her and grin his crooked grin and shake his shaggy, stupid head, delighted that such a sophisticated lady should take a fancy to him.

Winther took him aside for a serious talk. On the pretext of showing him a damaged boom in need of repair, he walked the big man away from his admirer, then sat him firmly on a coil of rope for'ard.

'Now cock your ear at me and listen well, lad. If I didn't admire you for a good sailor I'd leave you to stew, you silly young calf. That woman is poison. You've heard us all say it and you think you know better.'

Køne looked across the bay in the morning sun. 'It is all play, a bit of fun while we are in port,' he muttered. 'She likes me — where's the harm?'

'The harm is in what happens next. I've seen it happen to three ratings now — always a variation on the same evil game.'

'She's not so bad,' said Køne, ready as always to argue. 'I can handle a woman on my own, surely. She says you are all against her.'

'For good bloody reason. She is all sugar and spice today, but wait till she has you nailed. Which she will, if you go on mooning about her. You are acting like an idiot, lad. None of us wants to see you ruined.'

'Winther,' said Køne, nettled now, 'you talk of evil and ruin as if she is the goddess Hel herself. Perhaps you are jealous?'

Winther spat over the side. 'She might well be Hel. All beauty from the waist up and pure stinking rot below. She has a passion to see a man lashed, lad. Every time she comes aboard she takes a fancy to some young fool of a rating. Once she has him hooked and in her bed, as it were, she will let fly with accusations and demands to have the man lashed or punished in some other ways that we are not privy to. It would turn your stomach to see her. At each lay of the lash her blue eyes darken and glitter. Her pretty white hand reaches for her own breast. She breathes faster and cries out. She will clutch at some officer, feigning horror, but all the time rutting against him like some dog on heat. I have seen it twice and am still sick to my stomach thinking of it.' He spat again. 'No, lad, no; I am not jealous.'

Køne laid his hand on the damaged boom, fingering the sharply splintered wood. 'Well,' he said, 'you have warned me. I will take care.'

'More than care is needed, boy. Keep your eyes on the deck when she is around, walk the other way when she comes near. She has her hook in you already.'

Køne nodded. Privately he thought old Winther must be exaggerating. The officers seemed to like her, especially Lieutenant Dahl, whose young face showed something like adoration when she walked on deck with him. And wasn't she good company with the ratings of an evening?

'So what timber should I use to mend this break?' he asked.

THE next two weeks were edgy ones for those ratings and officers still aboard the *Jylland*. First Winther fell ill. He developed a fever: dark spots appeared on his neck. Fear spread quickly. Typhus or plague were more deadly than war in the close quarters below decks. The men demanded Winther be set ashore. The coughing old man, protesting his health, was unceremoniously dumped ashore and told to report to the naval hospital. No one wanted to accompany him.

Then crew returning from shore leave brought back depressing reports. The London Conference was stalled. It was said that Prime Minister Monrad held firm, but that the wily Prussian general, Bismark, outsmarted him at every turn. Whenever an agreement seemed possible, the general added a new demand to the treaty. The English were sitting on the fence as usual.

One day the sailors heard that the conference had failed and the blockade would be resumed. The ship was readied and provisioned, then word came of a new compromise and a last-ditch attempt at a reconciliation. The *Jylland* was to remain at Nyholm.

The on-again, off-again nature of the war and the fear of disease had the officers rattled. They took it out on the men, ordering yet another pointless holystoning of decks already spotless, or checking every inch of rigging already tarred and mended. The ladies came and went and were, in the captain's opinion, a welcome distraction to his men. He was not aware, perhaps, of the developing tension between one of his junior officers — Dahl — and that giant young Faroeman with the strange name. Køne had filled out now into manhood. He towered a good head over officers and ratings, was quick up the rigging and fearless over any task that involved strength and agility. His looks had matured too; the square jaw and blue eyes, the shock of blond hair, his songs and laughter had more women than Boline Fomisen casting glances his way.

'Ahem,' says Anahuia, 'are we speaking by any chance of the man who lies now beside me?'

'Is the description not accurate?'

'What a whakahihi! A little modesty would be welcome.'

'Ah well, now, sweetheart, you asked for a true story this time. What can a fellow do?'

'Conrad Rasmussen, you are an impossible man.'

'But a good storyteller, no?'

'A good storyteller, yes!'

YOUNG Lieutenant Dahl, brown-haired and smart in his uniform, yet still a boy for all his arrogance, could not bear the attention Køne was earning from the ladies. Especially from Boline. Dahl set Køne to tasks he thought would humiliate him, like hanging him over the side in a basket to scrub the windows of the captain's day-room. Køne made a game of it, swinging and singing in time to his swabbing, until Boline and the other ladies came running to lean over the rail and wave and laugh and ask for more. Køne hung upside down from his platform and swabbed in that fashion, still singing, until his foolish head filled with blood and his eyes turned red.

'Disorderly behaviour!' yelled Dahl. 'I'll have you in irons!'

But the ladies petted and patted the furious officer and begged him to let Køne continue, until poor Dahl was twisted so tight between rage and desire he could scarcely make a move.

Well, this was all harmless, silly fun, until the night when that evil Boline set her trap and Tall Køne walked straight in with his empty head high and his brains somewhere a good deal lower.

First there was a night of grog and music. Boline danced, showing a good fine ankle, placing a hand here and there on Køne's willing body and flashing her dark eyes at him until the poor lad was all aflame.

At one stage in the evening little Mikkel danced up to Køne and, still fiddling away, whispered, 'Watch out! She has those glittery eyes Winther talked about. She will make her move tonight.'

But Køne was lost to it. When Boline dragged him up onto the deck, he followed like a lamb. The other ratings, sickened by Køne's foolish arrogance, let him go. Loyal Mikkel, still clutching his fiddle, crept after the pair, but what could a ship's boy do when a big Faroeman had set his mind on self-destruction?

Above in the sweet night air, Boline led Køne aft towards the officers' deck and there, under the shadow of the mizzen mast, undid her bodice and pulled his hot hand inside.

'Come on, my big honey-bear,' she whispered, her fingers busy at his trouser-strings. 'Show me what you are made of, you lovely fellow.'

If her eyes lacked the fire of her words Køne was ignorant of it. The invitation was clear and the Faroeman came to the party with gusto. Up rose his member, stiff as a pole. Down tumbled trousers, lady and man all in a heap on the deck. Boline lay there, smart skirts up around her waist, smiling and cooing, but all the time keeping her knees clamped tight to drive the hot man crazy. At the very moment she opened her legs wide and Køne lunged, she let out a scream to wake all the dead souls of Niflheim.

'Get off me, off!' she screamed, raking with her talons at his back and face.

Køne, thinking this was part of her pleasure, clamped a hand over her mouth and kept at it. But by now the officer of the watch — Lieutenant Dahl by ill-fortune — was on the scene, and a few others besides. They shouted, the lady screamed again and Køne leapt to his feet, trying to haul his trousers up over his unruly prod.

'Oh, oh, oh!' wept Boline. 'He has shamed me, has taken my maidenhead! Officer, help me! I am ruined!'

And so on. Some of the officers turned away, knowing the woman for what she was, but Dahl, inexperienced and bearing a grudge, leapt swiftly to her defence.

'Shame, shame!' he cried with gusto. 'Where is the sergeant-at-arms? Put this man in irons! He has brought shame to the Danish navy! Shame!'

And *so* on. All was chaos and screaming, even little Mikkel adding to the din with his shouts of accusation against that black Boline, and the lieutenant commander himself coming out to see what had disturbed his peace. This officer was inclined to take the matter seriously. Perhaps he was the husband; perhaps an admirer. At any rate, the upshot was that Tall Køne found himself confined in the hold, in irons: locked into a tiny cupboard with nothing to do but stare into the blackness and reflect on his own foolhardiness.

How long his confinement lasted is difficult to tell. Dahl took pleasure in bringing him rat-fouled bread and stinking water, drawing the bolts and letting in light for the least possible moment before clanging the hatch shut again. Twice that evil woman stood outside, whispering through the hatch of all the terrible punishments Køne was about to suffer. Hard to credit this was the same sweet Boline who had danced and sung with him. Køne kept silent, cramped and agonised as he was, lest he gave the demented lady further pleasure. What use was rage when you were bent half double, clamped to ring-bolts in the dark, and thinking hour upon hour of the flogging to come?

After an age, it seemed, Mikkel was scratching and whispering at the hatch. He had a plan, he said, involving escape from the ship and the navy both. Mikkel would come too, he said, and they would make their way to foreign parts on a fine full-rigged merchant ship. Køne had his doubts about Mikkel's plan. The boy was a born dreamer. Often in the night he would rattle on about places he had heard of and sights he planned to see. Mikkel's father — or stepfather, you would have to think, as no one else in the family had darkness in his skin — was a seaman himself and had filled the boy's head with tales of southern oceans; of palm trees and coconuts and great swimming turtles; of New Zealand, which Mikkel imagined being peopled with Danes from Zealand, but also with exotic men and women, dark-skinned like himself.

'Perhaps I am part New Zealander,' he said. 'Perhaps my mother met a dark man from the southern ocean who had come to port while Papa was offshore.'

'Perhaps,' Køne had said, unwilling to dash the boy's dreams. The curly black hair looked just like that of the tall African with amazing blue-black skin who worked at the naval docks. But who was to say what a South Seas man might look like?

'We could both sail,' Mikkel would say, 'to that new sort of Zealand, where people like us would be welcome and free to make our own fortunes.'

'Who knows?' Køne would mumble, half asleep. 'Now pipe down, dreamer, this man is sailing another ocean right now.'

So Køne held few hopes for his friend's plan. Another misjudgement. Young Mikkel might have been a dreamer and a fiddler of talent, but he was also sharp and quick as a ship's rat. He had noticed what was afoot on the *Jylland* and planned to make use of the diversion.

That night a deputation of important men came aboard to speak with the captain. Admiral Suenson was there, but also some others — foreign, maybe, or royal, in red and gold jackets and white trousers, fancy swords swinging at their hips and all the trappings as well.

'All the officers will be eating and drinking in captain's quarters,' whispered Mikkel, 'so here is my plan. When I have finished serving them, and they are all drunk, I will let you out and we can both scoot.'

'The officer of the watch will just nod and let me pass ashore, I suppose?' said Køne. 'And I am to tear these damned irons out of their sockets? Mikkel, lad, it is fanciful to think I can go ashore.'

'Wait and see. I'll be back.'

Off went Mikkel Waag, ship's boy, confident as a cricket, leaving Tall Køne puzzled in the dark. Was the boy turning soft in the head? Or did he really have some plan up his sleeve?

Which the good lad did. Some little time later, Køne heard his friend scratch again at the hatch, but this time to more purpose. Both bolts were drawn and the hatch raised. For a moment Køne saw Mikkel's bony frame silhouetted against lamplight, then all was dark again as the boy crawled in, letting the hatch fall to behind him. Quickly he worked on the irons with a large key almost too heavy for the boy to handle. Finally one leg was free and Køne helped turn the key in the stiff lock of the other.

'Don't come too close,' growled Køne. 'I stink like a piss-pot.'

'God's truth!' Køne could hear the grin in his voice. 'We'll have to do something about *that*. Now, wait and be ready quite soon. I must get this key back before it is missed.'

Another age passed. It was one of the worst times the Faroeman could remember. Dirty and cramped, Køne tried to rub life back into his numbed limbs. He worried that his legs might not work when called to action; that Mikkel's plan might involve swimming to freedom; that if they were both caught escaping an even worse punishment would be meted out; that he was allowing a naive boy to endanger himself out of loyalty for a stupid friend. Hungry, dispirited, ashamed, he could not even allow the dim light of hope to illumine his waiting.

At last Mikkel came. This time the hatch was opened wide. Silently Mikkel lowered a canvas bucket of seawater down on a rope.

'Clean those trousers,' he whispered. 'Don't worry about the rest.'

Køne did as he was told, then hauled the dripping garment back up his legs.

Now a richly braided coat was passed down.

'On with it and smartly, friend. We are needed ashore.'

This was more like it. Køne grinned as he crawled out of the hatchway. Bent double, he followed Mikkel through a storeroom, then past a snoring ship's cook in the galley and up on deck by the foremast. Mikkel made a dancing, exaggerated bow and handed his friend a high-domed officer's hat, also richly braided in gold.

'Now, sir,' whispered Mikkel, 'you are drunk and a little uneasy in your stomach and I am to lead you back to your quarters on shore.'

'Drunk is good,' muttered Køne, staggering along the deck, 'for my legs are not behaving to my head's orders.'

'Hand on my shoulder. I will lead.'

Køne had to marvel at the young fellow's composure and wit. He began to enjoy himself, stumbling and muttering his way past a pair of sailors. When they came past the brig and the officer on watch there, Køne lowered his head to keep it in shadow.

'I am to take this officer ashore, sir, to his quarters in Krokodille Street,' piped Mikkel, all open innocence. 'He is in need of some assistance.'

'And what is that you carry?' asked the officer suspiciously, indicating the violin case the boy gripped.

For a moment Mikkel was silent, but Køne cut in quickly, keeping his voice gruff and slurred to hide the Faroese accent.

'This boy here, officer, can fiddle like an angel. He is to . . . entertain me . . . in my quarters.' He swayed and made a hawking sound as if vomit were on its way. The officer stepped back smartly and waved then on.

Ashore they stumbled slowly until they were out of sight, then ran like the wind, Køne's legs beginning to behave as they should. They searched along the dark quay until they spotted a rowboat, its oars neatly shipped, tied at the bottom of some stone steps as if waiting especially for them.

'Oho, luck is with us, little one,' laughed Køne. In an officer's ringing tones he ordered, 'Step aboard, lad, and secure my vessel for me.'

'Aye aye, Captain,' said Mikkel, grinning. 'And see, sir, they have left us a gift!'

Bundled under canvas in the prow of the little boat was a flagon of beer and, even better, a sacking bag containing shirt, trousers, a thick jersey, a seaman's cap and a Bible. Køne left the book, for he thought it bad luck to steal a man's religion, but said a word of thanks for the clothes and squeezed into them. The officer's finery he carefully folded and stowed in the bag. 'Who knows when we might need it again?' Winking at the boy.

Into the dark of the canal they rowed, away from the Nyholm and towards the soft lamplights of Copenhagen. Every now and then one or the other chuckled to re-live the night's triumph.

'I have brought your knife and your two carved pipes and your carved ship. They're all hidden with my fiddle,' said Mikkel, full of pride for his deeds.

'You are a wonder of a boy, and the ship will be yours.'

'To keep?'

'To keep for ever.'

'And I will be like your little brother and we will sail the southern seas in search of marvels, shall we?'

Køne rowed silently. He had time, now, to think on the consequences of his action.

'And one day,' said Mikkel, shivering in the stern, 'you will be captain of your own ship, and I your first mate.'

'My friend,' said Køne, 'you will be the captain, and likely before me. You are a quick and clever boy. But oh, Mikkel, you have ruined a good life in the navy to save me. And I have allowed it, which was not quick and clever at all.'

Mikkel's dark eyes watched him as he rowed over the black water. They were both silent now, the excitement giving way to reality.

'What will your father think — and your mother?' said Køne at last.

'They will be proud I saved your life,' answered the boy. His voice trembled. 'And anyway, merchant shipping is good enough for Far. Why not me?'

Køne could have turned the little boat then, could have rowed back to his prison and his flogging, could have explained that the boy had only obeyed his instructions and was not to blame. But, he argued in his head, surely it was too late now? The boy would no doubt be punished too. What good would returning do? Also, it must be said, the feel of the oars in his hands, the freedom of choosing his own actions, the call of distant seas — all these heady emotions were too strong for Tall Køne. He rowed on towards the canals of Copenhagen.

'Row a little to port here,' said Mikkel, through chattering teeth. 'This is Nyhavn Canal. There is a place I know.'

Køne slid the boat silently up a dark canal, pulling it forward by gripping the rough stones of the side walls.

'Here,' said Mikkel.

Hidden in the shadows, under a stone bridge, was a worn set of steps, slippery with slime, ascending towards a filthy dock. The stench of rancid whale oil was almost overpowering. The two tied the rowboat to an old iron ring and slithered their way up to freedom.

FREEDOM, it turned out, was near as miserable as being in irons. No sooner were they were on dry land than a drunken sailor, roaring up from a rowdy basement tavern, cannoned into them, almost knocking them back into the canal. A fine carriage clattered past, the horse snorting and startling at a group of tattered ladies shrieking with laughter at some joke, and already eyeing Køne. Mikkel pulled his dazed friend into a darker, quieter alley, away from the taverns and ships. The boy was racked with the cold. He had come away without any of his outer clothing. The spring day had been warm and full of summer promise, but at night, in the city, the frost glittered almost as bright as the stars. The seamen had already forgotten how much colder land can be. And how much dirtier. Clearly it had not rained recently. The open drains down the centre of these cobbled back streets were mostly blocked with unimaginable filth. A night-soil man, struggling down one lane swinging a full barrel of sewage at each end of his pole, tripped as he passed and sent a stinking splash down Køne's leg. Rats ran everywhere.

Køne felt lost in all this clutter and stench. He hugged the shivering Mikkel tight. 'You will need clothes,' he said, 'and the best place for that is your own home. Also, your father should know where you are, and where you are heading.'

'Does *your* father know?' asked Mikkel, who wanted always to be the same as his hero.

'Yes,' said Køne, and wondered whether dead Róland, the ballad-singing father whom he had never known, was watching; whether he could possibly care about his foolish son.

They came to a many-storeyed brick building, crammed among others and backing onto a fetid canal. No lamplight showed, and no sound came from any window.

'We live at the back,' whispered Mikkel, 'above the animals.'

Quietly the two crept through the arched gateway into the yard. A little lamplight leaked from a window here and there, where a family might be late abed — or early rising — but it was easy to keep to shadows. At the back of the square courtyard the smell of livestock rolled out richly from the lower, larger doorways. Rows of shuttered windows showed grey against the dirty brick for three more storeys.

'The horse stables are on the ground floor, then the cattle above,' said Mikkel, pointing. 'We are next floor up, along at the far end. See, over there.' He looked at his friend anxiously. 'Ours is not the worst place. There are poorer ones higher up. More crowded.'

Køne had no idea where the lad meant. The idea of so many families crowded side by side into one building, so many eyes that could be watching, unnerved him.

'Stay here,' whispered Mikkel. 'I will creep in and out.' Fear in his voice.

Køne stayed outside, pressed against a wall with only a pile of soiled straw for company. His own feet were cold, his shame forming like icicles around his heart. When noises began to erupt from behind a tiny window on the third floor — the cry of a baby, other children's voices and then, suddenly, the angry roar of a man — Køne moved out from the shadows and stood in full view. Shutters flew open. Lamplight fell in a shaft and Køne, trembling a little, stepped into the light. A woman's voice cried out — in joy, perhaps? And then a high keening wail. That was Mikkel. More shutters opened as other families lit lamps, shouting questions above Køne's head. He wanted to run, but the thought of Mikkel kept his feet planted.

Now came the sound of clogs on the stairs and the high whinnying of woken horses.

'Thor's hammer,' muttered Køne, 'we might have been safer back on board.'

A small door between the larger stable doors burst open. A thickset man, grey locks unruly, clad in underwear and cap, raged out. One hand reached for Køne's shirt and gripped there. The other smashed into nose and mouth with a sickening sound that echoed off the cold stone. Someone above cheered.

Holding Køne upright, the father shouted for all the neighbours to hear. 'You filth and scum! You cowardly shitbag! You have ruined my son's career, which we have fought for and planned for. A small boy! Jesus and Mary! You have let our lad take blame in order to save yourself from a simple flogging!' Again his fist crashed into the pulp of Køne's nose.

For once the Faroeman did not fight back. The words struck even more cruelly than the blows. His bloody head hung low, his knees threatened to buckle.

'Herr Waag,' he said at last, 'your son loves me, though as you say I do not deserve his devotion. Let him come to sea with me and I will promise to care for him like a father.'

Smash came the fist again. 'The boy already has a man who has been a father to him. And who can take him to sea in a merchant ship. The *navy*! The navy was the dream. Now what navy will take him? Or my other sons? Eh?'

From the open window above, Mikkel, changed from a confident ship's boy to a little child, leaned, nose bloody and eyes streaming. 'Let me go with him, Father! We will go together. Please, Far!'

The childish wail stung Køne sharper than if he were sliced open with a fish-knife. Here was a small boy lost.

Waag shouted up at the window. 'Get the boy inside!' A woman's thin face appeared briefly, and then the wailing boy was dragged back into the rumpus of the crowded tenement.

Køne tried once more, hardly able to speak through his ruined mouth and nose. One eye was closing. 'Surely,' he said, 'the harm is done now. I am truly sorry for it. Let me mend the matter by caring for the boy.'

Waag roared some insult and pushed at Køne, who lost his balance and all but fell into the pile of horse-dung. Perhaps he lost consciousness. By the time he found his feet the high façade was closed against him, the lamps extinguished, the shutters closed.

That was the last time Køne saw Mikkel. For three days he returned to the building, hoping to leave a message or to catch sight of his friend. Once the mother came out. When she saw Køne she growled something and walked past, hatred in her eyes. On the third morning Køne dared to stand in a corner of the yard and sing a snatch of a shanty Mikkel had loved. The Waag shutters remained closed, but a neighbouring window opened and an old man leaned out.

'He is gone, and his father with him,' said the old fellow. 'To sea.'

'Where bound?'

'Ah, as to that . . . French ports most like. Maybe north up the Baltic. Waag doesn't venture far these days. You would do well to get out too, while you can.'

Køne thought the old man referred to his escapade with the navy, but it turned out other more dire events were on his mind.

'Denmark is done for,' he said. 'Haven't you heard? Prussians have bombarded our army out of Als. It will be Copenhagen next. Your navy is off to sea again but what can they do? We are beaten on land.'

'What?' Køne couldn't take it in. His head ached, one tooth was loose and sending jabs down his neck, and now this old fellow talked about the defeat of Denmark?

'You been walking around with your head underwater, lad? We've lost the bloody lot. The duchies, Jutland, Als. If something doesn't happen quick we'll all be Germans. The king is after Monrad's hide, Monrad blames the army, the army is blaming both of them, and ordinary folk are running around Copenhagen like headless ducks. Look around you — half of the inner islands are sleeping in our streets. Als is evacuating. It'll be Funen next.'

'But the ceasefire? The conference in London? Wasn't Monrad going to sort it out?'

The old fellow was working himself into a fine rage. 'Monrad couldn't sort out a spat in a fish market! He refused to accept the peace terms, didn't he? Which were dreadful, God knows, but it'd be better than this. We're the bloody laughing stock of Europe, strutting around laying down the law and then wiped out after one day's bombardment. Don't give me bloody Monrad! I tell you, lad, if you can get a place on board anything that floats going anywhere, take it. Otherwise better start learning German.'

He squinted up at the cheerful morning sun as if it, too, were a dire enemy, spat again and slammed his way back inside.

Køne picked up his sack, which contained one scarlet officer's jacket, one braided hat and an empty beer flagon, and walked down to the docks.

He signed on as Conrad Rasmussen.

'And then . . .' says Anahuia into the silence.

'That's the end of the story, sweetheart.'

'Where did you go?'

'Wherever a ship sailed. To London. Then to Australia, because Mikkel had dreamed of the South Seas. Then back again. I always hoped to see that little black-head, so lively and determined; I thought he might make it but I never found him. Then, on one voyage south, the bishop and his family and six stout Danish lads were aboard. Wanted to settle his sons where the Monrad name wouldn't bring a curse down on them. He said he would give me work whenever I wanted, so the next year I stopped off for a look.'

'And stayed for a while.'

'Well now, my eye fell on this beautiful woman, didn't it?'

'And our story has a sad ending too.'

'Ah, sweetheart, don't rub it in.'

'I liked the parts about Mikkel. Was he real?'

'He was. I liked him too. I often look up, if I am working near the bishop's house, to hear a child's laugh. I think Mikkel might have made it here, as I did, drawn to a Danish settlement. He was so set on his new Zealand. But of course he would have a man's laugh now. And has no doubt forgotten me — or if not forgotten might hate.'

'And Dahl? That bad officer? Was he real too?'

'Well now, you have me there! He was a real man and a real hater, but a Dahl? That was a storyteller's little addition. I never knew his name. In my head, you see, I am thinking of returning to my homeland — and of the family of Dahls who have grown up not forgiving the Rasmussens. Perhaps it was my fear that turned the officer into a Dahl. Can you understand?'

'Of course. Grudges held for years are a fearful matter. In my own case the grudge against my family was settled quickly and done with.'

'Done with? You are still a slave! To take a person away from family — that is worse than keeping the grudge, surely?'

'I am not a slave.'

'So you say.'

'I choose to stay here and wait till you come back. Then we will see. You are going back to a grudge still burning.'

'Perhaps it will be different now. Napoleon said Magnus was dead.'

'Perhaps. But are you different? Is Otto? Will you pick up old matters and put them on like a well-known cloak and forget this place?'

'I want to come back, Anahuia, my dear one.'

'I will wait here. And if things change, remember that I will be back with my family. Ask south for the Pukeroa hapu. I will be waiting. I need you to come back, Conrad Rasmussen.'

5.
Flight

NEW ZEALAND
1868–71

1.

ANAHUIA GIVES BIRTH only days after Conrad has left. Winter is past and new spring growth shows pale on the trees. Pink and white blossom cloud the wild cherries and peaches along the banks of the Manawatu River. The river runs brown and sedate between its banks, ducks bobbing and up-ending in the shallows. A hopeful time of year, early spring: misty mornings and clear days to make you sing at your work.

On this morning Anahuia is indeed singing — one of Conrad's shanties — while she prepares eels for smoking. She leans forward to reach for another slimy black body and is surprised to feel a little tug inside and warm water run down her leg. Then a long, dragging pain. She gasps, looks to see who might be there to help, but for once her kainga seems deserted. No children running down by the river; no other women preparing food in front of their huts; even the old men, usually chatting in the sun seem to have gone off some-where. Matene, her . . . owner . . . has been away for days and his wife must be visiting downriver.

Anahuia knows that her lowly status will not afford her a proper whare kohanga, where she can stay, warm and sheltered, with women beside her, until the birth is over and her tapu will no longer contaminate the village, but she has hoped that at least old Pakura will come. Pakura has never cared whether you were slave or high-born; she listens to the trees and the spirits and will give any man or woman, rangatira or commoner, the rough edge of her tongue if she feels so inclined. Pakura has a soft spot for the strange, grey-eyed Anahuia, and has given her medicine to help the baby grow properly. But at this moment the whole kainga lies quiet and deserted in the drifting tendrils of mist. Anahuia longs for another face, even a scornful one.

The pain comes again. Surely this is too early? The bishop's wife said not for two or three weeks. Anahuia sighs deeply — and again — to keep the pain in her back quiet. Moving with difficulty, she picks up the flax rope and the stout stick with which she had planned to hang the eels. Taking these and her blanket, she sets out for the place she has marked but not yet prepared.

Beyond the boundary of the kainga, under the shelter of trees, she finds the small clearing. Here she will be close enough for someone to come and help, but far enough away to give no offence. She lashes the stick between two saplings, low to the ground, as Pakura has told her that women alone at birthing should do.

The pains are coming more swiftly now. Clumsily Anahuia gathers green fern fronds and spreads her blanket on them below the lashed branch. Surely the baby can't be coming yet?

'Ahhh, ahhh!' she cries in panic now. 'Ahhh!' It seems an age that she crouches there, moaning with each spasm. The grey river-mist rises chill around her, clinging to blanket and hair.

Panting now, she kneels beside the horizontal branch, knees well apart. She pushes the great bulge of her stomach up against the pole. She has been told this is how you push the baby out — but it hurts. The branch is not well prepared; knobby parts dig into her. She doesn't want the baby to come with no one to catch it. Tears run down her cheeks. Anahuia has never felt so alone.

'Conrad! Conrad!' she shouts, though she knows he is far away. 'Conrad!' Again she pushes at the stick.

'Aue! What kind of woman are you to call on a man? And look at you! Where is the blanket for the baby? Or at least some moss! Lazy girl.'

To Anahuia the scolding is sweeter than honey. Old Pakura, still muttering, bustles into the bush for moss.

'Now,' says the kuia, returning with an armful, 'here I am. Forget that old stick.'

She kneels behind Anahuia, tucking her old warmth into the younger woman's back. Her strong arms encircle Anahuia's belly and push down with her. 'Come on now, woman, don't leave it all to me or I will be worn out before we are done.'

Anahuia smiles at the grumbling voice. She relaxes, pushes, and almost immediately feels herself split in half as the baby slides out.

Pakura leaps back, laughing at the speed, to catch the little fellow.

'Small,' she says to the panting Anahuia. 'Small, but all parts in place.'

As she wipes the blood and mucus away her chattering voice changes to one of awe. 'But what is here? Have you given birth to a patupairehe? A fairy of the mist? Aue!' She looks around fearfully at the mist that hangs low among the branches, drifting upwards from river to sky. 'Your baby is pale like a ghost. Have the fairies bewitched you?'

Anahuia is too busy to look. The first cry of her son is drowned by her own. Pakura turns from her cleaning to see a second baby, also a boy, also pale as mist, slide out.

The kuia is too nervous to touch him. Anahuia must turn herself to pick up the tiny screaming bundle and hold him close. Amazed, she reaches for the other. Their cords still reach inside her, purple ropes connecting mother and sons.

She laughs at the silent old woman. 'No, Pakura, this is no bewitching. The father is a man, don't worry — the pale man up at te tihopa's block.'

'All very well,' mutters Pakura, 'but I see no sign of decent Rangitane blood.' She frowns at Anahuia. 'Or Te Ati Awa. What are you doing producing such uncooked babies? And two of them! So ugly! Matene will not be pleased.'

Later, when the after-birth has been wrapped in moss, ready for burial, and Pakura has returned with a square of blanket to wrap the boys, the old woman smiles at last. 'There! At least those horrible white slugs are hidden from sight now.'

Anahuia, tired but comfortable, rests on the bed of fern, looking up through the trees. The mist has risen now, and shafts of sunlight stab down to warm the earth.

'Thank you, Pakura,' she says. 'I was frightened.'

'Anahuia frightened?' snorts Pakura. 'I thought I'd never hear those words!' But her eyes soften to see the three lying there. 'Well, well, why shouldn't I help? You are part of our whanau, even if only a slave.'

Anahuia lets the remark pass. The babies are asleep in her arms. The sun warms her. She cannot remember such pleasure, even with Conrad. It is as if she is drugged from a night of feasting and drinking.

Pakura, groaning, lowers herself to the ground beside the young mother. She strokes Anahuia's dark hair and sings to her. Anahuia drowses.

'Sleep then,' says Pakura, 'You will need to be strong to feed two. And let's look on the bright side — the babies may grow good black hair soon. I have never seen such baldness at birth! Thank goodness the summer is on its way. You can leave the boys out in the sun to finish off properly.'

Anahuia grins sleepily at the woman's chatter.

'Better perhaps not to speak of that Conrad,' continues the old woman. 'After all, he has gone now, has he not? The bishop, now. Or his older son — that man is pale. They would give your babies more mana. I would advise naming the bishop's son as the father . . . Matene, though, what does he expect? Good brown sons from his own bloodline?'

Anahuia shakes her head. Matene had tried to lie with her only once. Neither enjoyed it.

Hours later, when Pakura steps into the little clearing with a pot of eel stew and potatoes, Anahuia is sitting up, fresh and smiling, a pale baby on each brown breast.

'Matene is back. I've told him the news, but not the colouring,' says Pakura, nodding her grudging approval to see both babies sucking away. 'Anyway, he is more taken up with news from the north. I told the elders they should not side with the Pakeha. Unwise, I said. Bad will come of it. Do those old fellows listen to a wise kuia? They do not. Our man Te Peeti may be a great leader but I can see through him. All he wants is some Pakeha guns to teach Ngati Raukawa a lesson. What does he want meddling in land wars of the north? Let the Pakeha fight their own war, I said. They are the ones took the land away. Did he listen to his old auntie? No, he did not. And now that handsome Titokowaru from the north is winning.

And so he should — it's his land. The Pakeha — and Te Peeti's men with them — are beaten up at Moturoa. Our people have chosen the losing side.' She pauses to take breath, wags a finger angrily as if she has Te Peeti in her sights. 'When will those old men listen to sense? It seems the war is coming our way.'

2.

A FEW DAYS after the birth, one of the bishop's Danish workers rides into the kainga with a great clattering of hooves. He's looking for Anahuia. The chief, Te Peeti Te Awe Awe, is up at the big house with an important letter: a warning from the Minister of Defence himself, in Wellington. Will Anahuia come, if she is able, and help with the translation?

Anahuia is pleased to go. She has missed the bustle of life up at Karere. She puts on a proper dress, ties the babies into a sling.

'I will walk up,' she says to the impatient Dane. 'These little ones will not enjoy bouncing along behind you. Tell them I am on my way.'

The fellow frowns at Anahuia's easy words. He has caught the air of panic up at the house, and here at the kainga there are signs of people leaving. Two families are already paddling downriver, their canoes piled with baskets, a whining dog running along the bank after them. Anahuia's family seems already to have gone.

And so has Anahuia. While the Dane's horse frets and stamps, she is already walking steadily upriver, the babies slung over her shoulder, her bare feet slapping the hard mud of the track. She laughs and waves to him, cheerful as the sun itself. He lays heel to flank and gallops away, nervous to be on his own, unsure whether the Maori here are friendly, whether some warriors have remained in the bush to strike where they can.

TE PEETI is in the front room with the bishop. Anahuia leaves the two babies with a delighted Olga, smoothes her skirt and knocks as she has been taught. Both men are frowning over the paper Te Peeti Te Awe Awe holds. The chief is dressed very formally. His tall leather boots shine, his coat and waistcoat are tightly buttoned, his hands encased in white gloves. A gold watch-chain stretches across his front. This is an imposing man. In his working clothes Monrad, bishop and ex-prime minister, seems dowdy in comparison.

The bishop can speak with the chief in halting Maori or better English, but in this important case he wishes to make sure. The official letter is in Maori, and addressed to Te Peeti and other local chiefs. The two men wait while Anahuia reads.

'This man, the Defence man,' says Anahuia, rather outraged by the tone of the letter, 'wishes the chiefs to warn their Pakeha settlers that the uprising in the north has spread our way.' She looks up. 'We know that already. He also says that the Pakeha should look after themselves, as no military assistance is available. He advises settlers to move to safer areas with blockades, like Te Awahou.'

'Yes,' says the bishop, 'that is what I thought. But is the letter genuine? It could be a trick to make us move.'

Anahuia looks down at the paper. 'The words are well written,' she says. 'I would guess the man who wrote it is an official. But how would I know?'

Te Peeti listens to this Danish exchange and then speaks in Maori.

'I have already advised this man that in my opinion the risk is small.'

'You think we should stay?' Anahuia asks him.

'I refer to the bishop, not you. I think he should stay, yes. But tell him that I am about to attend a meeting of all the important rangatira in the district. They are to discuss whether to join the war or take the way of peace. I will bring back news of the meeting. Some favour Titokowaru's Pai Marire movement. Others do not. I, as te tihopa understands, have already fought on the side of the English queen. And will continue to do so.'

Anahuia translates the speech for Monrad, who reaches for the paper again. Studies it carefully. 'Other settlers have already gone to Foxton,' he says.

Te Peeti frowns. He does not favour the name change. 'To Te Awahou,' he says. 'But as I say, you will be safe here. You are under my protection.'

Monrad nods, then looks for the first time directly at Anahuia. 'What is your opinion? Should we stay? Are we in danger?'

'I think you should stay,' says Anahuia, as firmly as she is able. It will not suit her at all if the Monrads go. When Conrad returns he will come to Karere. She wants to be here, safe with this household, until that day.

The bishop's sharp blue eyes watch her for a moment longer. Then he nods again. 'We will stay for the moment. But will take the precaution of packing our most valuable possessions in case of sudden news.' He rises and Te Peeti follows suit. They shake hands. 'You are a good friend,' he says to the chief in Maori. 'Go in the love of God.'

'And you.'

In the kitchen, voices are raised; the thin wail of babies penetrates the quiet room. Olga knocks and enters. One of Anahuia's babies, red-faced and screaming, is in her arms. She greets Te Peeti in Maori and smiles apologetically at her father-in-law.

'Sorry for the interruption but I can't do anything with this little one. Hungry, I'd say. And now my own fellow has joined the chorus!' She hands the baby to Anahuia and hurries out of the room. Further screams and the calming voices of women come through the open door.

Te Peeti looks at Anahuia's baby and then at the bishop. Anahuia opens the blanket a little to expose the pale belly and arms. Te Peeti nods gravely but says nothing.

The bishop clears his throat, holds the door for Anahuia. 'Thank you. That is all now. Feed your baby.'

She is not sure how he has interpreted Te Peeti's small approving nod. Smiling, making sure the chief sees her proud manner, she walks out to join the other women.

BUT all Anahuia's hopes for a calm future are dashed next day, when West, who works for Monrad, gallops past her hut, heading for the larger kainga of Tiakitahuna.

'The Hauhau are two hours away!' he shouts. 'I'm sent to Jackeytown to ask the chief for a large canoe. We are leaving today.'

Old Pakura, taking blankets inside, for the clouds are threatening, snorts. 'If there's one thing makes me mad, it's the way those Pakeha get everything wrong. Hauhau! Can't they say Pai Marire? A good peaceful name, which that fine Titokowaru has chosen to show he is a good man. And Jackeytown! What is that supposed to mean? Are their ears stuffed with wool that they cannot hear properly?' She hawks up phlegm and spits. '*Jackey*town! Horrible!'

Her manner is more sombre when she comes into Matene's hut a little later. Thunder rolls over the river and the first heavy drops are falling. Anahuia is alone with the babies.

'Well, after all, it seems we are moving too,' sighs the old woman. 'Pack up, girl. Matene has sent word that we are all to join his cousin downriver at Ngawhakarau. Or further, if those northern men keep coming.'

'But we will be safe here.' Anahuia is alarmed at this sudden change of plan. 'They won't attack us.'

'Why not? Hasn't our chief fought with the Pakeha? The fool. Aue!' Pakura rubs her hip bones. 'These old legs won't walk far. I hope there is room in a canoe for me. They have sent the big one up for the bishop's family.'

A short time later Anahuia is walking downriver, alone. Pakura has found a place in her brother's canoe; the rest of Anahuia's adoptive family has already left. As they hurriedly paddled out from the bank, they shouted instructions to Anahuia: to bring the dog; to bury anything left in the hut; to hurry, she would be needed at Ngawhakarau.

Anahuia plods along the narrow track, head down against the rain. Her normal good spirits have deserted her. She has the babies slung tight under her breasts, but neither her blanket nor her flax coat can keep them dry. All three are soaked. The dog, tail between his legs, water dripping off his ears, slinks along at her heels. What if the northern tribes win after all? What if they take the bishop's land and even the Rangitane land? How will she get news to Conrad if Matene's hapu move away to some other part of the country?

One of the little babies moves a little, finds her wet nipple and begins to suck. Anahuia walks on.

After another hour the sun comes out and her blanket steams. The babies, lulled by the steady movement of her feet, sleep. Around a bend in the river comes the big canoe, moving in the centre of the river, the paddlers working with a will. She waves but the Monrads do not see her. The bishop, his wife and two daughters, also Olga, the daughter-in-law, with her little boy, all sit near the stern, a great pile of possessions covered with tarpaulin occupying every spare inch of space. The two Monrad sons are not with the group. They are away north, fighting on the British side and protecting their own blocks of land. The sale of this land is now disputed, they say. It is common talk in the kainga that the land was unfairly confiscated from the tribes in the first place.

The canoe disappears around another bend — this lazy river winds through every point of the compass on its way to the sea. Anahuia will reach Ngawhakarau almost as soon as the canoe. She heads west now, away from the meandering river. Her path skirts the great flax swamps full of water-birds and frogs. As far as she can see to the south the dark glossy flax bushes grow, their giant grassy leaves crowding this way and that in the mud like the busy jostle of a great war-party. Last year's woody flower-stalks bristle like spears among the greenery. New spikes are just forming, their more hopeful green tips pointing skywards. When the dark red flowers open the air will be full of the songbirds — tui and bellbird — eager for the nectar, but now it is the rasp of frogs that accompanies her passage.

Anahuia leaves the bush behind and walks in open scrubland, the ground soft under her toes. Countless floods have laid their gentle muddy foundation under her feet. Sand is here, too, blown inland year after year by the relentless westerly wind off the sea. The sun is warm and the breeze brings an occasional sharp spike of salt air with it. Memories of her home on the beaches to the south come back: of her grandmother steaming pipi on an open fire, the sweet smell of the burning driftwood combining with the tang of the shellfish to make saliva nearly choke her with hunger; of playing in the dunes, sand in her hair and toenails and gulls screaming overhead. She walks on with long, even strides, the babies asleep, the basket of food bumping gently on her back. The freedom is intoxicating. From time to time she searches the tussockland north for signs of raiding parties, but the landscape is empty.

Late in the day, as she is sitting on the side of the path, feeding her babies, a cart draws up — a pale young Pakeha couple with their two children and few possessions, a horse pulling the cart and a reluctant cow shambling behind, tugging at its rope and bellowing. The man looks anxious and flustered. He greets her in English, asks a question which she doesn't understand. Anahuia shrugs, tries Maori and then Danish. Neither works. She points south and urges them on, indicates with gestures that they will find a place to sleep soon. They indicate that they have no room to offer her a lift and are sorry about this. She smiles and waves them on; the village is close by and she is in no hurry.

When Anahuia arrives she finds the village at Ngawhakarau crowded. More than twenty canoes line the riverbank; temporary shelters of canvas or fern frond dot the shore and smoke is rising from dozens of fires. The atmosphere is relaxed, festive: no hint of panic. On higher ground near the marae three carts, still laden, attract a group of children eager to explore the treasures aboard. A kuia shoos them away, waving her switch at them.

Anahuia looks first for the Monrads. Their big canoe lies on the shore, guarded by one of the Danish workers. The family will no doubt be fed and housed up at the marae. But Anahuia has never been formally welcomed onto this marae and is too shy to ask these strangers to bring her in. For a while she stands on the edge of the clearing, waiting. People are bustling back and forth to the eating house and the big wharenui. She glimpses Te Peeti's wife and sister, but they do not notice or acknowledge her.

The night closes in. No one will see her now. When one of her babies starts crying she turns back to the riverbank. She has already seen where Matene and his family have made their camp and she heads there, dragging her feet. Her day of freedom is about to end.

Pakura waves furiously. 'Come on, come on, girl — where is that basket? I have the potatoes boiling to mash and no eel to flavour them. Have you been sleeping in the sun? Matene is in a worse mood than usual and I have no eel to sweeten his temper.'

Anahuia dumps the basket of dried eel, and sits beside Pakura, stirring the big iron pot with a stick and feeding her babies at the same time. She is tired now, and happy enough to listen to the old woman's chatter.

'You have missed all the sights with your dawdling. Did you see the bishop's family in the canoe? What a load: I felt sure they would overturn before nightfall. A good thing the river is lazy today. And then at Tiakitahuna, we were on the bank just taking aboard that silly young nephew and some extra potatoes when the big canoe came down. All Te Peeti's people ran down to the river to say farewell. Singing, of course, and loading the canoe with more food than was wise. And the bishop's wife and daughters threw handfuls of flowers from their garden into the water and all the girls of the village waded out to take them. Such a sight! All colours of the rainbow drifting on the water! I'll say this for the lady bishop — she is a good gardener, very good. She will grow ten beans to my one — I've seen her garden, which will now go to ruin, I suppose. It's a sad end.'

Pakura pauses for breath. Tastes the stew. 'This will have to do. Run over to Matene with a bowlful and then I will tell you a piece of news to make your ears curl.'

Anahuia nods down at her two babies, both sucking away.

'Couldn't it wait a moment?'

'No, it could not. My old legs have done enough work for today. Here, give me those fat little huhu grubs. A pause in their guzzling won't hurt them.' Pakura slings one baby over each shoulder and Anahuia takes up the food. As she walks away the old woman is singing a slow, solemn song to the babies. The singing is gentle; for all her grumbling, Pakura has a soft spot for the pale pair.

Matene is sitting at another fire, with a relative Anahuia has not met. They are both drinking liquor and laughing. Anahuia hands each man a bowl of food. Matene looks up, frowns for a moment as if he has forgotten who she is, then grunts and starts eating. As Anahuia walks away he speaks over his shoulder.

'Things have changed.'

Anahuia is not sure whether he speaks to her or the other man. She waits and now he turns to her.

'Matters are different now.'

Anahuia speaks with her head down, not looking directly at Matene. 'What matters?'

'Ask the kuia, she will tell you.' Matene waves a hand to dismiss her and turns back to his food.

Could the war have taken a worrying turn? One or two men are carrying guns over their shoulders but there seems to be no hurry to reach a fortified pa or a Pakeha blockade. What matters have changed then, since this morning? Anahuia walks back past the other fires. Chatting families squat close to the flames, slapping now and then at sandflies; the heads of drowsy children poke out under the arms of blanketed women. The marae is quiet. Inside the wharenui lamplight flickers. Te Peeti will be entertaining the Monrad family and the other settlers who are heading for the blockade at Te Awahou. No one would think these people were fleeing from a raiding party. Anahuia begins to think the whole scare has been exaggerated. Perhaps they will all return home tomorrow.

Pakura is quick to hand back the grizzling babies. 'They are waking the whole camp! Those two have Pakeha voices, nothing surer. And see how their skin glows in the night! You won't hide your babies from those raiding parties. Titokowaru will eat them for breakfast.'

Anahuia quickly tucks them under her blanket. She is used to Pakura's gloomy forecasts, but even so . . . She eats with her fingers straight from the pot, which Pakura has kept warm by the fire, and smiles to feel the babies tugging at her breasts, sucking out the sustenance as fast as she can gulp it down. She is ravenous.

'What is this matter that has changed?' she asks at last. 'Matene said to ask you.'

'That lazy man would get someone else to carry him to hell. I am tired now; we'll leave the news till morning.' She glances sharply at Anahuia. Both know she would rather die than go to sleep with gossip undisclosed.

'Well, goodnight then,' yawns Anahuia. 'Sleep in peace, Auntie.'

'On the other hand,' grumbles the old woman, 'Matene will not forgive me if you wander away in the morning with the matter unspoken. Listen, then.' Her black eyes gleam in the firelight and she chuckles as she speaks. 'You are free to go.'

'Go where?'

'What does it matter where? Home. Back to your own tribe. Away. Matene has released your obligation and that of your family.'

'What! When?'

'Today. Up on the marae. I heard it with my own ears.'

Anahuia can hardly believe what she is hearing. The news she has longed for, and yet now it brings only dismay. 'But why?' she asks. 'Why now, when he has gone?'

'What are you talking about, you ungrateful girl? You should thank the gods for Matene's generosity.'

'Conrad is gone. I could have gone with him.'

'Listen, girl, that pale north man is a dream. You live in this country. He lives in another world.'

Anahuia frowns in the dark. She would like to argue with this hidebound old woman but holds her peace until the story is out.

'So what were his words? How did he speak it?'

'I was up there in the eating house giving Ereni a hand. Te Peeti and Matene were having a bite and discussing the war. It was Matene spoke first of you. He asked if Te Peeti still found you useful and the chief said if the Danes were leaving then he had no need of a translator. These men are quick to throw away a tool when it becomes blunt. No thought about sharpening it. I well remember when my husband was still alive and my childbearing days were over . . .'

'Old woman! You are wandering away from the meat of this story.'

'Well, and what I was about to say would be good advice, no doubt about it . . . but now you have made me forget it.'

'Matene . . .'

'That old fellow is all bluster and no balls. He is afraid — that is my opinion, though of course I would not say so to his face. He fears that your pale babies will attract the attention of the Pai Marire warriors, that they will think Matene is a lover of Pakeha, that they will kill not only your babies but him too, and eat his heart to give them strength.'

'But the Pai Marire are not even in sight! Where are these fearsome eaters of men?'

Pakura drinks noisily from a water gourd. 'Don't you be too

sure, girl. My cousin's husband's brother has gone to join them, and his sons with him, and they live only a half day's walk from our kainga. There's plenty of followers lurking in the bush. Titokowaru has said he is coming to clear out the whole Manawatu, that's what I heard, and why not believe it? Our people will come flocking to his banner, take my word. The Pakeha are right to tremble; they are right to flee to their blockade. Next they will maybe retreat to Wellington itself, and I will be able to pick all the tobacco I want from the bishop's garden.'

Anahuia is impatient with the old woman's chatter. 'Pakura,' she says, 'you are worse than doomsday itself. What does Te Peeti say about all this?'

'Te Peeti says for the settlers to go back to their farms; they will be safe; the tribes will not harm them. And so on and so on. Of course it is to his advantage. He is their friend and they continue to buy the land that he considers is his to negotiate. Oh, I am on to that greedy man! But the settlers are going. You will see tomorrow. The bishop and all his family will be gone to Te Awahou and then far away to their own country. I heard the bishop say so in his own poor attempt to speak our language.'

'Pakura, you know he speaks quite well.'

'It sounds like boots on gravel. Too loud, too harsh.'

'So anyway . . .'

'Do you need me to spell out every word? The matter is as clear and straight as the path to the sea. Matene had a debt to pay to Te Peeti. True. Some dishonour he laid on a young nephew of Te Peeti's, I forget the detail. So Matene paid it by offering you to the chief to be his translator with the bishop. True again. But now the Danes are running away and you are no longer useful so Te Peeti has discharged the debt. The way Matene sees it, you are now more a threat with your pale babies than an asset. So he announces that the debt with your family is discharged. The matter is finished. Lucky girl.' Pakura packs her pipe with tobacco leaves, pulls a glowing twig from the fire and touches it to the wad. 'Naturally,' she goes on, blowing clouds of smoke, 'no one has consulted this kuia. Who will fetch and carry for me, now that you are going? Who will bring a hot stone to warm these old bones, or weed my garden and dig my food? Eh?'

But her old eyes are sad and she pats Anahuia's knee. 'Don't mind an old woman's chatter, girl. I will miss you, even though you are strange and have produced the ugliest babies in the world. You are a good one in your heart.'

Anahuia smiles, shifts closer to the old woman and rubs the crooked back, easing the twisted muscles so that Pakura can lie down in comfort. As she kneads she thinks of her quiet walk today and the freedom she enjoyed, of further days stretching ahead: whole days and weeks in which she can walk where she pleases. The thoughts grow large in her until her fingers dig too hard and the kuia cries out.

'Aue! Are you trying to extract some precious piece of my insides? Enough of your digging. Help me to lie down now, close to this warm fire.'

Anahuia scoops a hollow in the soft river-sand and helps to make Pakura comfortable. Then, tucking her own blanket tightly around her and the babies, she walks to the water and stands, facing the slowly moving river. She moves her feet in the cool mud. Up at the marae there is singing. No doubt many farewell speeches and songs will be performed tonight. Anahuia, tired from the day's walking and from carrying the babies, is happy to stand there in the dark, letting her thoughts drift. She is not sure what she wants or where she might belong now. Not sure whether she wants to belong anywhere. One purpose is clear, though. She will move on tomorrow, before Matene changes his mind. But her own family — her old family? Will they accept her now she has been tainted by another tribe? Anahuia sighs. Long ago she lost feeling for the hapu who let her go. Conrad has become her homeland but he has gone and will be away a year, maybe even two.

She stands there, tall and blanketed. In the east a half-moon rises above a low bank of clouds. Its white light frosts the water and Anahuia shivers. One of her babies startles and cries out in his sleep. Anahuia smiles and holds him tighter. Singing softly — a tune from her own childhood, a whaler's ballad that her mother adapted as a lullaby — she moves back to the fire and settles to sleep.

3.

THAT SPRING MORNING, November 1868, was a day Anahuia remembered always. Even when she was an old woman, sitting in her own home, at her own table in a distant place, she would tell the story to her children and grandchildren.

'Tension was sharp in the air,' she would say, 'with the fear that Titokowaru's men might at any moment come around the bend in their canoes or creep up through the swamps and kill us all. All! Not only the Pakeha! Our people had fought on the side of the Pakeha so could expect the same fate. So at sunrise, at that place in the river that some called Half-Crown Bend but was in truth Ngawhakarau, everything was noise and shouting. Horses were harnessed to carts and canoes loaded. Two or three Pakeha families rattled off on the track to Foxton before my babies were awake. The sweet smell of hot food cooking came from the marae. You could be sure everyone up there would be well fed before they set out.

'Imagine, little ones, what thoughts ran through my young head that morning! I was free to go where I chose, but how would I fare with two white-coloured babies and no family to support me? If I stayed the Rangitane would feed me, but what respect would I command? None at all. If I returned to Te Ati Awa, would they welcome me? Often I had imagined the cries of joy, the welcoming tears. But perhaps they would think I had run away. More than likely they would drive out this dishonourable woman. But I tell you, those fears and dark thoughts buzzed in my ears that morning no louder than a swarm of tiny gnats. The great swelling chorus I heard was my freedom! On that warm, clear morning I breathed a different air; I stood in a different manner. You children who have walked freely all your lives could not imagine.'

And Anahuia would tell of the great farewell. How the chief Te Peeti Te Awe Awe, dressed in his white gloves and his polished boots, ordered his young men to carry the Monrad ladies and the bishop himself to their canoe, for fear their clothes might become muddied. And how they all stood on the bank singing a farewell while the men's haka echoed off the water. Some women held their babies high for the bishop to bless them and the high, sad voices of many karanga rose above the chants.

Anahuia stood close to the canoe, for she wished to get a message to the Monrads, but in all the fuss and grandeur she was not able to catch their attention. She would not wade into the river as other women did, for fear of dowsing her babies, and all her waving and calling came to nothing, drowned in the general heart-felt farewell. Out swung the big canoe into the current and slowly, slowly it moved around the bend and out of sight. All day the Monrads would be paddled, winding this way and that, through the great Ohutuiti Swamp, until the slow and muddy river reached the busy port of Foxton.

'Never mind,' said old Pakura, whose sharp eyes had watched Anahuia's manoeuvring. 'I will be back home at the kainga to give your young man a message, should he ever return, which I doubt. And should I live long enough, which is also in doubt if you are set on leaving.'

Anahuia then outraged the old woman by suggesting she come to Foxton, where they could help each other.

'And leave my tribe? Are you out of your mind?' cried Pakura. 'That Matene might be lazy and a coward, he might forget from time to time that this kuia is in need of food and warmth, but he is family. How could I leave him? What a wicked suggestion. If I were younger I would take a stick to you.'

Then Anahuia would tell her grandchildren of her long walk to Foxton, with a basket of food on her back and the babies strapped in front. On the first day she kept close to the river, walking steadily through bush and scrub. At the Oroua River she exchanged a little of her precious food for a ferry ride. Without the babies she would have swum. From the village of Puketotara her path led away from the river, west in a straight line over land as flat as a table, the salt sea air growing sharper in her nostrils with every step she took. Ahead, in the distance, the forest-covered hill Omarapapaku stood as a signpost to the mouth of the great Manawatu River, and to the town of Foxton.

At times the flax grew close to the path so that she walked inside a tall green tunnel. Then she would come to a patch that had been cut out and only tussock grew in the sandy soil. Several times she met groups of men and women — she did not ask their tribe and they did not ask hers — busy with their sickles cutting the long spears of flax and tying them into bundles ready for carting to town.

I could do that, thought Anahuia; or I could scrape the flax leaves, or spin the fibre into rope. I could learn to make beautiful rope. She remembered Conrad's tales of the sea: of how he climbed the rope ladders high up masts and loved to work there, his bare feet on trusted rope yards while he worked to repair yet other ropes that might secure or release sails that would drive a ship across oceans. Perhaps at this very moment, she thought, his feet are on ropes made from flax that grew right here beside me. And she sang as she walked in the sun, one of Conrad's sea-shanties — 'Tom Bowling' it was, she remembered — a sad song but with merry music. When the flax-cutters heard her song they waved their sickles and no one would have thought that war parties from the north were in the area.

As the sun began to sink on the second day Anahuia walked into Foxton. 'It was the busiest town you could imagine,' she told her mokopuna. 'Wooden houses each side of several roads, all with their iron roofs and brick chimneys, each one with a wooden fence around a square of yard as if the owners feared that some unclean foot might walk on their small patch of grass. At one jetty I could see two little steamboats and several barges loaded with flax, all tied to each other. Further down the river a larger sailboat was moored, its masts black against the evening sky, and on the banks there were more canoes than I had ever seen in one place. I tell you, my eyes were snapping this way and that to see it all! In the street more than one cart carrying goodness knows what. You children would not blink an eye, living in this great city, but to me it was such a sight! So many white people all in one place. So many Maori of many tribes.'

And if the grandchildren ran outside, tired of the old stories, Anahuia would smile and wave them off, and be happy to remember in peace those days when her life changed and she became almost intoxicated thinking and planning what she might do next.

IN the yard of the Presbyterian church, Reverend Duncan is supervising the building of a stout wooden blockade. He smiles to see Anahuia with her babies and asks her a question in English. When she does not reply, he repeats it in Maori. 'Are you English? Perhaps not.'

Anahuia replies that she is both Danish and Te Ati Awa and that she has been working for Bishop Monrad. At this news the kind churchman nods and smiles, all the time casting a sharp eye at the pale babies.

'This blockade is for white people,' he says, 'but you are welcome to shelter here anyway. If you are looking for the Monrads, they have gone to Langley's Inn, down by the sea.'

'Thank you,' says Anahuia. 'I will stay for the moment and help with the building.' And, she thinks, I will learn to speak this English. It seems everyone uses it these days.

During the next few days she helps with the blockade, letting her babies, who are greatly admired by the Pakeha women, lie in the sun on their piece of blanket. One of the Pakeha men — a strong young fellow with wild dark hair and bushy beard — begins to show more than a casual interest in her. One of his legs is damaged in some way, which makes him walk leaning to one side like a ship in a storm. His attention is unwelcome to Anahuia but because of his disability she finds it hard to push him away. The man, whose name is Samuel, brings her food and sits in the sun to eat it with her. Anahuia needs to eat — is desperately hungry — but her acceptance of the food seems to carry a special significance for Samuel. He brings his bushy face too close to hers, whispers something she does not understand, puts a hand on her knee. Anahuia smiles and moves away. He watches her go with hurt eyes.

Anahuia likes the reverend. He notices that her babies are in need of clothing and arranges with some ladies for their provision.

He speaks with everyone, Pakeha or any tribe, without discrimination. A kind and fair man. Anahuia tells him her story, and of her fear that her family might not accept her, might not believe that Matene has spoken his words.

'If you have difficulty I will help persuade your people,' he says. 'Slavery is no longer lawful in this country.'

Every day he speaks to the workers and reads to them from the Bible in English. Anahuia begins to remember the words she learned as a child and to string them together into sentences.

'You are a quick learner,' says Reverend Duncan. 'When you can say the catechism I will baptise you into the Presbyterian church and God will welcome you and your babies into his arms.'

Anahuia smiles and thanks him but keeps her own counsel.

THE blockade is completed but now the danger from the Pai Marire seems less urgent. The Maori tribes of the Manawatu have decided not to join the movement. Then news comes that Titokowaru is retreating. The great fighter lacks support to continue his campaign south, so is retrenching back into Taranaki. One family of settlers decides to return to their farm, but most stay safe in Foxton for the time being.

One day Reverend Duncan speaks to Anahuia carefully, using the Maori language.

'Anahuia, have you a husband?'

'Not yet,' she says, 'but I expect a man, the father of my babies, to return to me.'

'Have you asked yourself why he has left you?'

'He had an obligation back in his homeland — an island far from here but near to Denmark.'

The minister gives her a sad little smile. 'Anahuia, my dear, that country is very far away. Settlers who return to their homelands do not often return. I would advise you against hope.'

He speaks to her as if she were a child. Anahuia straightens her back. She is taller than him by a good head. 'He will come back,' she says.

The reverend nods, but speaks as if he has not heard her strong words. 'There is a man here — a good man — who has offered to take you as a wife and to look after your babies. It is an honourable offer, Anahuia; he has asked me to speak to you. He is willing to enter a proper Christian marriage. His name is Samuel McLean. A Scot. You have noticed him?'

The reverend mistakes Anahuia's silence for acquiescence. He smiles warmly at her. 'It would be a good move for you. A fortunate move. Samuel has land and is a hard worker. Your two little boys will need someone to protect and feed them.'

Anahuia feels tears of anger gathering. Her voice chokes but she drives the words out. 'Please explain to Samuel McLean that I am not free. Please tell him thank you but no. Tell him that I have a family south of here who will help me provide for the boys until my Conrad Rasmussen returns.'

Surprisingly, the reverend's face splits in a wide smile. 'Conrad Rasmussen? The big Dane with the white hair?'

'He is a Faroeman, but yes, he is the father.'

The reverend laughs at some memory. 'A great fellow. A Viking! Sings like a hero and strong as an ox. I have see him lift a horse for a bet. But he is surely a wanderer, my dear. I would pick him for a man of the sea. Take Samuel; he will be the safe husband. And a Christian father. Think carefully.'

'I do not need to think further. Please tell him not to hope.'

Anahuia walks away then, but the conversation has unsettled her. Later that day she sees Samuel's dark eyes following her as she washes out the babies' rag napkins and hangs them to dry on a bush.

I must move on, she thinks, or there may be trouble.

She decides to move down to the guest-house — Langley's — where the Monrads are staying. She wants to leave a message with them so that Conrad will know where she is when he returns.

A light wind blows off the sea. Tussock and low bushes lean inland as if pointing her in a different direction. She talks to her babies as she walks.

'Look,' she says, 'how everything lies in one direction. To the grasses life is simple: if the wind blows they lie flat to make the passage easier for the wind and for themselves. I could do the same, my children. Could return to that kainga, to Pakura and Matene, work for the Monrads, maybe, and wait for Conrad. But what I have in mind is to stand against the wind for a while and test my strength. The wind can be strong, but a person can usually lean into it and make progress.' She shifts the sleeping boys in their sling to ease her back. 'Let us hope there is no wind-blown storm on its way, eh, my chickens? And that you do not grow into big fat lumps too quickly!'

Fru Olga Monrad is at Langley's with her little boy, Ditlev, but Anahuia is surprised to learn that the bishop and the rest of the family have already gone to Wellington. Emilie was not well, Olga says, and also the bishop was disturbed by the news of Te Kooti and his ferocious war-party. What if he crossed the island and attacked families in the Manawatu? Also, the Monrads had been greatly upset by the death of their good friend and worker Heie, who had been found down by the river with a terrible axe wound in his head. He had been ambushed a short way up the coast, had been attacked and then had crawled — goodness knows how — to the riverbank. Olga tells how Emilie nursed poor Heie all night until he died. What terrible person, cries Olga, would attack a peaceful man from behind? Surely it was the work of the Pai Marire rebels. The bishop's wife cried and then coughed all night. Her health was certainly affected by that ghastly death. Now, says Olga, the family have sailed down to Wellington to wait for a ship home.

She looks tired. Her strong brown hair is not pulled back in its usual tight bun but straggles over her ears. The death, last year, of her second baby must have dispirited her, and now the other women are all going back to Denmark while she remains. Anahuia is curious about this woman, who followed her husband to a strange new country and is now left alone while he fights Titokowaru further north. She agrees readily when Olga suggests they walk to the beach.

'Let us take my son down to the water; he is driving me crazy with his questions,' she says. But her feet drag as the little fellow pulls her along, and she is soon ready to sit in the sun, sheltered from the wind by a tall sand dune. Little Ditlev occupies himself sliding and jumping in the warm sand while the twins kick and gurgle on their blanket, bare-skinned, waving small arms to grab at air. Beyond the little group the beach stretches north and south, wide and flat. Here and there on the grey, wind-whipped sand bleached driftwood lies, embedded at odd angles, pointing at the sky. Far to the south a group of tiny figures dig for shellfish at the edge of the water, but apart from them the landscape is empty of people. Anahuia begins to feel a pull towards the kainga of her childhood. The sounds and smells of the shore are rising in her blood.

She turns to the quiet woman beside her. 'Will you go back to Karere?'

Olga's smile is tired. 'I expect so . . . If the Hauhau leave us in peace . . . and if Viggo returns safely. Our plan is to settle here.'

'But do you like it here? Would you prefer to go back to Denmark with the others?'

Olga remains silent.

Anahuia watches her stir the sand slowly and then push back her dark hair. There is determination in the movement, but sadness too.

Anahuia decides to risk her question. 'Can I ask you something, Fru Monrad?'

'Of course.' She smiles. 'It is a pleasure to talk our language and at present there is no one else.'

Anahuia is not quite sure that her Danish is up to this conversation.

'Forgive me if my words seem blunt,' she says, 'but my Conrad told me about the war in your country, Denmark, and how your father-in-law, the bishop, did not want his countrymen to give in to the Germans.'

Olga turns to look at Anahuia in surprise. 'You know about all that?'

'And how the bishop, who was also prime minister, made speeches to the Danish people that they should shed the last drop of their blood to defend sacred Danish soil.'

'The bishop is a strong-willed man, with strong beliefs.'

It seems that Olga is not taking offence, so Anahuia dares to continue. 'My Conrad told how your own husband, Herr Viggo Monrad, fought in terrible battles in your own country; fought for land that the Danish people, over many centuries, believed was theirs. But then,' Anahuia pauses to pick the words carefully, 'then this same famous bishop sends this same son to fight tribes in the north, here in this country. Tribes who are fighting because their ancient land has been taken unfairly from them. Is it not the same?'

Olga pulls at a clump of tussock. Anahuia looks away, fearing she has maybe said too much, but speaks again at last, this time gently.

'How do the bishop and your husband feel about this present war?'

Olga sighs. 'Viggo would rather be farming than fighting.'

'Then why does he fight? Surely your husband and the bishop would understand Titokowaru's claims? Surely they would be more ready to fight on his side against the English?'

Olga laughs at this. 'Oh, Ana, it is not so simple as that!'

'But why not? I don't understand it at all.'

'Viggo fights because he must. He became an officer in the army here so he could be given land. That land is up north in Patea. If he leaves the army he will lose his land.'

'But you have land here at Karere.'

'That is his father's land.'

'And now that his father is leaving?'

'Viggo will come back to farm it if he is allowed.'

'Oh. Then would he give his Patea land back to the Taranaki tribes?'

Olga stands and walks over to little Ditlev, whose mouth is full of sand. She clears the gritty stuff out with her finger, lifts him to the top of a little dune, laughs and claps at his bold jump. When she returns she looks directly at Anahuia and speaks quickly.

'You must understand that things are very different for us,' she says. 'Denmark is a small country and so is England.'

'And so is New Zealand.'

'But this country is almost empty! Where I come from every inch of the land is in use. The families are suddenly large — ten, twelve children. My grandmother was one of four only, with six babies dead before they reached one year. Now our babies live . . .' for a moment she falters in her strong speech, '. . . mostly, and the land is too small. The farms are divided and divided till you cannot grow enough to eat. Can you understand that?'

'Yes, of course. It was the same for my father's family, but . . .'

'More than a third of Danish land is lost! It is a great tragedy, yes. It is quite unjust to lay the blame on the bishop, as many back home do. He had no choice. But all the same, the land is lost. So now the bishop wishes to make sure his sons are well settled on enough land to feed them and their families for generations to come.'

Anahuia is shocked to hear about the Patea land. It seems greedy to her. 'Karere is a very large piece of land . . .'

Olga frowns. 'The bishop has been generous to us, but also he believes that his sons should work for their own land.'

'Even if that land is stolen?'

'Ana, do you think Viggo knew that? Of course not. He joined the army here and waited patiently and then was given his land, which he accepted in good faith. The war is nothing to do with him.'

'Nothing to do with you? It is *everything*!' Anahuia scrambles to her feet. She finds that she is enjoying the argument. Standing her full height, she points to the roofs of houses dotted all along the riverbank towards Foxton. 'Look! Everywhere in sight are Pakeha houses. Foxton is full of Pakeha — whole families. Show me a Pakeha in Foxton who isn't trying to buy more land. Fru Monrad, there are more of you than Ngati Raukawa and Rangitane and Ngati Toa put together, and all wanting a farm of your own. A large farm.'

Olga stands now too. Perhaps she is astonished at the change in this woman, who has been a quiet servant for the past three years.

'But Ana,' she says, 'look around you. The empty dunes here. The empty hills. The empty hills beyond them. There is *room*. Plenty of room. Europe is all used up. Would you deny homeless people a chance to live a decent life? That is so selfish!'

Anahuia feels the warm sand between her toes and listens for a moment to the gulls screaming overhead. It would be stupid to antagonise this good woman, whose help she needs.

'Of course I would not deny you . . .' she says, ' . . . if the land is sold. If the land is *taken*, well, that is another matter.'

'We bought the Karere land fairly. It was land that Te Peeti sold in the proper manner.'

Anahuia would like to argue again over the Patea land but sees that she has angered the other woman, who is, after all, loyally defending her husband.

'Well,' she says lightly, turning to tickle her baby's fat tummy, 'it is all hard for me to understand.'

They leave the matter then, and talk a little of babies and of the doings of Foxton: the new flax-mill, the growing school. Olga suggests that Anahuia might like to return to work at Karere when the war is over. Anahuia thanks her without accepting.

'But Ana, do you not feel Danish yourself?' asks Olga as they walk back to the guest-house. 'Half of you carries our blood. You speak our language.'

'No! How can I feel Danish when I have never set foot on that soil?'

'You do feel Maori, then?'

Maori. Anahuia smiles at the strange word. As if all tribes are the same. 'Fru Monrad,' she says, 'I am only just free now to find out where I might belong. Perhaps in a year I will come and tell you. I am not Rangitane, that is clear to me. But Te Ati Awa? I will have to go to my birthplace and see.'

'And Rasmussen? The father of your babies?'

Anahuia speaks with confidence. 'He will certainly be part of my life. Certainly.' Then adds, 'Fru Monrad, I need a favour of you. When he returns to Karere will you tell him I have gone to my people at Wharemauku and will wait for him there?'

'I will.' Olga's face shows her doubt.

'Tell him he should come down by boat or by land and I will be waiting.'

At Langley's Inn Olga stops at the door and asks Anahuia to wait for a moment. When she returns she holds a bag made from the white cotton cloth of a flour sack.

'A farewell present,' she says. 'Your boys will need clothes and I have seen how quick your fingers are at stitching. I pride myself in my needlework but your hands are made for the work. You see,' she laughs, 'you have some good Danish blood in you, whatever you say.'

Inside the bag are several pieces of material, sewing cottons and a small square of flannel bristling with pins and needles. The hard lump in the bottom of the bag is a large pair of scissors, a treasure that Anahuia has never dreamed of owning.

'But all this . . .' says Anahuia, astonished at such generosity, 'are you sure?'

'Take it with our blessing. You have been helpful to our family. And go with God.'

Anahuia is so overjoyed she finds it difficult to maintain the usual dignified reserve with which she clothes her bare life.

'Thank you,' she says, adding a blessing in her own language: 'Arohanui ki a koe.'

WHEN Anahuia set out on her journey south her possessions, as she became very fond of stating, were these:
- a tight-waisted dress that once belonged to the bishop's wife
- a plaid blanket
- a flax kete in which were the precious sewing bag, a few strips of dried eel wrapped in flax leaves, four potatoes, some well-washed rags and two babies' smocks

- a cloth sling for her babies and a piece of blanket to keep them warm
- identical twin boys, pale-skinned and bald-headed, aged one month
- one gold guinea and one gold half guinea and two shillings given to her by Conrad, and now hidden inside a patch she had stitched invisibly to the inside of her bodice.

'And just see what I have come to!' she would exclaim to her grandchildren, sweeping her arms wide to encompass the large house, the polished furniture and, more than likely, a well-dressed client waiting to be served in the little studio. 'Who would believe it?'

4.

ANAHUIA, ENJOYING A ride in a canoe down the coast towards her birthplace, her possessions and her babies bundled at her feet, imagines Conrad well on his way to the other side of the world, but in fact he is still in Wellington. He has secured a position on the sailing ship *Asterope*, but delay after delay has beset the sailing. A consignment of flax fibre arrived late; a southerly storm dashed the ship against the wharf, damaging several timbers; and then six of the crew disappeared one night, lured, no doubt, by dreams of becoming landowners in the new colony, or at least of owning their own businesses. The captain has seen it all before on other voyages. He might rage and curse but has no power to seek them out or force them back aboard. Fortunately, experience has taught him that if he waits a week or two, disillusioned settlers, bankrupt or exhausted or homesick — or all three — will decide to leave the land of their dashed hopes and return. Soon enough the captain will find his crew.

Meanwhile Conrad tars rope, mends timber and cools his heels. He exchanges a ship he has carved from the tooth of a sperm whale for a battered accordion and teaches himself to play. Soon other sailors gather in the lengthening evenings, drawn by the music. They sit on barrels and boxes, tapping feet, piping and singing. Their songs come from all over the world — slave songs and love ditties from America, long rolling ballads from England, high haunting shanties from islands off Scotland and from Scandinavia, and whaling songs from the oceans of the world. Conrad knows dozens, and picks up more as quickly as anyone can sing them. His deep voice echoes off the new timber of the Wellington wharves, where there are always two or three big immigrant ships moored alongside Australian traders and a host of smaller steamers and sailing boats that trade up and down the coast. The air Conrad breathes, smelling of timber and tar, of fish and seaweed and sacking, seeps into his blood again, heady as wine. He would be entirely happy if other matters did not tug at the corners of his attention. Napoleon's death. Anahuia and her baby.

One night Conrad talks to a sailor who calls regularly at the Foxton port. The fellow has never heard of the Monrads, nor of Anahuia. He says that the settlers are panicked, that they are building a blockade because of rumours that the Taranaki war will spread right down to Foxton or worse. He has seen no sign, he says, of any trouble, though, and reckons it is all those nervous settlers seeing ghosts in a landscape too dark and spooked for their English minds to handle. Conrad decides to write a note to Anahuia but then the trader's boat is gone again and the idea leaves his mind.

On the night before, finally, they are to leave, Conrad and his fellow sailors are sharing a farewell jar or two of beer and a bit of music when they see passengers and their luggage being driven by a smart pair of horses and carriage onto the wharf. Bishop Monrad, his wife and two daughters are among them. This is a surprise. Conrad, uneasy to see them, needs to ask questions but they are escorted with some ceremony to their quarters. At least, thinks Conrad, the sons are not there. Nor the daughter-in-law. Perhaps all is well at Karere. He leaves the singers and climbs the gangway. But the door to the deck passengers' quarters is closed, and sailors are forbidden to mix with such people. Conrad stamps around in the dark for a few minutes, then returns, with a shrug, to his beer and his friends.

Three days into what turns out to be a hellish voyage, Conrad finally learns that he is the father of twin boys.

5.

Anahuia tells a story of
death and escape

'IMAGINE,' ANAHUIA WOULD say to her grandchildren, choosing to speak in English as they listened best in that language, 'imagine what I felt that evening when I arrived at last at the kainga where I was born. For three hours I had walked, carrying my bundle and those heavy babies, one of whom' (she would tap a fair head) 'was your father. Walking along that beach, tears came often to my eyes and don't think it was only the sand blown into my eyes! There was the beautiful island Kapiti standing offshore, its six peaks deep purple against the setting sun; there to the south the blackly etched islands and mountains of Te Wai Pounamu, which they now call the South Island. Such a dull name! Those early settlers showed no imagination in their naming. North Island, South Island, East Cape, West Coast — points of the compass or dead Englishmen. No poetry at all. Nothing to tell the story of a place. Thank goodness a few of the old names survived.'

Then a small dark hand or a fair one would tug at their Nana's skirt and remind her of the story, for this part of her life was one told many times for its dramatic and frightening events.

'What a shock, little ones, to walk down off the dunes to the bend in the stream where our kainga had always been. Where were the well-swept yards, the neat brushwood fences? Where were the fish hanging to dry and the dogs to bark at this weary traveller? Where, above all, were the members of my family?

'Understand that all the hours that I walked I had been rehearsing in my head the words to explain my freedom, my babies, my life over the past nine years and my many plans for the future. But now no one stood in the untidy yard to hear my call. Two huts leaned crazily towards the ground like old drunk men; the pataka, which is the food-house, children, and should be high on stilts to keep away dogs and to allow the air to freshen the food, that pataka had lost its thatch, showing the whole world how empty it was. Only two huts still stood, both in urgent need of repair. It was a scene of desolation and emptiness and my heart sank to see it. Had I come all this way for nothing?

'For a full minute I stood looking down from my dune, the setting sun warm on my back, the darkening kainga below chilling my heart. There was menace in that place: I could feel it. Quietly I scooped a hollow for the sleeping babies (your father, your uncle) and laid them in the warm sand, wrapped in their blanket. Then, alone, I walked, without calling any greeting, into the place where I was born.

'As soon as I reached the yard I could hear a terrible rasping sound. Harsh as a saw trying to cut through the toughest maire-wood. My first thought was that a mad dog, eager to tear at me, was strangling on his own rope. Then the coughing began and I knew it was a human sound. The smell, too, was by now in my nostrils. Carefully, but less fearful now, I approached the smaller of the two huts. I called but no reply came — only the dreadful hawking cough and the slow drag of breath after breath being pulled into the body. Again I called, and this time there came a croaking reply — a woman's voice.

'Yes, children, as you know, that voice came from your great-grandmother Paora, who lay dying and alone in her hut. To begin with she seemed like a stranger to me — wasted as she was, the glands in her neck swollen as big as apples, and the rest of her no more than skin and bones. Around her mouth and dribbling down to the sand was bloody foam she had coughed up. The stench in the hut made me retch. I stared at the dark figure, gave my name. She cried out at my voice and began coughing all over again. It was not until I had made up the fire and raised her head to take a little hot water that I realised this poor sick woman was my own mother.'

Usually Anahuia would pause here in her story, tears beginning to run down her old cheeks, and a grandchild would run quickly for a glass of rum with hot lemon, for this was the best part of the story, and if they were not careful their old Nana would drift into her own world of memories and forget to speak aloud. A long sip of the fragrant brew, a smile at the little one who wiped her tears with an embroidered handkerchief and then Anahuia would resume.

'Where was everyone? My mother's brothers and their wives? My grandfather and grandmother? I could see someone must have been caring for my mother, for the ferns under her were green, even though she had soiled them, and a tin bowl of fresh water lay beside her. My mother would not — or could not — speak. I do not know to this day whether she truly recognised me. Mostly her eyes rolled back into her head and all her concentration was on drawing one painful breath after another. I had seen this disease before, at a kainga downriver from Karere. The settlers called it scrofula but did not seem to suffer from it often. With our people, death always came after a painful swelling of the neck and much coughing.

'For fear my babies might catch this terrible scrofula I made a small shelter just outside the hut where I could hear them but where the putrid air inside would not seep into their newborn lungs. I smiled to see them wrap their little arms around each other and suck the other's thumb, under the stars. Inside, I cleaned my mother, sang to her and waited for her death. To be honest, I prayed for death, each breath was such a battle, and her moans so hard to bear. I tried propping her up against me but she thrashed and kicked as if I were the enemy, so I laid her down again. It was certainly not the joyful return I had imagined.

'Then — oh, it would have been towards morning, as I had already crept out to feed the babies and settled them back to sleep — I heard a sudden noise outside. A bundle of sticks and something heavy were dropped to the ground and a heavy commanding voice shouted, "Who is there?" (He spoke in Maori, you understand, but you sluggards would not understand if I told it in that tongue.)

'I called out quickly that I was a friend caring for a dying woman and that he should lower his voice in respect. "Ha!" he answered — with another rude word which I will not use. "Come out and show yourself in the proper way!"

'I stood in the doorway, fearful at the rough voice and afraid my babies would wake, but also angry that he should interrupt my mother's death. A tall man stood in the yard, clear in the moonlight. At his feet lay firewood and a bird of some sort — pukeko, perhaps — already plucked and beheaded. He wore dirty canvas trousers held by a leather belt, and another belt diagonally from one shoulder across his bare chest. Various things hung from the shoulder-belt: a powder-horn, a tin box, a small axe and other things I did not recognise. The rifle in his hands pointed at my chest. His dark hair hung wild and matted to his shoulders. Everything about this dark man was intimidating, you understand, but inside the hut each breath my mother took might have been her last, so I found courage to speak.

'"My mother here is dying," I said, trying to keep my voice from shaking, "and you are not helping with your loud voice and your rude manner."

'His black eyes glittered in that almost-morning light. For a moment longer he stood, and then he lowered his rifle. "That is my mother, not yours, stranger," he said, "so leave her hut. I have come to feed her."

'Imagine my astonishment! Could this tall warrior be the young brother I had left so long ago? I called him by his name, Hoani, using my own, Anahuia. The tall warrior drew a sharp breath and walked closer, keeping the gun in his hand. I think he feared an ambush. It was clear to me that this man was fearful of something or somebody, because anyone could see that I posed no threat.

'He repeated my name. I took a step out into the moonlight so that my face could be seen, thinking that if mine had changed as much as his then he would not see a sister in it. But, children, he did. Suddenly that stern and fearsome visage, with the whorls and lines of a proud moko outlining his nose and cheeks, broke into a wide grin and I saw the young boy.

'"Anahuia?" he said again. "This is very good you are here. But do not call me by that old name. I have a new one — Turi, after the ancestor of Titokowaru himself."

'His words told me that my brother Turi was a follower of Pai Marire, which explained his furtive manner. The tribes in our area, though perhaps sympathetic to the cause, had taken the decision not to join. But this was not the moment for explanations. Our mother was dying. Together we went in to her.

'It was too late for food. Almost immediately she slipped into unconsciousness. Still her strong body fought to drag in air, but every breath she took was followed by fierce coughing and then a choking flow of blood. Before morning she was dead.

'It was a truly sad time. For a day I sat beside her, wailing and singing as was proper, but we could not bring other hapu to the tangi because Turi, it turned out, was on the run, hunted by the volunteers of the colonial militia. Together we buried her. Turi dug a place for her in the family graveyard and made a cross from two beautiful pieces of driftwood, bleached white by the sea. He carved onto the wood some marks that I did not recognise but which he said were Pai Marire symbols. He spoke a strange karakia over the grave — prayers I had never heard the bishop speak, nor those at my other kainga. Our mother, said Turi, had favoured Titokowaru, who was related by marriage to Te Ati Awa. She had seen her son go north to join the movement and had blessed his going, even though by then the family had shrunk to but a few. My mother's last surviving brother, who was himself dying at the time, agreed that Turi should wear the moko of this hapu, as he was the only remaining son.

'My brother wept many tears for his mother, whom he had loved dearly. We remembered our old life and spoke warmly of her, even though I still felt some old anger that she had let me go all those years before. Turi said he thought his mother had blessed his journey north in order that he might escape the terrible disease that was wiping out the family.

'Those two days were both happy and sad for me. To find a brother lightened my heart. Though he was darker we looked a little alike: both tall and lean, both wearing this nose, which is a gift to all our family from your great-grandfather, Johan Gerhard Jensen.

The sadness, of course, was that we two were the only ones remaining of our hapu. All the others had died, one by one, of this scrofula — even the babies.

'"Perhaps," I said, as we ate a quiet meal of potato and pukeko, baked over hot stones and scented with driftwood, "perhaps we have survived because of our Pakeha blood."

'That made my brother angry. He stabbed his knife into his food, then waved his portion in my face. "I have no Pakeha blood!" he shouted. "That is all renounced, along with my baptised name."

'And here, my children, is where the story grows dark, so close your ears if you are fearful. Now, up to this time, although of course Turi knew that I had babies with me, he had not seen them. I fed them a little distance from the hut. But the night was cold and our fire warm so I went to their little shelter and brought them close to the fire. Turi's shouting woke my two little fellows. The fire shone on their fat little bodies and I held one up so that my brother could admire his nephew and feel proud that the family line would continue strongly. How wrong I was!

'My brother started back with a cry almost of fear. He stared at one wriggling little baby and then at the other already sucking at my breast.

'"They are Pakeha," he whispered. "You have lain down with the enemy!"

'I laughed at such dramatic talk. "What nonsense," I said. "Conrad, the father of these babies, is a good man, a Dane like our father. You would like him."

'"I have renounced our father too," shouted Turi, "as you must. I am the head of our hapu now. Our father was a bad and ungodly man."

'He kept staring at my babies with such hatred that I grew fearful. Quietly I removed myself from the fire and sat at a distance to feed and clean them. I decided to sleep that night with them in the little shelter I had built. But first I had to talk with this newly found brother to see why this hatred ate at him.

'When I returned to the fire he was calmer, but the warmth between us had disappeared. I tried to talk quietly to him about my life with the Rangitane and with the Monrad family. I told him about Conrad — his skill with carving, his singing, how everyone liked and honoured him for his music and his stories and his great strength. How I was a fortunate woman that he chose to lie with me. Well . . . I *tried* to tell him all this but Turi twitched this way and that, snorted and interrupted.

'"He is a Pakeha," he growled. "They are all the same. They kill us and take our land and poison us with their filthy disease. We must rid our lands of this scourge. Drive them away or kill them if they will not go."

'He recited his words as if they had been drummed into him. I could not recognise my brother when he spoke like that. His eyes showed red as he looked at me.

'"You have turned into a Pakeha," he said.

'"I am no Pakeha," I replied sternly, "and my Conrad has taken no land nor killed any of our people, Rangitane or Te Ati Awa. You speak like an angry child, not the head of our family!"

'He made me angry, you see, with his strong views, allowing for no shades of colour, only pure black or white. It was in his nature, I think. A bullying side to him. From a small boy he was the one who demanded to be first for a canoe ride or to take first turn on the rope-swing above the river, pushing the other boys away. Then, perhaps because his father had dishonoured the family, he felt the need to stand prouder than the rest, and fiercer. And yet there was the warmth, too: his love for our mother and his gentleness towards me before he suspected me of going over to "the enemy".

'I tried, that night, to reason with him. I am not one to give in when a difficult task needs attention, as you all well know! "Turi", I said to him, "you who now bear the name of the ancestor of Titokowaru himself. A quiet and gentle name. What do the words Pai Marire mean? Does the movement not stand for goodness and peace? Don't they call your general a great peacemaker? Would Titokowaru himself want to drive away and kill peaceful farmers?"

'"Of course he would. Those farmers have stolen the land!"

'"Not everywhere," I said, "not down here. The families I know have bought their land from chiefs who wish to sell."

'He wasn't listening.

'"And don't preach to me about Titokowaru!" he said, stirring the fire until the sparks flew up, "I no longer follow that man. At his best he was a great general but now he has lain with another man's wife and dishonoured our movement. He speaks again of peace. Peace! Now the strong warriors like me are leaving him," he said, rolling his eyes to look fierce and warlike. "We have no interest in retreat or peace. He is crawling back to his own pa — retreating to Taranaki in disgrace — but I am heading towards Te Kooti in the east. He still fights. He will keep hatred in his heart for our enemies."

'I could have slapped my brother for his stupid puffed-up manner and proud words, but also I began to fear him. His beliefs inflamed his mind as liquor maddens a drunkard. In this mood my brother was a dangerous man. But yet I tried to turn my brother from his burning beliefs.

'"Why do you feel so strongly?" I asked. "Have you seen much killing?"

'He spoke with pride. "I have been at victorious battles up north where we have killed many and been killed. We have hunted the retreating Pakeha through the bush and picked them off like flies.

We have ploughed up the land they stole and killed the surveying parties. I have myself killed seventeen Pakeha."

'Now, my chickens, you must not hate your great-uncle for this. Not the fighting in battle. As a soldier he fought an honourable war. That Titokowaru was a clever general. Very clever. And right was on his side. The land he fought for had been stolen, no doubt about it, and he fought his great battles only after trying the peaceful way. But bitterness had entered my brother's heart at some stage — or perhaps the taste of killing had a flavour he enjoyed in some dark way so that he wanted that taste again and again, whether the Pakeha were soldiers or not.

'The matter of the Dane, Heie, and his murder was different. I told you about the Danish worker whom the Monrads found axed and dying on the banks of the Manawatu River, you remember? Well, that night by the fire I learned that my own brother had killed Heie, a hard-working man who had fought in the battles, yes, but was now returning peacefully, walking alone through bush belonging to Ngati Toa, who were not at war.

'"You killed that man?" I cried out. "But why?"

'"He was alone. He had fought in the battles. He deserved to die."

'"You crept up behind and put an axe to his head? Then left him in pain to die alone? What kind of warrior is that?"

'"A Pakeha does not need to be killed in an honourable way. They have not been honourable to us," he said. But his head hung a little low as he spoke. I like to think he felt perhaps a crumb of shame at such a cowardly and cruel act.

'He spoke to me then in a quiet and urgent voice, his eyes shining, his words as slippery as an eel. My babies, he said, were a danger to me: they marked me as a follower of Pakeha ways. They were so pale they would grow up as Pakeha, speaking their language

266

and stealing our land. I was breeding children who would help destroy all the tribes. It would be an honourable thing, he said, to put them to sleep for ever so that they might not live to be a scourge to our people. What warrior, he asked, scorn in his voice, would take such a woman as a wife if she clung to these cursed babies?

'He urged me to follow the Pai Marire way myself and work towards banishing the white man from this country. Titokowaru, he said, preached that Maori women of all tribes should bear many children and Pai Marire men take many wives so that our race might survive the dreadful diseases that even our own family had experienced.

'Turi scratched in the sand as he spoke, as if already digging a small grave for my babies. I tell you, my dear grandchildren, my mokopuna, that those quiet words chilled me more deeply than all his fierce ranting. He had become a fanatic, you see, and fanatics are dangerous people, to be avoided and feared like a terrible disease, worse even than the scrofula that killed your great-grandmother.'

And here in the story one of the children would tug again at the fine cloth of their Nana's skirt to remind her of the story, for they had all heard the bit about fanatics many many times: about good warriors with worthy causes who turned bad and bitter because their eyes looked at the world through a single narrow hole and so on and so on. It was their Nana's favourite lesson.

'Well, my heart was chilled by his words, as I said, for I could see only too well Turi's strength. I was strong too — and fierce, believe me — but I would be no match for him if it came to fighting hand to hand. So I pretended to listen, all the time thinking about escape.

'"We should do it now," he whispered, in his dangerous, mad voice, "while they are asleep." But I said that I needed time to prepare for such a deed and that we would wait until morning. I lay down next to my babies, covering them with my body and shaking with fear at the unthinkable act my brother planned. In the end he settled by the fire, and when I heard him snoring I slipped into the hut and gathered into my kete a little food and my few possessions. I left them close to the doorway, innocent-seeming but ready to be picked up at a moment's notice.

'As I stepped past his sleeping body, he stirred. Firelight reflected in his open eyes as he silently watched me go back to my babies. I tried to seem calm but those cold eyes watching . . . ! Turi had the sharp reflexes of a warrior. I decided that the time to escape would have to be morning, while he was engrossed in his prayers.

'At first light my brother woke. I pretended to be asleep still, but watched through slitted eyes as he prepared to pray. Further away from the hut Turi had planted a rough imitation of a niu pole, which was the symbol for Pai Marire followers — to mark a place where they should gather and pray. He had thrust a tall post cut from the kanuka tree into the sand near to the stream and lashed two sticks across it, high up and pointing in the four directions of the compass. He had hoped to draw followers from those directions to his cause and had already told me how angry and disgusted he was that our people had not responded to his call. Only one young man, from a different hapu, had been prepared to travel with him to join Te Kooti.

'Turi stood under the pole, one hand raised to heaven. Soon his strong voice started the karakia. Slowly he walked around his niu pole. The words of the prayers spoke of a just god and a peaceful one, and of the survival of the righteous and of the lion lying down with the lamb. But I knew that Turi would not lie down peacefully with my two lambs. I crawled to the hut, picked up the basket and scrabbled back to the babies. The prayers continued. Turi walked more quickly round and round the pole, his voice rising with the quickening pace. He went into a sort of trance as he prayed — I had watched him before — and afterwards washed slowly in the stream. A kind of ritual cleansing, I think. So this was my choice of time to leave.

'Oh, that was a difficult time, believe me! At every stumbling step I feared a hand on my shoulder, pictured my babies torn from me and axed before my eyes. He would not hurt me, I thought, but even of that I could not be sure. Lucky for me (and for some of you children, of course) that a high wind blew off the sea that day, driving great waves towards the shore. For a short time I walked at the edge of the water and then, where the waves crashed right up to the tussock of the dunes, I turned inland, hoping that all footprints would be smoothed by the rising tide.

'For an hour I walked inland, until I reached the hills. There a track headed north and south through the low bush of the foothills. Under a clump of taupata trees, which bent low to the ground forming a screened tent, I hid, watching the track as I attended to my boys. No one passed. A long time I sat there quietly, watching and thinking. At last I saw him — my brother Turi — running towards me, north along the track. He carried his gun in one hand and axe in the other, running bare-chested and silent over the dusty track. I pressed each baby to a breast for fear they might cry, and sat there more still than a watching owl, as he passed by. My brother was in a hurry, looking this way and that. His manner was furtive, not vengeful. I thought that he had already forgotten me and was hurrying to join Te Kooti across the mountains, fearing as he went that he might be arrested for his murder of the Dane.

'Soon he was out of sight, lost among the rattling bush — the last time I ever saw or heard of my brother. He could have been a good and brave man, and perhaps he was to some eyes. I like to think he survived the wars and perhaps turned to more peaceful ways as he grew older. I pray that his narrow thoughts broadened, for as you know, my children, fanatics are dangerous men . . .

'Oh, the wind blew strongly that day! Even in my shelter, trees thrashed. My eyes and mouth were full of dust. You young ones would not even begin to imagine the winds of my birthplace: the sea that rages night and day; the sand whipped up and streaming low to the ground, stinging your legs worse than a thousand needles; the seagulls screaming high above, hanging still against the wind and then sloping away in the buffeting air, enjoying the ride as if they were on a Sunday picnic.'

Anahuia would sigh then. 'Oh, I miss that fierce weather of my birthplace,' she would say, and add, smoothing her skirts and preparing to get on with her tasks. 'So I travelled south, two days' walk, to Wellington, where I met your other grandfather.'

6.
Whale-road

THE FAROE ISLANDS AND NEW ZEALAND
1870–72

1.

AN IRON-GREY SKY presses low over the islands the day Enok
Rasmussen returns. Down at the stone dock old Niclas Patursson, on
his usual bench outside Parliament on the point at Tinganes, stamps
his feet and mutters to himself. He hates this dark and oppressive
weather — no room for a man to stretch his thoughts. Three days
now the sky has hung thus — leaden, windless, not a sea-bird aloft
nor even a rolling mist to break the sense of pending doom. Where,
in the name of Thor, is some breeze to break the mood?

Leaning heavily on his stick, the old man rises and makes his
way to the water's edge, peers over the wall at the sea below. It
heaves silently, sullen as the sky above, no friendly slap slap against
the stone, nothing of interest to see in its depths. Niclas sighs. On a
day like this he feels ready to leave this world. He looks south down
the sound. Nothing. But north, yes, at last some distant thing that

273

moves! He narrows his eyes, unsure of what he sees, but guessing, correctly, that a ship under steam is on the way.

'Well, that will make a change, at least,' he mutters. 'I will watch it unload, and there will be people coming and going.'

Back on his stone bench he watches the ship grow larger, its sails hanging slack, its funnel belching black smoke. Now he can hear the hammer of the engine and the ringing of bells as the schooner slows and the anchor-chain rattles its way towards the sea-bed. It is a medium-sized vessel, no doubt from Copenhagen with the usual load of provisions and timber. Since the war, visits have been less frequent. Everyone is feeling the pinch.

From the wharf sheds several fellows emerge, each greeting Niclas with a nod or a touch of the cap. They jump into a large rowboat moored at the dock and bend to their oars. This ship is too large to come alongside: goods will be rowed ashore. Niclas stands watching the activity on board the schooner. In the stern a lone mariner at a capstan hauls down the heavy triangular sail. A strong man, that, to do it alone. The man straightens, eases his back and stands looking shorewards. There is something strange about his stillness, the way he scans the hills. The man's peaked cap is pulled low on his forehead, the collar of his dark jacket high around his ears against the cold. His gaze lowers to take in the infield and the houses near the shore.

But now the big fellow's arms spread in a gesture familiar to old Niclas. Familiar, too, is the voice roaring across the water. 'Is that my old teacher Niclas Patursson come to greet me?'

Niclas clears his throat but no sound emerges. In frustration he stamps and nods, banging his stick hard on the cobbles, tears running down his old cheeks.

Enok flings down his rope and disappears from view. In a moment he is back, a canvas bag over his shoulder and some other bundle in his arms, making the dangerous leap into the loaded boat below. Someone aboard shouts at him to come back, in the name of God, and finish the task in hand, but already the oarsmen are pulling shorewards, laughing and greeting their returning country-man.

Enok runs up the steps and stops in front of the old man. He, too, has tears in his eyes. 'God bless you, my friend and my teacher,' he says.

'And you, and you,' chokes Niclas. 'The teacher welcomes the pupil: this one standing before me, who is like a son returned at last, just before this old man leaves his lonely life.'

Old Niclas lets his stick clatter to the cobblestones as he seizes tall Enok by the elbows, holding him at arm's length while he squints up to search the face. He sees a man where there was a boy. He sees the same eagerness to take life by the horns, the same infectious impatience. But also a shadow. He nods, releasing the boy — the man — and says quietly, 'But you have come with sad news?'

Enok looks away, up towards the dark hills. 'Are you a seer too, teacher?'

Niclas would like to claim that skill, but seeing Enok's lowered brows he decides on the swifter truth. 'A letter from that Danish bishop came for old Haraldsen. They say it warned that you brought bad news.'

Enok bends to hear more clearly. His question is anxious. 'What else did the letter say?'

'Am I the recipient? You will have to ask him.' The old man shakes his head sadly and adds, 'But any fool can imagine, when one returns without the other, what that news might be.'

Enok nods. They are both silent for a moment.

'Well then,' says Niclas at last, 'the news must be spoken first to the proper ears. Will you take a mug of beer with me before you walk up?'

'I will. Gladly.' Enok smiles then, and slaps the flax basket under his arm. 'There is a gift here for you, teacher, and another thing that will interest you. I have brought more than gloom. And wait till you hear, old man, the sights I have seen!'

The old man chuckles and his step is lighter as the two make their way over the uneven stones of the pathway. New stories! Now *that* is better than brandy to warm an old man's bones!

Enok slows his pace, dances on the spot until Niclas puffs level, talks of giant trees and strange dark people, his arms flinging this way and that to show improbable size and shape. Already he has forgotten, it seems, his sad news.

At the doorway Niclas points to the eaves, where dark blocks are hanging in the cool air. 'Reach me down meat and blubber,' he says. 'They have been hanging there waiting for some tall fellow. As you see, these old bones have shrunk even since I hung them three months back. Come in, come in, the smoke-room will be warm still.'

Enok reaches down a stick of the dark whale meat and one of the lighter blubber. Already his mouth is watering. Inside, the air is scented sweetly with burning peat. Niclas places a pan of milk among the embers in the firebox and stirs in barley meal. While they wait for the porridge to thicken, Enok unstraps the canvas roll and brings out a small bundle wrapped in soft leather. Grinning, proud, he turns away from Niclas while he selects something from the bundle, then turns back, his great hand cupping something small.

'For you.'

Niclas takes the carving, holds it close to his old eyes to examine the detail. 'Whale ivory,' he says, pleased with the smooth and golden glow of it. 'Beautiful. Very clever. But what is this thing, Enok?'

'A bird.'

'So? You have invented this creature? A mythical beast?'

Enok laughs. 'No, old man, it's real enough. I have eaten its flesh and heard its cry in the night. It is a bird from New Zealand. Kiwi, they call it.'

'But where are the wings? You don't have a bird without wings. How could it survive?'

Enok is delighted to be the teacher for once. The two down their beer and whale meat while the words tumble out of Enok, and the old man, sitting upright on his bench by the fire, listens and questions, his blue eyes alert, his aching knees forgotten.

'But listen,' says Enok suddenly, 'what do you think? I have learned the third kvæði! Wait till you hear! There is a book!'

He jumps to his feet, but before he has taken a step towards his swag there comes a boy's shout from outside and a pounding on the door.

'Enok Rasmussen! Is Enok within?' More pounding.

Niclas Patursson frowns. 'What manners! Let him knock until he learns better.'

But Enok only laughs, and opens the heavy wooden door to reveal a blue-eyed lad clad head to toe in black sealskin — jacket, pants, boots and cap roughly stitched and rather too large for him. He is still gasping from his run up the hill, his breath steaming in the cold air.

'You Enok?' asks the lad, grinning, but before Enok can answer, Niclas has reached the door and gripped the strings of the boy's cap, jerking his head up.

'Lars Larsen,' he grumbles. 'I might have known. Your mother would turn in her grave and your father die of shame!'

The boy, clearly used to such outbursts, only grins. 'Sorry, sorry, old father. Good evening to you, old father. God bless you, Niclas Patursson, and keep you well, but I am sent in a hurry to catch this man if he be Enok Rasmussen.'

'Haste never yet caught a fish, nor bad manners a civil reply,' says Niclas severely. 'Now stand still like a proper lad and say who sent you.'

Enok smiles to see the boy, son of a famous Nólsoy fisherman, whose mother died at his birth and who was only a toddler last time Enok saw him. Lars smiles back, but stands still and delivers his message as ordered.

'I am sent by the teacher's assistant, who says she will be free shortly, and will accompany the man Enok to her father's farm if he will wait. She says I am to run ahead to warn the household while it is still light and that she will bring a lamp for Enok's journey.' The boy taps his chest proudly. 'I am as fast as any skyd; they will have plenty of time to prepare a welcome feast.'

Lars looks to Enok for a response but the mood of the tall man has changed. He stares out through the doorway and down towards the village.

'Clara,' he says, and sighs.

There is silence in the room, Lars looking questions at both men.

Old Niclas wags a finger at the young boy. 'Off you go now, lad. Take your message. And watch the path over the tops: the ice makes it treacherous.'

'Hey! Just watch how I go!' boasts the boy, and speeds away up the hill, his oversize jacket flapping.

Niclas groans. 'That boy will never make a decent Faroeman. His father was old when he married and has not married again since his wife died. He does his best, but look at the lad — not a stitch of good wool on him. Young Lars runs wild, with no one to teach him the proper way of things. He will not fit in.'

'I was perhaps the same,' suggests Enok. His mind is on other things, though.

'You were not the same!' says the old man sharply. 'You were brought up knowing our old ways. Our old kvæði. There is no comparison.'

Enok is reminded of Bishop Monrad's book and the ballad he has learned. He hands the treasure to his old teacher, explains what it contains.

'All the Sjúrðar kvæði are here. And some we never even heard of.'

Niclas Patursson glowers at the book.

'To start with, I didn't want to,' says Enok, suddenly anxious to find, in his teacher, an ally. 'And then, on the long voyage, I was curious. Now I have learned to read our language — think of that! And have learned the third part with only the book to teach.'

'That,' says the old man flatly, 'is not possible. I am surprised to hear you boast of such a thing.'

'Wait till you hear!'

Enok chatters on, explaining how he memorised the ballad verse by verse, drawing on the cadences and rhythms of the earlier two to suggest the tune for the third; how he had sung to the gulls that followed the ship; had bellowed verses into the wind from the top-gallant.

Old Niclas shakes his head at it all but smiles, despite himself. He loves to hear the boy so enthusiastic. Enok hasn't changed at all. About to face a difficult and sensitive interview with the Haraldsens, his pupil has latched onto the intricacies of story-telling, completely forgetting what is to come. But when Enok tells how he cunningly wove sections of the kvæði into hauling chants for the sailors, Niclas has to draw the line.

'This will not do, my friend,' he says firmly. 'You are babbling nonsense.'

'Nonsense? It's the truth, I swear!'

'You will not be ready to sing that kvæði until you have spent a year up north in Borðoy with Finnur Jakobsen. You may have learned the words, but the spirit will be wrong.'

Enok puts down his beer and stands, almost hitting his head on the low ceiling. He laughs and gives the offending timber a casual slap. 'I am grown even taller, don't you think? But, teacher, is it not possible to add a new flavour to an old tale?'

'I am surprised you even ask! Of course not. The proper way is master to pupil, down through the generations. How else can the old ways remain intact?'

Enok taps the book. 'Now the old ways are written here. They *are* intact.'

Old Niclas slaps his knee angrily. 'They are *not*! Those are some words only. And more than likely half wrong if some Dane wrote them down. Enok, Enok, my friend, take care. There is danger in what you say. Your travels have — how can I say it? — lured you in a wrong direction. It is timely that you return.' He notices the stubborn set of his pupil's chin and softens his tone. 'But it is good that you have begun to learn the words at least. I will arrange with Finnur Jakobsen. He will teach you gladly. A good man, if a little slow these days.'

'Wouldn't you at least hear what I have made up? I think it is good. Your teaching has been kept in mind.'

'No, no. It would only annoy me. Forget that, young man. If you want to make up your own, think of a táttur. Make up a funny song about our politicians. That is perfectly permissible. You might be as good at it as I was in my day.'

Enok slumps to his chair and drains his beer. Never one to give up on an argument, he is about to launch a counter-argument when there is a sharp knocking on the door.

'God bless you, Niclas Patursson, I hope you are well. This is the teacher's assistant wishing it and hoping she may enter.' All this said in a rush, the voice greatly out of breath.

'Let her in,' says the old man gently. 'And think carefully how you speak.'

Enok nods, slaps at his rough seaman's trousers as if it could make a difference — or perhaps to gain time — and opens the door.

'Clara,' he says. His smile is careful. 'Come in.'

Her smile also is careful. A small, anxious flash, with hope in it — and something else that Enok finds difficult to read. 'I won't come in, but thank you,' she says. 'Enok. You are welcome. If you are ready we should set out.'

Her words are formal. No doubt she fears what she is about to hear, and is hesitant for that reason. Enok cannot tell whether she is pleased to see him or not. She is wrapped warmly in a heavy woollen coat and scarf. The flying golden hair that Enok remembers must have been pulled back in a bun, as none of it is visible beneath her knitted cap. Her cheeks are pink — perhaps she is blushing? She stamps her feet against the cold and shouts in to Niclas, 'Forgive us if we leave you so rudely.'

'Off you go, off you go.' Niclas smiles at the rosy woman. 'They will be waiting. This old man will hear the news at a later time. Go, Enok, my son.'

Enok touches her sleeve gently. 'He is dead, Clara.'

She sighs. 'Yes.'

He shrugs into his jacket, shoulders his bundles and follows her outside. Up the narrow path they walk, and west into a drizzling rain. Already, at three in the afternoon, it is completely dark. Clara leads with long strides, Enok following, rehearsing in silence the story he will tell.

ENOK tells the story well in the Haraldsens' warm smoke-room, where a coal fire burns in a modern iron stove and food lies ready on trays. There are fourteen sitting silent and formal on the benches against the walls — Haraldsen's family; his brother's family; young Lars, wide-eyed, in the corner where the old grandfather used to sit; and Enok.

No one will eat until the story is told. And story it is, not the uncomfortable truth. Enok lays out Napoleon's few possessions — his warm woollen coat, the carved boat Enok made him, the cheerful letter he wrote to his family a few days before his death, his knife and the papers releasing him from the Danish army.

Enok sits in the place of honour, next to the stove. 'Your son,' he says, taking in the assembled group, 'your brother and nephew, your cousin and friend, died bravely. He was my closest friend, and I have travelled the whale-road over the furthest oceans to bring you news of his death and the manner of it.

'You would find it hard to imagine the farm in New Zealand where Napoleon and I worked. Every single thing about it was different from here: the bishop's land flat as a table and covered in giant trees that had to be felled before his sheep could find any open land to graze. But Napoleon was a champion and learned quickly the new ways. Bishop Monrad himself often praised my friend for his speed and agility. You would have been proud to see him mount and ride a horse as if born to it. Proud at the way he laughed and shouted, galloping over the stumps and leaping his mount over streams just for the enjoyment of it. My task was to fell trees; his to herd the sheep.

'Listen! That distant land may have been flat where we farmed, but further inland were high and dangerous mountains. These dark inland heights trapped the rain-clouds which would suddenly, without warning, drop their rain by the bucketload, filling the valley streams that then ran to greater rivers, until by the time the rivers reached our farm great torrents swept down, wider than this whole valley, in places deep and treacherous, in others shallow and swift. It is difficult to explain to a Faroeman, familiar with our small streams and waterfalls, the breadth and strength of these rivers. Especially the way in which they changed from peaceful to treacherous within a short hour.

'Well. On this day, the last of Napoleon's tragically short life, his task was to drive a herd of cattle from a distant town where they had been purchased, to the bishop's farm, further inland. Unknown to him and his two companions, it had rained heavily that night deep in the hills. The river was rising. Napoleon, atop his fine white horse, encouraged the reluctant beasts towards a place in the river where carts and animals were accustomed to cross. In English they call such a place a ford. Leading the way, Napoleon negotiated the river safely and the animals began to follow.

'But as fate would have it, a few of the herd strayed from the shallow water of the ford to a place where the river ran more swiftly. One of Napoleon's companions, a Dane from Funen, shouted warning and drove his horse into the water, which minute by minute was rising. The Dane managed to head the cattle successfully towards the bank but his horse stumbled, throwing its rider. When Napoleon saw his friend in difficulty he showed no hesitation, even though, as you know, he could not swim. His white steed was set at the river, Napoleon leaning low in the saddle to grab at the tumbling man's coat. The Dane, spitting and choking, gratefully held to the saddle, the strong white horse turned towards the shore and all seemed safe again. But by cruel misfortune a heavy log, rolling in the now wild river, struck the threesome, dislodging Napoleon, who was swept away in a moment.

'Horse and Dane reached the bank with difficulty and then rode swiftly down the bank seeking a place where Napoleon might be brought to shore. Alas, though Napoleon struggled against the current, the river grew wilder and deeper moment by moment. The horrified Dane could only watch as the boy who had saved him went under for the last time.'

Enok pauses in this dramatic story and looks around at the silent family. 'Napoleon Haraldsen saved a life and lost his own doing so. When the desperate men rode into the farm with the news I ran out into the dark night, downriver, calling in our own language in the forlorn hope he may be lying injured. Many others followed. When grey dawn arrived there was still no sign. At last a sad procession of native Maori brought his body back to the farm. They had found him downriver, swept far from the Monrad block.

'In death, his face appeared peaceful; there were no marks upon his body to hint at his struggle with that powerful river, which is called Manawatu — a name that means in the native language "heart stood still". I was told . . .' Enok's voice faltered for a moment and he looked down at the floor, 'by a native Maori that a great chief once came to the river and felt his heart stop with fear at its grandeur and size. Hence the name. Alas, the heart of our brave friend and son, Napoleon, was also stilled by the River Manawatu in that far colony. We could only hope that the drowning was swift.

'He is buried in the cemetery at Jackeytown, which the natives call Tiakitahuna, the bishop himself saying the words of committal. I carved a simple cross with his name and family, his dates and the words "A Brave Faroeman".'

Enok took a deep breath, looked around at the silent family. At last he spoke a simple truth from the heart. 'Every single day since,

I have missed him and cursed the friendship that brought him to that far place in search of Enok Rasmussen, this wretched man standing here before you.'

'May my son rest in God's peace,' says Harald Haraldsen into the silence.

All are in tears. Clara, though she also weeps, gives Enok a questioning and thoughtful look, which he notices with discomfort.

That night, warm and well fed, lying in the bed kept for important guests, Enok wonders why he had not mentioned Anahuia or the twin sons he has never seen. During the evening he had told stories about the far colony of New Zealand: about Bishop Monrad's establishment there, about the death of the ship's captain on the long voyage back, about his frustration waiting for a passage from England and then an even longer wait in Copenhagen for one to the Faroes. He drew a smile from the grieving father over the strange way the bishop farmed his sheep, and a proud 'Yes, of course!' from the mother when he told how Napoleon had charmed the bishop's daughters. But Anahuia, who had been so important in his life, had never surfaced. For a moment or two he puzzles over his silence but then shrugs the matter away and sleeps soundly enough.

It took young Lars Larsen, walking beside him next morning, to put his finger on a few home truths. They walk in the cold half-light of mid-morning. Already Clara has disappeared over the hill, to reach Tórshavn in time for her work. Lars flaps along in his oversize sealskins, full of questions and pronouncements. The lively twelve-year-old has long finished with school. He works, when weather permits, on his father's fishing boat, practises to be a champion rower or a champion skyd and is a fount of knowledge on the private lives of everyone on Streymoy. Now he has a new ambition — to travel the world like Enok.

Coming over the brow, they stop to puff and look down the long sloping fields to Tórshavn. Lars peers through the mist, points out a wheeling guillemot — sign, he says, that the mist will rise. Then he looks back at Enok, head cocked to one side, and grins.

'That story,' he says in his cracking half-man's voice, 'about Napoleon's death. That was dressing up the sheep, eh?'

'What?' Enok has been thinking other thoughts.

'You told them a story they wanted to hear, I reckon, because the true one wasn't so pretty.'

Enok frowns at the boy. 'What makes you think that?'

'I watched your face. You were enjoying the story too much. The daughter of Haraldsen could see that too.'

'You see more than is there.' Enok sets off down the track at a pace that forces Lars to run.

'No, but . . .' the nimble boy hops and chats, keeping up with ease, 'No, but listen, Enok, why *not* dress up the story a bit? To make them happy. It was good.'

'Thank you, sir,' says Enok dryly. He is worried, though, to think that Clara might have noticed.

'Clara Haraldsen is holding a lighted candle for you,' says Lars. 'A very bright one. She watched you all the time last night. She has been waiting for you to return — everyone says so.'

'You are the oracle as well as champion skyd, then?'

'Yes, I suppose. Will you marry her, Enok?'

Enok laughs then, to hide his confusion. Snatches off the boy's cap and throws it into the field. 'Cheeky pup!' he roars. 'I have been here one day and you are matchmaking! Get away with you!'

'Is that a yes, then?' shouts Lars. And before Enok can answer he has grabbed up his cap, jammed it back on and flapped off down the hill. By the time Enok reaches the dock Lars is already setting out across the sound, rowing his father's small boat as if he were a one-man competition.

Enok stands on the dock watching the boat grow smaller. But what he sees is a woman's blue dress floating down a distant river, and his best friend drowning to save it.

2.

BY AFTERNOON ENOK'S mood and the mist have both lifted. Clara, beaming her congratulation, stands with him outside the schoolroom.

'But that is marvellous!' she says, clapping her hands and laughing. 'The third kvæði? That is perfect, Enok! We will call a special gathering to launch our newspaper, and you shall sing at it. It will set just the right note. Can you stay here in Tórshavn a few weeks more?'

Enok grins, enjoying the praise. It is Saturday and school is now over. Clara, eager to show off her modern ways, walks with him down to the little meeting room next door to the brewery. They drink beer together and chatter in the fading afternoon light. Soon, Clara promises, the others of their group will arrive to talk and plan and read Faroese poetry of their own making. Meantime, Enok brings from his pocket a carving for her — a small scene, carved from whale bone, of a group of sheep and lambs, grazing under a spreading fern.

'It might remind you of Napoleon,' he says. 'He was a farmer at heart. Already his taste for adventure had been quenched and his eyes were looking home.'

Clara strokes the little carving. 'You are so clever, Enok,' she says. 'Everything you touch . . .' Then, looking straight at him and blushing, 'And you? What about your taste for adventure? Do your eyes looked homeward now?'

When Enok remains silent she says suddenly, all in a rush, 'Enok, it is *so* good to see you again. I hope you stay now. Well, we all do, of course. Especially me. I have waited . . . I mean we have all waited . . . I mean . . . Enok, say you'll stay.'

There is something urgent about the plea. And embarrassed — the younger, sweeter Clara now showing beneath the surface of her severe hair and sensible clothes. Enok can't help smiling back, and her returning beam is like the sun coming out.

'Oh, we have such fine things planned,' she says, the confident, capable woman taking over again. 'You will be impressed. We are going to make big changes, Enok. Five of us who have all been to study in Copenhagen are back now. Over there we learned to read and write in our own language. Our teachers encouraged it.' She laughs. 'Imagine that! We wrote pamphlets and poetry and now we are going to establish a patriotic Faroese newspaper. You have arrived back at just the right time, Enok.'

Enok lets her chatter roll over him. He feels lazy and at ease in this fuggy room, the fumes from fermenting barley next door almost as heady as the beer he drinks. Clara's cheeks are pink, her blue eyes bright and animated as she outlines the group's plans. The old folk are too conservative, she says — they would let the old ways die, out of sheer inertia. The Faroese Poetry Society will bring energy and intelligence to the task of preserving the language and culture before it is swamped by the all-pervading Danish influences. With the help of her father they have purchased a second-hand printing press, and soon every Faroeman and woman will be able to read news of cultural and local events and, of course, enjoy Faroese poetry, once a week, all in their own language.

Enok smiles and nods, admiring her energy but only half engaged. Outside it is dark. Rain batters against the window. Enok finds it hard, now, to adjust to these closed and brief winter days. For a year and a half he has sailed across wide, open seas, in oppressive heat or bitter storm but always with a sense of great expanse and ever-changing light. He would have liked to walk over the hills this afternoon, but only a madman would walk in the icy dark of these treacherous islands with their plunging cliffs. Beyond the door he hears voices. He reaches out to touch Clara's hand, to stem her flow.

'They are here. You will have to introduce me.'

Outside they can hear boots clanging against scrapers and coats being shaken to free them from damp.

'No, no,' smiles Clara, leaving her hand, warm and small, under his, 'you will know them. Old friends.'

And in they come, four men, laughing and talking, removing caps and slapping them against their thighs. Petur and Johan and Símun — old schoolmates. The fourth is Otto Dahl. His quick green eyes notice the two hands on the table. His laughing chatter with the others ceases and his smile is careful.

'Hello, Enok.'

Enok rises quickly, knocking his tankard (fortunately empty) to the floor.

'Otto!' Enok looks quickly to Clara, angry that he has not been warned. She shakes her head gently as if to dismiss his agitation.

'Well, cousin,' says Otto easily, 'you look as if you've seen a ghost! No greeting, then?'

Enok recovers himself, clasps his cousin's offered hand as warmly as he is able. 'My friend, I have spent the last several years thinking you were indeed a ghost and regretting the blow that I thought had made you so.'

The others laugh. The story is obviously well known.

'I am no ghost but a merchant and proprietor of this very brewery and warehouse. The blow was nothing and is forgotten. Welcome back.'

'By God, I am glad to hear you say that, cousin. Also, my condolences on your — our — grandfather's death.'

Otto's laugh is easy but the voice has an edge to it. 'Do not pretend sorrow for the end of that life, Enok. Magnus was a hard man and I neither liked nor respected him. But for all that, he made me heir to certain important concerns. And one of these I would like to discuss with you later.'

The two men have been standing face to face during this exchange. Clara, still seated, watches the two. Otto is tall, narrow-shouldered and hipped. The fair hair of childhood has darkened to a deep honey-gold. His green eyes are striking in a handsome, narrow face. He looks a good few years older than his cousin, is more contained, carries a settled and prosperous manner with ease. Enok, taller, broader, his ash-blond hair wild about his slabby face, seems unfinished still, not quite grown into his expanse of skin. He shifts from foot to foot as if impatient to move on, uses his hands when he speaks. He is noticeable, and not just for his size. The openness draws people, Clara included, as sea-birds are drawn to the promised feast of a returning fishing boat. She can't help smiling as he now greets the others, as if he were the host and they the newcomers.

'Clara,' says Otto. He has been watching her and moves now to take her hands in his. 'I am looking forward to hearing your poem. Shall we begin?'

There is a great scraping of chairs and clearing of throats as fresh beer is poured and places are taken around the table. Otto conducts the session, inviting contributions and leading the following discussion. He is quick to praise and equally free with suggestions for improvement. Enok listens. He is surprised by Clara's piece. After all her fervent and patriotic talk he had expected more of a call to action, but her words are gentle, praising the joys of home and hearth, likening the role of the good Faroese mother to that of a prudent farmer: she nurtures the soul while he the land. Otto praises the work fulsomely, and Enok of course applauds, but in truth he finds all the writing a little dull.

When Otto looks to his cousin, Enok smiles easily. 'Well, I have nothing written, but how about I sing something I made up for the sailors on the way over here?'

'It must be in Faroese,' says Otto quickly. 'That is our rule.'

'I have gathered that, cousin,' says Enok dryly. He leans back, tilting his chair dangerously, and sings — in Faroese — a lively and saucy ditty about a fisherman who rows his boat across the sound to meet a lovely girl who is, alas, betrothed to another. The chorus makes a word-play about creaking oars and creaking bed-boards. Enok invites the group to join in the second chorus and they do, smiling and laughing, while he whips out his whistle and accompanies them. After the third ribald verse and enthusiastic chorus, Otto, who hasn't joined in the singing, holds up his hand to interrupt the flow.

'A good song for a sailor,' he says, 'but your tune is Danish. I heard it last year in Copenhagen.'

Enok crashes his chair back onto its four legs, ready to argue. 'But surely a tune has no boundary. Who is to say where the Danes found this one? Maybe some wandering sailor brought it back from America? Often I have heard one tune serve to tell different stories in as many languages as you can imagine.'

'Well, that is all very well for sailors. But we are scholars and are dedicated to preserving the culture of these islands. Think, Enok: if we let every new word or fashion take root here, Faroese would be swamped. Already this is a danger. Surely you of all people, with your background in kvæ∂i, recognise this.'

Otto's patronising manner irritates Enok. 'But you would cut yourself off from so much!' he cries. 'The Faroes have a great and interesting history, but we are so small. So . . .' he hesitates to use the word but then throws caution away, 'so *limited*. We are a conservative people who need opening out, not preserving in a museum.'

The others murmur and shift at such strong words, but they look to Otto to respond. He is clearly their leader. Nothing seems to provoke Otto; he is calm and in control even in the face of Enok's passion. Now, as Enok leans forward, enjoying every minute of the argument, his fist pounding the table, demanding a reply, Otto shakes his head as if to say that it is beneath his dignity to answer.

But before he speaks Clara laughs out loud. 'You two!' she says. 'Stop and listen to your words! I seem to remember an argument a few years back in realskole. My memory says you have changed sides. Enok, you argued for learning the Faroese language and Otto called you an old stick-in-the-mud! Surely you remember?'

Enok opens his mouth to speak, then shuts it again. Slap! Down comes his palm on the table and he joins the laughter. 'Clara Haraldsen, you have taken the wind out of my sails fair and square! Yes! It's true!' He leans across to cuff his cousin on the shoulder. 'Well, friend, this smart woman has caught us out properly!' Standing now, he paces the room, interested in the new direction of the discussion. 'But how strange that we have changed our views.

Or am I simply a little drunk and argue for the enjoyment? What does the oracle say?' He turns, laughing, to Clara, arms spread, inviting her decision.

'Clara,' says Otto quietly, 'is going to read us her next poem.'

'Well, actually,' says Clara, still flushed from Enok's praise, 'I was going to make a suggestion. About the launch of our newspaper. Come and sit down, Enok.'

'No,' says Otto, 'I want to hear your poem. We will have suggestions later.'

The meeting resumes, but the mood has been broken. Clara is aware of the change — Enok has brought a different energy to the group, one that both disturbs and excites her. On the one hand she agrees with Otto's views, but then as soon as Enok opens his mouth she finds herself listening to him, enjoying the fresh breeze he brings.

Before they go out into the black damp of the evening, Clara outlines her plan: to have Enok sing the last of the Sjúrðar kvæði at the launch of the newspaper.

'Everyone would come to hear him!' she says. 'Think what good publicity it would be. A dance, a great ballad singer and the first copy of the first Faroese newspaper all in one parcel. Perfect!'

For the first time all evening Otto seems agitated. He stands, comes behind Clara and places his hands on her shoulders: a formal and proprietary gesture. 'Let us think carefully about this,' he says, dampening the enthusiasm of all. 'The newspaper is the important thing, surely. We do not want it overshadowed by a performance — however good — that has little to do with our endeavour. Also, we should remember that the proper time for kvæði is Christmas or St Olaf's Day.'

Clara sits still under his hands. Enok wills her to defy him, but the pressure seems to drain her of animation. She nods slowly and smiles apologetically at Enok.

'Perhaps he is right,' she says. 'They are two different matters.' Seeing Enok draw breath to defend the idea, she gives him a small dismissive sign that wounds him more than sharp words.

Otto smiles now, pats her shoulders smartly, then walks to the door. 'Good, then. Perhaps if we are finished I might have a word alone with Enok. A private matter.'

He holds the door open while the others file out, shrugging into coats and caps as they go. Rain is still falling and the wind has risen. The houses of Tórshavn are obliterated. The dim glow spilling out from the meeting room and a single light down at the jetty are the only signs that a town is here. As Clara leaves, Otto compliments her writing, praises the improvement. Clara blushes proudly, but her last smile — regretful and warm — is for Enok.

LATER, when Otto has shown his cousin around the brewery and the warehouse, explained the breadth and scope of his business interests, he seats Enok in his cramped office and produces, with a flourish that is meant to impress, a bottle of brandy and two glasses. Enok, already glowing from the beer, accepts a shot and downs it. Otto refills both glasses, then, warming his hands at the meagre glow of the oil-lamp, explains the nature of his 'private matter'.

'My grandfather left my uncle the marks of land here and in both Vagar and Sandoy. Also his trading ship, *Thyra*, named after his wife, our grandmother. The same ship you arrived on last week. To me he left these businesses, and also . . .' Otto pauses, enjoying the moment, 'also the three marks of land in Suðeroy. Now. I have no great interest in farming, and no time to supervise a manager on an island so far south. I propose to make those marks over to your name. You are, after all, of our blood.'

Enok remains silent, looking down at the large ledger on the desk and waiting for the catch.

'You are not pleased? Your mother and her family are already aware of my plan and are deeply grateful. Their store has not done good business recently.' Otto fails to mention that he has undercut their prices. 'And the price of wool is favourable at the moment. There is a good living to be had off those marks.'

Enok wishes his head were clearer, wishes also that he did not suspect his cousin of some trick. 'Naturally,' he says, 'it seems generous — more than fair. Does my family farm the land now?'

'No, no, no. The transfer is to *you*. Once we heard you were returning, I had the deed drawn up. If you — personally — do not wish to farm the land it will revert to a more distant cousin on the other side of the island.'

Enok clears his throat. 'I am more of a sailor these days —'

'The choice is yours, cousin.'

'If I should have children?'

'They will inherit. Certainly. As long as the mother, also, is from Suðeroy.'

Enok frowns. 'Why? Why should it matter where she was born?'

Otto smiles easily, 'Call me a patriot. I would not want Suðeroy land to fall into other hands. More brandy?'

Enok drinks. 'But this is a nonsense! *I* am from Suðeroy — that should be enough.'

'As I say, the choice is yours. Take the document: it needs only your signature. Go down to your island and inspect your marks. You are a strong man, Enok, and will make a good farmer. Think carefully.' Otto's green eyes are now slightly unfocused as he smiles at his cousin. 'I mean you well, Enok. All that bad blood in our family is not worthy. A true Faroeman supports those of his blood first. Let us be friends.'

'Does Clara know about this? Do the Haraldsens?'

Otto stands suddenly and almost loses balance. He is even drunker than Enok, it would seem. 'This has nothing to do with them. With her.'

'No?'

'No.' Otto steadies himself against the table. He won't look at his cousin. '*No.*'

Enok, befuddled as he is, finally sees that the gift of land has everything to do with Clara. Otto wants him out of the way.

'Cousin,' he says, grinning, the words coming thick against his tongue, 'I will not stand in your way with Clara.'

He moves to clap Otto on the shoulder but the smaller man is quicker. Enok finds himself pushed up against the wall, Otto's swimming eyes only inches from his own.

'It is nothing to do with her!' shouts Otto. 'Nothing! And another thing — she shouldn't look at you like that. And *another* thing — keep your eyes off *her*. She is betrothed to me. *Me!*'

Tears are rolling down his face now. He lurches back to his desk, sits with a crash and flicks the pages of his ledger as if searching for something. He dashes a hand across his face and seems surprised to find it wet. At last he finds the paper he wants and rattles it in the air.

'An important letter from the king's bailiff here to the sheriff in Suðeroy,' he says, his voice and manner back under control. 'Come from Denmark on the same boat that brought you. The skyds will be running it down tomorrow. You could go too, if you can keep up.'

Enok leans against the wall, unable to control his foolish grin.

'Your mother will be pleased to see you,' says Otto.

'Oh Jesus, you *are* keen to get rid of me,' says Enok, shaking his big shaggy head. 'I can't think straight.'

'You're drunk.'

'We're both drunk, friend, and best out of each other's company.

I'll go down if I can clear my head quickly enough.'

'First skyd will leave seven in the morning. God speed.'

3.

THE TIME-HONOURED manner in which the official letter is delivered to Suðeroy (Enok travelling on its coat-tails) — indeed the only postal service the islands knew — is this:

First the skydskaffer in Tórshavn makes out the roster, choosing, on every island, runners and boat-owners who have not been called upon recently. No one enjoys giving up a day for skyd duty but fortunately official letters are rare, and so are travelling priests or sheriffs, who also have the right of skyd transport. Enok certainly has no such right and will be expected to put his back to an oar. The skydskaffer, a pompous fellow and a relative of Otto's (a fact that has Enok wondering if the letter is a fabrication), hands the sealed leather pouch containing the letter and the roster-card to young Lars Larsen, runner for the Streymoy leg.

'Make sure that lazy man in Kirkjubøur sets out smartly,' says the skydskaffer, 'and signs the paper before he hands it on. Off with you, then. If the big man can't keep up, leave him behind. This is king's business.'

Lars loves the duty and would run it every time if asked. He runs into the low mist on the tops, sure-footed even in this icy dark, leaping small streams and rocky outcrops, scattering the few shaggy sheep still in the outfield. Here and there patches of snow glow eerily. It will not be light until mid-morning, well after they have arrived in Kirkjubøur. At the brow he turns south, shouting to the labouring Enok to hurry, then disappears into the mist as he runs the five kilometres along the cliffs and down the steep southern slopes to Kirkjubøur, on the coast. Enok, strong as he is, cannot keep up. He arrives, puffing and coughing, just as the farmer whose turn it is, prepares to row out.

'Excellent,' says the farmer, eyeing Enok's size. 'You can take an oar and save my youngest son half the distance. He hasn't the strength yet for the return trip. And a sail will be no use to us in this weather.'

While the crew waits for the last rower to don his woollen coat and sheepskin boots, Enok speaks quietly to Lars. 'Take a message to Clara. Tell her I will come back at Christmas to sing the kvæði. Ask her to find a house for it.'

Lars grins. 'The old man's house, of course. Niclas Patursson.'

'No, perhaps not. He does not approve.'

'Well, he is old. I will approve! And Clara will be happy. Is she your sweetheart now?'

'Enough of sweethearts!' Enok's words come out sharper than he intended and he gives the boy a friendly pat. 'Thanks, friend. Tell Clara I'm sorry to leave so suddenly.'

The boy scuffs his boots against the pebbles of the beach. 'I wish I was coming. Never seen Suðeroy. Nor even the northern islands.

You have clapped eyes on the whole world.'

Enok laughs, his spirits restored. 'Well, a good chunk. And you will too, is my guess. God speed, friend.'

The six oarsmen set out across the sound to Skopun on the island of Sandoy, while Lars waves them off. No doubt he will run all the way back just for the fun of it.

At Skopun the new skyd takes charge of the letter (Enok is not a notified skyd and will not do) and the two run steeply up the hill, into mist again, past the lake, then beside the stream for two hours, thankfully downhill, over to Sandur on the south coast. Three hours of running. Enok is tired. And wet. A spiritless kind of daylight has finally arrived, and with it a soaking rain. Two more islands to go.

The Sandur skyd, whose turn it is to row to the next island, remembers Enok. 'Ho, Enok Rasmussen av Suðeroy!' he shouts. 'I would recognise that frame any day of the week! Here is our ballad singer returned. Take an oar, man. This skyd duty is a bloody curse, for I have important work on the farm.'

'Jesus, man, I am far cut,' pants Enok.

'Then stay behind — there's no room for passengers. I have a cousin on Skúvoy will row back.'

Clearly there is ample room for a passenger, but Enok is in no position to argue. He climbs aboard, happy enough at least to sit down for a while. Once out in the channel they set a sail, which helps, but the oars are needed. The current is against them. Another three hours and they reach Skúvoy in pitch dark. Enok climbs wearily up the icy stone steps to the village, sinks onto a pile of hay in the farmer's shed and falls asleep without eating.

Next morning the clouds run high and grey across the sky behind a stiff breeze from the north. On this tiny island there is only one farmer of any note, so the skyd duty always falls to him. He grumps his way down the stone steps to the tiny jetty, where Enok, chewing on a strip of dried fish, is throwing stones at the diving skua. Down fly the screaming birds, undeterred by the stones, beaks and talons ready to rake the intruders.

'Jesus, man,' muttered Enok, 'let us get under way before I am torn to ribbons! How do you live with these demons?'

The farmer is not inclined to talk. He jerks his head at the boat, indicating that Enok should get aboard and prepare the sail. Mercifully, the wind will allow them to scud down under sail — just the two of them manning the small craft, with a minimum of rowing. The sea runs with them — choppy, but no big swell. Enok sits amidships ready to luff the sail, and closes his eyes against the stinging spray. He remembers the story of Sigmund Bresterson, the ancient hero of the island they have just left, who was perpetually in scrapes with the church and the law and who had to escape across to Suðeroy by swimming this very sea. When he crawled ashore, Thórgrim the Evil killed him for the jewelled treasures he carried. Enok has always loved the saga, which his stepfather recounted with great style. As a child he imagined that the jewelled ring his father had found in the sea, and which hung even now on a thong around his neck, had come from that treasure, dropped by the hero as he waded ashore.

Enok thinks about swimming and how neither he nor Napoleon — nor any Faroese he can think of — have ever learned. And how the gods in the old stories could always swim prodigiously, and many of the heroes too. And how his own father walked into the sea on the very coast they are now approaching, knowing that he could not save himself if suddenly he changed his mind. Enok trails his hand in the cold grey water and shivers. He loves the sea — is never happier than when sailing on it — but the thought of swimming through it, of letting that deep expanse hold him up, fills him with dread.

His chance to learn the skill comes more quickly than he imagined. Enok, unable to keep up a silence for long, begins to expound one theory after another to the dour farmer. First a new way to secure the sail so it will respond more readily to the wind, and then a different kind of knot. The farmer eyes him sourly and says new theories are invented by the devil. Enok smiles and shakes his head, which seems to enrage the farmer further. Next it is the fishing tackle.

'But you should surely use a long-line in these waters,' says Enok. 'You would catch many more.'

The farmer grunts. 'What was good enough for our fathers is good enough for me.'

'You won't even try?'

'If you can't show respect, shut your mouth.'

The farmer's response should be warning enough, but Enok has to pursue the matter.

'We use a long-line in Sumba. Would you let Suðeroy go ahead of Skúvoy?'

The farmer spits into the sea and then changes tack abruptly. The swinging boom knocks Enok clean out of the boat. For a moment the farmer watches the thrashing boy, then he throws him a rope.

'See if your famous new theories can get you back aboard,' he growls, making no attempt to slow the boat or change its direction. Enok clings desperately to the trailing rope, half submerged, his fingers slowly numbing and losing their strength in the icy water. He has never felt such fear, the black sea closing over him. There is no way he can haul himself aboard. In that darkest moment it is Anahuia he thinks of, and his two unseen boys. He would call to them if he had breath to do so.

At the moment when he feels his fingers loosening and the sea about to claim him, the farmer pulls in the rope and helps to heave him over the stern. 'Now perhaps you will learn to trust your elders and your betters,' he says with some satisfaction. That is the last word he speaks to the shivering Enok. They run ashore at Hvalba and Enok, wet and exhausted, starts walking south to Sumba.

4.

Else Rasmussen tells the story
of her son's return

I SAW A tall man walking along the shore from the direction of Lopra and knew it was him. A mother knows. He leapt, reckless as ever, from one rock to another, and then onto the path, shading his eyes against the low sun. I watched from the house, afraid to move in case he disappeared by some trick of light and water and I was left with a dream of my own making. But oh, it was him all right, my great first-born son, greeting the fishermen down on the shore, clapping them on the shoulder as if he'd never been away, then striding up through the village, a bundle slung over his shoulder. By his walk alone I would have known him: that swinging gait, head high, looking side to side, open to anything or anyone that might come his way. Inviting the world in.

I should not let myself be seen when fishermen are setting out, nor is it proper for a woman of my status to stand in the doorway and shout for everyone to hear, but that day I surprised even myself. 'Enok!' I called, and then again, louder, 'Enok!'

He looked up and saw me. Broke into a run and near mashed my ribs, hugging me on the doorstep in front of the whole village! But you had to laugh. That was Enok all over — never one for the rules.

Safely inside, away from prying eyes, I could look my fill at this boy who had come back a man. Such a size! I am no slip of a thing but my head came only to his shoulder. His clothes, a sailor's canvas trousers and wool jacket, were in poor shape — I could see my needle would be busy — his hair every which way and a good few days' growth on his chin. But for all that, my son filled the room — the house! — with his — what is the word I search for? — with a kind of high spirit that is hard to resist. My good solid Hans laughed when I told him that. But I felt quite sure, on that first day, that here was a good man come back to bring his family joy. I was wrong, yes, but only partly wrong.

I set out dried whale meat that night, *and* boiled us each a stuffed puffin. We had potatoes and a kind of seaweed pickle I make and sheep's cheese with barley bread and honey. A feast! Hanna was there, of course — she had been slow to find a husband. She trotted in from the drying shed and greeted Enok calmly, as if he had never been away. Times enough I would like to put pins in that girl, even if she is my own daughter. The two boys and Hans came in late from the outfield, where the men had been working to get the last pluck of wool finished. A fine day is not to be wasted. They had already heard the news but still the boys were jumping and shouting, full of questions, until Hans had to settle them for prayers with a sharp word. Dorthe promised to come over later and bring the children to meet their lost uncle.

I was so happy that night, all the family around the fire. I know well enough the saying that the hearth-fire is the heart of the house, but unless the whole family is around that fire, the heart, for me, does not beat strongly. After dinner and the Bible (Enok fidgeting like a small boy — he was always better at talking than listening) we finally heard his story. Stories I should say: they were wonderful tales, full of sights and happenings you would never dream of. Can you imagine that he worked for the prime minister of Denmark, Bishop Monrad himself? Enok was his right-hand man, and sat often at his table and talked to his daughters and sons. That is something, even if the prime minister is no longer so important. Also Enok saved the bishop's little grandson from drowning in a lake full of eels and other strange creatures.

And the things he had made! Such beautiful scenes scratched into the surface of whale bone like the sailors do. One for me of a native house and a native woman sitting outside it and a native bird with no wings beside her. Enok swore it was all as he had carved it, smiling at me from eyes so blue and open; I was sure he was making half of it up.

Hans gave special prayers of thanks for the return of our son, and then allowed everyone to stay up late. Enok sang to us and played a wonderful instrument, pulling it out and in like breathing until it made sounds like a choir singing. He said there was no word in our language for it. We all sang along with him — a new tune he taught us but with old words that we knew. But the languages *he* could sing in! The boys were agog. Enok loved every minute: a blind woman could see that. Late in the evening he rummaged in his sailor's sack and brought out a wonderful scarlet coat, embroidered in gold and with a silver star on the chest. He put it on and struck nautical poses while the grandchildren screamed and wanted to touch. Then he told a story about how he got it. There were icebergs and sea battles and mysterious women of the sea; I remember Odin and Thor themselves had a hand in the adventure. All nonsense, of course. The jacket was far too small for my boy so you had to wonder, but the tale was a masterpiece. Even Hans, who prefers the truth of Bible stories, was caught up. Oh yes, Enok was happy to be home that night, I am sure of it.

The next day he helped carry peat from the far field, where it had been stacked to dry (Hans a little put out, I think, that my boy could carry twice his own load), and then the four men walked over the hill to the marks of land that had belonged to Magnus. A large area, as I knew well, having grown up there, with a big house, a little separate from the village, its own infield and two drying sheds.

Hans knew about Otto's gift — we all did — and had already laid plans for the future. On that land there was coal, which had been mined in the past, and Hans thought the mine could be opened up again. That night Enok, who had no great interest in farming — never had really, though we had forgotten that — entertained us all with crazy ideas for getting the coal out and down to the jetty. Some scheme of pulleys and ropes and brakes — I didn't understand half of it. He had a clever mind, always leaping this way and that — hit and miss, hit and miss — until he settled on some theory, and then you couldn't budge him off it. His stream of ideas annoyed my Hans, who has a slower way of thinking. Slow, but steady as a rock. Our boys — Hans's and mine — are like him: good farmers, hard workers. They will make fine husbands. No wild stories in their heads to draw them away.

Well, that good time didn't last. Enok couldn't settle; day by day he faded. I fed him good barley porridge and sheep's cheese, but nothing seemed to bring him into himself. It was as if his own hearth-fire had burned too low and threatened to die. He would walk off to the valley, spade in hand, ready to dig peat, but could not point to a single sod cut by day's end.

'Wake up, man,' my Hans would admonish him. 'You have lost the way of working. Daylight is precious and given to us by the good Lord for labour.'

Enok had begun to look right through you as if you were a ghost. He would shrug and say, 'I was thinking,' or, 'I had an idea.' Something like that.

'Thinking won't fill bellies,' said Hans. He was never really angry with Enok but you could tell he found the boy's dreaminess irritating.

After about a week of this I found him — Enok — sitting outside the sheep-drying shed when he should have been inside hanging the new carcasses. He looked out to sea, south, past the island. For a good minute I watched him and he never noticed. Just let the rain soak him while he hummed some soft tune over and over, all the time fiddling with a piece of wood — not carving it, just turning it in his hands. Humming and fumbling his wood like Sørine's boy on the other side of the valley, who is daft in the head and doesn't know better. It frightened me to see him like that.

I spoke quietly, not to startle him, 'Come inside, Enok. We must have words.'

He came like a lamb, smiling again. So beautiful, my boy. Taller even than his father and so like him. I wanted to hold him, to rub him dry, but of course he is a man now; it is not done. I feared for him, you see — feared that the darkness that had entered his father would take him too. It is not healthy to approach the dark months of the year with a mind that is also in shadow. It was February his father walked into the sea. So I spoke to him.

'Any mother can see you are unsettled, son, and that is unsettling the whole house-full, so out with it.'

Enok sat there like a big baby, put his head in his hands and groaned. 'It is too complicated,' he said. 'I cannot sort it all out.'

'Well talk then, you great oaf,' I said, 'and perhaps a wiser head can do the unravelling.'

Enok cast his eyes this way and that, over to the hearth and down at the floor, still fiddling with his piece of wood. His hands were never still.

'Is it a woman, then?' I asked him, for we were getting nowhere.

He looked me straight, then. 'It is,' he said, 'and more than a woman. It is two women — or even three — and a death, and two babies, and three marks of land.'

'Is this some kind of riddle?' I was sharp with him. I am one for plain speech.

'It is a riddle to me.'

He sighed then, and tried to tell me his woes. It was a woman, all right. A name I couldn't catch. Ana-something. She was half native, half Danish and some kind of slave, it seemed. Enok told me I would not approve and he was right. She lived in a simple native way but at least she did not eat human flesh, I was pleased to discover. He had heard that she had borne him twin boys, though he had never seen them.

'I cannot get her out of my head,' said my son. He seemed puzzled, though any natural man would think now and then of two sons he had never seen. 'She is there all the time. Waiting. I promised I would go back.'

'Well, that is one woman,' I said, now we were getting to the nub. 'I trust the other two are closer to home.' I was hoping he would mention Clara Haraldsen, who would be a very good match, and words already spoken between Hans and her father.

'Clara Haraldsen,' he said, reading my mind, 'is a sweet and lovely woman.'

Enok smiled at me then, some of his cheekiness returning, I was relieved to see, and told me he thought Clara preferred him over others.

'Over who?'

'Over my cousin Otto Dahl, who says he is betrothed to her.'

'What rubbish!' said I. 'I have not heard any announcement. In fact her father, Haraldsen, has spoken a favourable word in the ear of your stepfather just last week.'

That Otto Dahl was always a slippery boy — and more slippery than I had imagined when we came to the third woman.

'The third is whoever I must marry to hold the marks of land here on Suðeroy. Otto has stipulated that my wife must be from here or the deal is off.'

I had to close my mouth and think about that piece of news. Naturally, a good Suðeroy girl would be easy to find — several suitable and no doubt willing candidates sprang to mind. But Enok had education and travel in his life, as did Clara. The two were better suited. Also, that young puppy Otto Dahl should not dictate to his elders on the matter of marriage.

'Your stepfather will sort the matter out, count on it,' I said to my poor mooning boy. 'Otto Dahl does not enjoy the status of his grandfather. Hans Høgnesen is a senior priest and a landowner of importance. He has stood up to Dahls all his life and is not about to stop now.'

In all this talk of marriage, which is naturally a topic of great interest, I forgot about the death in his riddle. Finally Enok told the tale, and a sorry one it was. How he had had some stupid notion of freeing his native sweetheart and how his ruse backfired, causing the death of Napoleon Haraldsen. And how I was the first he had told. *And* how his conscience troubled him that he had not owned up. By the time the tale was told, the big lump was in tears, as well he might be.

'Enok of Suðeroy,' I said, 'it is past time that you must stop all this dreaming and storytelling and settle to a man's life. You were right, mind,' I said quickly, 'to keep the truth from the Haraldsens. It would do more harm than good and cause more pain. But it is good that your stupid act is off your chest and we will bury it together. Is that agreed?'

He seemed to accept my words. Certainly the next days he whistled at his work and brought home good catches of fish. There was a keenness in his eye again and a strength in his step as he walked over the hills. Unburdening your heart to another will untie knots that seem impossibly tangled to a single pair of hands. I began to plan for a wedding. June, I thought, or even St Olaf's, although that festival might hold memories too dark for Enok.

As I expected, Hans thought nothing of Otto's demands.

'Sign the paper, lad,' he said, 'but put a line through the part about the marriage. We will see who carries more clout if it goes to the Løgting for settlement. If Haraldsen and I join forces we will not be beaten by a boy, even if he is a Dahl. After all, you also are a Dahl, and should inherit, whether your cousin says so or not.'

On the matter of the kvæði, Hans was less encouraging. Naturally. He knitted his brows at the news that Enok had learned the third section.

'All the verses? From a *book*? How can you know it is right if you haven't learned from Finnur of Borðoy?'

Enok sighed and said he had heard it all before from old Niclas Patursson.

'Well, and isn't he right? That great man.'

Enok was never one to give in when words were involved. He said that the book was respected, that his version might be a little different but why not? That he had brought to his memorising the skills learned from the other two.

My wise husband was very doubtful. He saw the pitfalls. 'Are you ready to sing this section, lad?' he asked in his serious, careful way. He pointed out that the earlier stories dealt with heroism and dragons, with treasure and battles. 'That is your strength,' he argued. 'You are quite brilliant at reciting heroism. But the third tells of love and betrayal. Of subterfuge and death. This section is more subtle. I would not judge you old enough yet.'

Enok argued all night but got nowhere. Until he mentioned that he had promised Clara that he would sing, and had asked her to arrange a house for the performance. To my mind, naturally that put a different flavour on the project. Before the kvæði a betrothal would be announced. Afterwards a betrothal feast. Very suitable and proper.

Later, when we were alone, I made my suggestion and Hans was swayed a little, I could see that. Haraldsen had no son now. A union between our families would be highly advantageous for both. In the end he suggested to Enok that he devised a táttur and sang that instead of the kvæði. A satirical piece ridiculing Otto and the way he was unfairly undercutting other merchants, he suggested, would not go amiss. Make them laugh, he said, and you are halfway to destroying your rival.

Enok received this clever suggestion strangely. I expected him to argue again but he nodded in a quiet, thoughtful way — unusual for Enok — and walked straight out of the house, up the priest's path to the east. Everyone knows there are strange mist-folk up there among the cliffs. No man should walk there alone in winter. All that day until darkness set in I saw him on the skyline, pacing back and forth. That boy is so reckless! He knows the story as well as any, that if you walk between certain stones you will not live out the year or will grow suddenly old — wrinkled, white-haired and wasted in a matter of hours. But Enok was the kind who could not resist tempting fate. I would have sent Hanna up to drag him to his senses but the wool needed carding and fish cleaning and splitting for drying, not to mention food prepared for the evening meal, so I prayed to the good Lord and left the watching to Him. Enok came back the same age, at least. Do not laugh. These things happen.

SO we had our Christmas in Sumba, a good family time with candles and roast sheep. My husband preached a fine sermon about the three wise men and how their wisdom came from careful study of ancient prophecy and how they recognised the truth of the new event — the birth of Jesus — because they were wise in the old ways. I fancy the homily was pointed in Enok's direction, but we all took good advice from it.

Hanna, who had been even quieter and slower than usual since Enok returned, surprised us all on Christmas Eve. There we all were, warm and full of good food and listening to Hans read the Bible. A good peat fire glowing on the hearth. Perhaps it was the beer loosened her tongue. We had all drunk a mug of beer, which is a treat Hans allows on Christian feast days. For the past three years he has forbidden strong drink in the house as a general rule, to set a good example to the village, where more than one family are known to drink themselves silly far more often than is proper.

Well, after the Christmas hymn and a sea-song or two from Enok, Hanna suddenly asked her brother about going to New Zealand! Could a woman with no passage money and no husband go? she asked. That certainly brought a silence to the proceedings. Hanna — who could not settle to any husband for fear of leaving the family home; who would sit happily all day on her backside, growing fat while her mother toiled, if she were not prodded into action ten times a day. Naturally, I suspected the drink. Enok humoured her (as I thought then); said he thought there was a way. Some nonsense about a scheme to pay the passage of Danish girls who would marry Danish men-settlers and help to start up a Scandinavian colony there in that wild, savage country. Fool that I was, I laughed at the far-fetched idea and thought no more of it.

So the day came, twelfth night, when we set out for Tórshavn — Hans and me, Enok and Hanna — to hear Enok sing and to arrange a wedding. The boys preferred to stay with Dorthe and her family and enjoy our own island's festivities.

The few hours of daylight were blessedly clear, both the wind and the current in our favour.

'God is smiling on our endeavours,' said my good husband, who loves to sail, even though he is a priest and of Danish stock. 'We will easily make the harbour before nightfall.'

Enok smiled too, the wind in his hair and his face always set to the horizon. He spoke little on the voyage.

I do not like to remember the day of the performance but it must be told: it is part of his life. To me a good story is one you know already, from the Bible or from the Viking sagas, and if the ending is a sad one at least there are no surprises. That day of the twelfth night in Tórshavn took one strange twist after another until I didn't know whether I faced north or south and I longed to be home before my own hearth, living the straight line of my peaceful life again.

My husband said he had every reason to believe that the betrothal would be acceptable to all parties. Clara's father was in favour, but being a modern man with education he left the final word to his daughter. And everyone said she had eyes only for Enok. I could not get a plain word out of Enok on the matter, however cunningly I worded my questions. He smiled and said wait until after the singing. But there was a secret in his eye, which I thought meant he and Clara had come to an agreement and were teasing their elders by drawing out the moment. So I began the day cheerful and busy helping with the food. The head teacher had offered the school, which was generous in size but to my mind not as cosy as a house would have been, but we did our best with a warm peat fire and oil-lamps against the dark day. Icy snow rattled at the windows and froze the pathway, but a good and cheerful crowd gathered.

Enok would perform last. First there was poetry by this modern poetry club they have in Tórshavn. The good Lord spare us another. Let us get that Clara down to Suðeroy quick, I thought, in front of her own hearth and with babies at her side. Clearly she has too much time on her hands. The men were no better. Not a good tale among them — no story, nothing to stir your blood. Don't ask me what they were about, those poems: it was all a blur of high hopes and scenery in fancy words which they said were Faroese but which I would never use in a year of plain talk. Well, best forgotten quickly, like their newspaper, which has already gone out of print, they say. We are not ones for reading like the Danes and it is wasted time trying to force us against our custom. It is the same story as the plough.

So we came to Enok. He stood at the front of the classroom, splendid in the scarlet waistcoat I had embroidered for his father and his coat with its silver buttons, silver at his knees too. He stood easy, the fingers of one hand tracing the treasured ring on the other, smiling at them all. The whole roomful, who had been fidgeting through the poetry, were suddenly silent. Old Niclas sat in the corner, leaning on his stick, frowning at our boy as if willing him to do well. He looked frail, poor old soul: the winter is hard for the old ones.

So Enok signed for the circle to form and sang an introduction that was not like any kvæði nor even a táttur — more like one of his sea-songs. The chorus he gave us was different too. Not right, somehow. Old Niclas tapped his stick on the floor as if calling the dancers to their senses, but up they jumped, eager to begin. I thought to myself, these young things with their poetry and their newspaper and their fine words about holding on to the old ways do not always know as much as they think they do. There were a few smiles from the elders.

Hans and I let the young ones start; we would join the line later. I wanted to watch Clara, anyway. Otto took his place in the circle next to Clara, which did not please me, but her sweet smile was for Enok, which did.

> *Lend ear to the saga of Sjúrður and his Brynhild,*
> *Of their ill-fated love in far-flung land,*

sang Enok, his voice strong and warm.

> *New in its forming, nor sung e'er by man*
> *Now hear this sad tale, join heart and hand.*

Of course this was the next surprise. Who could tell whether that stubborn boy was singing a kvæði or a táttur? Sjúrður and Brynhild's ill-fated love is at the core of the third Sjúrður kvæði, but a new tale sung by none before? That would be a táttur. Old Niclas's head was wagging back and forth in disapproval but Enok was away and you had to listen.

The story started well enough, in the old style. A saga, no doubt of it. I have heard Finnur of Borðoy sing it once when I was a child and Enok captured the style wonderfully, from what I remember. No doubt Niclas Patursson would disagree. So we had Sjúrður journeying far, in search of adventure, forgetting his love for Brynhild. And we had those wicked Nibelungs plotting with their wile and guile to kill that hero. All in the room were well into the swing, the circle of dancers grown until it broke and began to snake around the room.

Then Enok changed his rhythm. It was so subtle you couldn't tell how he did it. I was dancing by then and suddenly found my feet stepping differently. I can't say what it was. But for a while we kept the line and the step going. The story was changing too. Of course we all knew the real version but suddenly that boy had us all ears over a completely new story. Oh, it was a ringing tale — but one of Enok's making, the cheeky boy. I thought Niclas would have a heart attack on the spot, the way the blood drained from his face.

Slowly the dancing ceased, the chorus faded away. Everyone was drawn into the new saga but you can't dance if you don't know how it will turn out. So we stood there facing him as he sang alone. I am one for the old ways, as you know, but I have to say he had me spellbound. Say what you like about the uproar when it was over — in the telling he was a master. My son is a storyteller born. Oh, the way he held us that night — his voice so strong and lively, singing the words directly into our hearts. I swear not a soul thought of criticism while the tale lasted.

And what a tale! Brynhild and Sjúrður and that wicked Nibelung clan were still the main characters, but in Enok's version the freeing of Brynhild told of a cunning ruse involving a perfect replica of the maiden, fashioned out of wood and branches and clothed in a beautiful embroidered gown. The replica was thrown into the river to fool the Nibelungs. But Sjúrður's plan misfired, because his companion and true shield-friend tried to rescue the dummy and was killed in the attempt, and of course Sjúrður was consumed with guilt.

Here Enok's voice changed. Somehow the tune was richer, deeper — more complicated, I suppose, than a true kvæði. Haunting and lonely, it sounded. That lamentation of Sjúrður had all our hearts aching. Enok took from his pocket a piece of carved wood on a string — a New Zealand singing stick — and whirled it above his head as he sang, making the loneliest, saddest moans you could imagine, like ghosts crying in the dark. My tears flowed rivers. I heard Clara Haraldsen sob out loud, for all her later protestations about lack of purity.

It was so skilfully done, so dramatic, that only later did I recognise the story. That soft-headed son of mine was making a disguised confession. He was singing about Napoleon Haraldsen's death! Only Enok would turn his own anguish into a story. And such a good one. At the end of the lamentation the despairing Sjúrður bared his breast to the tyrant's sword. The hero knelt, drew off his fabulous and cursed ring and offered it to the king of the Nibelungs, thus passing on the curse.

As he sang the last dramatic stanza Enok drew off his own ring — his father's ring, treasure found in the sea so long ago. In a great open gesture he held the ring towards us, as if he were offering it to any taker. There was not a sound in the room. No one knew what to do. Finally Enok broke the mood with a laugh and a bow.

The uproar and the argument that followed were almost beyond belief. Old Niclas stayed out of it, I'm pleased to say, but the young ones all had to have an opinion and to voice it loudly. The children loved it, of course, leaping around Enok as if he were the hero himself. That wild boy Lars Larsen tried on the ring, then feigned a horrible death, screaming that the curse had got him. But the students and the poetry club were another matter. How those noisy students argued and fussed! Enok had desecrated a sacred saga; the portrayal of Sjúrður was too unflattering; the use of instruments was not correct. Otto Dahl commended the performance but suggested the style was incorrect for a saga — his condescending praise more damning than the loud criticism. Oh, they were so full of them-selves, those young puppies, I could have slapped the lot of them!

What do they know of the real heart of a saga? Clara was clearly puzzled. 'Why, why?' she kept asking him, her eyes sad and hurt. 'After all we have done to preserve the sagas . . .'

Of course I knew. I could recognise the story well enough. My worry was whether any of the Haraldsens would make the connection. Then where would our betrothal be? Alas, I need not have worried on that score, as it turned out.

Finally old Niclas Patursson rose from his chair and began to hobble towards the door. Not a word said during all the pandemonium. Our Enok, who also had remained stunned and silent like an island in a stormy sea, broke from the mess of cheering children to bar his way. Others saw this and fell silent.

'Will you not offer an opinion when all the world seems to have one?' said my son, shaking his head as if to clear it of an annoying buzz.

The great old man leaned on his stick then, and looked up at his pupil. All waited to hear his words. 'Unfinished,' he said, and then after another silence while all waited, 'Not yet ready to be performed.'

Enok spoke only to him, quietly at first and then, as the argument developed, with a kind of force that betrayed his hurt.

'Must the performance always be perfect?'

'Yes.'

'Always follow the old rules?'

'Of course. The rules are there because they are right. Good.'

'But surely a new saga could follow new rules?'

Old Niclas moved his hand slightly as if to brush away cobwebs. 'Then it would not be a true kvæði.'

Enok's question was almost a cry. 'How, then, can we ever change?'

Old Niclas remained patient but would not give the boy an

inch. 'Our kvæði need no changing. They have already been perfected.'

He was right, I suppose, but oh, if only he had bent a little I might still have my son, and live to hear him sing again.

Enok had by this time worked himself up into one of his passions. Once he has his hook into an argument there is no way to reason with the boy. I have seen it all before.

'Perfection!' he cried. 'Perhaps your perfection is another word for reeled in and skinned and laid flat — and *dead*!'

He was going too far, as he always does. But I'll say this for old Niclas, the strong words did not anger him as well they might have.

'Enok, my son,' he said, forceful himself now and strong in his beliefs, 'the kvæði are old, yes, but additions may, from time to time — occasionally — be made. Listen to me, my good pupil. You have more talent than any ballad singer I have known, even your father. Your bold attempt tonight was very impressive, deeply moving and strong, though in several places incorrect in style and the content of your narrative unfinished, in my opinion. It is a brave man who wishes to create a new kvæði. But if you work at this piece for some years, if you incorporate important truths and tie the story more carefully to the old sagas (you have been surprisingly careless in this case), if you perfect the style and rhythm, then, *then*, your creation may, in generations to come, be accepted into the great body of Faroese kvæði. There could be no more noble endeavour. That is my advice as master to pupil.'

Enok took a deep breath. He could have been fighting tears. 'I cannot!' he cried. 'How can I do what you ask? This one here,' (and he thumped his own chest) 'is a different man from the pupil you taught. I have learned much from you, master, but also so much more now. From distant people who treasure different customs.

From ballad singers and dancers in other lands. My head is bursting with songs and stories and sights from more countries than I have fingers. How can I keep them locked away? How? I have no choice, and if I had I would not want to. They creep into my ballads, they knock on the closed doors of the kvæ∂i demanding entrance. I let them in gladly. "Join in!" I say. "Let us see what we can make together." '

Here Enok paused and cast his eyes over us all. Searching, I think, for someone who would agree with him. He knew what he was saying, though; knew his words would shock. With a small laugh that was also a question, he said, 'Surely my new tunes and instruments will only breathe fresh life into the old songs? After all, we must admit our kvæ∂i are at times a little dull.'

Dull! When he said that I knew he would go away. Already in his mind he was separate from us. Clara, I think, also saw that. Saw but could not understand. For all her education, she loves our traditions and would not rock boats or look for new ways. She is a good girl and I am sorry she is now only my niece instead of my daughter-in-law.

ENOK took very little with him. His scarlet storyteller's coat and a fresh set of clothes. A few tools. Also he took Hanna. That quiet girl had her fare to London saved up and was all prepared to leave! It nearly broke my heart to see her go. To think that she could prefer a life in that far country, whose name I will not speak, to a warm hearth here on her own island. Foolish, foolish girl.

As he left, Enok kissed me in front of everyone and then pressed into my hand the ring his father had passed to him.

'It belongs here,' he said.

I couldn't speak a word to save myself but held it out for him to take back.

'No,' he said, 'give it to someone else. I will make my own stories now.'

Those were his last words. You never knew what would come out of that boy's mouth, and half the time I don't think he knew either.

Thus I lost a son and a daughter. Their father had always dreamed of riding the whale-road to some imagined shore — of catching a wayward current. And so with these two. They reach for things beyond their grasp. If I had known Hanna harboured such desires perhaps I might have armed her against them. But how do you arm your children against dreams? Last year we had a sheep that would not stay within our village outfield but had to wander into the next. The boys tied that sheep to an old wise one until she learned better ways. So a sheep is taught. But with children? Alas, there is no way to tether them to the hearth-fire.

I fear Hanna and Enok will end their lives alone and unhappy.

Often now I think about that night when Enok sang. That argument between him and Old Niclas. Enok was playing with fire, of course, wanting to change our old ways (and never, *never* will I find our kvæ∂i dull), but still I hear echoes of that beautiful lament streaming in off the sea to ruffle the edges of my quiet life — and sweeten it.

5.

FOR SIX WEEKS, in 1872, Enok and Anahuia are both living in
the mushrooming settlement of Wellington, though neither knows
of the other's presence. For one thing, immigrant ships are flooding
the port with new arrivals, and for another, Enok and his sister
Hanna, sailor and assisted passenger aboard the ship *England*, are
stuck on the little hump of Somes Island in the middle of the
harbour. The voyage out was disastrous: sixteen deaths, most from
smallpox. Crew and passengers were promptly quarantined until
danger of spreading the epidemic was judged over. Enok raged and
fretted, anxious to get up to the Monrads' farm and see his sons, but
Hanna was happy enough, having met handsome Jens Olsen. Jens
walked off his farm in North Slesvig soon after the Prussians marched
in. The Germans, without word or warning, had lowered the Danish
flag over his town's post office and raised the Prussian one.

'I am not one to serve under people like that,' said Jens stoutly. 'They can have the farm, which was poor anyway. I will make a fine new one in this country.'

Jens escaped the smallpox that ravaged the ship, but his friend Las was the first to go down. Half the passengers blamed Las for bringing the scourge aboard from Europe, where an epidemic raged. Indeed, Las blamed himself. He wept and prayed to his God every day to save the children, but one after another the smaller and the weaker ones died, even though they had been vaccinated. On the other hand, Hanna and Enok stayed well, even though they had never even heard of vaccination, a mystery that led several desperate passengers to inquire what powerful and merciful god the Faroe Islanders prayed to.

Enok was amazed by his sister's transformation. Quiet, stolid Hanna was busy all day on the voyage out. She tended the desperately ill without fear, was never sea-sick, always cheerful. Enok, busy as he was with his duties, could hardly recognise this older sister, who had been renowned in all Suðeroy for her lazy ways.

'Well,' she laughed, 'now I have an adventure of my own to be cheerful about. Back home I was simply sitting waiting for it to happen.' And off she would bustle, a favourite among all the immigrants, especially Jens.

On Somes Island the two were married by the ship's captain, who was incarcerated with them. Winter was setting in and that day a cold wind howled unchecked between headlands and up the harbour, bringing rain and hail to batter the little island. Inside the long wooden hut, salt-encrusted windows rattled, walls creaked and draughts chilled the travel-weary Scandinavians. But for all that, the wedding was a cheerful affair. Enok sang and led the dancing. No one had money for a feast, but after all the deaths the Scandinavians were pleased to witness a new life beginning. Besides, new cases of smallpox had been absent for three weeks, and soon they would be free to go. Hanna and Jens danced together in the centre of an applauding crowd, a strong and handsome couple.

The very day the quarantine is lifted, Enok finds work on a coastal trader bound for Foxton. Hanna and Jens are headed for the Scandinavian Camp, up over the hills and then east into the deep bush of the Wairarapa. Jens has been allocated twenty-five acres of tree-covered land. Now the couple owe the government twenty-four pounds and six shillings, which Jens will pay off by working on the new roads. There is grumbling and even a formal complaint from some immigrants, who expected to go to the more settled areas around Foxton or the new town of Palmerston North. Hadn't Viggo Monrad, son of the bishop himself, written of the opportunities there? And of Scandinavian families already settled and ready to welcome them? But Jens puts an arm around his buxom and glowing wife as they farewell Enok, and says they will manage somehow.

Hanna looks up at her young brother, tall and strong, the fair skin of his face cracked and wind-burnt from the long voyage, his bleached hair tied back with a plaited leather thong. High on his shoulder sits his dirty canvas bag containing all he owns in the world.

'Thank you, brother,' she says. 'Thank you for this chance. I hope you find your Ana.' Hanna speaks quietly. Her Jens would not approve, perhaps, of such a relationship. 'I would like to know how it turns out,' she adds. This said without much hope: communication of any sort in this big raw country is going to be difficult until she learns to speak English.

Enok grins and shifts his feet, ready to be back on the water. 'Get someone to write to the Monrad farm, maybe. But I won't be there long. This time I will find a way to bring her with me.'

Hanna tut-tuts like a big sister should. She knows, by now, the true story of Napoleon's death. 'Well, keep your head out of the clouds and your boots on solid ground. You have children to think of, remember. If you can manage it, which I doubt, try to be sensible. Time to grow some roots.'

Enok laughs. 'Well, I will try. And write to "Conrad": that is how I am known here.'

Hanna groans. 'There you are! Off again. Inventing some imaginary fellow. I heard about the navy — how you changed your name there too. But why, silly boy? Anyone would recognise you on a dark night in a storm just by your size. What is wrong with Enok?'

The tall man shrugs. 'It just happens. New adventure, new name, I suppose.'

'Running away from old adventures, more like. Grow up, Enok.'

For a moment it seems that Enok will argue, will stand there on the windswept wharf extolling the virtues of invention, but a cry from the leader of the Wairarapa expedition catches their attention. The cavalcade of drays, laden with people, supplies and tools, is setting out. Jens and Hanna run to take their place, while Enok climbs the plank of the little coastal steamer, heading for Foxton.

ANAHUIA never discovered how she managed to miss him. Perhaps she was up at the Methodist Mission, or collecting seafood along the bay with Erenora, the day he came ashore from Somes Island. You would think, with Scandinavians in town, she would have been particularly vigilant, or that one of the labourers on the wharves might have noticed the blond giant and reported it. But on a cold day, with the wind whipping the spray into your face, you pulled your cap low and hunched your shoulders and got on with it.

So Conrad was missed.

6.

IF CONRAD HAD taken time to ask a few questions at Foxton, his life for the next several years might have taken a very different turn. But then, as the blond giant himself liked to point out, many strange and interesting experiences would not have been available for later storytelling. Coal descending from the sky in great wagons for example, or deformed monsters who could quote every word of the Bible.

And other stories.

Had he taken a walk through the bustling town he might have exchanged a few words with Reverend Duncan Taylor, who was visiting a newly arrived settler down by the river; he might have greeted Tomas Uppadine Cook at the door of his hotel or paused to kick a ball with some of that man's many children. Any of these people could have told him that Olga Monrad was at that very moment in town with a sickly child, visiting the German doctor. They might have laughed and told the story of how every time she visited the doctor — which was often — Olga insisted that he turn to the wall the portrait of Bismark that hung behind his desk. Not a word would be exchanged until the face of that hated Prussian leader, who had destroyed her father-in-law's fortunes, disappeared from sight.

Had Conrad waited to greet Olga Monrad or even to beg a ride back to Karere in her trap, he would have learned a different story about Anahuia. But on this fine and chilly April morning, 1872, Conrad is in a hurry. At the little Foxton wharf he steps off his trading steamer, spots a young Maori lad sitting smoking a pipe in the stern of his waka tiwai and negotiates with him by sign-language and a few rusty words of the native language. Within an hour he is helping to pole the canoe upriver through the great Ohutuiti Swamp. Conrad always prefers to travel on water if the opportunity presents itself.

Apart from Conrad's canvas bag, they are transporting two sacks of flour and one of sugar, a small bag of salt and a battered old tin full of something precious, which the lad keeps close to him. Conrad has not the language to ask what is in it and the lad doesn't offer. The wind is mercifully at their backs and the river lazy, which makes the journey easy. Conrad kneels in the prow, incongruously large in this small canoe made from the trunk of a young totara. Gradually he learns the rhythm of the long punting strokes that drive the canoe inland against the seaward flow. The lad in the stern poles too, laughing and righting the balance effortlessly when Conrad's enthusiasm threatens to overturn the craft.

All day they pole upriver in their private world, hemmed between high walls of flax plants and rushes. Ducks clatter into the air as they approach but the brilliant red-legged pukekos ignore them, stalking on through the shallows, intent on their prey. The sun warms their backs, the flax shelters them from the breeze, and soon the two are sweating. Gradually they leave the great swamp behind. Now there are patches of cleared land; willows, planted by farmers, lean over the river. They skirt numerous mud-banks and low-lying islands of this broad and meandering Manawatu River.

'Manawatu,' says Conrad aloud, remembering the meaning. His own heart, though, does not stand still: it pounds, rather, and not only with the effort of poling. He has no plan. Has not the language to negotiate with Anahuia's hapu. It is growing dark.

When the lad points to a small collection of huts on the bank and indicates that this is the end of his journey, Conrad is glad enough. He turns down offers of a meal and shelter, and walks on alone up the riverbank, gnawing on a cold potato as he goes. He begins to recognise landmarks in the dusk. Where a wild peach tree stands on a raised bank he stops. The peaches are small and sour but he eats them anyway, looking down at the quiet water. This would be close to the place where Napoleon charged into the river and drowned. Conrad gathers ponga fronds and pig-fern for a bed. He pulls his heavy coat around him and sits there in the dark. After a while he takes the carved flute from his pocket and begins to play: a high sad lament of his own making. The notes echo across the black water. Then far away, from the other bank, a morepork calls. Conrad stops to listen. Blowing softly into his flute he tries to imitate the two tones and to elaborate on them. The owl answers, its two notes steady, perhaps disapproving of the decoration. Conrad smiles in the dark, his heart eased. He sleeps.

IN the morning, dirty and unshaven, he walks into the kainga where Anahuia had lived. It looks smaller, the low huts dilapidated, the flattened mud of the yard sprouting weeds. A fire surrounded by stones smokes in front of a hut, a blanketed young woman tending it; a bone-thin dog barks. He stands at the edge of the clearing and calls her name.

'Anahuia!'

He is both excited and apprehensive. The young woman looks up for a moment, then turns her attention back to the pot over the fire. Something feels wrong.

'Anahuia!'

A big man crawls out of a hut on the other side of the yard. He stands, shading his eyes against the morning sun and then, grinning, shouts a welcome.

'Te Ma! Haere mai! Tena koe!'

Conrad grins back, relieved. This is Rua, the easy-going man who organised the eel drive, who first named him Te Ma — the white one — and who admired Te Ma's abilities in singing and carving. Rua says something to the girl, who comes to offer Conrad a tin mug of hot, sweet tea. Both men squat to drink their tea in the sun. Rua sings a phrase of a song Conrad had taught the hapu. He puts his own actions to it, then laughs uproariously, slapping Conrad's shoulder and shaking his head. Conrad would like to join in but is too anxious. Where are all the others? Matene and his family? Perhaps Anahuia is up at the big house? When it is clear that Conrad has forgotten most of his native language, Rua switches to halting English.

'Anahuia? But she long ago went. Not here.'

'She was free to go?' Conrad tries to keep his voice and face neutral, not wanting to offend, but the news is exciting. Anahuia free! 'Where did she go?'

'I te kainga. Her home.' Rua holds up his hand to halt further questions and indicates the door of the hut. 'Hou mai. Come, come. Pakura knows answers.' Rua waits while Conrad removes his boots.

'Pakura very sick. This girl and me must wait here. When she die we go to the whanau. We all have gone downriver. Better place. Hou mai, hou mai!'

Inside it is dark and strangely warm. The old woman lies on the floor wrapped in blankets, at her feet a small heap of stones — the source of the warmth. The girl removes two cooling stones and takes them to the fire outside, then, using an old shovel, brings two hot ones to replace them. The old woman murmurs something. Her eyes are closed. Rua motions Conrad to sit to one side of her, then seats himself at her head and leans low to speak in her ear.

Conrad tries to follow the conversation but is lost immediately. The old woman's voice croaks; often the words trail away into silence. He hears the word Anahuia and his own name — Te Ma — but can make out little else. At one time Rua frowns, looking quickly over to him and then away again. He asks another question and breathes in sharply. Conrad shifts uncomfortably. Something is wrong. The air in the hut is thick; a smell of decay comes off the old woman. She opens her eyes and slowly turns her head to look at Conrad. The black eyes are fierce and desperate, but recognition is there, too. Conrad feels her strength like a strong presence in the hut, as if she is holding tightly to life and will not let go. She speaks again and this time Rua answers strongly. Conrad feels that he is reproving her. He waits. Finally, after a long silence during which the old woman seems to have fallen asleep, Rua tries to explain.

'The news is bad,' he says, 'but she knows all this kind of thing. That woman Anahuia is dead.'

'Dead!'

'All her whanau, whole kainga dead. Pakeha sickness dead them all.'

'Her children?'

Rua speaks to the old woman. 'Nga mahanga?'

'Kua mate,' whispers Pakura. 'Kua mate e rua.'

'Both dead.'

Conrad sits in silence. It has never entered his head that he would come all this way and find her gone.

'Is she quite sure?' he asks finally.

'She say Anahuia a bad girl because she don't come back . . .'

The old woman interrupts, her voice stronger. Rua smiles and pats her blankets. He jerks his head towards the doorway and Conrad follows him outside.

The sunlight is bright after the dim and smoky hut. Rua hawks up phlegm and spits. Conrad walks away and then back. He can't keep still, wants to run or shout or hit something.

Rua giggles and looks down at his feet. 'Sorry,' he says, 'my words not good.'

'What did she just say then?'

'That kuia says we speak too loud. Want to sleep.'

'Was she angry with Anahuia?'

'Ae. Say Anahuia should stay, look after old Pakura. Not go away. Say Anahuia sickness is utu — punishment. Curse. That kind of words. No one left to cook her food and warm her.'

'Rua,' Conrad places a hand on the man's shoulder, and again the big man giggles in embarrassment, 'Rua, are her words true?'

'True, yes. Of course. Those Ati Awa got sickness bad. Many kainga all dead. Pakura knows all that things.'

Conrad groans. It is too hard to speak further. With a nod that he hopes conveys thanks, he walks away from the little settlement, into the bush beside the river then up towards the Monrad farm. Now the peaceful scene is hateful to him: the flat fields scarred with ugly stumps, the muddy and slow-moving river, the still air which seems to be waiting for some further terrible news. He breaks into a run, leaping logs and scattering sheep, but the feeling of doom, of being cursed himself, keeps pace with him.

Close to the big house a single man is hoeing weeds in a field of potatoes: not someone he remembers. Conrad tries Danish and is absurdly pleased to hear his greeting answered. He learns that none of the Monrad family is at home. Herr Viggo Monrad is in Palmerston North pursuing business there. His wife and a child are unwell. Fru Monrad has taken the children to Foxton to consult the doctor. He is unsure when they might return.

Claus produces bread and cheese. Together they sit on a log, eating and exchanging news. Conrad finds himself telling this stranger the story of Anahuia and his long voyage back to find her. Claus has never heard of the woman, never heard her mentioned.

'She was so strong and full of life,' says Conrad, still unable to believe it. 'How can she suddenly be dead?'

Claus is of the opinion that the native Maori are very prone to disease and for that reason he will never marry one. 'Even though good Danish women are hard to find, I would rather wait.'

Conrad, lost in his own world, doesn't hear. 'I thought I could feel her waiting. You know? I could *feel* her. But now they say she was dead, maybe all the time I was sailing here.'

'Take my advice and marry your own kind. Don't rush is the best thing, friend.'

'I never saw my two sons. Never even knew their names.'

'You are young. Others will come. Good Danish sons.'

Conrad stands, weary of this stolid fellow.

'Please give my greeting to Herr Monrad and his wife when they return.'

Claus stands too and stretches. 'I will. You won't stay?'

'No.'

'What now, friend? There is work here, if you want it.'

Conrad looks around sadly. 'I am not a farmer. First I will visit her kainga by the sea. Maybe there is a grave. Then who knows?'

'Are you interested in mining? They say there is still gold in the south.'

Conrad makes a sound that is part laugh, part sob. 'Mining! There was coal on my own land on my own island half a world away but I left it for this new adventure. I am a simple fool.'

But an hour later, swinging down the long track south, through farmland and bush, heading into a rising wind, Conrad Rasmussen, Faroeman, feels his heart lift again at the thought of new sights still unseen and of oceans yet to be sailed.

7.
Change

WELLINGTON, NEW ZEALAND
SYDNEY, AUSTRALIA
1870–82

1.

ANAHUIA'S FIRST MONTHS in Wellington were not as rosy as she might suggest in the later telling. The experience unsettled her more than she would admit.

'You won't find it easy,' warned a farmer who had given her a ride in his cart, on the last few miles into the town. Anahuia sat beside him on the seat, her babies wedged between bales of flax and sacks of potatoes behind her. The farmer, a Ngati Toa from Porirua, regularly brought food to sell from his tribal acres, but had no time for the rapidly growing capital.

'Rules for this, rules for that, and militia-men to put you in jail for no reason at all,' he grumbled. 'You should have stayed in the country with your own tribe.' He looked critically at her light eyes and light skin. 'If you know it,' he added.

'I am Te Ati Awa from the Pukeroa hapu,' said Anahuia with as much dignity as she could muster, given the jolting cart and crowded seat.

It seemed this was worse than not knowing. The old fellow spat into the dust at the side of the road — a road broader and smoother than any Anahuia had seen.

'Oh, well then, you'll be set and sitting pretty,' he said, a nasty glint in his eye. 'Your lot are in with the government and have plenty of land, not to mention fine houses and all the trimmings. You'd do best to go to them — old Te Puni and all his family. Sold our land as well as his own, the son of a dog. And Ngati Raukawa's. And Ngati Mutunga's. He's the one got us into all this mess. It's no use him apologising now and saying he was tempted by the muskets and blankets. What about us? He sold the land right under the pa belonging to my relatives down here. Came down from Taranaki not so long ago and then hopped into bed with the Pakeha the minute they arrived. You'll get on fine with that lot with your Pakeha looks. They'll find you a husband to look after you.' He spat again.

Anahuia remained silent, unsettled by his vehemence. Her brother's fierce beliefs and now this tirade. She decided to keep the babies well hidden for the time being.

As they came down over the hills and reached the beautiful harbour, ringed with hills, the farmer pulled on his reins sharply and pointed up the valley. 'Pito One — that's your way. Te Ati Awa land. I'm headed for the wharves. Go on, off you hop.'

He gave her no choice. Anahuia climbed down and stood at the edge of the road as he clucked his horse into motion again, headed south towards a large collection of buildings rising up from the water's edge. Slowly she slung the babies across her shoulder and took up her bundle. Pito One looked a good distance away around the shore, and anyway Anahuia was more interested in being near the wharves, where Conrad might arrive one day in the future.

On the broad road that skirted the shore a carriage approached then rumbled past, the finely dressed men seated high and frowning ahead, the women inside looking out at her as if she were some interesting curiosity. A heavily loaded dray pulled by two enormous horses passed the other way but the driver gave no sign of noticing her, let alone offering a lift. Anahuia sighed and set out north in the direction the farmer had indicated. She would need shelter and help if she were to survive in this busy world. And it sounded as if this branch of Te Ati Awa did not share her brother's abhorrence of all things Pakeha. Surely her babies would be safe.

Five minutes along the road a woman's voice called from above.

'Eh, girl, come in and rest. I saw that good-for-nothing Ngati Toa excuse for a trader dump you in the road — may his bones be picked bare by birds! Come on, come on in, you poor soul, loaded down like that. Come on up and rest.'

A large woman, dark-skinned, her black hair wild around her head and a tattered dress hanging limp over a pregnant belly, stood in a garden a short distance above the road. The land there formed a broad shelf, and behind the rows of vegetables Anahuia could see three huts set close together. The roofs were rusted iron, though the walls were built of traditional ponga logs. Over a brush fence three small children watched her, their black eyes interested. Dogs barked.

The woman leaned on a hoe and gestured vigorously with the other arm. 'Don't mind those stupid dogs. They would bark on their way to heaven. There's no shelter between here and a good distance north. You will be caught out if you go on. Hoani! Carry the woman's kete for her! Himona! Open the gate!'

And so she continued, introducing herself and her five children as she guided Anahuia up the slope through the neat rows of cabbage and beans and potatoes to a bench in front of the largest of the three huts.

Erenora, for this was her name, was philosophical about the babies' colouring. 'Oh well, we have seen plenty of this, my dear, haven't we? Never mind. They are good healthy boys, which is a blessing these days and rare enough. I have lost three. Are they baptised?' When she heard they were not she advised against Bishop Hadfield and his Church of England (even though he spoke good Maori) in favour of the Methodists, whose mission ran a very generous kitchen. But Erenora's loudest exclamations came when she heard Anahuia's lineage. 'The Pukeroa hapu! But my husband is related by marriage to them! Your good mother Paora's second brother — or was it the youngest? — married one of Tipene's cousins! Wait till Tipene hears this! You're Te Ati Awa from further up the coast then? Exactly! The very same! Sit here and rest, my dear, while I call Tipene.'

A month later Anahuia was still living with the family. She was happy enough to rest, to work in the garden, enjoy the games of the children and Erenora's cheerful chatter. Her twins, following Erenora's advice, were duly baptised at the Methodist Mission in Wellington and received clothes and a Bible and a fine Sunday lunch of meat stew and potatoes. The good ladies of the mission welcomed her and promised to keep an eye out for any Conrad or Enok Rasmussen who might come to the port. Anahuia loved that visit to the town — the crowds in their fine clothes promenading on the Sunday afternoon, the bristle of ships' masts in the harbour, the amazing size of some of the buildings — they could surely house hundreds! One week she offered to help Tipene take his vegetables to the market and proved herself useful, negotiating a good price. Anahuia had a quick ear for language, it seemed, and could soon converse in English more comfortably than the slower Tipene.

Erenora's husband was a large man and older than her by several years. He was good-natured enough, though often silent from morning until night, sitting on the bench outside the doorway, smoking his pipe and watching the traffic pass on the road below. Sometimes he saddled the horse and headed north to the Hutt Valley where he had relatives, and would be away for a few days. Erenora, Anahuia and the children worked in the garden. Anahuia's skill with needle and thread delighted Erenora.

'Aue! You have fingers like the wind. These rough paws of mine would make a rats' nest of it in three blinks of an eye.' And she would find another child's shirt in need of repair.

Both women commented on the ridiculous fashion worn by English women. Anahuia could not believe they would waste so much material, bunching and fluffing the stuff behind, yet hobbling their poor legs in front so they could barely walk.

'What do they hide under those big bottoms?' laughed Erenora. 'I would like to unwind a fine lady and see!'

But Anahuia was fascinated. On her visits to town she watched closely the way clothes were cut. She loved the look of the fine, smooth materials in glowing colours, the way one colour was matched to another so that a dress was striped and banded and tucked in patterns as complicated as the markings on Erenora's ginger tabby. Back home she would try to imitate the fine embroidery and tucks, altering her one dress over and over until she was satisfied. Learning new skills and a new language, her days passed easily enough.

In time, Anahuia began to feel Conrad might be expected. He had been gone more than a year. Enoki and Hoani, the twins, were now walking, staggering their way into mischief, bigger already than Erenora's two-year-old. Anahuia took every opportunity to visit the wharves and make inquiries. She was well known there by now, often earning a shout of greeting — or a rougher invitation

— from a sailor or trader working there.

'Here comes the lovesick lady!' they would shout. Or 'Here I am, sweetheart — just call me Conrad and I'll serve the purpose!'

She would smile and nod but hold on to a reserve that none could break — or only one, and he regretted it for a good month afterwards, nursing a thick ear and a bruised face and having to endure ribald comments from his mates.

The only sailor who had seen or heard of the big Dane was the one who had sailed with him aboard the *Asterope* on that first voyage back to England.

'A grim voyage, lady,' he said. 'The cap'n were sick before we left this shore and then croaked on us not two week out. Just as well we had that Danish bishop on board. A useful kind of a fellow in a storm, for he read the last rites for the cap'n and then gave our poor first mate, who were thick as a plank on his navigation, a helping hand. But for that bishop we might of fetched up on God knows what wild foreign shore. Your man Conrad were a right darlin' of the crew, too. Sing! He could find a tune for any occasion — doleful or merry — and argue a point till he had you turnin' your thoughts about-face without knowing it. Cunning bastard. But we loved that foreign giant for his big heart and his grand voice. Useful aloft in a storm, too.'

'And when you reached England?' Anahuia asked.

'He was off, wasn't he? Along with the bishop and his mess of lovely ladies. Never saw him again. The world's a wide old place when you're on the sea: you can lose a man soon as blink your eye.' And then, seeing Anahuia's face, added, 'Good luck to you, sweetheart, anyways. I can surely understand your liking for the fellow.'

As she returned to Ngauranga after one of these trips, riding on the cart's plank-seat with Tipene, he removed the pipe from his mouth and spoke to her — an unusual event.

'Time to move,' he said.

Anahuia waited for more but none came. The wind was keen this late afternoon; small white-caps broke against the shore, flecking the cart and its occupants with spray. Tipene hauled an empty sack from the tray behind them and handed it to her. He had been courteous over the past months, and generous, but she had never felt drawn to him as she did to Erenora. Now she received the sack gratefully and huddled under it.

'Time for who to move?' she asked.

'For you.'

Anahuia thought about this. She also was feeling a desire to move. Did silent Tipene recognise more of her feelings than she realised? She waited for more.

After a plodding mile Tipene said, 'My cousin in Pito One. His wife is dead. I have an obligation to him. I have offered you.'

Anahuia drew breath to protest but Tipene raised a hand to silence her. The imperious gesture reminded her of Bishop Monrad: the way he liked to conduct an interview.

'He is a good man,' said Tipene, looking straight ahead. 'Not so big a garden as us but enough. There are four children who need a mother. You need a man to protect you and your boys.' The big man nodded, as if pleased with this long conversation. Before he replaced his pipe, signalling the end of the conversation, he added, 'He has agreed to take your Pakeha boys.'

Perhaps, thought Anahuia, he takes my silence for agreement. In fact her feelings were so strong she feared to open her mouth. She pulled the sack closer so he could not see her face. She glared out at the wild sea. Here was another man willing to trade her against an obligation, who assumed she was available for such a purpose. This time, she swore, it would not happen — no way would she let it happen. On they plodded, in silence. What to do now needed some thought.

Erenora, seeing her grim face, greeted her with some anxiety. 'He has told you?'

'Yes,' said Anahuia, bending to pick up Enoki, trying to remain calm.

'I know that man, Whiri,' said Erenora. 'A little old perhaps, but not so bad — you could do worse, and after all, it is better to have your own husband. And your own house to care for.' Grinning, she dug Anahuia in the ribs. 'You will need more babies. Why not some good brown ones for a change, eh?' She looked for a moment at Anahuia's set face and added quietly, 'There is nothing to be done, girl. Accept it. Tipene has made up his mind. And you must think of this — so many of our people have died it is our duty to have babies.'

'I'm sorry, Erenora,' said Anahuia, unable to keep her peace any longer, 'but I cannot agree. My Conrad will return soon . . .'

'Conrad, Conrad — we have heard enough of him! Forget your lost Pakeha man, girl; everyone knows he will never come back. A stubborn heart is no use to anyone. So then, be happy! No more talk of the big Danish man. Whiri is the husband for you.' Erenora turned her attention to a crying child. 'Now, give me a hand with dinner. Did you bring the pork?'

TWO days later, news came that the chief Te Puni had died and there would be a great tangi at his marae. The government had declared a bank holiday for their good friend, and all the important men in the capital would pay their respects at the funeral. Tipene made preparations to take the whole family, along with a slaughtered pig and sacks of vegetables to help provide for the occasion. He also planned to introduce Anahuia to her new husband.

'Since we are going that way,' rattled Erenora, bundling children and provisions into the cart, 'we can leave you and the babies with Whiri after the tangi. All his family will be there.' She sighed. 'It will be their gain and our loss. They are lucky to be getting such a clever woman into their household.' Smiling, she embraced Anahuia, smoothed her hair and admired her dress. 'I'll miss you, my tall friend. But it is kind of my man Tipene to find a good place for you, so look a bit cheerful, girl. It is not *your* funeral.'

Anahuia had other plans for the tangi, but held her peace.

THE celebration for Te Puni's death was indeed impressive. So many dignitaries from the capital wanted to attend that a ship was commandeered to bring them across the harbour. Anahuia, already arrived at Pito One beach, stood on the tray of the cart with the children and cheered to see the *Rangatira* steam across, its decks crowded with top-hatted men, Bishop Hadfield standing out from the field of black suits — a single purple flower. On the beach, tents had sprouted overnight like mushrooms and there must have been fifty canoes pulled up. The old chief might have earned enemies in his life but who would deny him respect at his death?

From the marae came much wailing and calling on of dignitaries; on the beach a haka party challenged those who stepped ashore, whether they were men from the government or important parties from allied tribes. In all the bustle and noise Anahuia found it easy to slip away from her little party on the pretext of chasing after her toddlers, who were into everything. She had seen someone she knew — a deckhand from the *Rangatira*. Tom stood at the end of the jetty, leaning against a bollard, enjoying the sun and the spectacle.

'Hey there, Ana,' he grinned with a wink and a cuff to the little boys. 'Here's one face I know, then, in all this boil. What a to-do! Are you part of it all?'

'I should be up there peeling a mountain of potatoes but the boys are determined to get into that water, as you can see!' She laughed and hauled a dripping fellow out of the waves. 'Noki here would walk straight out to his death if I'd let him.'

Tom was surprised to find her so ready to chat. Ana had a reputation on the wharves back in Wellington: friendly up to a point, but definitely not for sale, nor any other favour if you pushed your suit. Best, everyone said, to keep your distance. Silly Notso Gully nearly had his block removed when he tried, one drunken evening, to get too close. But today Ana had a purpose, which soon became clear.

'Tom, could you get me on board, do you think?'

'What, on the *Rangatira* here?'

'Me and the boys. I need to disappear — don't ask why — and these lads are too heavy to carry all the way back to the capital.'

Tom was intrigued. Also keen to join in a bit of an adventure that would earn him a pint, maybe, in the retelling back at the wharves.

'Well now, can't see the harm,' he said. 'There'll be a crush going back and I'd say you'd not be noticed, but for your clothes. The ladies are trussed up like pigeons in all their finery and bonnets.'

'Don't worry, I'll tuck away quietly.' Ana gave Tom her hand like a man. 'I'll remember this, friend. Would you keep a quiet tongue on you for the time being?'

'Ah well, I would if the lady would promise to tell me the story first when it is available!' Tom let out a guffaw. 'I don't mind betting there's a man in it, and he won't be your lost Conrad, for no one has set eyes on that deserter!'

Ana gave Tom a chilly smile and he decided to press the matter of the mysterious Conrad no further.

'I'll be back later,' she said. 'Just before the official party come aboard.'

Back peeling potatoes alongside Erenora she chatted and worked cheerfully, until that woman paused in her work to wipe away a tear.

'I'll miss you about the house, and so will the children, but I can see you've come to realise you have a better life ahead of you.'

'I have,' said Anahuia. 'Thank you for your friendship and your care. I would not have survived easily if you had not welcomed me. I'll remember you always.'

'Eh, girl,' laughed Erenora, 'you are only moving up the road! We'll see each other at family occasions. You won't have to remember this fat old face for long before it is in front of you again.'

'I hope so,' said Anahuia quietly.

2.

A letter to Olga Monrad,
Karere, via Foxton

16 Jervois Quay
Wellington
12th March 1871

Dear Fru Monrad,
Please go with God.

I hope that you are well and your children thriving. A sailor on the wharves here has brought news that you and Herr Viggo Monrad are back at Karere and that the wars are no longer dangerous in your area. I am glad to hear it.

My boys are doing well. I have named them Enok and Johan after their father and my father, but mostly they are called Noki and Jackie. I have taken the name

Rasmussen as my second name. Here it is important to have two names, particularly with two babies. My boys walk and are beginning their first words. I will teach them Danish, but first English and our native tongue. I have baptised them and myself in the Methodist religion. There is no Lutheran church here. The ladies at the mission have been kind and find me work.

You will be pleased to know that your gift has helped also in finding that work. I live in a small room close to the wharves and take in sewing to mend. Also I am beginning to stitch new clothes, which are a great shortage here. Again I am thankful to you, Fru Monrad, and to your mother-in-law, who have taught me by example the skills I need for this work.

I have learned to speak and write English, so please forgive if my Danish is not correct. This is my first Danish writing. Also this is my first letter. A kind woman from Copenhagen is helping me.

There are very, very many people here. This was a big surprise to me. I thought Foxton was the biggest town. Perhaps Foxton also is growing a big city? Every day more people arrive. Some from Denmark but they went to another place they call Seventy Mile Bush. Not your side of the mountains. But perhaps anyway you meet them and help them?

I have a favour to ask, if you please. Please tell Conrad Rasmussen my address here as written at the top of this page. Perhaps it is too early to expect him back but just in case. I keep watch over the ships arriving here but there are so many it is hard to know. I might miss or he might arrive at Wanganui or

Nelson. I do not expect him to arrive until maybe a few months more, but please keep me in mind because no other person can tell him. My mother and family are all passed away or gone so I have come here.

While I wait I am happy. I send greetings to you and to Herr Monrad and to little Ditlev.

Live with peace.

God bless you and your family

Arohanui

Anahuia Rasmussen

3.

A STORY ANAHUIA never tells her grandchildren is the one she thinks of as The Night the Whalers Came to Town. Often it comes back to her and she smiles as she sews — or sheds a tear — but the events of that night are too personal, too charged with conflicting emotions for her to turn them into a good tale, so she keeps this one for herself.

IT is November 1873 and the boys, Noki and Jackie, are almost four years old. Anahuia Rasmussen, seamstress, now rents three rooms above James O'Halloran Saddlers on Jervois Quay. The ladies who visit the ships — and there are many, be assured — favour Mrs Rasmussen because she asks no questions and because she has a wonderful eye for draping the bustle just so, or for matching surprising colours that will catch a sailor's eye (and consequently his purse-strings).

The seamstress is respected down on the waterfront but she has few close friends. Sometimes Erenora comes to town with her gaggle of children and the two women walk along the wharves chatting while the children run wild among ropes and bales and drays laden with goods from all over the world. English is the only language heard around the ships and Anahuia is always pleased to slip back into her first tongue. 'You can have a good laugh in our language,' says Erenora. 'English is too solemn for me.'

Erenora has forgiven her friend's disobedience but her husband has not. Tipene is still outraged that Anahuia should flout his arrangements and embarrass him in front of his wider family.

'Where is her family respect?' he raged to Erenora when he discovered her disappearance. 'An unnatural woman. No sense of tradition. Do not speak her name in this house again.' So Erenora, who admires her friend's enterprise and enjoys her company, keeps quiet about her visits and hopes her children do not chatter too loudly about the antics of the 'Pakeha mahanga': no one can tell the 'Pakeha twins' apart so they get lumped together with the common name.

Apart from Erenora there are few who would claim Anahuia as a friend. Annie O'Halloran, the saddler's wife, speaks to her on occasion, but disapproves of her clientele. Tom, deckhand on the *Rangatira*, likes to lean over the rail and chat. The ladies at the Methodist Mission fuss over the 'beautiful' twins, and bring Anahuia their mending. But the seamstress keeps her distance. The reserve is perhaps in her nature, but her past has also made her wary. Looking back, Anahuia recognises that she was, at that time, probably lonely, but also that she valued the freedom, found real pleasure in making beautiful clothes and earning money from her skill.

Everyone loves the outrageous twins. As soon as they were able to walk Noki and Jackie — or Jockie, as many call whichever one happens to be in sight — toddled across the road and into the ships. Anahuia, sewing at her window, often sees them both riding atop a dray piled with bales of flax fibre or barrels of liquor, waving to passers-by and shouting at them to watch while they perform a handstand or a hornpipe or some other trick. The boys show only slight traces of their Maori blood. The skin is lightly coloured like well-milked tea, and their hair flaxen. Not the ash-blond of their father but honey-gold. Only the lashes around the green-grey eyes they have inherited from their mother are dark. They are strikingly beautiful — as the ladies at the mission note, tall for their age and as active as fleas. In summer the colours of their skin and hair change places: skin darkens to the colour of malt and their wild hair — always in need of a good cut — bleaches white. Sailors teach them to knot and splice ropes and to fish off the wharves. Anahuia never fears for their safety. Remembering Napoleon, she has made sure both boys can swim. Now the lads will jump off the wharf, diving for whatever their sailor friends might throw in to tempt them, and come up triumphant, streaming and laughing, the trophy held aloft in small fists.

When a new ship arrives in port they'll be among the first to wheedle their way aboard. 'Have you seen our father, Conrad?' one will ask, as they have been taught, of sailors freshly arrived. 'He is a very tall white man who tells the best stories.'

'And sings,' the other will add, 'and carves things and is a Faroeman from way in the north.'

No one has seen Conrad.

Anahuia has not lost hope. 'He will come,' she says to her boys. 'You will see your father one day. He'll come roaring in and scoop you up in his strong arms and tell you all the stories of the world and far places.'

She believes this. She feels him about in the world — sometimes in danger but always alive. When Jackie, who is the quieter and more thoughtful of the two, asks why his father is taking so long, she answers, 'Your father is a storyteller. On his way north and then back here again he might see things or places that will make a good story, so he just has to follow that thing.'

'What kind of thing?'

'Maybe a beautiful ship going to a strange country. Or a golden city he must explore.' She smiles. 'I am not the storyteller so I can't say.'

'I want him *now*!' Noki demands, and Anahuia smiles again at her fierce little son. 'He will come. The longer the wait, the more stories he will have to tell. Now, bed!'

But this day — the day of the whalers — she is forced to doubt. In the morning a farmer delivers a letter from Fru Olga Monrad. The busy woman is apologetic: she should have written much earlier. At last there is news of Conrad but it is not good news. A farmhand happened to mention to Olga that the big man called in a good while ago. Evidently he was told by the Maori down at the kainga that Anahuia and her babies were dead. Conrad had spoken to the farmer but then left without seeing anyone else. (Here Anahuia, reading the letter, cries out and clutches at her bosom, fearing she might faint.) The farmhand, writes Olga, got the impression that Conrad was headed back to sea. Olga advises Anahuia to forget the sailor — he would never be a settled husband. Men of the land, she writes, are best.

Anahuia runs into the street without her hat or coat to find the Danish woman who works in the post office. The lady reads the letter carefully. Sadly she confirms that what Anahuia has slowly spelled out for herself is indeed the truth of the letter. Too sick at heart even to nod a thank you, Anahuia leaves the busy hall and walks home. All day she sews in a daze. What now? Where is he? What far ocean is he sailing, thinking I am dead?

Gradually the steady movement of her fingers in and out of the lovely material calms her mind. But a change is taking place; a different purpose is growing. If Conrad is at sea, he is more likely to arrive at a large port than this far colony. Perhaps she, too, might sail to a different land. Where she carries no labels. Not slave or half-caste or native-convert-who-sets-a-fine-example, but just Anahuia Rasmussen. A seamstress. The idea begins to excite her.

In the evening, when the boys are asleep, she goes downstairs to ask if one of the O'Halloran girls could keep watch while she goes out for a while. It is an unusual request: not quite proper for a single woman to go out alone. But Lucy O'Halloran, who loves to collect brightly coloured scraps of cloth for her dolls, runs upstairs gladly, while Anahuia, beautifully dressed and bonneted in green and blue satin, walks out onto Jervois Quay.

Across the harbour the hills glow purple and red in the setting sun. All week the wind has blown up whitecaps on the sea but tonight the air is calm; the lamps, glowing for'ard and astern the docked ships, are deeply reflected in the darkening water. Most of the wharf drays have disappeared now; an occasional dog-cart or cab wheels past, the horses' hooves skittering stones; a bowler-hatted man strides along, his cane tapping a counterpoint to the hooves. But the clerks and the businessmen have long gone. Anahuia walks steadily, enjoying the tang of tar and rope. I could leave this, she thinks — there is nothing to hold me. It is dreadful to think that Conrad believes she and the boys dead, but also there is this other feeling: I am a free woman!

Further along the quay, at Barrett's Bar and Saloon, she can hear distant sounds of music and singing. The hotel is lit brightly and from inside come the stamps and shouts of whalers. Anahuia recognises the flavour of the voices from her childhood and smiles to hear them. The season must be over and the whalers come from Tory Channel to spend their lays. Well-bred settlers frown at this time of year, and avoid the public houses down near the wharves. It brings the colony a bad name, they say, these rough fellows, stinking to high heaven and drinking themselves to death. The whalers, on the other hand, jeer at the sober-sided 'jimmy-grants'. What's the point, they roar, in travelling half around the world to make a town just like the one you've left? We work hard to earn our money and we drink hard to spend it. Live your life while it's under your nose; no point bottling it for later! Anahuia has heard it all the past two seasons and enjoys their free-wheeling ways.

She stands in the dark listening. Someone roars out a song her father used to sing; another sings him down with one Conrad knew, though the song has different words; several beat the rhythm with pairs of spoons. She steps a little closer to hear, but will not risk going inside alone in her fine clothes: an entirely wrong message would be sent to these rough and jovial whalers, who will drink the night dry — and the next day or two — and assume any female in sight is on offer.

Then a fiddler starts up and the men pause a little to listen. Some ship's boy, perhaps, adds his piping voice to the fiddle and soon everyone is stamping.

> *Weigh Hey, my fair lady!*
> *Oh, you New York gals*
> *Can't you dance the polka?*

The fiddle takes off then, faster than any foot could dance, and the men roar their approval. Anahuia has to see. The music is so gay, so wild. She can't imagine any whaler's fingers being delicate enough to manage the intricacies. She stands in the shadow of the verandah and presses her face to a small pane in the corner of the building. It is dark inside. Oil-lamps swing from the rafters and pipe smoke hangs like a curtain over the scene. Some are sitting on benches but most stand, their wind-burnt faces even ruddier with the drink and the heat of the crowded room. Dirty caps are jammed over unwashed, unkempt hair. Through the closed window she can still smell the oily, fishy stink she remembers so well.

In the centre of the crowd the fiddler is whirling and playing like some madman. He is a tall young man, beanpole thin, his shirt-sleeves torn off above the elbows and his once-splendid waistcoat bright with embroidered patterns. Anahuia can't see his face in the dark of the room. She moves to another pane. Now she can see that it is the *man* who is dark. His long, skinny arms are the smudged colour of wood-ash, his black hair short and tightly curled. He laughs as he plays and the teeth show white in the shadowy face. Anahuia is fascinated. Forgetting propriety, she moves into the doorway. Surely this thin and breakable man cannot be a whaler?

A black-coated gent, better dressed than the whalers, who has been leaning in the shadows against the back wall, now steps forward and taps his cane smartly on the floor. Abruptly the fiddler stops his playing and bends to pick up the cap at his feet. This, too, is embroidered in gold and red. Now Anahuia recognises the fancy waistcoat and cap as imitations of a performing monkey's uniform. The fiddler hands the cap around and the whalers toss in coins. One drunken fellow tries to land a smacking kiss on the lad's cheek, but quick as a flash the black-coated man brings his cane down between the two.

'Back off!' he growls. 'Any suchlike is extra. And paid for in advance.'

The whaler laughs and turns to his mates, clutching at his trousers to suggest an agony of need.

Anahuia frowns and is about to leave this sordid scene when she hears the fiddler speak.

'Tak skal han ha', mange tak. Det var venligt af herren,' he says in response to a generous payment. Reaching to secure his tip, he looks up, meets her frowning stare and shrugs as if to say, what else can I do? The gesture is both smiling and shamed — more the look of a naughty child caught out than a grown man selling himself.

That child's look and the Danish words of thanks make the improbable connection for Anahuia.

'Er du Mikkel Waag?' she whispers. 'Var du ven med den høje mand som hed Køne?'

The lad stops as if shot.

'Er du Mikkel Waag?'

For a heartbeat or two he is utterly still, then slowly he arches his head back, bares his teeth and screams at the smoky ceiling. The pain in that howl is terrifying. Even the whalers are silenced. The black-coated man is over in two strides. He lays one firm hand on the boy's shoulder and cuffs him about the head with the other.

'Calm down, calm down. Good boy. Good Ali. Good Ali.'

Mikkel shakes his head from side to side and screams — a wholly animal sound. The man knocks him to the ground, stands over his prone body and speaks to Anahuia.

'This is no place for you, madam. My Ali can be dangerous, and these whalers are not much better. Unless you are in the business of . . .'

Mikkel heaves himself to a sitting position, silent and crouching, like the monkey his master has made him. Anahuia is more angry than she can remember being. For a moment she stands looking directly at the black-coated man. She is taller than him and in her own way formidable. The whalers murmur and crowd around, ready for a confrontation, but the woman speaks in a level voice.

'I have taken a fancy to your musician. How much do you charge?'

The man turns to the whalers with a bark of derision. 'This native pigeon is not so fancy as her clothes, eh? She wants a piece of my pretty boy!' He names a sum. Anahuia produces it from her purse.

'I will take him away for an hour.'

'He stays here.'

'He comes with me. And his fiddle. I fancy his music.'

The black-coated man jeers. 'Mary and Joseph, madam, I am no fool. If I keep the fiddle he comes back, eh, Ali?'

Anahuia nods. 'Well, keep the fiddle. I will take the man.' She holds out her hand to the cowering Mikkel, who rises slowly, still watching his master's face.

The black-hearted man pats Mikkel gently on the cheek. 'Remember the sweet dreams I will give you on your return, eh? No monkey-business now!' And roars at his own joke.

The look she sends him would silence the dead. At the door she turns to the whalers, who are ready now for other sport. 'Make your own music, friends,' she says, 'and leave me to mine.'

They cheer her spirit and leave her free to go.

Outside, Anahuia turns sharply down a narrow alley between buildings and stops there. She speaks quietly, in Danish, to the lad, who stands waiting where he has been stood, against the wall.

'Stay exactly here. I am your friend and the friend of your Tall Køne. I am going back for your fiddle.'

At the back entrance of the saloon she collars young Jimmy Smart, the wash-boy, and gives him a penny. 'Get your dad and quick about it. Not a word else.'

The publican comes out, grumbling, peering into the dark to see what has excited his son. Anahuia comes to the point quickly.

'I aim to winkle this man's boy away, Frank. We have a history of a sort. Now listen: first, I want his fiddle; second, I want every whaler's son in there to keep his trap shut about where I live. I'd pay you for the fiddle but have no money till next week.'

Frank grunts. 'Keep your money. The fiddle belongs to the boy; he shall have it. I'd be glad anyway to see the back end of that Josiah and his performing freaks. Last year he brought a mangy cur could stand on his hind legs and bark messages. Half starved. That was bad enough. This is worse — that poor boy with his talent, brought so low. Tell you what, though — the whalers won't remember any moment of it by tomorrow and I'll not remind them.'

Anahuia smiles her thanks. 'I'll send for the fiddle tomorrow. Just make it disappear somehow.'

From inside comes a roar of laughter and a new round of songs. Frank turns with a brief wave and Anahuia moves back into the shadowed lane.

LATER that night a quiet and shivering Mikkel Waag sits wrapped in a blanket while Anahuia mends his torn shirt. He will not tell his story: is ashamed of it, he says. All Anahuia can discover is that he is 'about twenty-two years of age' and has sailed many oceans in search of Køne. Anahuia speaks to him slowly (for her tongue is rusty in the Danish language) of Conrad and the stories he has told: of the escape from the Danish navy, and Conrad's hope he would meet Mikkel again. At first Mikkel listens avidly, his quick grin lighting his face. Once he laughs — a rich gurgling, like a tickled baby, and Anahuia laughs with him. A new bond. But then his eyes begin to wander; he listens with only half his mind. From time to time he glances at the door, at the windows. He pulls the blanket tighter. Once he stands as if to go, shuffles his long bony feet, then sits again. He moans softly like a dog in pain.

'You are safe, Mikkel,' says Anahuia. 'He won't come here.'

Mikkel shakes his head and moans again. He reaches one long dark arm out to hold her hand. 'It is the sweet dreams,' he whispers. 'He gives me the sweet dreams every night. Do you have some?'

Anahuia doesn't like to think what he can mean. She shakes her head. After a while he whispers, 'Just three drops in water. That's what he gives me. I need it.'

Anahuia understands then. He is speaking of laudanum. Some of the women she sews for are addicted — would do anything for a few drops of the dreamy stuff.

'There is none here,' she says, 'and will be none. You must give it up.'

Mikkel moans.

'Act like a man!' says Anahuia sharply. 'You are not the silly monkey he has made you.'

Mikkel sighs and looks at the floor. His lanky body seems to shrink and fold. Anahuia wonders if she has been a fool to rescue him. What will happen when her boys wake up? You can't keep those two mouths shut, not at any price.

'Do you want to go back, then?' she asks. 'You are no prisoner here.'

Mikkel scrabbles along the floor to lay his black curly head in her lap. 'I want to stay. I want to see Køne again.' He adds sadly, 'I need my fiddle.'

She strokes his back gently. 'Your fiddle will come. Be strong. Stay.'

'Yes.' But his big dark eyes are doubtful.

She makes a bed on the floor for him and leaves him to his restless movements. In the middle of the night she hears the door to her bedroom open. Soft as a cat, Mikkel slips in beside her. He is shivering. She holds him like a child and slowly he relaxes, warms against her. She thinks he is sleeping, and perhaps he is; perhaps he moves in his sleep to pull down her nightdress and take her breast in his mouth. For minutes he lies there, tongue and lips gentle on her, sucking like a baby. One arm is tucked under his own curled body; the fingers of the other hand play a soft tune against her arm. Up and down they run. Up and down, soft as mice.

Now it is Anahuia who moans. This is all too much. The flickering and swelling in her lower parts is part maternal but also something quite other. In time her own need becomes too great to withstand; her warm hands begin to play their own counter-tune up his bony back. Mikkel sighs, moves in closer. His narrow fingers steal up under her gown to caress her back and behind. She feels him stiffen and begin to move against her, slowly as if in an underwater world. They make love in silence, both so deeply absorbed they could be dreaming.

I will regret this, thinks Anahuia. But as sleep comes she is smiling.

4.

ANAHUIA LOVED SYDNEY. From the moment she stepped ashore with Mikkel and the boys everything about the bustling, raw, noisy city delighted her. She loved the crowds; the way the houses crawled up and over the hills, joined side by side, row after row. No one turned a hair if she walked right into one of the grand buildings — the town hall, St Andrew's Cathedral with its tall spire — on no particular business except to stare.

'Look!' she would say to her gawking boys. 'Look at the statues, the archways — see how the carved staircase curves around!'

The busy wharves, crammed with ships from all parts of the world, gave her hope that Conrad would one day sail into this sprawling harbour. Especially she loved the elegant carriages and longed to ride in one. Perhaps one day she would. Everything seemed possible in this wonderful city. Any day of the week she could pay her penny and ride a ferry to the other side of the harbour, or take a horse-bus out to the beach, or sit quietly in Hyde Park listening to the screech of the strange Australian birds.

She talked easily with smiling, friendly women who asked no questions but gossiped in the streets in front of their crowded houses. A strange accent or a different shade of skin caused no comment here. A few eyebrows were raised when Mikkel staggered into the wrong doorway one night, out of his mind with the laudanum, but when he took his fiddle down to Hyde Park next Saturday and played to the promenading families he was forgiven. Mikkel became known and loved as a musical genius who shared his talent freely; he was therefore allowed to be different.

Anahuia painted a sign: *Madame Ana, Latest Ladies' Fashions. Finest materials and workmanship.* She placed it, along with a beautiful gown, in the window of her rented rooms. Soon she had more work than she could manage on her own. Her satisfied customers spread her reputation until 'Madame Ana' could boast a large clientele of smart society women who swore her fashions were the most up to date in the colony. Her business flourished.

Anahuia rented and then bought a larger house in Surry Hills, where all the fashionable clothing establishments were concentrated. She hired well-bred seamstresses, paid them good wages and made sure orders were filled on time. Soon she was supplying fashionable garments to David Jones Emporium down on George Street. When Madame Ana walked up the Surry Hills streets in search of the best fabrics or the latest ribbons she was greeted with respect. Her imposing bosom would be resplendent with tucks and ruches, her skirts draped just so, her smile radiant. Tall as a man and beautiful, she turned many a fellow's head, but never looked for favours. Sometimes dark Mikkel Waag drifted in and stayed the night. More often he frequented the dark opium dens in the winding streets down at the Rocks. Anahuia's two daughters, born a year apart, were clearly his. She never took his name, though.

In the first years, on fine Saturdays Anahuia would take a horse-bus from the rail terminus down to Circular Quay or to Darling Harbour and then walk about with the boys, asking after their father. Once or twice there was word of a blond giant who could be Conrad; one ship's master laughed at some memory and vowed he had definitely employed her Conrad on the long haul to England.

'I was sorry to lose him,' he said. 'A useful pair of hands. Kept us all in good spirits with his songs and antics. I reckon he took off east — Singapore or Ceylon, maybe. It would be a full-rigged ship: he couldn't abide steam. But listen, sweetheart, it would be needles in haystacks finding that adventurer, if you get my drift.'

Anahuia was hungry for further details: was he happy? Healthy? Did he have a wife? But the master was suddenly called away to some emergency and she had to make do with those few words. By afternoon the ship, all sails set, had moved majestically away, out towards the heads.

One night, five years after they had come to Sydney, Anahuia woke, overcome with dread. It was Conrad, she was certain of it, in danger. It felt like a storm. She felt Conrad fighting for breath. An hour she sat, alone and sweating in her comfortable bed, but fighting, breath for shuddering breath, with him. At last the breaths came more easily. She sat quietly then, until morning, keeping watch, feeling for his presence, and finally knew him to be alive.

Then there was no news at all year after year. Anahuia began to visit the wharves less often, favouring rather a Saturday walk in Hyde Park or Victoria Gardens, where her two dark and beautiful daughters, flounced and beribboned, would be admired, and the boys, Noki and Johan, fooled around with the other lads, kicking balls in and out of the promenading families. Sometimes Mikkel came with them. He would find a good spot under a tree, take out his fiddle and play. His little daughters would caper around him, waving their arms and singing wordless songs. No one thought it strange: on Saturdays the park was full of entertainers. Once a man lit a fire under a huge balloon and sailed away out of sight. Noki declared he would become a balloonist or a trapeze artist — he hadn't decided yet.

Mikkel came and went, never staying long. Anahuia was his anchor but laudanum his deepest love. The ships he worked on kept close to shore, trading up and down the coast, or inland up the Parramatta River, never across oceans where he would be too long away from his 'sweet dreams'. Anahuia loved the gentle fellow, who was part-child, part-lover, mostly loyal friend. She learned that lecturing him on his addiction was useless. Worse than useless — it drove him to it. In happy times, when he felt no pressure or anxiety, he would stay away from the laudanum for a while. Then he taught Johan to play the fiddle and threw his little girls in the air, and at night in the big bed upstairs, over the sewing rooms and the consulting salon, he played Anahuia's body like a virtuoso until her moans of pleasure woke the house. But when Madame Ana was busy — distracted with clients and children, and her growing staff of seamstresses — he would wander out in search of his 'sweet dreams' and return days later, dirty and starving. Anahuia always welcomed him back.

NOKI grew to be a handful. Energetic, large, restless — like his father, Anahuia thought, but not a dreamer like him. He hated school and left at twelve to go to sea. It was a relief to his mother. At the same time Anahuia apprenticed the other twin, Johan, to a carpenter. Johan — Jackie to his few friends — missed his brother; had always been the quiet one, often unhappy. He hated wearing shoes and would leave his fine clothes lying lost on a wall while he wandered, barefoot and dreamy, among the trees and flower-beds of the parks. His master set him to work on the great Garden Palace being built for a grand exhibition — a centenary of something or other.

At first the apprenticeship seemed to work. Johan came home full of the building they were creating: what a marvel it would be, how grand the carvings and paintings, how gigantic the ballroom. He seemed to enjoy working with tools. Anahuia praised him and stopped worrying.

When the edifice was completed she went down to the Botanic Gardens, along with the rest of Sydney, to witness all the lords and ladies arriving for the opening gala. The palace towered over the surrounding houses, acres of it, its spires and turrets lit like a Christmas tree and a huge decorated dome floating high above it all. Anahuia, accustomed now to buildings on a grand scale, thought it rather pretentious. For one thing, it blocked the lovely gentle view down to the sea. For another, your feet ached just walking through all those rooms full of exhibits trumpeting Sydney's achievements. (And scarcely a mention of the dressmaking trade!) But she would not speak these thoughts to her son. Johan pointed out the section where he had worked, shaping the timbers into decorative curls. Anahuia smiled and nodded, pleased that this son who so often railed against Sydney — how dirty it was, how black with smoke, how noisy — was at last settling down.

But then, two years later, that grand Garden Palace burned to the ground and Johan's life seemed to collapse. Anahuia woke early in the morning to the clanging of bells. Fire engines were racing down Macquarie Street from all points of the city. She saw the Surry Hills fire-cart, pulled by half-dressed firemen, clattering down the street, and then a steam fire engine belched its way around the corner, rocking and clanging, almost a fire disaster of its own. People poured into the streets in the grey light of dawn and ran to see.

'The Garden Palace is burning down!' they shouted. Johan ran with them.

Anahuia stayed in Surry Hills with her screaming daughters. Watching from the upstairs window, they saw fire run along the parapets to flower from the arches of the four high towers. Then they heard a booming crash, far louder than the cannon salute when the royal duke visited from England. They cried aloud in awe to see a great fireball light the sky, followed by shooting flames and black smoke. Crash after crash echoed across the sky.

Jackie came home later, black with soot and crying. 'It is all gone,' he shouted. 'Every bit of it burned!' All day he mooned and moaned and stamped about the house, upsetting his sisters and driving Anahuia mad with it all. 'The plants!' he cried. 'Those beautiful plants. Every one shrivelled. Black corpses dead on the black soil.' Anahuia had admired the garden of thirty thousand plants that Dr Moore, the chief botanist, had planted around the palace. Its destruction was a shame — sadder, she secretly thought, than that of the showy palace.

But even so, the boy's mood was out of all proportion. The disaster, after all, did not affect his livelihood any more. Johan sobbed that he hated Sydney, always had. Hated its smoking chimneys, the cold, raw stone of its buildings. He railed against all the dark sides of the big city — the rats and squalor of the Rocks area, the stench of the markets, the belching factory chimneys at Darling Harbour. Anahuia washed her son and rocked him. Finally she spoke sternly.

'This is our place,' she said. 'I rely on you, now that Noki is at sea. You must learn to find your way here.'

But Johan Rasmussen would not be comforted.

NOT long after the fire Anahuia begins to feel again that pull she has always connected with Conrad. It moves inside her like the steady flow of a river. In the past, when the feeling came, she imagined Conrad in trouble and asked more diligently down at the wharves. And sent steadying thoughts into his mind. For several years, now, she has not felt that pull. It meant, she thought, that he was settled and happy somewhere and she was glad. But now it is back again, and strong. She never talks about these feelings — the down-to-earth neighbours and friends would find her strange. To Anahuia, though, premonitions are as natural as food and drink. Her grandmother always knew when her sons needed help, even if they were many miles away. The death of Anahuia's father was 'felt' in the kainga long before the news arrived.

So when Conrad's river begins to move again in her, she takes the feeling seriously and resumes her search. She goes back to the wharves, asking for news of a big Scandinavian, who would be sixteen years older than when she knew him, but surely still a man of prodigious strength, still a renowned storyteller. He will think her dead, of course, which makes the search one-sided, but she has a growing sense that they will meet soon. Her feeling is urgent and close. Maybe he is in deep trouble, or maybe nearby.

Practical Noki makes light of his mother's premonitions, says he is embarrassed to ask his seafaring friends. Surely their father would now be happily settled in some other part of the world with a large family. 'Leave well alone,' he says, but then, seeing the anxiety on his mother's face, adds, 'I might ask. As long as they don't laugh at me.'

Johan, moody, unsettled, living in his own uncomfortable world, ignores or perhaps simply does not know about his mother's search.

Mikkel understands, of course. Dreams — glorious visions and strange landscapes — are increasingly the stuff of his life. It is poor emaciated Mikkel who brings the news that a man answering the description of Conrad has been sighted in Hokitika, New Zealand. A sailor on shore leave, drinking down at the Rocks with Mikkel, said he had seen such a man working on the wharves at Hokitika.

'Hokitika,' says Anahuia. 'I have heard of it. In the south. Do you know it, Mikkel?'

He nods. 'That man — the one you rescued me from — took me there once.'

'What is it like?'

'On the West Coast of the South Island. Wild. A bad place. Full of storm. Full of men in a fever over gold.'

'Mikkel, all that would be past by now. The gold rushes are over. It will be an ordinary town now.'

Mikkel shakes his dark head, avoiding her eyes. 'No, still bad, I think. Don't ask me.'

Anahuia smiles. Always this man knows what she is thinking before the words are formed. 'Mikkel,' she says gently, 'listen to me. It would be a great thing for you if you found him. Think of it. Your friend and mine. Think how the boys would cheer! How pleased I would be.'

Mikkel smiles uneasily. 'You might forget this man.'

'You know in your heart I could never forget you. Mikkel, I would go if I was free but the work . . . Will you go? See if it is him and bring him back? I think he needs us.'

Mikkel wrings his hands, wags his head back and forth. 'Across the Tasman Sea. It is a long way . . .'

Anahuia knows what holds him back but will not give in this time. 'For goodness sake, you have sailed the world in better days. The Tasman is nothing. It will do you good, Mikkel. You have been living in too many basements. The open ocean, I think, will clear your head.'

Mikkel smiles sadly. 'It may not be him.'

'Also it may.' A new idea comes to her. 'No, listen, Mikkel, I tell you what. I will send the boys with you. I have been thinking of sending them to see where they were born. After all, they are fifteen now, nearly men. Go to Hokitika, and then, whether you find Conrad or not, take the boys to see that place. It might settle Johan to know where his whenua is buried.'

'His whenua?'

'The afterbirth. As I buried your daughters' ones here, remember? The boys' is under a totara tree by the Manawatu River. They know the story.' She smiles at Mikkel. 'This is a mission for you. A double mission.'

His eyes begin to focus then, and a liveliness creeps back to his face. 'If it is him . . .' he says, 'if it is him, and I bring him back . . .'

'You will be a hero, my dear,' says Anahuia.

8.
Hearth and Homeland

HOKITIKA, NEW ZEALAND
SYDNEY, AUSTRALIA
1884

1.

IN MOST OF Con's stories a storm is a predictable player and the way Con tells it there's a black storm that day in Hokitika. Con's mood is just as dark as he tramps down Gibson's Quay in search of his boat. His head is down against the blinding rain and hail that sweeps in sheets up the long wharf, pinging like gunshot on the iron of the wharf sheds. The woman known as Eva, drunk, sodden inside and out, trails him all the way, shouting and cursing, then trying a few tears — any trick to hold him from going. Rolling waves, driven by the sea-wind, surge up the river, tossing ships against their moorings. A forest of spars and rigging wave back and forth with much creaking and groaning, like spectators jostling for a better view. Con shakes rain out of his eyes, unable, in all this fury, to read the names of the ships. Where, in the name of God, is the *Mary Emmanuel*?

Under an awning, in the lee of the weather, a rough group of rock-miners, in from the bush, are celebrating their day off in the usual manner. Con met them earlier, in town — attempted a greeting but quickly gave up. Even then they were surly-drunk, having been tossed out of Pritchard's Saloon Bar for disorderly behaviour. On the coast, 'disorderly' has a fairly lenient interpretation so their behaviour must have been bordering on criminal to earn them the heave-ho. Con gives them a wide margin.

The barque *Mary Emmanuel* is tied up at the seaward end of the quay, her master and crew struggling to bring a load of logs aboard.

'Come up quick, man!' shouts the master to his new crewman. 'We are fighting a losing battle with this lot.'

Con turns for a moment to the pleading Eva. 'I'm off, then. This is the end of it, Eva.'

She strikes at him, fingernails drawing blood down his cheek. The miners cheer. 'Traitor!' she shrieks. 'Deserter!' Then softer, 'Will you be back, at least?'

'I will not!' shouts Con into the wind, despairing. 'We are nothing but poison together. And have ruined a child's life.'

He turns away then, leaving the wild woman alone on the wharf. Swag on shoulder, sure-footed, he runs up the plank. Stepping aboard is like coming home. He groans. Why, in the name of Thor, has he stayed ashore so long?

Hauling on slippery ropes, cursing at the tangling tackle, Con and the rest of the crew struggle to swing the wet logs aboard and stow them below in the tossing hold. The heavy grinding work helps to ease his pain. He tries to ignore the woman still shouting on the quay, but notices how one of the miners — a black-bearded thickset ape of a fellow — approaches her to offer a swig, tries to put an arm around her. Eva, in no mood for play, knocks the jar from his hand, shouts some obscenity, and at last marches back towards the town. For a moment the furious fellow goes after her, but when she turns and bares her teeth, even he thinks better of it. Con eases his shoulders for a moment and watches her go. He does not regret seeing the back of her.

Further away, a thin man is making his way up the quay, staggering and weaving against the rain. He stops at each ship, shouting a question up to whoever might be there, waits for an answer and then tries another. Con sees him shout his query at Eva, sees her shake her head angrily and push him away. On he comes, unsteady but dogged, towards the next ship. Here the vessels are double-banking and the man scrambles across one to check the other. He is nimble across the heaving deck: a sailor. Con is curious but must turn back to his work.

When next Con looks, the thin man has reached the unruly miners, who are at that moment quarrelling among themselves, shouting drunken insults. One presents a fist in another's face. They are spoiling for a fight. For a moment the thin man hesitates, but some kind of foolish obstinacy seems to be driving him. He approaches the knot of men. Careful, tentative, he asks his question.

Another log swings aboard. Con struggles to control its lethal passage. When next he looks up the thin man is on the ground, writhing and kicking. His cap is knocked off and the poor fellow is trying vainly to protect his dark head from the boots of the miners. One of them heaves the skinny fellow to his feet, spits in his face, and flings him to the ground again. The fellow's scream slices through the storm.

'Hey there!' shouts Con, leaning over the side. 'Get off the poor sot!'

The ship's master pulls Con away. 'It is only some idiot of a black fellow. No great loss to mankind. He has wasted our time already once, asking for someone. Out of his mind.'

Con doesn't like the master's tone. 'Well then. Who does he ask after?'

'Something foreign. Rasmussen, perhaps. Conrad. Nothing to do with us.'

But Con leaves the log swinging and the master cursing. He is over the side and into the boil of miners.

In Con's telling, the battle is heroic: he bestrides the dazed Mikkel, and, deadly accurate, fells his adversaries one by one as they fly at him from left and right. The truth is darker. The fight, at first a rescue, becomes, for Con, a release. The shattering despair and humiliation of the past few weeks explode out of him in a berserk fury. He picks up a lump of timber as if it were kindling and sweeps it at two of the miners, breaking ribs and smashing them to the ground. Another he hurls against the iron wall of the shed. By the time a fourth is retching on the ground, his face a bloody pulp, the rest have scrambled off, leaving their victim motionless in a puddle.

Con bends over him. The dark man's skin has paled to an unhealthy grey; an arm angles sickeningly from a dislocated shoulder; blood oozes from an ear. One eye is swollen shut, the other stares up.

'Conrad,' he croaks. Tries to smile, then passes out.

Con picks up the shattered body, light as a bundle of sticks. He holds him gently but even so he can feel bones grate. By now several of the crew are hanging over the side of the *Mary Emmanuel*, watching the show. Con shouts up into the wind and rain that he is taking the man to a doctor. The master threatens but Con walks away.

'Is it you, little Mikkel?' he murmurs. 'After all these years, friend?'

Con walks down the quay, treading softly. From the other end two men are approaching — lads, more like, same size and height, heads down into the wind. As they are about to pass, one stops and signs to the other, nods towards Con's burden. The other curses and comes in a fury at Con.

'What have you done to him?' he shouts. 'Give him over here or I'll knock you flat!' A brave threat, given the mismatch in size.

'Hold your hair on,' mutters Con. 'I have rescued your friend. There is no need of further blows.'

But the two lads are now stock still, staring. Con stares back. What Con sees are two boys, identical and handsome. Pale gold hair and skins the colour of milky tea, large open faces and broad shoulders. Unused to seeing his own image, he does not make the connection. The boys, on the other hand, have looked at a living mirror image every day of their lives. They stare now at a larger version.

'It's him,' whispers Johan.

Noki gapes.

'This man needs assistance, lads,' says Con.

Johan clears his throat. 'Are you Conrad Rasmussen?'

'That is one of my names,' says Con. 'I have others.'

Mikkel seems to be unconscious but now his lips move into the smallest of smiles. 'It's them,' he croaks. 'Your sons.'

Con hears the words. He looks again and knows it. 'Jesus, Mary and Joseph,' he whispers. The boys look at each other, gape back at Con. It seems no one can make the next move.

Finally Con speaks. 'How are you named?'

'Enoki and Johan,' says Johan. 'Some call me Jackie. We are Rasmussen.'

'Ah, Jesus!' cries Conrad, looking from one to the other. He all but drops Mikkel.

'Why didn't you ever come?' shouts Noki roughly. He is not yet ready to forgive this new father. 'Our mother waited!'

'I thought you dead. And your mother. *I was told you were dead*!' Con howls the words into the wild air. Then stops as if shot. 'Your mother?' The words are barely audible.

The boys nod together. 'We are all alive,' says Noki, frowning. 'No thanks to you.'

A fresh shower of hail rattles down the quay. Mikkel moans.

'Quick,' says Con, taking charge now. 'Where is your ship? We must get this poor bugger under a roof and then a doctor to him. The stories can come later.'

BY nightfall the coastal steamship *Waipawa* is pounding north in rough seas. Mikkel lies smiling and dreaming on his bunk, loaded to the eyeballs with laudanum but a dreadful colour. The boys, who are signed on as passengers, sit with him. Con is on deck, taking over Mikkel's duties. Before they left Hokitika the doctor, drunk himself by the smell of his breath, and careless over the fate of a black man, diagnosed broken ribs, bound them and prescribed a heavy dose of an opiate. Announcing that nothing more could be done, he hurried ashore to more savoury patients.

When Con's watch is over he comes below to the crowded little cabin. He sits on the bunk and holds Mikkel's cold hand. The broken man hardly raises a lump under the blankets. His breathing is ragged and his cheeks flushed. Occasionally a pinkish foam bubbles from a corner of his mouth. Con tries to prop him up, but Mikkel cries out with the pain. They give him more laudanum.

All night the boys and Con talk in low voices, telling their lives. Sometimes Mikkel smiles. Perhaps Con's stories are entering his dreams. Con tries a quiet song, but Mikkel becomes agitated, calling for his fiddle and coughing up blood. They calm him, hold his hand.

At one time Con reaches into his trouser pocket and takes out a crumpled piece of paper. Smoothes it, reads and sighs. The boys wait, smiling to each other, recognising the tricks of a storyteller.

'While you have been pursuing your decent lives in Sydney,' begins Con, 'I have been making yet another mess of mine on a high plateau up the coast a way. A hard place.'

Con talks of coalmining and miraculous engineering and whole towns isolated up in the mist. Of the ghosts of dead miners moaning through abandoned mines and of wagons derailing to crash thousands of feet down precipices. He describes a daughter — or perhaps, he says with a fierce growl, not his daughter at all — so pretty and smart that everyone took her to heart. The mother is not mentioned. There is a murder, too, and an evil, Bible-spouting blacksmith.

'Our lives in Sydney have been plain as milk, to hear you talk,' says Johan, not quite believing it all.

Con smiles sadly and strokes Mikkel's feverish brow. 'Plain can be paradise — don't forget that, lads,' he says. But the boys want more stories.

Con reads aloud his crumpled letter, written just six days ago by this same daughter. 'She took my last guinea, saved in case of further disasters, left the note and disappeared. Only seven years old,' he says, 'but more sense in her curly head than both her parents put together.' He points to her handwriting with pride — a neat, firm hand you would take for someone older than seven. The way the big man reads and re-reads the words, the way his tears run, the boys know some truth lies in the heart of the story.

I am going away, the words in the note say. *I don't want to stay with you and my mother any more. I can look after myself better. I don't want you to look for me, I will be all right.*

Rose

'She was right to go — she is better off without me,' says Conrad sadly. 'I thought I was protecting her but only made her life worse. Ah Jesus, boys, you had better be rid of me here and now!'

But he doesn't mean it, not for a minute.

LATER, as the *Waipawa* steams up the coast towards the North Island, and a calmer dawn is lightening the sky, Mikkel Waag smiles in his sleep and dies. They bury him at sea out from the island of Kapiti, close to the place where Anahuia was born.

2.

A letter from

Johan (Jackie) Rasmussen

Karere
3rd December 1884

Dear Mama,

Our new father says I must write to you if I am not
coming back so he can at least bring a letter. He is
afraid, I think, that you will blame him. But I think
you know. That I am not coming back.

I love this country, Mama. It is my homeland and
what I have been missing. The soil here has a beautiful
smell, dark and sweet. I love to take off my boots and
feel it under my bare feet. Mama, I am happy here,
please believe this and don't worry. The country is so

open, the sky so clear. On this farm the flat fields and the river and the patches of great trees are just like you described. We all walked down to find where our whenua was buried, but no one is living there — the Maori kainga you told us about has gone, so no one could tell us where to look. We found a tree by the river, a totara, and decided this might be the one and said a prayer there. Noki and I sang the song you taught us. I hope we got it right.

Mama, Sydney is good for you, I know that. But not for me. You must take some blame because of all your stories! I have work here on the Monrad farm for now but later I will go down to the place where you were born and see that. My plan is to one day have a farm of my own somewhere close to here.

We found a sad thing when we arrived at Karere. Herr Viggo Monrad met us at the door of his big house. He looked so thin and tired. His wife, Fru Olga Monrad, who you knew, has died just a few weeks ago. I don't know how — some illness, I think. There are seven children and the youngest only three years old. Herr Monrad is very sad and also finding it too hard to look after them all. He is going back to Denmark. He says he remembers you well and sends his greeting. He says his father, who you translated for, is back in Denmark and living happily. He is a bishop again, not a politician.

Mama, I have been thinking about how to explain this — why you went away from here and why I must come back. I have met Oscar Monrad. He is Herr Viggo Monrad's second son and a little younger than me but a big boy like us. We talked about this thing — leaving and coming back. I like him very much. He is friendly and laughing. You would think him older than he is. He loves this land too and knows everything about farming and cows and ploughing and all the things I have yet to learn. He says he must go back to Denmark to help his father with the young ones on the voyage, and to see his grandfather, but he is determined to come back soon. His father, he says, longs to see his homeland again, but Oscar and his brother know they will come back to live here. This is his homeland. And mine now.

In my head I see it as a kind of pattern. You and Herr Viggo Monrad and maybe Onkel Mikkel and our new father are different from us younger ones — your children. You are those who break away. You still have different voices calling you in different directions. It is easier for us. We don't hear all those distant calls. Maybe we are the ones who will settle, and then maybe our children will become unsettled and want to break away!

Sorry, Mama, this does not make much sense. You will say I am the one breaking away, but it doesn't feel like that. I feel as if I am coming home. I am doing what you would like to but can't. Think of me as your bridge. When I have a farm (perhaps you could send some money?) and a wife and children, I think you will find it easy to come back and love this land too.

Noki is angry with me and upset and of course I will miss him, but then he is already a man of the sea so we will be apart anyway.

God bless you, Mama, and keep you well. Please give my sisters a kiss.

Arohanui

Your Jackie

(Johan Rasmussen)

P.S. We all cried when Onkel Mikkel died. But he was smiling. He was happy to know that he was the one who found Conrad. The others will tell you about it. I wonder what you will think of our new father. He is very loud and big but a great storyteller like you said.

J.

3.

ANAHUIA CAN DESCRIBE every detail of the day they came back. Years later, she could tell you what colours she wore (deep purple tussore with narrow magenta stripes; mother-of-pearl locket and earrings to match), describe the day (hot and cloudless with a blessed breeze from the south), and the date (16 December, a Wednesday, close to midday). The grandchildren thought she remembered rather too many details. They preferred the stories about dark bush and savage wars and catching eels in muddy rivers. But to Anahuia the story of this day is a rich one, full of joy and fulfilment — and of pain. She loves to tell it.

She is standing on her own doorstep, having just seen off a wealthy client, and pauses for a moment to enjoy the fresh breeze on her face. The homecoming is imminent; she can feel their presence. Can almost feel his heartbeat. But also, mixed with the expectation, a loss, which puzzles her. She already guesses that Johan might not be with them and will only be pleased if he has found peace in that country. So what is this other loss? She sighs and shifts on the doorstep, reluctant to go back to work. Inside the house the air is stifling, even though the big windows of the sewing rooms and the cutting room are raised and the back door latched open. The staff are all heads down and fingers flying to finish a rush of Christmas orders, the girls at school. Across the road Mrs Andropoulos, her basket heavy with fresh bread and cheese, waves a hand jingling with gold bracelets.

'Good morning, Madame Ana. Already it is too hot to walk! What will the afternoon bring?'

Anahuia looks down the street. Looks again, narrowing her eyes. 'It will bring a husband,' she murmurs, 'and maybe a death.'

But her heart lifts to see him.

Far below, the familiar shapes of two men toil up from the railway station, canvas swags over shoulders. Mikkel's fiddle case swings from Noki's hand. A sign.

The figures appear to shimmer slightly in the heat off the road. They walk together, stride for stride, talking like friends. She waits. Their heads are down, leaning into the gradient, bowed by the heat. The bigger man pauses to peer this way and that at houses. Every movement is familiar. Then he looks up the street and sees her standing there. It is as if his heart has, for a moment, failed him. He turns to stone. Noki climbs on, unaware.

Anahuia suddenly finds it difficult to breathe.

Noki looks up too, then, and sees her standing, one hand on the door-post, the other at her throat. He turns back, his hand out to Conrad, who is standing stock-still below, in the middle of the road. No one speaks. They could be posing for a photograph.

Noki breaks it. He runs up to his mother, shouting in the

thunderous voice so like his father's, 'We have brought you a surprise, Mama! We have found our father!'

Anahuia manages a nod.

Slowly the big man picks up his bundles and continues walking, eyes on her every step of the way. He stops in front of her, ready to smile but anxious, waiting for a sign. Anahuia stands, proud in her splendid dress, at the door of her large establishment.

'Where in the name of all the oceans have you been?' she asks, her voice stern, tears running down.

'He thought we were dead!' shouts Noki. 'It wasn't his fault!'

'I know that,' says Anahuia. 'I know that.'

Conrad can hear the love in her voice. And the joy. Wordless for once in his life, he stands there, smiling, his throat aching.

Anahuia longs to touch him, to hold that bruised man tight and stroke away the great sadness in him. 'Come inside quick,' she gasps, 'before my legs give way.'

In the shadow of the doorway he opens his arms to her, pulls her dark head into his shoulder, smelling her fragrance. She rests there. Noki has never seen his mother so soft.

'Sweetheart,' says Conrad. And then, 'Anahuia.'

In other rooms the clatter of the establishment continues: shouts, running feet, the snap of shaken cloth. Here is stillness.

Finally Conrad sighs. 'We have many stories to tell. Songs to sing.' He smiles into her hair. 'Many foolish acts in my life, as you can imagine.'

'I can.'

'But marvels, too. Wait till you hear!'

Anahuia stands back from him then, laughing. 'Conrad Rasmussen, I have waited sixteen years for you. The marvels can no doubt wait another minute or two. Come inside, at least.'

LATER, when the seamstresses have gone home, and the house is quiet, they sit together in the cool back yard, looking over roofs and trees down towards the harbour. Conrad has wept with Mikkel's beautiful daughters over the death of their father. He has distributed gifts. A comb of carved walrus tooth gleams against Anahuia's dark hair.

In the fading light Conrad begins to sing. The slow beautiful phrases echo off the bricks of the house. On and on he sings. The others breathe the scented air and listen. To Anahuia the song is part lament, part homecoming. She hears peace in the strange, soft words. Noki hears the sea — he thinks of high-wheeling sea-birds. He picks up Mikkel's fiddle, fingers the strings, then leans in to whisper to his mother, 'What is it about? I can't understand!'

Anahuia smiles at her impatient son. 'Shh. Listen. The words are from the far north. From his homeland. Listen.'

THUS ends this saga of Enok of Suðeroy, Faroeman, also known as Køne, Con and Conrad Rasmussen. Storyteller. Carver. Traveller on the whale-road.

SOME REAL EVENTS RELEVANT TO
THE PERIOD OF THIS NOVEL

1822   First written form of Faroese published (by
                Danes): a collection of Faroese ballads about the
                Viking hero Sigurd.

1849   King Frederik VII of Denmark accepts constitu-
                tion, largely devised by liberal politician D. G.
                Monrad. Universal male suffrage. Two elected
                Faroese and two Greenlanders are included in
                Denmark's folk Parliament.

1850 July: Battle of Isted. Danish and Slesvig armies finally
                repulse invading Holsten and Prussian armies,
                driving them from Slesvig.
                Treaty of London signed: the duchies of Slesvig
                and Holsten must remain together, neither
                bound more strongly to Denmark than the other.
                (Monrad disagreed with this treaty.)

1851   Faroese Parliament (Løgting) reinstated as
                advisory council to Danish king's representative.

1855   Danish Trade Monopoly on Faroes abolished.
                Free trade permitted.

1860   Full-rigged steam frigate *Jylland* launched at
                Nyholm naval shipyard, Copenhagen. *Jylland* took
                part in Battle of Heligoland (1864) and is now a
                museum ship in Ebeltoft, Jutland, Denmark.

1862	Bismark appointed prime minister of Prussia.
1863	King Christian IX becomes king of Denmark.
November:	Danish Parliament ignores Treaty of London and passes a law giving people of Slesvig the same liberal rights as Danish citizens.
December:	Bismark uses this as an excuse for Prussian troops to occupy Holsten.
	Monrad appointed prime minister of Denmark.
	Danish troops withdraw to Dannevirke Line in Slesvig.
1864 January:	Bismark gives Denmark impossible ultimatum to revoke Slesvig constitution. General de Meza withdraws Danish army from Dannevirke Line to Dybbøl. Monrad offers resignation: not accepted. Prussian army follows into Slesvig. Digs in at Dybbøl.
March:	First major bombardment of Dybbøl and Sønderborg.
April:	Danish army defeated, withdraws to Als with many losses.
	Battle of Heligoland — Danish navy defeat Austro/Prussian squadron.
	London Conference begins, aimed at finding peace terms.
April	(in New Zealand) Pai Marire followers in Taranaki, angered at land confiscations, attack colonial forces.
June:	Monrad, at London Conference, will not agree to punitive compromise.

Bismark immediately crosses to Als. Danish army routed.

July: Monrad wishes to fight on. King Christian asks Monrad to step down. Other ministers sent to negotiate peace terms.

October: Disastrous peace treaty signed. Denmark loses 40 per cent of its land.

1865–66   (in New Zealand) Pai Marire followers in Taranaki are defeated by colonial troops, who lay waste to Maori villages and crops.

1865   Rangitane chief Te Awe Awe plays major role in selling a large block of land, Ahu-a-Turanga (now Palmerston North district), to the government.

December: Monrad, his wife, sons Viggo and Johannes, daughter Karen and daughter-in-law Olga sail for New Zealand aboard *Victory*, with six young Danish men and a quantity of equipment.

1866   Monrad buys land at Karere (part of the Palmerston North block). Builds house, breaks in land. Other Danes follow, including Monrad's daughter Louise.

1868   Pai Marire leader Titokowaru abandons non-violent resistance and leads several successful attacks in south Taranaki against colonial troops, who retreat to the outskirts of Wanganui.
            Many Manawatu settlers, including the Monrad family, flee to Foxton after warnings of an

imminent Pai Marire invasion.

Colonial troops mount attack on Titokowaru but find his pa abandoned, and the leader retreated to north Taranaki. Manawatu is never invaded.

1869	Monrad, his wife and daughters leave Wellington for Denmark. Two sons stay to fight in the colonial militia and later to settle. Monrad gifts to the New Zealand government his valuable collection of etchings and other artworks on paper.
1870	New Zealand Parliament adopts Treasury Minister Julius Vogel's scheme to assist immigrants with their passage. Monrad family helps to persuade government to include Scandinavians in the scheme. Many Scandinavians are settled in Manawatu and Wairarapa. Assisted settlers pay back their loans by building roads and railways.
1872	Disastrous voyage of immigrant ship *England*. Many Scandinavians aboard. Smallpox epidemic kills many passengers.
1870s	(in Faroes and Copenhagen) Faroese students fuel a nationalist movement, focused on preservation of language, poetry and culture.
1878	(in Sydney) The Garden Palace, a huge and ornate wooden exhibition hall, is erected in the Botanic Gardens. Many citizens are annoyed at the loss of the harbour view.

1882   (in Sydney) The Garden Palace burns to the ground — the most spectacular fire in the history of the fire-prone city.

1884   (in New Zealand) Olga Monrad, wife of Viggo, dies, leaving seven children. Viggo leaves for Denmark. His sons Ditlev and Oscar return months later to farm the Monrad block at Karere.

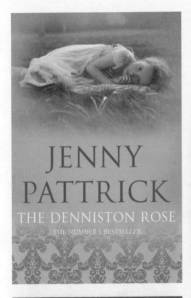

JENNY
PATTRICK
THE DENNISTON ROSE
THE NUMBER 1 BESTSELLER

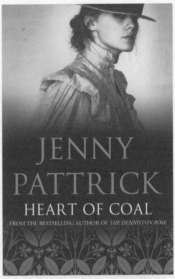

JENNY
PATTRICK
HEART OF COAL
FROM THE BESTSELLING AUTHOR OF *THE DENNISTON ROSE*

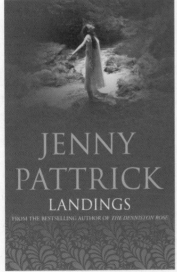

JENNY
PATTRICK
LANDINGS
FROM THE BESTSELLING AUTHOR OF *THE DENNISTON ROSE*

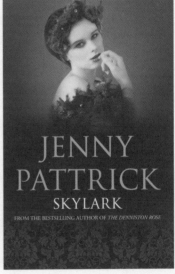

JENNY
PATTRICK
SKYLARK
FROM THE BESTSELLING AUTHOR OF *THE DENNISTON ROSE*

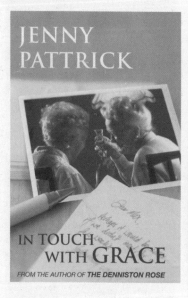

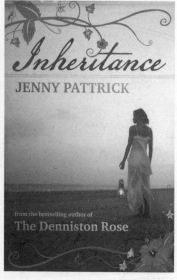